THE POSH PREPPER

The Posh Prepper

This book is a work of fiction. Any references to historical events, real people, real organizations, real products, or real locales are used fictitiously. Other names, characters, places, and incidents are the product of the author's imagination, and any resemblance to actual events or locales or persons, living or dead, is entirely coincidental.

Printed in the United States of America
Book Cover Design by ebooklaunch.com
First Printing, 2023

eBook ASIN B0BVNRQ4B4
Paperback ISBN 979-8-377381-27-3

THE POSH PREPPER

TODD KNIGHT

MEADOWLAKE
PRESS

To my wife, for her endless love and support.

Stay in touch.

Don't miss Todd Knight's next book.

Join his email list at:
ToddKnightBooks.com

Subscribers get early access, deleted scenes, and other exclusive content.

ONE

Katanga Cobalt Company
Democratic Republic of Congo
Wednesday, August 11, 2033

"TERRORISTS, natural disasters, disease outbreaks, mass violence, environmental accidents, food shortages, social instability, global war." A female corporate-marketing voice listed each disaster in an upbeat tone as a corresponding icon swooped onto the big screen. "We live in unprecedented times. And these are just a few of the threats facing your business today."

Nick Ritter scanned the faces of his clients, a dozen hardened African mine managers who clearly didn't care about a corporate safety video. They sat in a semicircle facing the conference-room screen. Most browsed on their phones. Two whispered by the coffee machine in the back. One dozed in his chair.

"You need a partner to help you navigate the rocky road ahead," the video continued. "At Thorne Global, disaster planning is our specialty. Our highly trained consultants will analyze your business from top to bottom and create a customized plan that covers the five phases of emergency management: prevention, preparedness, response, recovery, and mitigation." With each phase, an icon landed with a pulsing glow.

"When disaster strikes, you'll be ready to protect your assets, brand, and, of course, human capital. In our new world, disaster is inevitable, but crisis is avoidable. Let us focus on 'What if?' so you can focus on 'What next?'"

A giant logo faded in and sparkled. "Thorne Global, prepared for tomorrow."

Overhead lights flickered on. Oskar Zurcher stood and buttoned his flawless slim-fit suit. "Good afternoon, gentlemen." He spoke with precision and formality in a strong Swiss accent. "After the recent incidents at our Lomami and Red Hills mining operations, we have acquired a special advisor from Thorne Global to assess our disaster-response plans."

He gestured at Nick, who was seated against the side wall. "Mr. Nick Ritter is a top crisis consultant who has traveled from the United States to be here with us today. He has reviewed each of your mining operations in meticulous detail and assembled contingency plans for a range of disaster scenarios." He gave a formal nod. "Mr. Ritter."

Nick stood and took the front of the room. "Thank you, Mr. Zurcher. Gentlemen, I represent Thorne Global, an international crisis management, planning, response, recovery, and mitigation company. We design programs for…"

They judged him with half-awake eyes, a jury of ruthless miners frowning at this soft, clean-shaven, bright-eyed, thirty-something American in a shiny new suit.

"For all types of catastrophic events, including—"

A pot-bellied man in a drafty red button-down screeched back his chair and wandered to the rear refreshments table for a cup of fruit-infused water. He sipped with his back to Nick, staring up at a corporate poster above the water dispenser. At the top it said, "Katanga Cobalt" with their blue-gray logo and slogan, "We power the world." The center featured a globe surrounded by a giant ring of products that used cobalt: electric cars, solar panels, cell phones, tablets, laptops, batteries, power tools, scooters, jewelry, cosmetics, paints, medical devices, machinery, and dozens more. At the bottom was their ethical statement: "RESPECT. INTEGRITY. EXCELLENCE."

"Including…umm…"

To Nick's left, two managers muttered in French, then chuckled. To his right, a skinny man in a fedora leaned over to show his neighbor a magazine. Everyone else scrolled on their phones.

I've lost the room. In the first minute. A new record.

Nick straightened and switched to an informal tone. "Look, guys, I know the recent incidents are top of mind and, well, you're not alone. All my clients are struggling to keep their people safe. While I can't stop the next disaster, I promise I can teach you how to respond."

They were all looking at him now, half-interested, but listening. The manager with the fruit water turned to face Nick, his face skeptical, and finished off his ice-cold drink.

Nick started to pace. "Now, your three biggest risks here are mine collapse, riot, and looting." He picked up a thick binder. "In front of you is a binder. I've drafted disaster responses for those three situations, plus eleven more, ranging from earthquake to foreign invasion. Each situation has a detailed crisis-response plan customized for your particular operation. The plans include mine maps, escape routes, safety procedures, and much more."

He tapped the cover of the binder. "Study this. As you read, try and visualize each disaster scenario in your head. Play it out, step by step, like a movie in your mind. This is called 'emergency conditioning' or 'battle proofing.' If you practice ahead of time, in an actual crisis, your response will be automatic."

He placed down the binder and retook the front of the room. "Gentlemen, my training will teach you how to save lives. Maybe even your own." He shifted to a heartfelt tone. "I tell all my clients: You can replace your assets, you can replace your operations, but you can *never* replace your people."

They stared at him, a wall of contempt.

"OK." Nick clapped his hands in conclusion. "Well, my card is inside the binder. Please call with any questions, day or night. Thank you."

Zurcher stood sharply. "Thank you, Mr. Ritter. Gentlemen, please arrive tomorrow prepared to discuss the disaster plans for your particular operation. Thank you, and good afternoon."

The room shifted to murmuring and packing.

Nick was stuffing the binder into his briefcase when Zurcher stepped to his side. "Thank you, Mr. Ritter. That was quite instructive."

"I'm happy to help, Mr. Zurcher." He smiled politely.

"Before you leave, Banza will escort you to inspect the installation of our new emergency notification system." Zurcher gestured toward the door.

Nick turned to see a short African man in a faded t-shirt and shorts waving enthusiastically, his hand missing two fingers from the middle knuckle up, the other fingers crooked, like they'd been crushed. He beamed a warm smile, his bulging eyes bloodshot.

Nick raised his eyebrows at Zurcher. "Inspect? Here? You mean, in the mine?"

Zurcher smiled condescendingly. "Yes, of course."

"Mr. Zurcher, I apologize, but system functionality is outside my area of expertise. I'm the planner. Inspections would be handled by the equipment manufacturer or one of our local subcontractors. I'm happy to arrange something if you like."

Zurcher frowned, leaned in, and lowered his voice. "Your boss, Mr. Wasserman, assured me you would conduct the inspection *today.*" He pointed down for emphasis. "So that we may host a private tour for the chief commissioner of the Safety Bureau tomorrow morning."

"Mr. Zurcher, I'd like to help, but I wouldn't even know what to look for. I'm sorry."

Zurcher leaned closer and delivered his words carefully. "This is… not ideal. Given our recent safety incidents, a poor impression with the commissioner would be of *serious* concern to our Swiss parent company." He flashed his eyebrows and stared at Nick.

OK, Zurcher. Message received.

"I understand." Nick nodded. "Do you mind if I call Mr. Wasserman briefly?"

Zurcher straightened and beamed a condescending smile. "Of course."

Nick left the conference room and wandered down the short hall, looking for a private place to call Sam Wasserman. The mobile office trailer only had four conference rooms, all occupied, so he headed for the EXIT sign at the end of the hallway. He stepped out from the soft lights and air conditioning into the blazing African sun.

Nick flinched and squinted at the Katanga mining operation behind the trailer—a sprawling, muddy, pitted hellscape buzzing with workers. Men and women, baking under the heat and humidity, waded in cloudy pools, sifting mud through old rags. Children, caked in yellow mud and toxic grime, sat in circles pounding rocks, sorting cobalt flakes into wooden bowls. Conveyor belts, fed by underground miners, spit up rubble through holes in the ground. Guards were stationed throughout the site, dressed in camo fatigues and berets, gripping AK-47s, studying the miners behind big black sunglasses.

Nick dialed Sam and drifted away from the trailer. A stone-faced guard with a thick scar across his forehead trailed behind.

No answer.

"Goddammit, Sam," Nick whispered.

He scanned the area and considered his options.

Thirty yards ahead, a witch doctor chanted a blessing over a group of seated men who were about to descend into the mine. He tossed powder over them and waved his hands, then clapped and pointed at Nick, and a dozen angry eyes turned.

Nick spun back toward the trailer and dialed again.

Sam answered in his impatient Brooklyn accent. "Nick, what's up?" The background sounded like a busy conference room.

"Sam, sorry to bother you, I've got a quick question. I'm onsite at Katanga and Oskar Zurcher wants me to inspect some new emergency notification system before the commissioner of Safety tours tomorrow. Did you tell him we'd do that?"

"Ummm...I don't know. Maybe? Look, I'm in Zurich right now

trying to renew a huge contract with their parent company, so I've been promising a lot of things and I really can't keep track."

"OK, but…the thing is…I don't know these systems. I can't tell if it's operating safely." Nick looked back toward the miners and lowered his voice. "And this place doesn't exactly look up to code, if you know what I mean."

Sam gave a sharp laugh. "Nick, it's a cobalt mine, not a Toyota factory—what do you expect?" His voice was suddenly distant and muffled. "No no no—tell them I'll be back in thirty seconds. Then stall, goddammit." He returned, irritated. "Look, Nick, they're one of my biggest clients, and I'm hours away from signing them to a ten-year monster contract. So can you please just do it? Turn some knobs, pull some levers, say a fucking blessing—I don't care. Just make Zurcher happy. OK?"

Nick closed his eyes, dread gripping his stomach.

"Nick? You there?"

"Sam, this…this isn't some kind of warning or payback because of what I asked you…is it?"

Sam replied in a chummy tone. "Nick, buddy, come on—you worry too much. Just cut the ribbon on Zurcher's machine, I'll close the deal, and we'll talk about your question over a bottle at Ostra. I gotta go. Thanks, pal."

The background noise went silent.

Nick stared across the hellscape.

* * *

THE ELEVATOR CREAKED and groaned as it descended into the earth. Nick and Banza stood side by side, silent, as the rusty cage swayed down the craggy shaft. The sunlight above faded, replaced by a dirty brown glow from a greasy lamp.

Nick looked down at the worn inspection sticker: "Elevator inspected for Katanga Cobalt by DRC Safety Bureau: November 2025. Expiration: November 2030."

Expired three years ago. Great first impression.

The elevator jolted with a sharp bang, then shuddered and rattled.

Nick grabbed a railing and peeked sideways at Banza. The miner reached into his shirt and pulled out a necklace with dirty pink beads and a Christian cross. He kissed it and looked up to god.

"Good luck charm?" Nick nodded at the necklace.

Banza tucked it back under his collar and smiled. "My daughter." He did the voice of a little girl. "Daddy, this will keep you safe in the mine."

Banza pointed at Nick. "You have children, yes?"

"No. No children." Nick paused. "I travel a lot for work and—"

"Nine children." Banza pointed to himself with a huge grin.

"Nine?" Nick's eyes widened.

"Nine. Soon ten." He held up all ten fingers, including the crooked and stumpy ones.

"Wow, congratulations. What a blessing."

Banza nodded, glowing, his eyes gentle and warm. "Here we say, 'Big family, big heart.'" He tapped his heart.

Nick smiled politely, unsure of how to respond. After an awkward pause, he spoke. "Yeah, someday I—"

The elevator slammed to a stop at the bottom of the shaft.

Banza opened the latch and moved through the steel gate. "Come."

Nick followed, gesturing back. "By the way, the elevator…it needs to be inspected. It's past due."

Banza laughed and nodded. "Is OK."

Did he think that was a joke? Maybe he didn't understand?

They moved down a long tunnel, following a string of filthy lamps glowing sickly yellow against the sweaty walls. The air was cold and damp, heavy like a wet blanket.

Ugh, that smell…

"Banza, do you smell that?"

"Bad eggs."

"Yeah, it's stinkdamp, hydrogen sulfide. It's toxic and highly flammable. You're supposed to be pumping it out. What about the air filtration system?"

"Fan is broken. Today morning."

"Broken? What do you mean, broken? How are you still working down here?"

Banza gave a quick, confident nod. "Is OK."

They reached the first in a series of side chambers and Nick slowed, squinting inside. Four miners squatted under a little dome carved out like a rock igloo. They chipped away at the ceiling by the light of headlamps, working to a steady beat of pounding, banging, and the occasional cough. The chamber exhaled a sickening blend of rock dust and sweat.

Nick followed Banza down the hall to the next chamber. This one was larger, with six men chiseling away chunks of stone. Various logs and car jacks were wedged haphazardly around the room, supporting the weight of critical rock structures.

Then Nick saw it and froze: Children were seated around the chamber—no headlamps, no shoes—toiling like little ghosts in the dark. They crushed rock into small stones, filling bowls and baskets.

In the back corner, a child was sleeping, or maybe passed out.

A woman sat with her back against a jack, breastfeeding a baby as she sorted stones.

Something moved at his feet, and Nick looked down to see a little girl, no more than six years old, working just inside the entrance. She wore a muddy red dress and braids threaded with red beads. Looking straight ahead, she pounded rocks with a little hammer. Suddenly, she stopped...then slowly looked up at Nick, her pupils milky white.

He gasped.

She's blind. Of course. Perfect for mine work.

She cocked her head, curious, and her nostrils flared, giving him a little sniff. A warm smile spread across her face.

Even though she couldn't see, Nick smiled back.

Banza pulled him along. "Come."

The girl turned back to work.

Nick followed Banza to a wide room cut into the side of the tunnel. Men were emptying baskets onto a long conveyor belt that knocked and groaned as it streamed to the surface. Banza stopped and began speaking French to a group of children sitting on old tires along the belt, picking through the passing rubble like assembly line inspectors.

The stinkdamp was smothering. Nick rubbed his throbbing temples and tried to blink away the burning in his eyes as he waited for a break in Banza's conversation.

"Banza, the smell…is it getting worse?"

Banza nodded without looking back. "Is normal. Is OK."

A young boy in a dusty New York Yankees cap playfully quipped at Banza in French. Banza grinned, wagged a finger, and returned a short phrase in a sing-song voice. The children burst into laughter. Banza doubled over in a deep belly laugh. He continued chatting, rolling the beads on his necklace, smiling with bloodshot eyes. And then Nick noticed it: Banza had a chronic cough, a subtle, repetitive thump that rose from his chest like a hiccup.

This poor guy…nine kids at home, huffing fumes for pennies.

And these kids…I can't stand by and watch.

Nick interrupted Banza with a hand on his shoulder. "You know what, no. It's not OK. These fumes are dangerous. I'm going to tell Mr. Zurcher to evacuate until we can clean the air. Come on." Nick started back toward the elevator.

Banza stared, alarmed and confused. "I no tell Zurcher anything." He shook his head.

"*I'll* tell him." Nick beckoned with confidence. "Come on."

Banza followed cautiously.

Nick spoke over his shoulder as he strode along the tunnel. "I don't know how you're going to tour the Safety commissioner tomorrow. The elevator is three years past inspection, the air filtration system isn't working, the hydrogen sulfide fumes are overwhelming…I mean, this site is *clearly* hazardous."

Banza scampered to catch up. "Yesterday."

"Hmm?"

"Commissioner here yesterday. Nine a.m."

Nick stopped.

Banza continued a few more steps, then turned and looked back.

Nick squinted and gestured for emphasis. "The commissioner of the Safety Bureau…came down here…to tour the new equipment…*yesterday*?"

"Yesterday." Banza nodded.

Nick gazed ahead, his eyes dancing through the tunnel as he processed—connecting, analyzing, calculating. He turned serious. "Banza, it's not safe down here. We need to get everybody out. Right now."

Banza shrank back at Nick's tone.

"Come on." Nick grabbed him and started back toward the conveyor room. "I want you to yell out in French and tell everyone—"

BOOM.

An explosion blew out the conveyor room, blasting rock and dust and debris into the main passage.

Nick was on his hands and knees, ears ringing, the tunnel swaying. Blurry flames roared from the conveyor room, clawing the roof of the tunnel, riding a cloud of thick black smoke.

And then the smell flooded over him: gasoline and burning rubber.

Nick crawled to the wall, coughing, climbed to his feet, then helped Banza stand.

They rushed back to the elevator. The shaft was empty. The cage had been pulled to the surface. Banza frantically tapped the button. No response.

A group of men shoved past and forced open the gate, leaning into the shaft, pulling the cables.

"That's not going to work. Come on." Nick pulled Banza back into the tunnel and pointed toward the fire. "There are two other ways up—the conveyor belt, which is on fire, and there should be a personnel shaft on the left, halfway to the conveyor belt."

"Yes! Ladder!" Banza started down the tunnel.

Nick followed to the shaft, where a group of men blocked the entrance, yelling and pointing inside.

"What are they saying?"

"No ladder."

Nick pushed through and looked up. They were trying to scale the walls. A man would bury a pickaxe in the stone, climb up on it, and then anchor another higher up. But the pickaxes kept collapsing under the weight, sending the men tumbling down, knocking loose chunks of stone.

"It's gonna collapse," Nick said quietly. He grabbed Banza and pointed. "Tell them to stop or it's going to collapse."

Banza yelled at the men.

A big miner spun and barked back through missing teeth. He pointed at Nick and menaced.

Banza stepped to the man, breaking his glare, and raised his tone.

Nick pulled at Banza's arm. "Come on."

They continued arguing.

"Banza! They won't stop. Come on." He dragged Banza down the tunnel. "Listen, there has to be another way. Are there any—"

The men in the personnel shaft screamed and there was a sickening thud. The shaft rumbled, then collapsed, pulling down part of the tunnel with it.

Nick covered and coughed as a dusty cloud swallowed them.

The lights flickered off, plunging them into darkness, the only light coming from the fire. They were trapped between the flaming conveyor room ahead and the collapsed shaft behind.

Nick pulled out his phone, hand shaking, and turned on the flashlight. He swung it around the tunnel, trying to orient himself in the dust and smoke. The light jumped from horror to horror.

The big miner was sprawled across the ground, covered in dust, mouth hanging open.

The breastfeeding woman lay motionless beside a wall, clutching her still baby.

Outside the conveyor room, scattered bodies burned.

Children ran past in little blurs, coughing, screaming.

The ground shook. Another section of the roof crumbled and fell.

Nick whipped the light round and round—gasping, lungs burning, sucking smoke and rubber and gas and burnt flesh. Raw panic bubbled up inside.

Stop. Control your response. Focus on your options.

He took a knee, below the smoke, closed his eyes and began box breathing: four counts in, four counts full, four counts out, four counts empty. Repeat.

The mine faded and muted. His mind sharpened.

How do we get out?

The elevator is pulled up.

The conveyor belt is in flames.

The personnel shaft is caved in.

How do we get out?

Can we make a new exit?

Signal for help?

Is there another way up?

A memory clicked and his eyes shot open. "There was another shaft."

Nick rose. "Banza!"

Banza was frozen, staring down at the bodies.

Nick shook him. "Banza!"

His head snapped up, big eyes wide.

"Before the elevator was installed, there was a shaft for lowering equipment. The original plans showed it at the north end of the tunnel." He pointed past the fire. "Do you know where it is?"

"Closed. No more." Banza shook his head.

Shit.

Nick ranked their options and decided there was nothing better. "Show me."

Banza started toward the conveyor room.

"Wait." Nick pulled off his jacket, tore off both sleeves, and showed Banza how to tie a makeshift sleeve mask.

"Stay low." Nick crawled past the conveyor room, under a steady stream of smoke rolling into the tunnel. He pushed through rubble and baskets and shredded tires, passing bodies and headlamps and a smoldering Yankees cap. They made it to the other side and rushed past a series of side chambers to the far end of the tunnel. They stepped inside a large room and pulled off their masks.

Nick swung his flashlight around the equipment room, spotlighting piles of shovels, pickaxes, and baskets. By the back wall, three square-shouldered figures loomed. Nick aimed his flashlight and his heart sank: it was Zurcher's new safety system—shiny, top of the line, turned off.

There was no shaft.

"Closed. Long time," Banza said.

Nick sighed and lowered the flashlight to his side. Behind the safety system, at the base of the back wall, a tiny glint caught his eye. Nick pressed the flashlight against his leg, turning the room completely black, and squinted. He could see it clearly, a single pinprick of light in the dark.

Nick rushed to the wall, dropped to his knees, and clawed back rocks, blew away dust. Light spilled in. He reached up and rapped on the wall. It was wood. And it was hollow.

They threw a piece of plywood across the old shaft. Of course. Cheaper than filling it in properly.

He swept the surface looking for a gap, brushing off dust and grime, exposing a soft, rotten piece of plywood bolted to the stone. He tried to pry it loose from the wall, leaning against the center as he pulled up the edge.

A pickaxe blurred past his face and buried next to his head.

He looked up to see Banza gripping the handle, eyes sparkling.

Nick ran to an equipment pile, digging through, searching for a pickaxe. He rushed back to a cluster of children hacking away at the board with their little tools. One by one, rays of light beamed through. Within a minute, they'd torn the board free and opened the shaft. Inside, a dusty ladder with crooked tree-branch steps led up to a wooden cover sparkling light through its gaps.

A boy scaled up and threw off the cover. Light poured in and the children cheered. The rest of the kids streamed up.

Banza grabbed a rung and gestured to Nick. "Come."

Nick waved him off, backing out of the shaft. "Go. I'll be right there."

Banza started to climb.

"Wait!" Nick stepped back in. "How do you say 'come here' in French?"

Banza stopped and looked down. "Viens ici."

Nick repeated it back. "VEE-en EE-see."

"Good." Banza gave a thumbs up and hurried up the ladder.

Nick sprinted to the equipment room's entrance and waved his flashlight into the tunnel. "Viens ici! Viens ici!" He cupped a hand to his mouth. "Follow the light!"

Miners emerged from the darkness, rushing past him, squinting, coughing, stumbling. He pointed them toward the shaft.

Once they stopped coming, he crept into the tunnel and shined his flashlight into the first side chamber. Two boys huddled against the back wall, crouched over, covering their ears. Nick guided them out and pointed toward the shaft. "Follow the light."

He squinted up the tunnel, toward the other chambers, his head pounding and ears ringing.

Focus. Two more rooms, then out.

Nick sprinted to the next chamber and shined his light inside. A groggy teenage girl rocked a passed-out child. He put his sleeve mask on her and steered her toward the back shaft.

His vision started to vibrate as he rushed to a third chamber. All dead.

The ringing grew louder, sharper.

Go. Right now. Any longer and you're not getting out.

He backed toward the equipment room, aiming his light down the tunnel one last time. Dust, debris, equipment, bodies. Nothing moved. The ground began to quake. He turned and stumbled back to the shaft.

Nick started up the ladder, gripping the rungs as the rumbling grew stronger.

It's gonna go. The whole thing's gonna go.

He squinted up at the sunlight, a blurry Banza beckoning wildly. "Come! Hurry!"

Scrambling. Halfway there.

The ground jolted, a rung snapped and Nick fell, sliding down two rungs, catching himself before freefall. He grabbed the next rung with determination and glanced down the tunnel one last time. Something moved.

He froze.

Nick stooped down and aimed his flashlight into the dark. The girl with the red braids was feeling along the tunnel wall, inching toward the equipment room.

"Viens ici!"

She cocked her head in his direction and started moving more quickly.

"Viens ici!"

She tripped over a pickaxe and fell to her hands and knees. She stood, wobbled, felt for the wall, and kept moving forward.

The mine shuddered, raining dust and stone around her.

"Come now!" Banza's voice echoed above.

Nick weighed the odds.

Don't do it. You go back in there, you're not coming out.

He started back down the ladder. "Viens ici!"

The ground shook and he slipped, falling backward, collapsing at the base of the shaft in a heap, his phone hitting the ground and going dark.

Nick pulled himself up and started toward her. "Viens—"

A section of tunnel collapsed behind her and she disappeared into a cloud of dust and smoke.

Nick stumbled out of the shaft, wading into the haze, his only markers coming from the two sources of light—the fire ahead and the shaft behind.

He bumped against the tunnel wall and groped. Nothing.

He brushed the floor. Nothing.

"Viens—" He choked, throat on fire.

Swinging back and forth between the two blurry lights, disoriented, unsure which was the shaft, he chose one and staggered forward, then tripped over shovels and crashed to the ground.

Drowning in smoke and rubber and gasoline, he lowered his head and closed his eyes.

The ringing built to a deafening crescendo, then cut off.

Silence. Swirling in darkness.

A little girl's voice whispered, crisp and close. "Follow the light."

TWO

New Hampshire
Monday, November 22, 2035
6:00 a.m.

THE STEEL DOOR unlocked with a sharp crack and swung open, activating the lights inside the makeshift studio apartment. Twelve people shuffled in, single file—seven young men, three old men, and two middle-aged women. They were all dressed the same: white sneakers, blue jeans, and a maroon sweatshirt with big white letters, "New Dawn Travel Group—2035 World Tour."

The windowless studio was long and spacious, with bright fluorescent lights, gleaming tile floors, and cozy furniture, as if a real estate agent had staged a hospital lounge. Inside the door was a long mahogany dining table. Six tourists sat on one side and six lowered themselves opposite. The door slammed shut and locked with an echo.

Perfectly aligned at each seat was a small aromatherapy diffuser and a steel rack with three vials of cloudy yellow liquid. In silent unison, the tourists drew the first vial, twisted off the cap, and poured into the diffuser's water tank. Power on, gentle whir, soft red glow, and a plume of mist drifted from each spout. They leaned in, eyes closed, and inhaled the vapor.

A woman's voice came over a loudspeaker. "Slow, deep breath in…hold…and release." She led them through ten minutes of rhythmic breathing, then concluded. "Dose one is complete."

A red countdown clock above the door flashed "24:00:00" and began to tick down.

The tourists shut off their diffusers and moved into the room, which was organized into three distinct sections: The front held the dining table and a cozy kitchenette, the middle had a big-screen TV on the right and a round poker table on the left, and the back was lined with two rows of cots. A long one-way mirror reflected the dining table.

The seven young men moved to the right wall, crashing on plush couches and recliners around the TV. Over the next thirteen hours, they drank nine cups of coffee, downed three cases of Bud Light, smoked eight cigars, and notched over three hundred pushups. They laughed and hollered and chanted as they rotated between video games, college football, pro basketball, drinking games, pushups, karaoke, and arm wrestling.

The three old men hunched around the poker table and sipped bourbon, traded stories, played cards, and periodically barked at the young men to "knock it off."

The two women chattered, sampled wine, and prepped food at the kitchenette.

At 7:00 p.m., the women served a feast. The twelve tourists held hands and prayed over a steaming spread of buttermilk-brined turkey, country-bread stuffing, bacon-fat gravy, canned cranberry sauce, creamy mashed potatoes, garlic green beans, creamed sweet corn, buttermilk biscuits, and sweet tea.

At 10:00 p.m., a woman's voice came over the loudspeaker. "Second dose."

Dinner was already cleared and each seat again faced a diffuser and vial rack. The tourists sat and emptied the second vial.

"Inhale…hold…release." She guided their breathing for ten minutes.

Once dismissed, they moved to the cots in the back. They tossed and turned through the night, and most were already awake at 6:00 a.m. when the loudspeaker announced, "Third dose."

They sprung from their beds and gathered at the table.

"Inhale…hold…release."

After ten minutes, a man's voice came over the loudspeaker. "Good morning, my friends, and welcome to the most important day in human history. Today begins an unprecedented journey, a quantum leap, a chance to design our own destiny. From this day forward, you will be revered as brave pioneers and brilliant visionaries. Your sacrifice will become legend. Thank you. Good luck and Godspeed."

The countdown clock ticked to "00:00:00" and the lock cracked free.

The twelve tourists shuffled, single file, down a dim hallway lined with airtight plastic sheeting. At the end, they unzipped an entry flap and stepped out to a muted sunrise.

Cascades of hard rain darkened what little light peeked over the horizon. On the right, a canopy covered a plastic folding table with twelve backpacks, each labeled with a name tag. The tourists streamed past the table, grabbed their backpacks, and ascended into a short, white, school bus with maroon lettering, "New Dawn Travel Group."

The last to enter, an old man with a potbelly, dropped into the driver's seat, closed the door, and started the engine.

"Buckle up!" He chuckled and shifted into drive.

* * *

By the time they crossed the Massachusetts border, they were showing symptoms. A growing chorus of wet coughs and sneezes mixed with the damp air, fogging up the windows. By the time they reached Boston, they were stirring and twitching in their seats. A few scratched and picked at their palms.

The bus leaned onto a highway exit, and a young man scrubbed off a fogged window with his raw palm, leaving a pink smear. The exit sign rushed past, "Boston Logan International Airport."

A skinny old man in the first row turned and faced down the center aisle. He cleared his throat. "Roberts?"

A young man in the middle leaned forward. "Los Angeles. Thanksgiving Day Parade."

The old man nodded. "Burke?"

A woman raised her hand. "Sydney. Opera House."

"Parker?"

The other woman looked up. "Paris. Le Grand Rex Theater."

The roll call continued and each tourist answered.

"Tokyo. Shinjuku Station."

"Shanghai. Lucky Dragon Casino."

"Delhi. Skyline Convention Center."

"Sao Paulo. Museum of Art."

"Moscow. Harvest Festival."

"Cairo. Arkadia Mall."

"Lagos. Church of Redemption."

The old man paused, then added himself. "London. Wembley Stadium."

The bus turned toward the Departures terminal and the old man took a deep breath. "Listen up. Y'all got at least three hours until boarding, so stay active and work the space. Touch everything you can. When you land, work that space too. Next few days, you're gonna have Red Bull in your veins—make the most of it while you can. Whatever happens…" He paused, considering his next words, then straightened and raised his chin. "God bless us and God bless the United States of America."

The bus pulled up to the Departures curb and eleven tourists streamed out. The young man in front held the terminal door for the others, then followed inside, leaving red droplets on the steel handle.

The enormous hall buzzed with eager travelers grabbing coffee, checking bags, and rushing to make flights. The tourists fanned out toward their gates, and one by one, threaded into the crowd and disappeared.

Outside, the bus driver closed the door, pulled away from the curb, and headed for the airport exit. Fifteen minutes later, he arrived at Market Basket in downtown Boston and parked in a back corner of the plaza. He strode toward the entrance, pulling on a red vest as he skirted around two cars posturing for the same parking spot.

He was two steps inside when the manager swooped in. "Morning, Buck!"

"Morning, Dale."

"You're bagging on three today." Dale leaned in. "Listen, it's shaping up to be a real zoo out there. Everybody's getting a head start on their Thanksgiving shopping. I know you've got a double tomorrow, but is there any chance you could maybe pull a double today too?"

Buck looked past his manager at the checkout lines stretching down the aisles. He grinned. "Sure thing, Dale."

Buck took his usual position at the end of the register, coughed into his raw and speckled palm, and began bagging.

Turkey…cranberry sauce…stuffing.

Potatoes…sweet corn…green beans.

Inhale…hold…*release.*

THREE

"THE NUKE IS GONNA BLOW in sixty minutes. Go."

Marty Kettenbach took a quick sip of scotch, placed the glass on the table, and scooted forward in his plush armchair. In his late fifties, he had the smooth skin and thick hair of a twenty-five-year-old. Dressed to the nines—gold cufflinks, diamond-studded tie bar, Rolex watch, silk pocket square—his salt-and-pepper hair slicked back like a lion's mane, he looked like a guy who wanted you to know he was a rich asshole.

Marty straightened the sleeves on his pinstripe suit and cleared his throat. "OK, I'm at the office, so I need to gather my family and get to our fallout shelter. First I call my wife, then my boys, and tell them to head home ASAP. Then I call my driver…no wait, the operator…no, first my driver. And he brings me home. Once my family's safe inside the shelter, then I call the operator."

Marty cocked his head. "Hold on, how do I know whether we should go to the shelter at my house or my office?" He cocked his head the other way. "And what about traffic? What if it's rush hour?"

He waved a hand in frustration. "Ahhh, fuck it. I don't know. What do I do, Nick?"

Nick Ritter leaned forward in his armchair. He wore a dark suit, white shirt, no tie, two days of stubble, and cynical, tired eyes. He took a deep breath and winced at the hint of cigar smoke baked into the yacht club's Rockefeller Room.

"The first thing you do is call your operator. Always. The number is a favorite on both your phones, plus the satellite phones at all your home and office locations. Once you activate your escape plan, your operator will help you execute your next steps. They'll also give you the latest intelligence on the situation. That's important. There's a big difference between a lone wolf dumping a dirty bomb on the subway and Russia launching a warhead at the state house. So it's critical to gather as much information as possible from your operator." He leaned in and pointed for emphasis. "But you do that *on the move*. Never sit still. Always move and confirm."

Marty nodded like an attentive student.

"OK, so let's assume you've gathered all the info you can," Nick said. "Your number one priority is to get out of the blast radius and far away from any fallout. Food, water, shelter—all that can wait. None of it matters if you're in the blast zone. Depending on the size of the nuke, burns can reach up to ten miles away. Flash blindness up to fifteen miles. So when it blows, you want to be underground, at least twenty miles away. Preferably much more. That means any man-powered travel—foot, bicycle, whatever—it's out of the question. A car or train could work, but there's a high risk of traffic jams or break-downs. Plus you're among the general public, which, well, you don't want that."

Marty winced and shook his head.

"If you're near water, we have speed boats located up and down both coasts. But then you're stuck twenty miles offshore with no supplies and limited gas. I don't love it. Bottom line, in this situation, your number one exit path is private air. It's fast, safe, and adaptable. That's why we have multiple aircraft on standby everywhere you go."

Nick leaned back and summarized. "So, in a nuclear crisis, head for your closest aircraft and call your operator on the way. Get far away, as fast as you can. Focus on surviving and your operator will route you to one of your safe destinations."

"Yeah, but what about my family? I'm supposed to hop on a private jet and leave my wife in downtown Hiroshima?"

"Don't worry about your family. Your wife and sons all have their own escape plans customized to their locations, movements, and personal needs. If you call the operator and activate your plan, your family will be extracted to the nearest air strip and you'll meet up later."

"Extracted…what does that mean? Like a SWAT team snatching my wife outta yoga?"

"Pretty much." Nick shrugged. "The extraction teams are private military contractors, the pilots are Navy and Air Force vets, and the intelligence guys are all ex-CIA or NSA."

Marty gave a half-impressed nod, then picked up his scotch. "So when the shit hits the fan, how do I know these guys will show up?"

"Don't worry about them. They're all on contracts with heavy incentives. You can push them hard and they'll do whatever you need, or they won't get their payday."

"I like it." Marty winked and took a sip. "OK, but what if we don't have time to get to a plane? What if it's gonna blow in ten minutes?"

"If you can't get out in time, head to your nearest fallout shelter. There's one at your office, one at home, one at your Nantucket beach house, and one halfway between home and Nantucket. Again, call the operator, activate your plan, and they'll find you the nearest shelter."

Marty nodded, slightly dazed.

"Make sense?"

"Oh, it makes sense, Nick. But I can't keep track of all that. Maybe I should just call you." He took a sip, eyeing Nick over the glass.

"Don't call me." Nick shook his head. "The goal isn't to memorize the details, because no two disasters are the same and plans always go wrong." He scooted forward. "Look, Marty, there are really only two ideas you need to remember: save time and save yourself." He tapped his watch. "Time is your enemy. If you want to survive, every second counts. So whatever you do, don't hesitate. Always move and confirm."

"What do you mean, confirm?"

"There are three stages to disaster reaction: denial, deliberation, and decision. The goal is to skip the first, shorten the second, and optimize the third. It's that simple. On 9/11, most Trade Center survivors waited between six and thirty minutes before heading for the stairs. They checked the news, looked for coworkers, sent emails, shut down computers, cleaned desks, called loved ones. One woman got out safely then went back upstairs to change into a tracksuit so she could bike home."

Marty scoffed.

"Forty-seven minutes…that's the average head start my clients have before everyone else figures out what's happening. Do you know what most people do with that forty-seven minutes? They waste it. They debate where to go, argue over what clothes to bring, search for their phone charger. Hell, most people wait for four pieces of confirmation before they even start to act. Don't do that. Immediately execute your plan with cold, calculated precision. And don't get distracted. If you hesitate, the worst outcome is you die. If you overreact, the worst outcome is you spend two million for a family weekend in Saint Kitts."

Marty shrugged. "That's not even bad." He tipped back the rest of his drink.

"Second thing to remember, you have one job: Save yourself. Every member of your family has that same job. Don't worry about anyone else, they'll just slow you down. In a crisis, seventy percent of people freeze, twenty percent harm themselves or others, and ten percent save themselves. I've trained you to be in that ten percent."

"What do you mean they freeze? No one would just stand still in a burning building, right?"

"Wrong." Nick shook his head. "You have to understand, in a disaster, people don't optimize for survival. They optimize for psychological comfort. They stand around and chat with each other. They groupthink up plans that don't make sense. They irrationally follow social norms. They're slow and they're dangerous. The truth is most people would rather die with their group than survive alone. In a crisis, don't be a hero. Save yourself. Everyone else is added risk."

A sleazy grin crept across Marty's face. "Damnnn, Nick, that's cold. You shoulda been a banker."

Nick winced and looked at the floor.

Marty opened an ice bucket and lowered a perfect sphere into his glass. He lifted a decanter and forced an awkward chuckle. "You ever think, maybe, there's hope it'll all get better? Or are we too far gone?"

Nick looked up. "Why did you hire me, Marty?"

Marty paused, decanter half-tilted over his glass, and cocked his head. "Umm, because the world is fucked and I don't wanna die?"

"Right. All my clients say the same thing. The world's falling apart. Everything's corrupt. People are fatally flawed, easily manipulated, selfish, lazy, dogmatic, barbaric…beyond hope."

"And?"

"And if you want to survive, you have to go alone."

Marty nodded in acknowledgment as he poured his scotch, then pivoted to business mode. "OK, Nick, I appreciate the refresher. But the truth is, I can't keep track of all this shit. I'm a big-picture guy." He leaned in and lowered his voice. "Last week, when we had that little earthquake at three a.m., you know what I did? I called the pizza guy instead of the operator, then spent fifteen minutes trying to find my great-grandfather's watch collection." He gave a what-the-hell shrug. "That can't happen again, or it could mean my life."

"Those reactions are normal. We can refresh your training."

Marty scoffed and leaned back. "I've been top ten on Boston's Power Players list since 2020—you know why? It's not because I'm smart. It's not because I know the right people. And it's definitely not because I work hard." He chuckled and toasted his glass. Then he leaned in with intensity. "It's because I pick *winners.*" He leaned back with an arrogant shrug. "I've got a gift for it. My executive team, my money manager, my real estate agent…hell, even my tailor." He plucked his jacket lapel. "They're all winners. I pick winners, and they take me where I need to go. Nick, when it comes to keeping me safe, you're the winner. And I want you on my team."

"Marty—"

"What would it take for you to be on call to me, 24/7/365? You don't have to do a thing. Just coach me through whatever comes up, like my own personal 911."

"I'm sorry, Marty, but I don't do live support."

"I know, I know, you've got other clients. But I'll pay whatever it takes to be your number-one client."

"It's not about money, it's about safety. You'll be safer if you learn the playbook rather than rely on me."

"Oh come on, Nick. Don't bullshit a bullshitter. What's the problem? The money's good. The work's easy. You've got no family, so don't give me that work-life balance bullshit."

Nick wound up to respond. "Now hold on—"

There was a knock at the door.

"What?" Marty barked.

A butler stepped in. "Mr. Kettenbach, your guest has arrived. Would you like me to show him in?"

Marty waved him off. "Make him wait a minute."

Marty leaned in and pointed at Nick. "We'll come back to this later. But there's something else I need to ask." He put down his glass, scooted to the edge of his seat, and whispered. "If I wanted to make certain...adjustments to my escape package, could we do that?"

"What are we talking about?"

Marty leaned back, shifted uncomfortably, and brushed nothing off his pants. "Well, if I wanted to add someone...say, a special friend... but do it *discreetly*, like a separate, silent, self-contained plan outside my family's plan. Is that something we could do?" He cocked his head and flashed his eyebrows.

"I understand." Nick nodded. "Shouldn't be a problem."

Marty looked away and gave a half-satisfied, half-guilty nod. "Alright then."

The door swung open and the butler stepped in. "Gentlemen, Governor Sutton."

The governor strode in like he owned the club. He was tall, a big guy with big features and a simple, working-class haircut. In his early fifties, he looked one part friendly Boston neighbor and one part ruthless political boss.

A bodyguard wearing a suit and red earpiece posted outside the door.

Nick stood and shook hands. "Governor."

Marty, still reclined, swirled his drink. "Jesus, Ray, where'd you get that suit, the DMV?"

The governor unbuttoned his boxy, drab jacket with a crooked American-flag pin and looked at Marty with genuine surprise. "What, this? This is a fine suit," he said with a strong Boston accent.

"Can I get your usual, sir?" the butler asked.

"Mm-hmm." The governor gestured without looking.

"Mr. Ritter?" The butler turned to Nick.

"I'm OK, but thank you."

A second butler added an armchair to their table. They sat and the staff left.

Marty presented Nick. "OK, Ray, this is the guy. Nick Ritter, The Posh Prepper. He's the best in the business. Your one-stop-shop for high-end apocalypse insurance."

Nick shot Marty a look then turned to Governor Sutton. "Sir, I'm a crisis consultant. I design survival plans for high-profile clients with complex requirements."

"I appreciate you meeting me, Nick. Give me your background. What do you do?"

Nick straightened and took a deep breath. "Well, sir, I double majored in Social Psychology and International Relations at Georgetown. After graduation I moved to Boston to work for Thorne Global. I was there for eleven years, worked my way up to Junior Partner, ran multiple project teams." Nick hesitated. "Then, two years ago, I left and started my own practice. Now I design survival plans for ultra-high-net-worth clients, everything from wildfire to world war."

Marty raised his glass. "You should hear his nuke pitch. *Fantastic.*" He smirked and sipped.

"I heard about that unfortunate business in Africa." Sutton shrugged. "For what it's worth, I thought it wasn't your fault."

Nick looked at the floor and nodded.

The door swung open. They watched in silence as a waiter cruised in with a tray. He placed a frosty glass of beer and a nearly empty Sam Adams Boston Lager bottle on coasters in front of the governor. Then he put down a basket of roasted, in-shell peanuts and an empty bowl for shells. He turned and left.

Marty looked down his nose at the peanuts. "Ugh, I'm gonna be sick."

Sutton smirked at Marty. "Are you even from Boston? Let me guess, you're the prick who wears a Yankees cap in the luxury box at the Red Sox game."

"I don't wear hats." Marty ran a hand over his perfect hair.

Nick cleared his throat. "Governor, Marty said there was a sensitive situation you wanted my advice on. How can I help?"

Sutton shifted uncomfortably in his chair and looked at Marty.

Marty nodded. "Go ahead, Ray. He wouldn't have half the club in his book if he couldn't keep a secret."

"In my work, I need to know every detail of my clients' lives," Nick said. "Complete discretion is part of the job."

Sutton took a deep breath and his face turned serious. "I'm worried about something. And I'm afraid it's nonsense. But I'm also afraid it's real. This is gonna sound crazy. There's this…rumor, this theory, that for the last few years, our country has been engaged in some kinda… silent civil war. Soldiers, recruited by shadow governments in their home states, are traveling to opposing states and waging war."

"I'm familiar with it," Nick said.

"So you've heard of it?" Sutton raised his big eyebrows.

"Sure. Last year's Boston Harbor bombing was orchestrated by Texas. There are economic sanctions between northern and southern states. Ordinary citizens are being captured and kept as POWs, like that missing Globe reporter."

"Right!" Sutton pointed. "But it's all in secret. Nobody knows about it."

"Right."

"So, as part of this supposed civil war, there are rumors that there's gonna be an attempt on my life, which, whatever, that's nothing new. But recently, there've been a number of voices…trusted voices… telling me that something big is coming." Sutton leaned in and lowered his voice. "There's gonna be a full-scale invasion by a southern state militia. An attempt to capture the capital and take over Massachusetts."

Sutton sat back and raised his hands. "I know, I know. It's crazy, right? But also we don't know who did the harbor bombing. Staties don't know. FBI can't figure it out. And I've got credible people, smart people, telling me it's coming. So, if a southern militia invades Massachusetts, I don't wanna be around for it. I'd be top of their list. So I guess I'm wondering…is there an escape plan for something like that?"

Nick considered his answer. "Well, yes. I've done many military invasion escape plans, mostly for clients near conflict zones. Eastern Europe, Africa, South America. Places like that."

Sutton, locked on Nick, picked up his beer.

"But the thing is, Governor…it's probably not real."

Sutton stopped with the glass near his lips. "Not real?"

Nick scooted forward. "OK, so clients call me for all kinds of reasons. Usually it's because they think something big is coming. War with Mexico. Alien arrival. Extinction-level asteroid. I've heard it all. Most of it's…not credible. But it scares them and they call me. Who am I to question it? These are some of the smartest, wealthiest, most powerful people in the world. But if you trace these rumors back to their source, they're usually some kind of disinformation campaign run by a foreign government or private corporation. So, something like this, it's probably not real."

Sutton sat back and sipped his beer, mulling it over. "Yeah, you're probably right. But yesterday I received credible information that suggests otherwise. And I can't afford to ignore it."

Marty pointed at Sutton. "Take it seriously," he said in a heartfelt tone. "If not for you, for Connie and the girls."

Nick nodded. "That's what all my clients say. The cost of being prepared is nothing compared to the cost of being wrong."

Sutton placed his beer on the table and straightened to face Nick. "Let me ask you something else. Marty thinks I need a crisis planner. But frankly, I don't get it. I got a 24/7 state-police detail. I got private security. So explain to me, why would I need someone like you?"

"You use Kormann Group for your security?" Nick asked.

Sutton tilted his head, suspicious. "How'd you know that?"

"Most of my government clients use them." Nick nodded toward the door. "Plus, all their guys wear red earpieces. It's a branding thing. Don't worry, they're good. They'll protect you from any direct attack."

Sutton scooped up his beer and relaxed. "So you think I'm covered then?"

"Well…no."

Sutton stopped with the beer halfway to his mouth and squinted at Nick. "I'm confused."

"Governor, someone like me specializes in being a step ahead of everything that can go wrong. I provide my clients with seamless escape plans, 24/7/365. No matter where they are, no matter what happens, I get them where they need to be—quickly, safely, comfortably, with everything they need to survive and thrive. I know how crisis situations unfold…how people think…what they do." He pointed to the door. "If civil war breaks out, Kormann will rush you into a basement panic room to hide out for six months. Someone like me? I'd have your entire family on a private beach in the French Riviera before the first shot's fired, with your wife's favorite champagne on ice and your clubs polished for a nine a.m. tee time with Mayor Bouchard. To do that requires exhaustive threat analysis, a complex network of private contracts, extensive travel documentation, and hundreds of hours of scenario planning. I work alone, but I coordinate with dozens of partners to design an airtight survival package." Nick paused, then straightened. "I'm the planner who sees everything before it happens."

Sutton looked at Marty, who gave an impressed nod, then turned back to Nick. "OK, Nick. Marty tells me you're the best in the business. Everyone who matters in this city uses you. I want you to do a civil-war escape plan for me."

Nick froze, then looked from Sutton to Marty and back. "Governor…I appreciate it, and I'm happy to consult, but I'm not taking on new clients."

Sutton squinted at Nick for a long moment, then grinned and waved him down. "Yeah yeah, spare me the whole 'fully booked' schtick. I get it. You're exclusive. What's it gonna cost?" He grabbed a peanut.

"Sir, I took this meeting as a favor to Marty, he said you wanted advice. The truth is I'm retiring. I'm getting out. I'm happy to introduce you to other firms. Lockley & Partners is excellent in this area."

Marty lurched forward. "Wait, what? You're retiring? To do what?"

Nick paused, both men glaring at him. "I'm moving to New Zealand."

"New Zealand?" Marty said. "What's in New Zealand?"

Nick weighed how much to share. "I built a place. I'm retiring there in January."

"New Zealand!" Marty slapped his knee. "Don't they have more sheep than people? Nick Ritter the sheep farmer—ha!"

Sutton stared at Nick, gripping his peanut, dead serious. He leaned in, suddenly looking tired and worn. "Look, Nick, I want you to do this for me. The truth is I'm scared. My wife is scared. My girls are scared. And if you're the best in the game, I want *you* to do it. Just give me a basic civil-war escape plan. Surely you can finish that by January."

Nick shook his head. "It doesn't work that way, sir. Disasters build on each other. What starts as a civil war can devolve into a nuclear conflict or disease outbreak or martial law. To keep my clients safe, I have to consider everything. I'm sorry, Governor."

Sutton's face darkened. He stared down at his peanut. "You know, Nick, with a client list like yours, I bet you've learned there are people you say no to and people you don't." He crushed the shell with his oversized thumb, crumbling fragments and dust over the carpet, then locked eyes with Nick. "I'm someone you don't say no to."

The governor stared for a long moment, then leaned back and relaxed. "Plus, you owe me a favor." He tossed the nuts into his mouth.

"How's that, sir?"

"I pulled you out of that shithole in Africa."

Nick looked at Marty to see if it was a joke.

"Oh, you didn't know?" Sutton laughed. "What, you thought they just released you one day?" He tossed the shell into the empty bowl and grabbed another.

"Their prime minister—what's his name, Magoogoo something—he wanted to make you their whipping boy for the whole mess." The governor did air quotes. "'Negligent safety planning.' 'Corporate sabotage.' 'Colonial aggression.'" He rolled his eyes. "Please."

He cracked the shell and dust drifted across his pants, the chair, the carpet. "They wouldn't dare execute an American, so they were gonna throw you in prison for life. Your Thorne lawyers attacked for six weeks, but with the media frenzy around the collapse and all the dead kids," Sutton shook his head firmly, "prime minister wouldn't budge. Finally the whole thing got so ugly that your brother and Senator Swenson officially got involved. They were Co-Chairs of the Foreign Relations Committee at the time, and because you were a Mass resident, they called me."

Sutton tried to hide a smirk. "They asked my office to partner with the U.S. Ambassador to Congo to lead this formal, two-day negotiation session with these African…diplomats." He started to giggle. "Well, I had one too many Glenlivets at lunch, and ten minutes into this big conference I fly off the handle and threaten to end their humanitarian aid." He gave a sharp laugh and leaned forward dramatically. "Which, of course, I have *zero* control over. But they don't know that. They fly into a tizzy, and low and behold, an hour later, you're on a plane to Germany."

Sutton pointed his thick finger. "That's right, Nick. Without me, you're eating bugs in a Congo work camp." He flicked a peanut into his mouth and flashed his big eyebrows.

Nick swallowed the nausea rising into his throat.

Sutton smiled, leaned back, and crossed his legs. "So...what's it gonna cost?"

Nick considered for a long moment. "How many people?"

"Me, my wife, and our three daughters. Plus the dog."

"You want a bare-bones escape or the luxury package?"

"What do you mean?"

"Bare bones is a 700-square-foot bunker in South Dakota. Luxury is a ten-acre ranch in Portugal with a swimming pool and helipad."

Marty smirked. "Want me to call Connie, check with her?"

Sutton rolled his eyes and shook his head. "Better do the luxury."

Marty snickered and sipped his drink.

Nick took a deep breath. "Eight million."

"Eight million?" Sutton spewed peanut dust. "Are you crazy?"

"The house and land alone are three million. Golden passports for five people are two million, minimum. Plus you need dedicated access to private pilots, doctors, chefs, a staff of a dozen or more."

"Let's say four million." Sutton crushed another peanut. "Call it a government-employee discount."

Marty gave Nick a stern look.

Nick forced a weak smile. "I'd be happy to, Governor."

"Excellent!" Sutton flicked his peanut, tossed the shell, and dusted his hands.

"I'll need to interview you, your family, get details on all your lives. It'll take about a month to line up the contracts, integrate with your security team, stress test the plan. I have to think of everything."

Sutton picked up his beer. "How soon can you start?" He chugged.

"I can start tonight."

Sutton finished his beer and slammed it down on the table. "Beautiful." He wiped his mouth, stood, and brushed peanut dust off his jacket and pants. He extended a hand. "Thanks for your help, Nick."

Nick stood and shook. "Thank you, sir."

Sutton headed for the door.

"Same time tomorrow, Ray," Marty called from his chair. "I'll introduce you to my tailor."

Sutton turned and walked backward, smirking. "You know, Marty,

I'm having dinner with Dougie Chang tonight. Maybe I'll nudge him to approve zoning for that biker bar at your Nantucket place."

Marty gagged on his scotch and lurched forward. "Don't even joke about that."

Sutton laughed and turned back toward the door.

"Ray, come on. Is that because of the suit?"

Sutton opened the door and turned back. "Oh, Nick, I almost forgot. I need one more favor, buddy."

Nick gripped the chairback. "Anything, Governor."

FOUR

Nick strode through the skyscraper's lobby to an unmarked hallway in the back. Brushing past two armed guards, he moved down the hall and stopped at the steel door. He swiped his badge and stared into the camera's red eye. A big lock cracked free. Nick stepped inside and a guard with an earpiece locked the door behind him.

"Good evening, sir. Welcome home." The front-desk woman handed him a small white box sealed with a strip of red tape.

"Thank you." Nick took the box without eye contact and moved into the open elevator at the end of the room. He swiped his badge and the doors shut.

When the elevator reached the penthouse level, Nick hurried down the hall. A condo door at the far end opened and a Saudi prince in a robe and keffiyeh strode toward the elevator. They passed each other. No greeting. No eye contact.

Nick reached his door, swiped his badge, and moved inside. A screen on the entry wall glowed to life.

"Nick Ritter. Home," he said.

"System armed," a voice said. The condo lights faded on.

Nick exhaled, lowered his shoulders, and relaxed. He tossed his badge on the table and wandered into the family room.

Located in Boston's swanky Seaport neighborhood, his corner unit was walled with floor-to-ceiling windows, offering a breathtaking 270-degree view of the city. He stepped to the window and gazed over the sprawling city lights, then out at the sunset across the ocean. He drew a breath of crisp, clean, HEPA-filtered air and took comfort in seeing three escape routes at once: Logan Airport, Boston Harbor, and the highways heading north, south, and west.

Nick moved to the kitchen and began his usual routine. It was automatic now, like a well-choreographed dance.

Grab the white box.

Knife through the red tape.

Pull out the vacuum-sealed tray.

Chicken breast and veggies. Didn't I have that last night?

Pop it in the microwave. Two minutes. Start.

Break down the box. Squeeze it into the stack.

Open the drawer. Grab an aspirin.

Jesus, my head.

Make that two aspirin.

Fill a glass with water. Take the aspirin.

Set a place on the bar counter.

Position the laptop.

Grab the steaming tray.

Plop down on the stool.

Bon appetit.

Nick angled his laptop into its usual viewing position and clicked "Play" on a live video stream. A doughy middle-aged man in an ill-fitting blazer hunched over a desk in a podcasting studio. He shuffled papers as his intro music wrapped up, then pulled the microphone to his mouth. "Alrighty, loyal listeners, let's run through the news for today, Tuesday, November twenty-third, 2035." He spoke with a slight southern accent. "As always, I'm gonna give you the *real* story behind the story."

Nick sliced his chicken breast.

"Before we jump in, I wanna share something big that y'all need to hear. Last night, I had dinner with someone connected in state government. And he told me something that shocked me to my core. Now, y'all know there's a silent civil war raging across the country right now. We covered it many times on this show."

"Hey, maybe this is the governor's source," Nick muttered, then chuckled.

"Well, folks, we're on the brink. This kettle's been simmering for years and now she's about to boil. Last night, my source told me something so vile, so disgusting…I can't even believe it. But it *proves* this civil war is about to go from silent to loud as hell." The host leaned in and spoke in a hushed and serious tone. "A certain state senator's newborn baby girl has gone missing, captured as a POW in this war. And in response, his southern state has mobilized its militia and is preparing for a northern invasion." He leaned back and threw up his hands. "This is it, folks. This is how it starts. Now, I don't disclose my sources, so I can't say more than that. But I can say this: For y'all living north of the Mason-Dixon, it's time to get right with your three G's: God, Guns, and Gold. Don't say I didn't warn ya."

He always opens with an imminent disaster. Who falls for this shit?

The host shuffled papers and switched to a cheery tone. "Alrighty, on to the news. There was a mass shooting today, fifty-four so far this month, one shy of the record. It took place at Disneyland, with twenty-three people dead and twelve more in critical condition. Now, the mainstream media is saying the shooter was a man, Randy Joe Reardon, whose wife, Betsy Reardon, worked at the theme park, and that he snapped because she was, quote, 'fixin' to leave me for another man.'" He shook his head and chuckled. "Well, loyal listeners, I ain't buyin' it."

Nick pushed aside his half-eaten dinner and picked up his phone to browse emails.

"Here's something you won't find in the lamestream media. Last week, Disneyland employees started a campaign to unionize and negotiate higher pay. And well, surprise surprise, Miss Betsy is president of the union committee. Coincidence? I ain't fooled. Based on all the facts here, I'm ninety-nine percent certain this was a corporate-sponsored assassination gone horribly wrong. And I'll tell you why…"

The screen cut to an empty podium in the White House briefing room. It was flanked by somber-looking generals and men in dark suits. The word "LIVE" glowed red in the corner of the screen. A voice came over the feed. "We interrupt this program for an emergency broadcast from the White House. We are required to air this message under the Early Warning Act."

Nick scrolled through emails, uninterested.

The President took the podium, his face tired and grave. Cameras clicked and flashed. He gathered himself, then looked up at the screen. "My fellow Americans, I come to you with a somber message. Tonight, we are a nation at war. For the first time since Pearl Harbor in 1941, a foreign enemy has invaded U.S. soil."

Nick sipped his water and moved from emails to researching the governor.

"An hour ago, Saudi Arabia, a country we trusted as our ally, landed one hundred thousand Arab troops in my home state of South Carolina." He paused to steady his voice. "They have captured my hometown of Charleston and are storming west, through the southern belt of our great country." He glared with intense resolve. "We will *not* stand for this terrorist aggression." He banged the podium. "I *urge* you to rise up and protect our United States of America. Right now, please visit www.AmericanFreedom.biz/invasion on your computer or mobile device and make a contribution to save this great country."

The website address pulsed in red, white, and blue at the bottom of the screen. At the same time, the phrase, "*ADVERTISEMENT—simulated announcement," appeared in tiny font in the bottom right corner.

"Use promo code 'CHARLESTON' and any gift over two hundred dollars will receive a genuine U.S. government defense kit. This priceless kit contains an American flag lighter, an American eagle coffee thermos, an American—"

Nick closed the video and rubbed his eyes.

No wonder nobody knows what's real, everything's a lie.

He opened an email login page and typed in a username, "JohnSmith6353," and password and hit enter. He skimmed down the inbox, but everything was already marked "read," except the top email, which was new:

GoFundMe: New Hope Church sent you a message!
GoFundMe: Thanks for your donation to New Hope Church
GoFundMe: Thanks for your donation to The Ward Family
GoFundMe: Thanks for your donation to Turkey for Veterans Project
GoFundMe: Thanks for your donation to New Car for Lesley Rios
GoFundMe: Thanks for your donation to Adopt a Stray Club
GoFundMe: Thanks for your donation to Horizon Senior Center
GoFundMe: Thanks for your donation to The Nguyen Family
GoFundMe: Thanks for your donation to Lawrence Youth Project
GoFundMe: Thanks for your donation to Smokey's Leg Surgery
GoFundMe: Thanks for your donation to Spruce Street Shelter
GoFundMe: Thanks for your donation to Ms. Lily's 3rd Grade Class
GoFundMe: Thanks for your donation to Gabby's Tumor Chemo
GoFundMe: Thanks for your donation to Randolph Hurricane Fund
GoFundMe: Thanks for your donation to Wheelchair for Nana
GoFundMe: Thanks for your donation to Temple Shalom Roof
GoFundMe: Thanks for your donation to Craig & Kathy's House Fire
GoFundMe: Thanks for your donation to Kiley's Last Wish
GoFundMe: Thanks for your donation to Rebuild the Yusuf Mosque

He opened the top message: "To all donors: Please join Reverend Duncan live at 8:00 p.m. to celebrate reaching our fundraising goal."

He glanced at his watch, 8:07 p.m.

He hovered over the big green button, "Join live stream," and swirled his mouse, then clicked. A live video opened in a new browser tab.

The view was from a camera posted in the back of a small church. It looked down over crowded pews at a stage where a reverend was speaking behind a podium.

"...and during this week of Thanksgiving, we got so much to be thankful for here at New Hope. The blessings from our Lord and the blessings from each other."

The congregation murmured in support.

Reverend Duncan began to pace the stage. "For many folks in this congregation, it's been a difficult year. We seen hardship. We seen tragedy. The good Lord has tested our faith."

The crowd murmured.

"But through every misfortune, this community has been a guiding light—a place of love and kindness and hope. Which brings me to tonight's topic. Last week we started our first internet fundraiser for a handicap ramp in front the church. Now, we had many generous donations from this community and we was doing fine. But last night, the good Lord smiled upon us and sent us a genuine miracle." He stopped and turned to the congregation, his eyes wide. "Someone donated eight thousand dollars and we reached our ten-thousand-dollar goal."

The congregation cheered.

"Hallelujah!"

"Praise Jesus!"

"Lord heaven above!"

Duncan scanned the crowd with a big exaggerated nod. "Mm-hmm. Mm-hmm." Then he shushed everyone with both hands. "Now, y'all know the Lord works in mysterious ways, and I'd like to thank this generous donor, but their contribution was...*anonymous*."

The room buzzed.

Duncan lifted his voice above the hum, stirring their emotions. "No name...no number...no nothin'...just a genuine miracle, straight from the hand of God."

The crowd reached a fever pitch.

"Thank you, Jesus!"

"Oh, good Lord!"

Duncan nodded. "Mm-hmm. Mm-hmm." He waved them down until the church was quiet. Then he leaned in, poised to deliver something important, and spoke softly. "Now, Jesus don't have no credit card."

The congregation chuckled.

"And I *know* none of y'all that rich." He grinned with his hands on his hips.

The crowd laughed and clapped.

Nick smiled.

"Mm-hmm. Mm-hmm." Duncan milked the joke to the last laugh. Then he turned serious. "But whoever made this donation is a truly good and generous person. Their kindness will make a real difference to our elderly and disabled folks."

Duncan looked straight into the camera. "If you're watching, I want to thank you and show you what your gift means to our little community."

Nick leaned in, his eyes wide and glowing against the bright screen.

Duncan pointed to someone in the crowd. "What your gift means to Mr. Jerry Coleman, who uses his wheelchair to come play the organ for us every Sunday."

The crowd murmured with praise.

Duncan pointed to someone on the other side. "Or Mrs. Gloria Green, who ain't so steady on the stairs, but at ninety-three years old *still* bakes a cornbread that'll make this grown man weep."

The congregation clapped and hollered. "Amen, Reverend. Amen!"

Duncan winked and smiled. Then he looked at someone in the front row and his face turned warm and gentle. "Or little Miss Sandy Shelton, who just recently joined our community, and has been on the mend from the rickets."

The crowd gave a pained confirmation.

Duncan's eyes sparkled, kind and loving. "Miss Sandy, honey, you wanna come up here and share what this gift means to you?"

A girl in a red dress stood with help from her neighbors. Duncan extended a hand and helped her up the steps. She was thin, with bowed legs, and walked with an unsteady gait.

Nick leaned closer.

When she reached the podium, she gripped it for stability and turned to face the camera. A little girl with red braids stared up at Nick with milky-white pupils. He gasped and recoiled, blinking and refocusing until, suddenly, it wasn't her. Now he saw an older girl, eight or nine, with her hair in pigtails and dark circles around her eyes. She stared into the camera with a sweet smile. "Hi there, to whoever gave that generous donation, I just want to say—"

Nick slammed the laptop shut.

He closed his eyes and massaged his aching forehead.

The girl from the mine…her face flashed in his mind…smiling up from the chamber floor…disappearing into a cloud of dust…a whisper.

And then he smelled it: a hint of rubber and gasoline.

"No no no…come on."

He pressed a hand to his chest and began box breathing, trying to reset before it spiraled into a full-blown attack.

His phone gave a loud *ping* and he looked down at the notification: "New Zealand Immigration: Your Residence Application is Complete."

A surge of excitement ran through him. He grabbed the phone and skimmed the email:

> We have reviewed your New Zealand Residence by Investment application.
>
> Your residency has been: APPROVED.
>
> Effective immediately, you may travel in, out, and around the country as a full citizen.
>
> Thank you for your investment in our country. Welcome to New Zealand.
>
> – New Zealand Immigration

Nick looked out the window, across the dark sea, and imagined New Zealand lay just beyond sight. He let out a relieved laugh.

It's early. I thought it would take another month, at least.

He glanced at his watch, 8:27 p.m. Was it too late to start Governor Sutton's plan?

"Sooner we start, sooner we're done."

Nick tapped the table, jumped up, and cleared dinner.

* * *

NICK GRABBED a red dry-erase marker off the wall holder and eyed the three huge windows that overlooked the city. He rolled up his sleeves. "Alright, here we go."

He moved across the windows, writing one stage of disaster response at the top of each, narrating as he worked.

"Arrive. Get there safely."

"Survive. Outlast the threat."

"Thrive. Live in the new world."

In each window, he drew eight big bubbles and sketched a symbol in the center of each.

Airplane. "Transportation."

Fork. "Food and water."

House. "Shelter."

Cross. "Health and medical."

Shield. "Safety and defense."

Dollar sign. "Currency and assets."

Phone. "Communication and continuity."

Book. "Leisure and entertainment."

His approach was simple: Prep for each of the eight categories in each of the three stages of disaster response. After all, Transportation prep for the Arrive stage might require a helicopter for extracting the governor from a battle zone, whereas Transportation prep for Thrive might require a bicycle for exercise. And a category like Leisure & Entertainment wasn't important during Arrive but was critical during Thrive.

At Thorne, they'd used automated software to plan. It was fast and efficient and spit out impressive-looking reports, but it was too regimented, too formulaic—it missed things. So Nick came up with his own method, which relied on round after round of scenario analysis. He missed nothing.

Nick stepped back and took a deep breath. "OK, breaking intelligence report: A southern militia is heading north. What do we do? Talk it out."

He stepped to the Transportation bubble under Arrive and added a ring of spokes off it.

"Plan A is we fly private from Boston to Portugal. From Portugal, we can get anywhere. So we'll need on-call pilots across Massachusetts." He scribbled a note at the end of a spoke: "Private flights."

"We've got Logan Airport plus seven private air strips under contract here in Mass. That should be good." He made a note: "Air strips in MA."

"On the Portugal side, we've got Lisbon Airport plus three private air strips along the coast and three more inland, all under contract." He added a note: "Air strips in Portugal."

"We'll need Portuguese golden passports for five people, which will unlock visa-free travel to all twenty-seven countries in the E.U." Note: "Golden passports (Portugal x 5)."

"Oh, and we'll need a crate for the dog. Hopefully it's small." Note: "Dog (crate x 1)."

He moved to the Food & Water bubble under Arrive and added spokes.

"Private air should be fast, 6–8 hours depending on where we land. So two meals plus snacks should be enough." He scribbled: "Flight = rations for 12 hours."

"We'll have to check on food allergies and special diets." Note: "Allergies/diets?"

"Plus we'll need dog food and treats." Note: "Dog x 1 (special diet?)."

"In terms of numbers, we've got five clients." Note: "Clients x 5."

"And staff count…that's still TBD. We'll come back to that." Note: "Staff x ?"

He hovered over the Shelter bubble. "We shouldn't need shelter as part of Arrive because the flight is so short. Let's skip it for now."

A thought popped into his head and he reached up to the Safety & Defense bubble. "Since we use Kormann, we'll want private security the whole way." Note: "Integrate with Kormann."

He crouched to Health & Medical. "Obviously we'll need basic first aid kits, plus a doctor on staff in case of emergency." Note: "First aid + MD."

"And we'll need an inventory of emergency meds for the clients, plus the staff. Plus the dog." Note: "Meds (clients + staff + dog)."

Nick reached a state of flow, gliding across the windows in a smooth dance, playing out scenarios, talking through logic, circling, connecting, scribbling.

Time raced past as Nick planned:

Crunching a handful of granola as his eyes jumped between two bubbles—springing forward, circling two distant notes, drawing a line connecting them.

Staring at the ceiling, visualizing a situation, talking out loud, pointing with the marker—stepping to the window, marking up insights.

Sipping coffee, squinting down at a dense bubble—dropping to a knee, scrubbing off a note with his palm, scribbling a better idea.

He scanned and sidestepped and sketched, the city lights glowing behind his map, casting colorful patterns across his animated face.

He felt perfectly balanced: sharp, alert, energized, but also calm, focused, and creative. He felt alive.

Ninety minutes later, the windows were covered with a giant red spiderweb. Nick jotted one last note on a Shelter spoke under the Thrive window. "We'll want the ranch to be energy independent and fully sustainable. That means fossil as our primary with solar and wind backups. Plus batteries and generators for temporary outages." He squeezed a long note into a small space: "Energy: fossil, solar, wind, battery, generator."

He stepped back and squinted at his note, then shook his head. "Yeah, no way this is coming in under four million."

Nick scanned his work. What was once a ten-million-dollar view of the city was now a sprawling, tangled escape plan for a foreign invasion that would never happen. His reflection stared back from the window, clothes rumpled, palms smudged red, face tired and worn.

He exhaled. "Alright."

He stood in a daze for a long moment.

Then Nick took a sharp breath. "Plan B. Air isn't an option. What do we do?"

He jumped to Transportation under the Arrive window. "Boat is our next fastest option. Plenty of departure points in Mass and plenty of arrival points in Portugal. Five clients, plus a dog, plus security, a doctor...this thing has to hold ten people, at least." Note: "Boat (Plan B) = 10+ capacity."

He glided to Food & Water. "Depending on size and weather, a boat could take 3–10 days from Mass to Portugal. So we'll need a full menu. Five clients, plus the staff, plus the dog...yeah, we're gonna need a chef." Note: "Boat = chef for 10 days."

Nick spent the next forty minutes scouring his spiderweb, adding notes, circling ideas, drawing lines, solidifying Plan B. When he was finished, he stepped back and stared. His reflection stared back, wasted, eyes red, face oily, hair a mess.

"Alright." He gave a slow, tired blink. "Good."

He took a sharp breath. "Plan C. No plane. No boat. Go." He trudged to Transportation under Arrive.

"Eventually, we'll still need air or water to reach Portugal, so let's use cars to get out of Mass to an airport or seaport in another state. With five clients, five or more staff, plus the dog, we're gonna need a caravan of large-capacity vehicles. The usual Chevy Suburbans will work." Note: "Suburban caravan (Plan C) = 10+ capacity."

He continued for hours, dreaming up disaster scenarios and backup plans, until his vision was blurry and he was making mistakes. He stepped back and stared at the zombie in the window.

Nick glanced at his watch, 1:43 a.m. "OK, let's call it."

He capped the marker, took pictures of everything, and uploaded them to his secure planning app.

"Bedtime," Nick called to the security system.

The room went dark.

He staggered to the bedroom.

* * *

Nick climbed into bed, sat up, and blinked at the red clock on his nightstand, 1:56 a.m. He reached under his collar and pulled off a pendant necklace—a worn jet-black cylinder hanging from a chain—and placed it on the nightstand next to his phone. He turned on the white noise machine, filling the dead-silent room with a low hiss, and laid back, staring at the city lights cast across the ceiling.

Nick tossed and turned, his mind still racing from the planning session. As he watched the lights flicker and shift, a video flashed in his mind: the governor throwing a tennis ball into a cornfield, his dog racing through the rows to fetch.

Shit—what if he wants to stay in the U.S. but relocate to a neutral state?

Nick sat up and groped his phone off the nightstand, wincing as the bright light radiated his dark-adjusted eyes. He tapped a note into his planning app: "Gov needs shelter options in U.S."

He replaced the phone and laid back down.

He stared at the ceiling, time passing, his mind drifting.

Another video streamed: the governor standing by a desk, barking orders into a secure phone.

What if he wants to act as Governor of Massachusetts from a remote location?

Nick grabbed his phone and jotted another note: "Need continuity of government + communications strategy."

He laid down and gazed at the clock, 2:24 a.m. He closed his eyes. A video flashed: the governor in a safe room, surrounded by bodyguards.

If soldiers arrive before he can escape, Kormann will lock him in a safe room. Then we'll need a tactical team for a high-risk extraction.

He turned over, trying to forget it.

Leave it until morning. You can run it with the other scenarios.

He turned the other way, but the video was already streaming, fast and vivid:

Kormann guards surrounded the governor, guns drawn, and rushed him and Connie and the girls into a basement safe room.

Outside, rag-tag militiamen encircled the governor's mansion and cut the power. The lights flickered off.

Nick turned over and groaned. "Let it go."

The militiamen crept down a dark basement hallway, toward the safe room, guns raised. Kormann guards jumped out behind them and opened fire. The dark tunnel flashed bright, lighting their faces... crazed soldiers...loyal guards...men twisted in bloody pools on the floor. A burst of gunfire lit a downed face, a big miner sprawled across the ground, covered in dust, his mouth hanging open.

"No no no..." Nick gripped his blanket and the movie accelerated into a series of disjointed flashes.

BOOM...an explosion blew out the conveyor room, blasting rock and dust and debris.

A scream...a woman lay motionless, clutching her baby.

The stink of rock dust and sweat...children blurred past.

A charred smell...scattered bodies burned.

Nick pulled the blanket over his head. "Stop!"

The stench of gasoline...the girl with red braids groped along the tunnel wall.

Burnt rubber...the tunnel collapsed, she disappeared into a cloud of dust.

A whisper, loud and close. "Follow the light."

Nick shot up in bed, flicked on the light, and grabbed his necklace. He unscrewed the top of the cylinder and huffed a long, deep breath of lavender oil. He put a hand on his chest and began box breathing. The images dimmed, the sounds muted, the smells faded.

Ten minutes later, he was back to baseline. He put on the necklace and picked up his iPad. With a few taps, he pulled up the security system app for his New Zealand ranch and ran through the cameras.

Camera 1 (Dining Room): A long dining table with fresh flowers.

Camera 2 (Family Room): Two couches, three chairs, a big fireplace.

Camera 3 (Game Room): A pool table, ping pong table, big TV, bean bag chairs.

Camera 4 (Power): Green pastures, rolling hills, three wind turbines, solar panels.

Camera 5 (Gardens): An old woman with short hair, kind eyes, and a Maori tribal tattoo on her chin hummed and planted flowers.

Camera 6 (Livestock): A stocky old woman with a tight bun and dirty overalls stood with a hand on her hip, pointing to a barn and arguing with a fat sheep.

Nick laughed and relaxed his shoulders. A wave of calm washed over him.

So soon. Just finish the governor's plan, get through the holidays, and you'll be there by January. Then you can finally—

His phone ringer shrieked, volume accidentally set on high. He snatched the phone and glared at the screen. It was Marty Kettenbach. At 2:49 a.m.

"Jesus Christ, Marty…fuck off. I'm not your personal 911."

Nick declined the call, lowered the volume, and slid the phone back on the nightstand. He placed a hand on his pounding heart and tried to recenter.

The phone rang again.

Nick covered his ears and closed his eyes.

The ringing got louder.

"Forty-nine days," he whispered. "Forty-nine days."

Louder…in his head, rattling his skull, vibrating his brain.

"Forty-nine days," he shouted. "Forty-nine—"

An idea struck.

The ringing stopped.

He opened his eyes, grabbed the phone, and dialed.

"G'day, Nick, what a nice surprise. How ya going?" Her voice was gentle and peaceful.

Nick relaxed and met her tone. "I'm doing well, Maia. How are you?"

"Yeah, I'm good. It's a cracker day here, so I'm out planting sweet peas and alyssum in your garden. Oh, and I added something new, it's called love in the mist. I think you're gonna like it."

"That sounds wonderful, I can't wait to see it. How's Kora feeling?"

"Ohhh, you know Kora. She's out there arguing with the sheep all day even though the doc told her to rest."

Nick laughed. "It's good for her. She'd go crazy sitting inside all day."

"No, I'd go crazy." Maia laughed.

Nick laughed again, then paused for a beat of silence. "Hey, Maia, I wanted to ask you something. I know we talked about me moving there in January, but I was wondering…would it be alright if I came sooner?"

"Oh yeah, Nick, no worries. It's your house, come whenever you like. We'll get everything ready for you. When were you thinking?"

"Umm, maybe like two weeks? I have to wrap up one last project, then I'll head down the first week of December."

"Yeah, no worries at all. It's practically ready now. Won't take much to spruce up a few things."

"That's great. Thanks so much, Maia. I really appreciate it."

She paused. "Everything OK, Nick?"

Nick took a deep breath, pressed his aching chest, and forced a smile: "Oh yeah, no worries. I just want to catch more of the summer season…see your new garden and help Kora with the first sheep shearing."

"Aww, that would make Kora happy. Me too. Look, we'll get the house ready in a couple days, just in case you decide to come early."

"Thank you, Maia. Truly, thank you."

"No worries, Nick. We'll see you soon."

"See you soon."

He put his phone on silent and placed it on the nightstand.

"Fourteen days," he whispered as he snuggled into bed. "Fourteen days."

FIVE

"Thanks for waiting, Mr. Ritter."

Nick looked up from his phone at the peppy, young assistant bouncing with her iPad. With her short skirt and heavy makeup, she looked like a model. Nine times out of ten, when his clients had an assistant like that, it only meant one thing.

"T.J. just finished his morning meditation, he's ready for you now. Follow me."

Nick stood and glanced at his watch, 9:40 a.m.—forty minutes past his appointment time. He straightened his dark jacket, white shirt, and jeans, a neutral outfit that worked equally well for politicians, businessmen, and startup founders like T.J. Chandra. He followed the assistant across the ground floor of T.J.'s 5,000-square-foot Back Bay brownstone, weaving through a buzzing crowd of support staff—administrative assistants, agents, brand managers, media planners, press secretaries, and a plant-maintenance lady. The entire downstairs had been converted into an office and furnished with fun furniture, wacky art, and big-screen monitors swirling innovative graphics. A barista ran a free coffee bar in the back, making the whole place smell like a Starbucks.

She led him past two security guards in suits, down a hall, and opened the door to T.J.'s office. She gestured inside. "Enjoy!"

He stepped inside and she closed the door behind him.

It was a long office that had probably once served as the home's private library. At the head of the room was T.J.'s desk, and at the other end was a seating area with refreshments, a whiteboard on wheels, and a big-screen TV. Aside from the windows and doors, the walls were one giant screen, wrapping 360 degrees around the room, stretching from floor to ceiling. The screen streamed a coral reef, with fish of all shapes, sizes, and colors darting and swirling through a forest of coral and kelp.

T.J. was standing at a window, his back to Nick, hands clasped behind, watching people stream past a busy sidewalk.

Nick walked to the center of the room and cleared his throat. "Good morn—"

T.J. shouted, as if trying to break into an invisible conversation. "Don...Don...Don...the truth is they don't add value. We're not running a public service here. I mean, this is still free market capitalism, right? Did I fall asleep and wake up in China?"

T.J. spun and adjusted his Airpods. He was slim, with bright eyes, healthy color, and perfect hair. Under his gray blazer he wore a bright red sweater over a red tartan shirt. Despite being almost forty, he had a babyface, which made him look like a boy wearing his dad's suit.

He squinted at Nick, pointed directly at him, and whispered, "Grapes?"

Nick stared and blinked, then turned to see a big bowl of shiny grapes on the refreshments table behind him. He turned back to T.J. and nodded with a polite smile.

Nick walked back and scooped some grapes into a paper cup. He popped one into his mouth and pretended to watch CNBC on the giant TV.

T.J. erupted behind him. "You're wrong, Don. You're fantastically wrong. Across the global economy, the value of human capital is in secular decline. We simply don't need people to do these jobs anymore."

At the bottom of the TV screen was a banner, "CNBC: Economy Now." In the top right corner was a picture of T.J. titled, "CALLING LIVE: T.J. Chandra, Founder & CEO of Zencryptic." A host stared at the camera in shock.

Wait, is he...

The host spoke. "T.J., are you saying that computers and robots *should* replace people in the workforce? That's a good thing?"

T.J. responded behind Nick, way too loud for the room. "For most low-skill and back-office jobs, yes. Absolutely. It's economically irresponsible to put humans in jobs that robots can do more efficiently."

Nick spun and watched T.J. pace. "Look at Zencryptic, we're the largest social network in the world and we have fewer than two thousand employees. And most of those are lawyers to defend against our litigious government."

Nick swung back to the TV as Don responded. "Let's talk about that for a moment. Senator Galloway recently called Zencryptic, quote, 'a cancer of America's moral fiber.' And she wasn't talking about your hiring practices. She was talking about your privacy policy. What do you say to that?"

Nick turned to T.J. "First of all, Don, let's not pretend Senator Galloway cares about America or understands what Zen is. She's just another useless D.C. sock puppet regurgitating talking points."

Nick glanced back at the TV. Don's eyes popped wide and his jaw dropped.

T.J. strolled to the window, turned his back to it, and raised his phone in a selfie pose. He tapped the screen, smiled, and gave a little wave. "Second, let me clear up exactly how Zen works, because you guys *really* struggle to understand it. Zen is an invite-only, private-room, end-to-end encrypted, fully distributed, social platform. Put simply, we're a social network where anyone can create a private group conversation that can't be accessed by the government, or hackers, or anyone else. Complete and total social privacy. And because everything is hosted remotely on our user's devices, the company has no access to, and bears no responsibility for, any of the content." T.J. gave his phone a big thumbs up, then tapped and lowered it.

"OK, but T.J., let's be real about what's happening on your platform," Don said. "Criminal operations, child pornography, human trafficking, illegal narcotics, terrorism, insider trading. Just last week, classified government documents were leaked on Zencryptic, compromising national security and risking the lives of our soldiers overseas."

Nick wandered to a weird, futuristic chair against the side wall, halfway between T.J. and the TV. He sat and flicked grapes like popcorn, watching the debate volley back and forth like a tennis match.

T.J. strolled to a coffee bar against the wall and prepared a matcha tea. Using a thin wooden ladle, he scooped green powder from a small container and dumped it into a teacup.

"Hold on, hold on…you've made a mess of it, Don, as usual. First of all, those classified docs came from high-ranking intelligence officials acting as legally protected whistleblowers. They were exposing evidence of rampant government corruption within their own agencies so the public could see the truth."

He picked up a wooden brush and whisked the green powder as he poured hot water from a little porcelain kettle.

"Second of all, you're missing the bigger picture here, so let me simplify. Let's imagine you install a whiteboard and a box of permanent markers in a dark corner of the Boston Common. You leave it there for a week, and when you come back it's covered with all kinds of objectionable things: hate speech, bullying, secrets, whatever. Who's to blame? Is it the board's fault? Is it the marker's fault? Is it *your* fault? All you did was put up a blank page and walk away. It's the *people* who wrote on the board that are responsible for its content. They could've written poems or drawn flowers, but no, they…you know…did what people always do. It's the same idea with Zen. But our crooked politicians, rather than address their deeply unhappy and immoral populace, try to score points off me as a distraction from our national dumpster fire."

Don stared in disbelief, then started to nod. "Wow…alright then… well, in the past you've claimed that Zencryptic brings power to the people, but your company is under investigation for selling user content from secure forums to private entities. Is that true?"

"I can't comment on that."

There was an awkward silence.

T.J. lifted his steaming mug and began to stroll. "Listen, Don…the whole point, the reason I called in, is because I want to *help* the American worker. In every industry, technology is replacing human beings, and it's creating real economic misery." He softened his tone. "Look, I'm a self-made man from humble roots. After my parents moved to Queens from the slums of Mumbai, my father opened his own Indian restaurant. He didn't run that restaurant for profit, because, trust me, there was none. He ran it to provide jobs for his employees and food for his community. If his restaurant was staffed by robots, my dad never would've opened it in the first place." T.J. placed the mug on a coaster on his desk.

Don interrupted, respectful but stern. "T.J., we've heard your father's story many times on this network. He started a small business. He built it from the ground up. He ran it for the community. It's an inspiring story. Truly. But how has *your* entrepreneurship created value? Your company is a hub for criminal activity. You offer very few jobs, which, apparently, is a good thing. You're embroiled in a staggering number of lawsuits. And you've burned through five hundred million in venture funding without a penny in profit. What have *you* done to better our global community?"

T.J. stared straight ahead.

Don pressed his earpiece. "T.J.? Are you still with us…T.J.?"

"Sorry, Don, you've completely lost the thread. I gotta go."

T.J. tapped his watch and the TV shut off. He closed his eyes and took a few deep, meditative breaths. The room was silent.

Does he remember I'm here?

T.J. opened his eyes and spun, looking directly at Nick. "Hi, how can I help you?" he said in a cheerful tone.

Nick froze, then stood and walked to the desk. "Mr. Chandra, my name is Nick Ritter. I'm a crisis consultant. Governor Sutton asked me to meet you this morning."

T.J. pulled out his Airpods. "You want a Core Water?"

Nick hesitated. "Um, no thank you. I'm fine."

T.J. squeezed his watch. "Zelda, two Core Waters." He nodded at Nick's wrist. "You have a Z-Watch?"

"Huh?"

T.J. pointed to his futuristic watch. "Our new Zencryptic watch. You have one?"

Nick pulled up his sleeve to show a classic dive watch.

"Oh my god, dude, is that thing analog?" T.J. shook his head and gestured at the chair. "Wow. Have a seat."

Zelda entered and placed down two little boxes of water and two glasses. Nick stared at the label, a picture of a straw reaching through the gray earth to a blue circle in the center, with the tagline, "Core—The Last Drop."

"Please don't tell me you drink the tap water here," T.J. said. "The fluoride will rot your brain."

"Ugh, gross." Zelda made a yuk face.

"To find clean water these days, you literally have to go to the end of the earth." T.J. grinned at his clever joke.

Zelda touched his shoulder and laughed too hard.

Welp, that confirms it. He's sleeping with her.

"Can I get you anything else, T.J.?" She fluttered her big eyelashes.

"We're good. Thanks, Zel."

She gave his shoulder a little squeeze and walked out.

Nick cleared his throat and pointed to the walls. "This is an amazing display."

T.J. jumped up. "It's the Great Barrier Reef."

Nick feigned amazement. "Wow, incredible, such a detailed reproduction."

T.J. spun and glared. "It's not a reproduction. It's the *actual* GBR."

Ugh, not this one...

Nick smiled and nodded.

"Well, as much of the reef as still exists." T.J. strolled along the coral. "It's not a video. It's a living, breathing, digital simulation of the northwest segment of the reef. Everything in here has to eat, sleep, breed, live, and die, just like in the wild. Except, digitally, of course."

He grinned. "Crazy, right? We scanned what was left of the reef right before the Japanese bleached it. Lucky timing really."

The GBR conspiracy was a favorite among his clients. The theory was that the Japanese bleached the reef as payback for high Australian tariffs. However, one of Nick's Japanese clients claimed he had insider information that it was actually a false-flag attack staged by Greenpeace activists. An oil executive in Australia swore the reef never existed in the first place. And just last month, Marty Kettenbach showed Nick pictures of his family snorkeling the reef on vacation. In these situations, Nick found it best to simply agree with the client.

Nick beamed a patronizing grin. "Well, now I can finally say I visited the Great Barrier Reef."

"Ha! Right? And look, you can feed them." T.J. swiped his finger in a little arc, sprinkling down a rainbow of fish food. A school of fish attacked. He tapped the glass and they winced and scattered. He laughed.

Nick gave a polite nod.

T.J. dropped back behind his desk. "OK, so Sutton got you in here…let's hear it. Pitch me." He gestured for Nick to bring it on.

Nick hesitated. "Well, Mr. Chandra, actually, Governor Sutton asked me to meet with you because he's concerned about a high-risk event in Massachusetts."

T.J. twisted open a boxed water, sniffed it, and poured. "Oh, right! His civil war thing. Yeah, I did some snooping on Zen…it's bullshit. Actually, it's the opposite. Mass is sending troops south. Sutton probably knows about it."

Nick pulled out his business card. "Well, the governor wanted me to offer my services…but if there's no immediate threat, I can just leave my information and—"

"Sorry, what exactly are you selling?" T.J. sipped his water.

Nick blinked, trying to hide his annoyance. "I'm a crisis consultant. I design survival plans for high-profile clients."

It clicked and T.J.'s eyes widened. "Ohhh, you're the Posh Prepper! I know you. You're big with my friends in Silicon Valley."

Nick nodded. "I have quite a few clients in the tech industry."

"Yeah, Bryce at Greenseed Capital was raving about you. Also, Caleb from Humanoid. Very cool. So what's the pitch?"

"Well, here's the thing, Mr. Chandra—"

"T.J."

"Here's the thing, T.J. I'm not taking on new clients. The governor asked me to meet with you as a personal favor. But if you're not in the market for my services right now, I'll just leave my number." He slid a card across the desk.

T.J. smirked and tilted his head. "Reverse psychology? Artificial scarcity? I like it."

Nick sighed.

T.J. looked down at his watch, tapping and scrolling. "Look, to be honest, Sutton is like the fifth person to recommend you. You're here now, I get what you do…so pitch. What can you offer me?"

"Well, that depends on a lot of things."

"Just bottom-line it for me. What'd you do for Bryce and Caleb?"

"I can't share their plans, but my high-end tech clients all lean toward a certain…premium package."

"Oooh, let me guess, a backyard bunker and a lifetime supply of SPAM?" T.J. cracked up. "I'm kidding. What's the premium package?"

This guy's starting to piss me off…

Nick leaned in, focused and intense. "24/7/365 monitoring, protection, and extraction for every disaster I can think of. Survival training for you and your security team. A fleet of private planes, boats, and vehicles. A two-hundred-acre luxury ranch in New Zealand with an air strip, helipad, and independent energy. Fresh food from sustainable hydroponics, aquaculture, and agriculture, plus a lifetime stockpile of food, water, and medicine. We diversify your finances across countries and institutions to reduce risk, and build off-grid backups in paper currencies, crypto, and precious metals. Plus rescue all your valuables…art, cars, coins, whatever. For you, safe arrival is just the beginning. I'd focus on wealth preservation and business continuity…computers, internet, data centers. Whatever you need to operate seamlessly." He leaned back. "That's just the basics. The rest would be customized."

T.J. thumbed over his shoulder. "Yeah, but can you save my fish?" He burst out laughing.

"Absolutely. I do a lot of data redundancy for tech clients."

T.J. nodded, impressed.

"Entertainment is mandatory," Nick said. "Without it you'll get cabin fever or depression. I include a bowling alley, movie theater, library, golf course, swimming pool, game room, climbing wall, gym, spa, pets, horses...whatever you want."

T.J. picked up his phone and began to scroll. "Sounds fun. How much are we talking?"

"Package like that...twenty million up front, then two million per year."

T.J.'s eyes shot up. "Twenty? That's a lot. Can't we just buy a bunker somewhere?"

"Sure...if you want to live in a concrete box in the middle of a cornfield. We can do an 800-square-foot bunker in a disaster community in Idaho. Or a 2,000-square-foot condo in an underground missile silo in Kansas. But your friends are all buying big in New Zealand."

T.J. returned to scrolling. "Why New Zealand? Isn't it all sheep?"

Nick counted on his fingers. "It's a first-world country with a high standard of living. It has cheap, abundant, breathtaking land. It has political, social, and economic stability with no enemies. And it's isolated, yet easily accessible from all global hubs. It's survival paradise."

T.J. squinted at Nick. "I thought they closed the border after that Taiwan refugee incident?"

"They did...but that's what you pay me for. They have a residence by investment program, also known as a golden passport. It's complicated, but basically you make a significant financial investment in the country and in return they grant you full citizenship."

T.J. smirked. "Sounds simple, like a bribe."

Nick shrugged and nodded. "We'd do New Zealand, two fallback countries, and Portugal, where citizenship unlocks all twenty-seven countries in the E.U."

T.J. put his phone on the desk, leaned back in his chair, and tapped his watch.

Nick slid his card closer to T.J. "But again, you can think about it and call me down the line. You don't have to decide—"

T.J. lurched forward, stood, and extended a hand. "OK, Nick. If the other guys are doing it, I'm in. Draw it up for the lawyers."

Nick sighed, slowly stood, and shook T.J.'s hand. "Will do."

"Oh, before you go, let me grab you a Z-Watch."

"That's OK. I'm good."

T.J. waved him off and pointed at Nick's wrist. "No no no—you gotta replace that sundial with something digital." He squeezed his Z-Watch and chatted with Zelda.

Nick pulled out his phone. He had a stack of notifications: thirty-six texts and nineteen missed calls. The top one caught his eye, a text from his brother, Paul: "Call me now."

Nick froze, they hadn't spoken in a long time.

"Is there someplace I could make a call?" Nick asked T.J.

T.J. pointed to a glass door in the back corner of the room. "There's a conference room through there."

Nick stepped into the dim conference room and shut the door behind him. The walls contained a different part of the reef, and the fish were all much smaller and brighter.

He took a deep breath and called.

"Nick," Paul said over a stream of hectic background chatter.

Nick hesitated. "Paul."

"Listen, I know we haven't talked in a while, and I'm sorry to jump you like this…but there's something you should know."

Nick waited.

"You there?"

"Yeah, I'm here."

"I don't have much time, so listen carefully. There's been some kind of…outbreak. It looks like a deadly virus, possibly manmade, possibly natural…we don't know. They think it started here, at Logan Airport, but it's spreading worldwide. We've already confirmed cases in three other global airports. Nick…if you're in Boston, you should get out."

Nick strolled the reef and a school of fish followed. "Paul, I appreciate the heads up, but the thing is…in my work, I hear this stuff all the time. Yesterday Governor Sutton swore we're on the brink of civil war. Today you're telling me there's a deadly virus outbreak. Tomorrow it'll be a Chinese nuclear strike. Every day is some new disaster." He swiped the screen three times, and the fish swirled and gobbled the rainbow. "This virus…it's probably just localized hysteria or a disinformation campaign."

"It's real, Nick," Paul said in a serious tone. He was louder, had moved the phone closer. "This is from a top-secret briefing to the senate subcommittee on Emerging Threats and Capabilities…it's not some conspiracy blog. The FBI received an anonymous tip that the outbreak started yesterday at Logan Airport, otherwise we never would've caught it this quickly. In twenty-four hours, there are already a hundred and fifty airport employees sick, thirty of them in critical condition. The early transmission stats…the CDC says they shouldn't be possible. They're freaking out." He lowered his voice. "Nick, I've seen the medical reports…they're horrifying."

Nick watched the fish dart and swirl. "How confident are you on this?"

"Confident…but it doesn't matter. The White House is acting on it. They've activated the National Guard and they're locking down major cities right now. They have no plan, other than to stall and say there's a terrorist threat. Tomorrow the President will tell the public the truth." He shifted to a heartfelt tone. "Listen to me, Nick…real or not, you've got one hour before they lock down Boston, and twenty-four hours before all hell breaks loose. Get out. Get out while you still can."

Nick checked his watch. "OK, I'll go. Tell me about the virus. How is it spread?"

"Hey!" Paul yelled.

A voice bellowed in the background. "Sir, please come with us."

"I'm on the phone," Paul said.

"Senator, we have orders to extract you to a secure location."

"Get your hands off me!"

The phone scuffed and crackled. Silence.

"Paul? Paul?"

Nick lowered the phone and stared at the swirling fish. His eyes darted back and forth as he analyzed, calculated, ran the scenarios.

Information quality is high. Paul has no reason to lie. His data is fresh, credible.

The fish shimmered and swooped, eager for another feeding.

If he's right, downside is you get trapped in Boston with a deadly virus. If he's wrong, downside is you spend a million to move to New Zealand two weeks early.

Nick looked at his watch. The seconds hand raced ahead.

You're wasting time...make a call.

He winced, hesitating.

You're freezing...move and confirm.

"OK." He nodded. "Move and confirm."

Nick spun and strode toward the door.

SIX

Nick burst out of the conference room as he pulled up the operator's number, muttering to himself. "Drive north, activate your plan, clear the city in thirty minutes, then—"

Nick nearly slammed into T.J., who was standing just outside the conference room, Airpods in, clutching his cell phone in one hand and dangling a shiny Z-Watch from the other.

"Deadly virus outbreak?" T.J. said.

They stared at each other for a long moment, each man trying to size up what the other knew.

"What?" Nick said.

"On the phone…you said there was a deadly virus outbreak."

Nick thumbed back toward the conference room. "Were you listening to me?"

"Well…yeah." T.J. shrugged.

Nick brushed past. "I have to go."

"Wait, you can't just leave. Tell me what's going on."

Nick strode toward the office door.

"Come on, man. Help me out," T.J. whined.

Nick didn't look back.

"Hey, asshole!" T.J. shouted in his big-time-CEO voice.

Nick stopped halfway to the door.

"Five minutes ago I hired you to protect me from this shit. Now you're gonna walk out mid-conversation? You owe me an explanation."

Nick slowly turned. "There's a deadly virus outbreak. It started in Mass and is spreading worldwide. The military is locking down major cities as we speak, starting with Boston." He paused. "And I don't work for you until you pay the bill."

T.J. stared past Nick in a daze. "They predicted this on Zen..." He refocused. "How do you know it's real?"

"I don't. That's the nature of prepping—you have to be early. To survive, you have to act before the threat is here, before it's obvious to everyone. The only way to be one hundred percent certain is to wait and see what happens. I'm not taking that chance. I'm getting out, and I suggest you do the same." He nodded and headed for the door.

"Take me with you," T.J. blurted.

"I don't do live support," Nick said over his shoulder. "Your security guys will get you out."

"And then what? Hide in a concrete box in the middle of a cornfield? We *agreed* on the premium package."

Nick opened the door. "I'm sorry, I can't help you."

"Oh, you're going to help me, or you won't make it past Newbury Street."

Nick paused in the open doorway and looked back.

T.J. stalked toward him. "You're not going *anywhere* until my valet brings your car...unless, oh, were you planning on taking the subway? If you don't help me, I'll blow you up on Zen. I'm thinking," T.J. made a headline gesture in the air, "'Posh Prepper Nick Ritter just warned me: Deadly virus spreading worldwide. Released in Boston by POTUS. Flee your city now!' I think my hundred and twenty-five million followers would find that very interesting." He glared at Nick.

"That's not true—"

"Doesn't matter if it's true. Only matters if I say it."

"You'd be in FBI custody within the hour."

T.J. mocked innocence. "Oh no, my account got hacked!" He shrugged. "Happens all the time."

Nick checked his watch.

Two minutes gone…this guy's gonna get you killed.

T.J. stepped close and lowered his voice. "Look, I can help you. I've got money and connections…I can monitor the private conversations of two billion people worldwide. Take me with you." His eyes hung on Nick.

Nick gazed out the open door for a long moment. "How many people?"

"Just me."

Nick gave him a skeptical look. "You *sure* there's no one else?" He cast a suggestive glance into the hallway.

T.J. stared, unflinching. "Nah. We're good."

You're sitting around debating…move.

"OK, call my car."

T.J. grinned, raised his watch and swiped twice. "Done." He scanned his office. "I need to pack a few things, and I wanna call my CFO, and—"

Nick slammed the door and stepped to T.J. "Listen to me—if you want in, we need to get a few things straight. We do things my way—no debate, no bullshit. We move quickly and silently—no calling your buddies, no warning your followers, no picking up strangers. In a disaster, every person is added risk. We have a head start, but my clients are well connected, and soon they'll know. If everyone tries to escape at once, we'll run short on planes and pilots. So we need to move *now*, before they lock down Boston and everyone heads for the exits."

T.J. stared like a schoolboy getting a lecture.

"We're going straight to my ranch in New Zealand as fast as we possibly can. Once we get there, I'll help you make your own arrangements."

"OK, but—"

Nick leaned in. "This is what I do. If you break my rules, I will leave you behind. If you slow me down, if you put me in danger, I will leave you behind." He pointed. "And you pay me two million for the escape. Consider it a rush-order fee."

They were startled by a knock at the door, then Zelda's voice. "T.J.? Mr. Ritter's car is here. Everything OK?"

Nick locked T.J. in a take-it-or-leave-it stare and whispered, "We walk out that door, right now, or you're on your own."

They stood for a long moment, dueling cowboys waiting for someone to draw.

T.J. reached past Nick and opened the door to reveal Zelda leaning in. He brushed past her. "We're doing a brainstorm brunch at Ostra. I'll be back later."

She turned, watching him go. "Oh, OK…what about your eleven o'clock with Mindy from STEM Girls?"

"Reschedule," T.J. called over his shoulder.

Nick followed down the hall.

The two bodyguards fell in behind.

T.J. waved them off. "You guys can stay. I'm good."

They slowed and exchanged confused looks.

T.J. and Nick strode through the brownstone lobby, eyes locked on the front door, the buzzing crowd parting and watching them go.

They stepped out to a crisp fall morning. Nick put on his sunglasses.

"Your car, Mr. Ritter." A valet extended his keys.

Nick snatched the keys and popped the trunk on his jet-black Mercedes. He pulled out a black duffel bag, threw it in the back seat, and got behind the wheel. T.J. slid in the passenger side.

They tore away from the curb and turned the corner into a column of Back Bay traffic inching toward Storrow Drive. Nick tapped his phone and it rang over the car's Bluetooth system.

A woman answered after one ring, her voice focused and intense. "Operator."

"This is Nick Ritter. I need to activate my escape plan."

"OK, Mr. Ritter. I've got you voice verified. What's your passphrase?"

"Wantabo Lake."

"Confirmed. What's your situation?" She had a precise and direct tone, likely from prior work as an emergency dispatcher or combat mission coordinator.

Nick checked his rearview mirror. "I've got a credible report of a virus outbreak, with ground zero at Boston Logan Airport. Right now I'm in the Back Bay and I need to get outside the city ASAP. They're gonna lock it down. I have one passenger and I want to fall back to my New Zealand ranch."

"Roger that. Before we go any further, I'm required to remind you that if you activate your plan, we'll immediately deduct one million dollars from your escrow account. That fee is non-refundable, regardless of the situation outcome. Would you like to proceed?"

Nick paused. "Are other clients activating their escape plans?"

"I can't share information on other clients, sir."

Nick turned the wheel, merging into Newbury Street traffic. "Come on, you know who I am. Most of your clients are my clients."

She paused. "I can confirm we're seeing unusually high volume in your area, sir."

Nick nodded. He felt T.J.'s eyes on him. "OK. Let's do it."

The operator started typing. "OK, we're live. Your last ping was ten seconds ago…looks like you're at the corner of Berkeley Street and Newbury Street. Is that correct?"

"Yes. I'm in my car, headed to Storrow Drive East, planning to take Route 1 North out of the city."

"Do you need an extraction?"

"No. There's no immediate threat."

"Do you need medical care?"

"No. Just get me a plane to New Zealand, departing from north of Boston."

"Roger that." She typed. "Sir, I'm going to go silent for a moment as I plan your escape route. Continue moving north. If you need me, just speak up."

They merged onto Storrow Drive East in silence, listening to the operator type and horns blast.

"Mr. Ritter, are you still with me?" the operator said.

"I'm here."

"Listen carefully, sir, I'm going to run through your escape plan. You've got a pilot activated and confirmed—his name is Brian Donahue. Head directly to his home at 221 Highland Road in Revere. It's right off Route 1 North, approximately seventeen minutes from your current location. From there, he'll transport you north via Route 1, then 95 North up the coast until you reach New Hampshire. I've secured a Learjet at a private airstrip in Moose River, New Hampshire. To avoid the outbreak, I maximized your distance from Boston, so it's pretty far north, about four hours from your current location. You still with me, sir?"

"Keep going."

"Your flight is scheduled to leave on Friday, November twenty-sixth at five p.m. There's an estimated twenty-four-hour flight time, including three stops to refuel, which means you should arrive in New Zealand by Saturday evening. You'll be flying into a private airport on the South Island, near Lake Wantabo. We'll have vehicles and supplies waiting. From there, it's a thirty-minute drive to your ranch."

She took a breath. "I just texted you and the pilot all the details. Do not be late, Mr. Ritter, or you forfeit your plane. Do you have any questions?"

Nick steered around two cars abandoned by arguing drivers. "Friday? That's two days away. Don't you have anything sooner?"

"That's the soonest we have, sir. I'm having trouble securing a plane. There's been a spike in demand and we're experiencing a shortage. Do you want to be put on the priority waitlist? If anything opens up sooner and you're within range, we'll call you first. It's one hundred thousand dollars per person, non-refundable, regardless of whether anything opens up."

Nick whispered to T.J., "A hundred grand to get on the waitlist?"

T.J. shrugged. "Yeah, whatever."

"We'll do it," Nick said.

"OK, I've added you to the priority waitlist," she said. "I'll contact you if anything opens up."

"Where do we hide out until Friday?"

"Unfortunately all the fallout shelters within range of your airstrip are hosting other clients. So you're going to have to secure your own accommodations."

Nick squeezed the wheel and clenched his jaw. There was an awkward silence.

"Sir, do you want me to stay on the line until you reach the pilot?"

"No, we're good."

"Roger that. Pick up your pilot, get out of the city, and shelter for forty-eight hours. You'll be in New Zealand by Saturday night."

"Roger that," Nick said.

"Stay safe, sir." She hung up.

T.J. turned to Nick. "Friday? Why don't we just drive to Logan and take the next flight to New Zealand? We'll be there by tomorrow."

Nick shook his head as he tapped the pilot's address into the car's navigation system. "We're dealing with a virus, so we have to avoid crowds. We have no idea how it spreads, which means we can't go near anyone that could be infected. By flying private, we'll have five, maybe ten, interactions. If we fly commercial, we'll have seven hundred, maybe more with a trip of this distance." A map appeared on the display with an arrival estimate of fifteen minutes. "Plus this thing started at Logan. That's the last place we want to go."

Traffic inched forward. Nick tapped his phone until it started ringing over the Bluetooth system.

"Boston General ER," a woman shouted over chaotic yelling and ringing phones.

"Hi, I think my wife is sick with some kind of virus. What's your wait time there?" Nick asked.

She raised her strained voice over the sound of a loudspeaker announcement. "Sir, we're overwhelmed with viral patients right now. We don't have any beds. Sorry, you're going to have to go elsewhere." She hung up and the commotion went silent.

T.J. looked at Nick. "Oh, shit."

Nick placed another call.

"Southern New Hampshire ER, how can I help you?" She sounded calm and friendly.

"Hi, I think my wife is sick with some kind of virus. What's your wait time there?"

"Umm, it's pretty quiet here. She might have to wait a half hour, an hour at most."

"Thank you. We'll be there soon."

Nick hung up. He merged onto Route 1 North and accelerated.

"What does that mean?" T.J. asked.

"It means if we can beat the roadblock, there's a good chance it hasn't spread widely in New Hampshire. We still need to be cautious, but with fewer cases it's less risky than Boston."

Within two minutes, they were back to crawling in traffic, staring at an endless snake of red lights.

T.J. squirmed in his seat. "Come on, this traffic is killing me. Can't we—"

They winced as an ear-splitting siren shrieked right on top of them. They looked around but saw nothing. The siren wailed again and Nick turned to his passenger-side blind spot to see an ambulance trying to merge from an on-ramp. He made space to let it in.

The side of the ambulance read, "MERCY COMMUNITY HOSPITAL" in red block letters above a logo of two held hands. It passed and the next car slowly yielded to let it through. The next vehicle in line, a pickup truck, didn't move. The ambulance blasted its shrill siren, but the truck didn't budge. A car in the next lane made space, and the ambulance passed the truck, but then became stuck behind an unyielding white van.

"What is wrong with people?" Nick shook his head. "How can you not move for an ambulance?"

"Why should they?" T.J. scoffed. "It's probably some druggie taking a limo ride to a cut clinic on my dime."

Nick sighed.

The "cut clinic" conspiracy, another favorite among his clients. Last year, a law passed that allowed hospitals in low-income communities to provide patients with free care and be reimbursed by the federal government. But the law only covered medical emergencies. However, once a patient was admitted for an emergency, they could be treated for other "coincident comorbidities"—basically any non-emergency medical need—as part of the same covered bill. It was a strange loophole, passed with good intentions, but abused on the ground almost immediately.

Politicians claimed that patients would cut themselves and come into the ER with an open wound so they could get free care for some other medical need. The doctor would bill the government for the cut and submit the other items as coincident comorbidities. Critics called the participating hospitals "cut clinics."

There was a media frenzy around a woman who needed dialysis seven days a week for chronic kidney disease. Every morning she would cut herself, get a couple stitches, and then get her free dialysis. One day she cut too deeply and bled to death in her car, ten yards from the hospital entrance.

Most of Nick's clients believed cut clinics were a scam by the poor to get free medical care. Others felt they symbolized a tragic failure of a broken healthcare system. And a handful swore they weren't real, but Nick suspected that was because they had only experienced private medical care and had never set foot in a public hospital.

Apparently T.J. was in the first group.

Nick watched as the ambulance crept forward, blasting its siren at unyielding drivers, cutting from lane to lane, swinging through the breakdown lane.

"Jesus, what is that?" T.J. pointed out the window.

Nick glanced off the side of the highway at a sprawling tent city built up around the crumbling Bunker Hill Monument. The monument was built in 1825 to commemorate the heroic Battle of Bunker Hill. Two years ago, a portion of the peak collapsed, letting in the elements. The National Park Service closed it to the public, and it fell into disrepair. Now it was surrounded by hundreds of tents and tarps in all different shapes, sizes, and colors. The ground was covered in litter and the air was hazy from barrel fires.

"It's the Bunker Hill Monument," Nick said.

"Not the busted tower," T.J. said. "The tents."

"They call it Methadone Mile. It's a homeless encampment. People started camping there to access the addiction center at Bunker Hill Hospital—most of them never left. Now it's basically its own city."

T.J. looked down at his phone and scoffed. "And that's why you don't have cut clinics."

They crawled through traffic for another ten minutes, then took the exit for Revere. The traffic cleared and the navigation announced they'd arrive in two minutes.

"So who is this pilot?" T.J. asked.

"No idea. Never met him. Pilots are assigned based on location, availability, and skill set. They're all Navy and Air Force vets—you know, action-hero types, so they can double as protection if needed."

"So this guy's gonna drop everything, drive us to New Hampshire, camp out a couple days, and then fly to New Zealand? How do we know he won't bail?"

"We use certain…incentives…to ensure pilot compliance." Nick spoke like the words tasted bad.

"Incentives? The hell does that mean?"

Nick turned onto Highland Road. "Pilots are on call 24/7/365 to respond to any disaster situation. They get a few pre-approved days off, but they're not allowed to work anywhere else because they need to be reachable every minute of every day. We pay them well, but they only take home ten percent of their pay. The other ninety percent goes into escrow, to be released at the end of their contract—usually five or ten-year terms."

Nick scanned the house numbers. "If they fail to respond to an emergency call within ten minutes, they forfeit the money. If they're not packed and ready to go within ten minutes of client arrival, they forfeit the money. If they show up to a destination without the client…" Nick shrugged. "The only way for a pilot to collect his money is to finish his contract, or die, in which case everything goes to his family. So yeah, compliance is pretty high."

T.J. grinned. "Damnnn, I wish I could pay my employees like that. Has the Department of Labor seen those contracts? They're not big on withholding earned wages. Gives 'em flashbacks to indentured servitude."

Nick slowed and pulled off his sunglasses. “The lawyers found a way around it…phantom share award with a vesting cliff…something like that. Plus everything is run out of the Caymans, so DoL doesn’t matter.”

T.J. smirked. “I’d love to meet your lawyers.”

The navigation system cut in. “You have arrived at your destination.”

They pulled to the curb and stared at the pilot’s house across the street.

SEVEN

Even though the small ranch house was modest, it stood out because it was the most well-maintained home on the street. The paint was fresh and flawless, the lawn lush and perfectly trimmed, the American flag bright and crisp. Someone took care of this house on a weekly, if not daily, basis.

A jet-black Chevy Suburban sat in the driveway, facing the road, its rear liftgate open by the single-car garage. The Suburban was the standard escape vehicle issued to pilots. Roomy enough for up to eight clients and a driver, yet sturdy enough to withstand disaster situations. With its tinted windows, reinforced bumpers, and custom license plate that read "ARK-1," it looked like an FBI tactical vehicle. Parked curbside at the end of the driveway was an old beige Toyota Camry that had clearly spent its winters on the street.

A man burst from the house carrying a black duffel bag and headed for the Suburban. He was well over six feet tall, early fifties, with a military cut, jeans, and a worn leather flight jacket over a button-down shirt. Despite having the strength and posture of a military man—straight, confident, disciplined—he looked tired and worn. He crossed the lawn with a limp.

T.J. broke the silence. "Is this the guy? This isn't the guy, right? This is just the bag man. The action hero's inside…right?"

"Stay in the car." Nick locked the doors and placed a call on speakerphone.

A shrill ringtone blasted across the street. The man stepped out from behind the open Suburban and answered immediately.

"Captain Brian Donahue."

"Brian, this is Nick Ritter. I'm your client."

"Mr. Ritter, thank you for making contact. Are you en route?"

"Well, actually, I'm here. In the black Mercedes across the street."

Brian looked directly at Nick and T.J.

"Oh, perfect, I'll come get your bags." Brian started toward them.

"Brian, stay right where you are. I need to ask you a few questions before we get out."

Brian stopped and stared at Nick. "Yes, sir."

"Have you, or anyone in your household, been in Boston, or specifically at Logan Airport, in the last forty-eight hours?"

Brian hesitated. "Ummm, no, sir. My wife's been off work this week, my daughter's been off school, and I don't leave the house much because of my contract. So we've all been hanging out here."

"Are you, or anyone in your household, feeling sick?"

"Sick? Uh, no, sir. We're all fine."

"Have you visited with anyone that was sick?"

"My wife's sister came for dinner on Sunday, but she felt fine."

Nick stared at Brian for a moment and weighed the odds. "OK, we're coming out."

Nick hung up, grabbed his duffel bag from the back, and walked across the street.

Brian erased the confused look from his face, a practice he'd likely perfected after years of serving eccentric high-net-worth clients. He strode toward Nick with his hand extended, projecting an air of military formality and professionalism.

"Captain Brian Donahue. Let me get that for you, sir." He took Nick's bag.

Nick gestured over his shoulder. "This is T.J. Chandra. He's also a client."

Brian extended a strong hand. "Brian Donahue. Pleasure to meet you, sir."

"Hey." T.J. shook without eye contact.

They walked toward the Suburban.

"I spoke with the operator and reviewed the escape plan," Brian said. "We're heading north, hiding out for two days, then departing from a private airstrip in Moose River on Friday at 1700 hours. Is that right, sir?"

"We have a lot of details to fill in," Nick said. "But yeah, that's right."

"Sounds good, sir. Would you like to take your own car? Or all ride in one car?"

"One car. The Suburban."

"Would you like to leave your car in my garage? A luxury vehicle like that, in this neighborhood…"

"It's fine. Let's go."

Brian got the message. "Roger that. Let's roll out." He opened the passenger door for Nick.

"I need to pee," T.J. said behind them.

Nick and Brian slowly turned.

"What?" T.J. said. "Matcha goes right through me. You want me to hold it for the next two hours?"

Nick looked at T.J. like he was a whiny kid on a long road trip.

"No problem, sir," Brian said. "Come inside and use our restroom."

They stepped inside to a simple but cozy interior. Nick inhaled the smell of fresh pancakes, maple syrup, eggs, bacon, and muffins. He couldn't remember the last time he had home cooking.

"First door on the right." Brian pointed down the hall.

T.J. rushed to the bathroom.

"Can I get you anything, sir?" Brian asked Nick.

"I'm good."

"You mind if I step out for a moment?"

Nick nodded.

"Make yourself at home." Brian gestured into the living room and walked down the hall, toward the sound of a woman and girl chatting in the kitchen.

Nick stepped into the living room and looked around. The space was overflowing with hobbies, like an adult playroom. His eyes jumped around the cluttered space.

An old guitar and music stand.

A book, "Learn Guitar in a Week!"

A stack of worn Sudoku notebooks.

A line of model airplanes.

A book, "Spanish for Dummies."

A row of dumbbells sunk into a yoga mat.

A ten-book box set, "Epic Battles of History."

A half-finished game of solitaire.

This guy's bored out of his mind waiting around for a call.

Nick could hear Brian and the women talking in the kitchen, so he peeked into the next room. Inside was a dining table covered with a grid of papers. Red block letters jumped out:

"OVERDUE."

"LAST REMINDER."

"PAST DUE."

"FINAL NOTICE."

The same logos popped up again and again:

Mercy Community Hospital.

Boston General Hospital.

Veterans Mortgage Alliance.

Revere Community Bank.

Saint Francis Catholic High School.

In the center of each bill was a sticky note. The bottom row of papers had all green stickies, the middle row had yellow, and the top had red. They were triaging overdue bills.

Nick moved back to the living room and spotted a glass cabinet he hadn't noticed before. The top two shelves were filled with pictures of Brian and his wife with their daughter at various ages—at the beach, ice skating, opening presents—all laughing. A few of the pictures included a younger woman who looked similar to Brian's wife, likely her sister.

On the middle shelf, military medals flanked a picture of Brian and fifteen other soldiers in full gear, smiling and holding two flags: The first was a black flag with the SEAL trident and the phrase, "THE ONLY EASY DAY WAS YESTERDAY—U.S. NAVY SEALS." The second was a green flag with a snarling frog flexing his giant bicep and pointing a flaming trident.

On the shelf below was a framed Time Magazine titled, "The Men Who Stopped Captain Cairo," featuring a picture of Brian and four other SEALs in uniform. He looked young, bright-eyed, powerful—an elite soldier at the peak of his career.

Nick heard a creak behind him.

"Everything good, sir?"

Nick startled and spun. Brian, his wife, and his daughter were all staring.

"Uhhh, yup, all good." Nick gave the women an awkward wave. "Hello."

Brian's wife squinted with her arms crossed. Her hair was up in a messy ponytail and she had food stains on her apron, sweatshirt, and mom jeans. She looked annoyed, almost bitter—time had taken something from the young woman laughing in the photos.

Brian's daughter offered a polite smile. She looked about fifteen and was wearing black leggings and a food-spattered sweatshirt featuring a Christian cross inside a recycling symbol above the words, "Saint Francis Catholic High—Revere Beach Cleanup Day."

Nick's startled "hello" hung in the air. The daughter broke the silence. "Hi there, I'm Zoe, and this is Tracy. Welcome to our home." She projected warm, peppy energy. "Can I get you anything?"

Brian winced. He touched Zoe's shoulder and whispered, "Honey, no. Thank you…but no."

He must've flown enough paranoid clients to know that they wanted privacy and he wanted them away from his wife and kid.

A door slammed open down the hall and T.J. exhaled. "Whew! I had to piss like a racehorse." He strolled into the room and spotted the group. "Oh hey, what's up?"

Tracy's eyes jumped from T.J. to the seat he left up in the bathroom —then shot Brian a death stare.

"Umm, OK, gentlemen, let's head out." Brian ushered them toward the door.

They were halfway to the Suburban when Zoe called from the front steps. "Dad, you forgot something."

"You guys jump in. I'll be there in thirty seconds." Brian jogged back to his wife and daughter.

Nick climbed into the passenger seat and T.J. hopped in back. The windows were halfway down, and Nick couldn't help overhearing the Donahues.

"You forgot your sunglasses," Zoe said.

"Oh man. Thanks, Z-Bird." Brian grabbed the aviators and hung them on his shirt.

Zoe looked like she was holding back tears.

"Hug and a prayer?" Brian asked.

She nodded. They all took hands and closed their eyes. Zoe spoke. "Lord, protect my dad on this journey and show him a peaceful path home. Make him your shepherd, a gentle guardian. Make him your stone, a pillar of strength. And should evil come, make him your storm, a swift and mighty force. Amen."

"Amen. Love ya, Zo." He pulled her in for a hug. She snuggled into his chest.

Tracy leaned in and kissed him. "Be safe, hun. Don't do anything dangerous for these guys."

Brian looked from his wife to his daughter and back. "Guys, come on, I do this all the time. It's always nothing. A quick trip round the world, then back home for another delayed Donahue Thanksgiving."

They laughed and relaxed.

"Seriously, it'll be easy. Don't worry. I love you." Brian hugged them both with his wide wingspan. "Go time."

The women went inside and Brian jogged to the car.

He started the engine, checked the dashboard gauges, and tapped a few buttons. The navigation display lit up and the rear liftgate began to close. Brian buckled his seatbelt, slid on his aviators, and shifted the car into drive. "Good to go?"

"Good to go," Nick said.

"Holy shit, it's all over Zen," T.J. muttered, scrolling on his phone. "Roadblocks…Houston, Seattle, Atlanta."

Brian squinted at his rearview mirror. "What's the situation, sir?"

Here we go. This is why I don't do live support.

"We can discuss on the road," Nick said.

"It's happening, Nick." T.J. looked up. "We're next."

Brian removed his sunglasses and looked at Nick. "Sir, is there a situation here in Boston?"

Their window of opportunity was closing. If T.J. got the pilot worked up, it'd be twenty questions before they hit the road, or worse, he might bail. Nick's nose started to sting at the smell of burning rubber. He put on his sunglasses to hide his watering eyes.

"We need to go," Nick said.

T.J. lurched forward, poking his head into the front seats. "Hey, driver, let's fucking go. I don't wanna be here when this place turns Walking Dead."

"Walking Dead?" Brian put the car in park. "Sir, what are—"

Nick turned to Brian and snapped. "There's a deadly virus. It started at Logan twenty-four hours ago and is spreading worldwide. The military is locking down major cities, and if we don't get out in the next thirty minutes, we're *dead.*"

Nick turned back to facing forward, his last word hanging in the air.

Brian gazed at his house and spoke softly, "I can bring them…I mean, they've never come before…but if I want to, I can bring them… right, sir?"

Nick clenched his jaw and nodded curtly.

Brian looked at Nick with fearful eyes. "Look, I didn't want to say anything, but…I know who you are. Please, just tell me…is this real?"

Nick stared straight ahead.

Tell him it's real—more delays, risk a roadblock, get the wife and daughter as baggage.

Tell him it's not—lose him once he finds out, the wife and daughter probably die here.

Nick spoke, stone-faced behind his sunglasses. "Real enough to run."

Brian killed the engine and unbuckled his seatbelt. "I'm getting them. I'll be back in five minutes."

Nick turned to Brian. "You have two minutes. Then we leave and call a backup pilot." He pointed at Brian's hand. "Leave the keys."

Brian spilled out of the car and sprinted for the house.

EIGHT

TRACY DRIZZLED maple syrup over a giant stack of pancakes and Zoe topped it with a puff of whipped cream. "Ta-da!"

They plopped down at the kitchen table and admired their steaming brunch spread. Tracy grinned. "Sooo, where do we start?"

The front door slammed open. They jolted and locked eyes.

Brian burst into the kitchen, his face a mix of flushed and pale. "You're coming with."

"What…" Tracy held a hand to her chest. "What just happened?"

"I don't have time to explain, but you're both coming on the job with me, and we need to leave *now*."

"What? We can't just leave. I'm slow cooking brisket. I told Father Ray I'd bring it by this afternoon."

"Dad, I'm dog walking for the shelter at two," Zoe said.

Tracy crossed her arms. "Brian, what the hell is going on?"

"Listen, there's a situation…" Brian glanced down at his watch. "I'll explain in the car. But you can't stay here, it's not safe. And I can't do my job out there if I'm worried about you back here."

Tracy stood up and threw down her napkin. "What did those assholes say to you?"

"Tracy—" Brian tried to stop her train before it gained steam.

"No, Brian. How many times have you sat at this table and said," she did an impression of Brian, "'These guys are all paranoid, they're crazy, they're liars. They're running from imaginary space bugs and lizard people and Chinese robo-whatevers.'"

Tracy softened her tone. "You can't trust them, hun. If they're delusional, we should stay away. Far away. And if they're not, if there really is some situation, then you need to protect our family, not those bozos. So go tell them to find another pilot."

Brian scoffed. "You know I can't do that. I have a mission, and they're depending on me." He took Tracy's arm and guided her gently toward the door. "We'll talk in the car. We can—"

Tracy yanked her arm away. "Brian!"

"Dad, what's going on? You're freaking me out."

Brian looked at his watch, took a deep breath, and forced his calmest voice. "Listen to me—if we're not in that car in thirty seconds, we lose everything in escrow. Ten years of hard work, *gone*. But worse, we'll be trapped here, under military lockdown, during a deadly virus outbreak. Now, if I'm wrong—and I hope I'm wrong—we'll visit New Zealand and be home in a week. But right now, I need you to trust me. So *please*...stand up and get in the car."

Tracy crossed her arms and squinted.

NINE

NICK CHECKED HIS WATCH.

Ninety seconds and we're gone.

T.J. was peppering him with questions. "Why'd you let him get the girls? What happened to 'every person is added risk?'"

"It's in his contract—pilots are allowed to bring immediate family on any mission, otherwise we had compliance problems. You ask a man to ditch his family and he won't show up, no matter how much money you threaten."

T.J. huffed. "This guy's a joke, he's used up. Can't we upgrade?"

"We're about to…in seventy-five seconds."

Nick gave Brian the full two minutes, despite T.J. lobbying to leave early. As the clock ticked down, they stared at the house—it was still.

"They're not coming," T.J. said. "Let's go."

Nick lingered on the front door.

"Nick!" T.J. clapped. "What are we doing? Let's go!"

Nick jumped out and circled around to the driver's side. He started the engine and placed a call on speakerphone.

One ring. "Operator."

"We need a backup pilot. This guy's not ready."

"Roger that, sir. I'll deactivate him and get you rerouted. Give me a moment to see who's available near your current location."

Nick stared at the front door.

Denial and deliberation...this is how people die.

"OK, sir, I've got a pilot in Malden, eight minutes west. Can I activate him?"

Nick took a deep breath. "OK, let's do—"

The front door swung open. Tracy and Zoe rushed out, clutching a red duffel bag and a pink backpack. Brian followed behind.

"The fuck is this?" T.J. said.

"Sir? Can I activate the new pilot?"

Nick hesitated. "Never mind. He's here."

"*What?*" T.J. lurched forward.

"Are you sure?" the operator asked. "The new pilot is ready to depart."

"No, this pilot's good." Nick waved T.J. away. "We'll call back with any issues. Thanks." He hung up as the Donahues reached the car.

Tracy climbed in the rear driver side and Zoe jumped in the rear passenger side, squeezing T.J. in the middle.

"Hello, let's get comfy." Zoe gave an awkward smile.

T.J. stared straight ahead, red-faced.

Nick exited the driver's seat and headed back around. As they passed each other, Brian stopped him with a firm hand on the shoulder—he leaned in and whispered, "Thanks for waiting, man. I appreciate it."

Nick flashed a smile and rushed his eye contact. "Yeah, no problem."

* * *

Two minutes later they were cruising north on Route 1. Traffic had eased and they were on course to cross the New Hampshire border in fifty minutes, assuming no roadblocks.

Tracy had been staring out the window, arms crossed, but couldn't contain herself any longer. "OK, can someone please explain this situation that has my family fleeing home the day before Thanksgiving?"

Nick took a deep breath and told them everything. When he finished, the car was silent.

People struggle to process new information during a crisis, especially when it's emotional, so he tried to simplify. "Look, all we can do is focus on the next step. If we beat the roadblock, our chance of survival goes up dramatically. We can regroup from there."

"And if we don't?" T.J. broke the silence with attitude.

"It's not ideal. Then we try backroads, alternate air strips, boats—we'll figure something out."

Brian glanced at the navigation display. "Once we cross into New Hampshire—"

"What about Dana?" Tracy cut in.

Is Dana the sister?

"We'll call her as soon as our clients are settled in." Brian flashed his eyebrows in the rearview.

"She's an ER doctor, Brian. We need to call her *now*, before she goes to work with a bunch of sick people."

"Hold on, I thought they made her take the week off," Brian said. "She was leaf peeping in Maine with that guy…the dentist."

"Ew, Dad, no—that was like a month ago," Zoe said. "She dropped that creep."

Brian shrugged. "Well, then she's probably at home baking those weird little googly eyed cookies she makes every Thanksgiving."

"They're called Gobbles," Tracy said. "And yes, she's at home. Let's pick her up on the way. It's only ten minutes off the highway."

Nick felt Brian look at him. He gave a subtle head shake: We're not picking her up.

"Hun, listen," Brian said, "we can't stop now, but why don't—"

A call rang on speakerphone.

Nick turned. Tracy was holding up her phone.

A woman's voice answered. "Hey Trace, what's up?"

"Hey, Dana, are you home right now?"

"Umm, no. I'm at work." Dana sounded like she was rushing.

Tracy was silent.

"Hello?"

"You're at work? I thought you were off this week."

"Yeah, well, me too. They paged everyone a half hour ago, there's some kind of viral outbreak. They're out of beds, putting people in the halls…can I call you tonight?"

In the background of the call a horn honked, then an ambulance wailed. Nick hesitated, then leaned toward Brian and whispered, "She's still outside. Tell her not to go in."

Brian shouted into the back seat. "Dana, where are you right now, exactly? Where are you standing?"

"Brian? Am I on speakerphone? I'm in the parking lot, twenty feet from the hospital entrance. What's going on? Is Zoe OK?"

"Listen to me," Brian said, "don't take one more step toward the hospital. Do *not* go inside. Turn around and go back to your car right now."

Dana was silent.

"Dana?" Tracy said.

"Guys, what the hell is going on? You're freaking me out."

"Just do what Brian said and we'll explain," Tracy said.

There was a long pause. "OK, I'm walking back to my car."

"Lock your doors and we'll call you in five minutes," Brian said. "OK?"

"OK, I'm getting in now," Dana said, her voice unsteady. "Call me right back."

Tracy hung up and leaned forward, looking at Nick. "We need to pick her up. She's at Mercy Community Hospital. It's five minutes off the highway."

Brian forced a frustrated smile. "Hun, our primary mission is to get our clients across the border. We can call—"

"Primary mission?" Tracy's tone jumped. "I'm sorry saving your family doesn't fit with your *primary mission.* But these guys can—"

Brian shot her a death stare in the rearview.

"They can wait five minutes," Tracy finished carefully.

Nick tried to de-escalate. "If you tell her to drive north now, she'll beat the roadblock. She might even be ahead of us."

Tracy squinted at Nick. "And if she doesn't beat it? Or gets stopped? Or won't go? Then she's trapped here alone. If we don't get her, she'll go in that hospital within the hour—I know my sister. We are *not* leaving her behind."

"Dad, we can't spare five minutes for Auntie D?" Zoe said.

Brian tried to convince his family that Dana would be safer driving on her own. His words faded into the background as Nick watched a train of desert-camo humvees roar past in the fast lane. At the end was a flatbed trailer stacked with wooden barriers, steel fences, and orange cones.

"They're blocking the road," Nick said quietly.

The car went silent and everyone looked at him.

He pointed out the window. "We can't stop now. If we don't beat that roadblock, none of us are getting out."

Tracy unbuckled her seatbelt and leaned into the front seats. "Brian, I swear to God, if you leave my little sister here alone, I will—"

"Oh come off it!" T.J. threw up his hands. "Just tell her to drive north and she'll be fine." He looked at Brian. "Driver, get us to the border. Do your job!"

Tracy turned her cannons on T.J. "Excuse me? Who the hell are you? Are you part of this family? I don't think so. So you can—"

Brian slammed the dashboard. "Tracy! Leave it alone!"

Tracy turned back to Brian. "Her exit is in one mile. It'll take five minutes. Get over." She pointed at the far-right lane.

Brian kept cruising at a steady 80 mph. He flashed a side glance at Nick.

"We need to beat the roadblock," Nick said quietly.

Brian pushed them up to 85 mph.

"Brian! Get over!"

90 mph.

"Dad!"

"That's enough!" Brian glared into the rearview. "We're here to do a job. I don't want to hear—"

"Look out!" T.J. screamed and pointed.

Brian tapped the brakes and swerved to avoid rear-ending a minivan at 95 mph. The Suburban screeched and wobbled, nearly losing its grip on the road. Behind them, an eighteen-wheeler bellowed its horn.

A green sign flew past: "EXIT 1/2 MILE."

Tracy slid back, buckled her seatbelt, and shook her head. "You've lost your mind, Brian. You're gonna get us killed. Once we cross that border, drop us off. I don't want Zoe anywhere near you guys."

T.J. poked his head into the front and whispered, "Hey Nick, this is a fucking shitshow. I want a new pilot. Call it in."

"I've got it under control, sir," Brian said to T.J., then frowned into the rearview. "Tracy, enough—we'll finish this conversation in New Hampshire."

"This conversation *is* finished," Tracy said, and turned to T.J. "You want a new pilot? By all means, call it in."

"Tracy!" Brian glared, wide-eyed.

Nick stared ahead in a daze as the argument escalated. A blaze shot up both nostrils and met in his forehead. His eyes watered at the stench of gasoline.

EXIT 1/4 MILE.

Nick closed his eyes and began box breathing.

The crossfire of angry voices faded to a dull echo, like underwater yelling.

Beat the roadblock—get to safety, hide out two days, make the flight. The wife and daughter will be a problem every step of the way. If the pilot can't focus, we're all at risk.

Get the sister—five minutes there, two minutes load-up, five minutes back. Twelve minutes added time, fifteen with traffic. We might still make it. It'll calm the wife and daughter, focus the pilot. Plus we gain a doctor.

Nick opened his eyes.

Tracy was pointing at T.J. "…treat your employees, but no one talks to my husband like that."

NEXT EXIT 100 FT.

T.J. jabbed back. "Listen, lady—"

Nick pointed ahead and gave Brian a firm and unmistakable order. "Take the exit."

Without hesitation, Brian leaned the Suburban hard right, scanning his mirrors as he threaded effortlessly through three lanes of vehicles. He squeezed past the exit guardrail and caught the offramp with no room to spare.

The car was silent.

Nick waited until they pulled onto the main road, then projected his voice so everyone could hear. "If she went inside, we're leaving."

* * *

THEY FOUND Dana sitting in her blue Volvo station wagon in a remote corner of the parking lot, where she had moved to avoid the chaos near the hospital's entrance. Brian pulled up and idled so their windows aligned driver-to-driver.

"Hey Dana." Brian pulled off his aviators and flashed a tired smile.

"What the hell is going on?" Dana said.

She was in her mid-thirties, with dark doe eyes perfectly suited to a cut-clinic doctor—patients would find in them gentle kindness, critics would find fiery conviction. She wore blue scrubs and a white doctor's coat peppered with colorful pins:

"Vote YES on Question 3."

"Call, don't cut."

"Stand up for survivors."

"I got my vaccine!"

She was gripping the steering wheel, with pink, blue, and green awareness wristbands on one wrist and a silver bracelet with an inscribed heart on the other.

"We'll tell you everything," Brian said. "But first, I need to ask you a few questions."

Dana looked from Brian to Tracy, who was leaning out the rear driver-side window. "Tracy, what is this? Where's Zoe?"

"I'm here, D!" Zoe called from the third row, where she'd climbed to free up a seat for Dana.

"Just answer the questions, then we'll fill you in," Tracy said.

Brian started to run through Nick's script to make sure Dana hadn't been exposed to the virus. While he quizzed her, Nick scanned the parking lot. It was overflowing with cars—abandoned, double parked, idling at frantic angles.

A line of people snaked from the ER entrance, down the sidewalk, around the corner. Two nurses wearing N95 masks, goggles, full body coveralls, and face shields stood at the entrance, interviewing patients and marking clipboards. Two more nurses pushed a cart down the line, handing out water and first aid.

The people definitely looked sick, but in a different way than Nick had ever seen. They were coughing, sniffling, sneezing—like the flu. Even from the corner of the parking lot, with the Suburban's engine idling, he could hear soggy, raspy coughs that barked like someone stomping an empty soda can. Despite their obvious illness, most of them looked energized, almost upbeat.

People rocked back and forth in place, paced in little circles, danced around.

A woman and a little girl did jumping jacks.

An old man laid out his shirt to hold his spot, and jogged topless up and down the line.

The whole sidewalk was squirming, and if not for the horror of it, they almost looked like a line of circus performers warming up for a big audition.

But the strangest thing, the thing Nick couldn't look away from, was their hands. They were scratching, digging, clawing at some maddening itch deep within their palms, and no matter how far they went, they couldn't reach it. Their hands were shredded, split, raw—dripping little pools of blood on the sidewalk.

A man in a suit squatted, singing and rubbing his palms up and down the concrete.

An old woman comforted a boy and girl with dish towels duct taped around their hands.

A ragged homeless woman scratched alternating palms with a bloody fork.

The nurses handed out instant cold packs, which the sick clutched, seemingly unbothered by gripping ice on a chilly November day.

Up and down the line, they all looked the same: like they caught a vicious flu, chugged two Red Bulls, and kneaded poison ivy.

Is it normal for a virus to cause such consistent symptoms? How could—

"Nick?"

Nick turned to Brian. "Sorry, what?"

"She answered the questions. All good."

"OK." Nick nodded that he was satisfied.

Brian took a deep breath. "OK, Dana, listen carefully, because we need to leave here in sixty seconds. Obviously, there's an outbreak. We have intel that suggests it's deadly and spreading worldwide. The military is locking down major cities, including Boston. I have two clients in the car and we're heading to a safe location in New Hampshire. But we need to leave *now*, before they close the roads and we get stuck. So get in, and we'll fill you in on the way." Brian slid his aviators on.

"You want me to just…leave?" Dana looked from Brian to Tracy and back. She gestured at the long line of sick. "Look at these people—they need help. You want me to abandon my patients, abandon my team, right when they need me most?"

"Dana, they'll be OK," Brian said, like he was placating a child. "I'm sure the other doctors can help."

Dana glared and tossed her hospital-ID lanyard around her neck. She opened her door and stomped out. "If you want to run, *fine*. But I won't give up on these people."

"Dana, you can't save everyone," Tracy said. "If you go in there, you're exposed, and you can't come back to us."

"Auntie D, please, come with us," Zoe said.

"Twenty seconds," Nick whispered to Brian.

"Dana! Get in the car," Brian said. "We need to go *now*."

Nick looked down at the navigation display and his heart sank. A red dot of traffic appeared where Route 1 merged into 95 North.

That's where they'd block it. We're too late. It's already up.

Nick looked up. "Drive."

Without hesitation, Brian shifted the car into gear.

"Brian!" Tracy said. She opened her door. "Dana, get *in*!"

Brian looked to Nick for final confirmation.

Dana stood by the car, cheeks flushed, eyes shimmering as they jumped back and forth between the hospital and the Suburban.

Nick recognized it immediately: she was frozen.

It was common in a crisis—70 percent of people become overwhelmed by the combination of too many options, too many variables, very little time, and the high cost of a wrong decision. It was called "choice overload," and the solution was to narrow the options and give the frozen person a simple justification for taking one particular path—then apply pressure to commit or be left behind.

But choice overload didn't really make sense here. Dana was an ER doctor—every day she had to make complex life-and-death decisions under extreme pressure. There was something else happening... survivor guilt. Sometimes people felt they did something wrong because they survived a tragedy when others didn't.

Usually survivor guilt haunted the survivor after the tragedy ended, but Nick had seen people experience it during a crisis, hesitating to take an opportunity to save themselves because others were dying.

The solution was to release the person from their guilt by convincing them that saving themselves would also save others. The truth didn't matter—what mattered was that you provided an altruistic justification for a self-preserving action, relieving their guilt and validating their decision to save themselves.

Nick removed his sunglasses, leaned toward Brian's open window, and spoke in a clear and gentle tone. "Dana...Hey, Dana."

She peeled her gaze away from the hospital and looked at Nick with haunted eyes.

"You can't help these people, they're too sick. If you go in there, you'll die with them. But there are others that need care—trust me, this is just the beginning. If you come with us now, you'll save your family *and* help hundreds of innocent people before it's too late."

Dana stared at Nick for a long moment, rubbing her thumb over the inscribed heart on her bracelet.

Nick held her gaze and nodded gently. "Help us, Dana."

Dana stepped to Tracy's door and slid into the Suburban.

TEN

THEY IDLED behind four lanes of stopped cars, fifty yards from the roadblock.

They were five minutes too late.

The roadblock was a sloppy blend of wooden barriers, steel fences, and scattered road flares. Beyond it loomed a line of enforcers: a row of humvees and Army National Guard soldiers in camo, tactical gear, and N95 masks.

"Stay here in the right lane so we don't get trapped," Nick said to Brian.

The right border of their lane was lined with orange cones, reserving the breakdown lane on the other side for military vehicles. A convoy of humvees barreled past like a freight train, swaying the Suburban. A soldier at the roadblock waved them through.

After the last humvee passed, a blue pickup truck behind the Suburban screeched over a cone and followed the convoy down the breakdown lane.

"Oh shit, he's making a run for it." Brian pointed.

The pickup accelerated toward the roadblock. Four soldiers stepped out and aimed automatic rifles at the driver. One pointed just above and fired a warning shot. The pickup slowed to a roll, then stopped at the roadblock.

The driver pleaded something out his window, but before he could finish the soldiers swarmed, tore open the door, and launched him into a belly flop on the asphalt.

Dana gasped.

The driver, a skinny old man in a green trucker hat, went limp as one soldier kneeled on his neck, another kneeled on his legs, a third zip-tied his hands, and a fourth hovered, rifle aimed just off the pile. They lifted the groggy driver by his armpits, blood dripping from his mouth, and dragged him behind the roadblock. One soldier moved the pickup, and another assumed a guard position in the military lane.

"Oh my god, how can they do that?" Dana said. "These are just regular people."

"What's our move, Nick?" Brian asked. "Take the exit and try backroads?" He nodded toward an exit ramp twenty yards ahead.

Nick studied the exit and shook his head. "It's blocked. Look at the end of the ramp, you can see people outside their cars. They must've set up secondary roadblocks off the exits."

Nick peered across the grassy median at a matching roadblock on the southbound lanes. "Other side's blocked too, to keep people out of Boston."

Brian pointed to a strip mall on the other side of the southbound lanes. "We could try and cut across to that parking lot, then take back roads."

Nick squinted at the strip mall. "Yeah, that could work. Only problem is we've got three lanes of parked cars between us and the median. We'd have to plow through a lot of people, starting with this bus." Nick gestured at the school bus full of restless little faces on their left side.

"So we're trapped," T.J. said from the back. "We can't get through, we can't get off, we can't go back. We're trapped…fifty yards from freedom."

"We're working on a solution, sir," Brian said.

"Here's a solution," T.J. said, "maybe next time we should listen to

Nick. You know, the guy who does escape plans for a living? We should've headed straight north—like he said—instead of packing, and arguing, and picking up strangers like a goddamn school bus."

"Gee, thanks." Dana stared at T.J.

Tracy turned to T.J. and crossed her arms. "Tell me, Mr. Big Shot, what have you contributed to this situation, besides a whole lot of whining?"

"Tracy!" Brian said.

"Oh, here we go, not this again." T.J. rolled his eyes.

"Guys?" Zoe said quietly from the far back row.

The argument escalated.

"Hey, guys…" Zoe tried again.

T.J. and Tracy traded barbs.

"Guys!" Zoe shouted.

Everyone turned to see Zoe pointing out the back window. "People are getting out."

Nick scanned the windows and saw two dozen people had left their cars. Others were joining, and a crowd was beginning to trickle through the gridlock, toward the roadblock.

More soldiers stepped to the barrier.

"Some of these people are sick," Dana said.

Nick followed her gaze.

"Look, you can see they're symptomatic." She pointed. "Bloodshot eyes, upper respiratory irritation, pruritus of the palms."

"Lock the doors," Nick said.

Brian jammed the lock button.

There was a bang on their left side as four New Hampshire police officers squeezed between the Suburban and the school bus. As the last cop pushed through, he steadied himself on their left rear window, smudging a red streak in Zoe's face.

Nick's eyes jumped from the jammed exit ramp, to the blocked southbound lanes, to the distant parking lot—then settled on the growing horde streaming toward the battle line ahead.

"We need to go," Nick said. "Trust me, this doesn't end well."

He flinched as another convoy of humvees roared past in the breakdown lane.

There was a sharp crack. A big biker chick with frizzy, blood-caked hair and bulging red eyes rapped a skull ring on T.J.'s window. "Hey! You got any water in there?" She squinted inside. "Helloooo?"

"Hey Nick…" T.J.'s voice quivered. "What's the plan here?"

Brian scanned their surroundings and revved the engine. "I can cut across the breakdown lane, turn around and drive south on the grassy shoulder."

The stench of burning rubber flooded Nick's nose. He squeezed the door handle.

No no no…not now.

"Or we could plow through to the strip mall." Brian revved again.

"Dad, hurry, more people are coming," Zoe said.

"Talk to me, Nick," Brian said.

"Helloooo?" The biker chick hammered a fist against the window. Blood oozed between her fingers, spattering on the glass.

Nick closed his eyes and took a deep breath.

Focus. All your exits are blocked—forward, back, left, right. There are no good options.

What's the highest-probability path? How do we get through? How do we—

An idea snapped into place.

Nick's eyes shot open and he pointed to the breakdown lane. "Take the military lane."

"What? Are you crazy?" Tracy lurched forward. "Did you see the last guy that tried that?"

Brian shifted into drive and watched for an opening in the train of humvees.

The last humvee sped past.

Nick squinted down the breakdown lane—there were more approaching, sixty seconds behind. "Go now—cut in before the next convoy."

Brian tore into the breakdown lane and aimed for the roadblock. "I hope you know what you're doing."

Nick turned around to terrified stares. "Seatbelts off. We're gonna play musical chairs."

* * *

THEY ROLLED to a stop at the checkpoint, blocked by three soldiers with half-raised rifles.

Nick's first bet had paid off: they weren't facedown on the asphalt because with its tinted windows and reinforced bumpers, the Suburban looked like a law enforcement vehicle.

A young soldier with thick military-issue glasses and a clipboard approached. He wasn't wearing a mask, probably because this lane was only for military personnel.

Brian lowered his window and stared straight ahead.

"Sir, this lane is for military vehicles only," the soldier said. "I need you to move to the side please."

Nick pulled off his sunglasses and leaned toward Brian's window. "We have orders to deliver a high-value asset to a secure location outside the city," he said, trying to project authority with a touch of impatience.

The rear driver-side window rolled down to reveal T.J. browsing on his phone.

The soldier's eyes widened. He offered a deferential nod. "Mr. Chandra."

T.J. ignored him.

The soldier turned back to Nick. "Who are the other passengers?"

"I'm Mr. Chandra's head of crisis management, and these are essential members of his staff."

Nick pointed at Brian. "His driver and bodyguard."

At Dana in the rear passenger-side seat. "His physician."

At Tracy in the third row. "His chef."

The soldier squinted at Zoe sitting next to T.J. in the middle seat. "And in the middle here?"

"That's Mr. Chandra's personal guest."

The soldier squinted at Zoe for a moment, then turned back to

Nick. "Sir, we have strict orders not to let any civilians through. Now, I appreciate the situation, but my commanding officer—"

"I need to speak with your CO immediately," Nick said. "Mr. Chandra has been called to an urgent matter, and he's already late because of this mess."

The soldier jogged to a bald, older man who was already rushing toward him. They spoke briefly, gesturing in Nick's direction, then the CO marched toward their vehicle with the soldier scrambling behind.

As the CO approached, he signaled for two more soldiers to step in. The next convoy of humvees slowed to a stop behind them.

Well, we're all in now.

"I'm Captain Kravich." He pointed off the road. "Pull your vehicle over and step out." He had the flushed cheeks, bulging veins, and hoarse Boston accent of a man who'd spent many years screaming at people.

"Absolutely not." Nick met his intense stare. "Mr. Chandra has been asked to join a statewide emergency-response summit, and I have strict orders not to let him or his staff leave the vehicle."

"Whose orders are you operating under?"

"I can't disclose that."

"Where are you headed?"

"I can't disclose that."

The driver of the lead humvee honked and stuck his head out the window. "Let's go!"

Kravich signaled for the driver to wait and looked at T.J. "Mr. Chandra, could I ask you to please pull your vehicle over. You can—"

"Don't address him," Nick said. "Talk to me. And no, we're not moving. Mr. Chandra is needed *immediately* on a matter of national security and he will not be detained."

Kravich leaned in and squinted at Nick. "Look, son, you're interfering with a National Guard terrorism operation during a state of emergency. So unless you show me some orders, I have no choice but to remove you."

Kravich gestured to his soldiers. Two swung their weapons into firing position, three approached the Suburban.

Brian looked at Nick for a signal.

Ugh, I really didn't want to do this...

Nick pointed at Kravich and snapped. "You crack that door one inch and you can explain to Governor Sutton why his niece and Mr. Chandra were exposed to a deadly virus on their way to the governor's lake house."

Kravich raised a hand and his soldiers froze.

Zoe draped a hand over T.J.'s thigh.

Kravich squinted, his face shifting from confusion to disgust. He leaned into Brian's window and lowered his voice. "Central command is run out of the governor's office. I'm calling this in. We'll see what he says."

"Make it fast." Nick glared.

Kravich held his stare. "And who do I say is asking?"

"What? T.J. Chandra."

"No. What's *your* name?"

Nick hesitated. "Nick Ritter."

"Hey, what the hell's going on?" The driver from the lead humvee approached, trailed by four armed soldiers. "We gotta go go go."

Kravich held up a finger, raised his cell phone, and strode away.

Nick tried to control his breathing as he watched Kravich. It was a gamble, two gambles really. First that they'd be able to reach Sutton, and second that he'd clear them to pass. Nick's stomach turned—he really didn't want his name in this, especially since Sutton had already bailed him out once.

Kravich lowered the phone and walked back to the Suburban.

"OK, here's the situation—the governor is on a conference call with Washington. Central command will call me back as soon as they speak with him." Kravich gestured off the road and forced an accommodating tone. "In the meantime, I do need you to *please* pull your vehicle over so these humvees can pass. You are *not* being detained, you can remain inside, and I will clear you as soon as I hear from the governor's office."

Shit. That's it...all we can do is wait and hope Sutton clears us.

Nick gestured to Brian. "Pull ov—"

"Hey!" T.J. lurched to the edge of his seat, jerked to a stop by his seat belt locking. He leaned out the window, glaring at Kravich, straining against the seat belt like a man held back from a fight. "Hey, meathead...what's your fucking problem?"

Kravich's jaw dropped open.

"You think I'm gonna wait in a ditch for a break in Ray's schedule? You see my face. You know who I am. We all know you're gonna let me through. So stop wasting my fucking time."

Kravich swallowed hard. It must've been a long time since anyone spoke to him like that. "Sir...respectfully...without authorization, I cannot clear you."

T.J. flipped from outrage to disgust. "Oh please, cut the bureaucratic theater. I don't need you to clear me—you're irrelevant. It's me, Ray, and a dozen other players holding this shithole together. You're not at the big table. You're not even in the big house. You're off in the woods shoveling horseshit off the trail. So get the *fuck* out of the way and let the big boys work."

T.J. aimed his phone at Kravich like a gun. "Because if I have to run down my contact list until I reach someone you recognize, I promise you'll be working at McDonald's within the hour."

Kravich stood frozen, eyes wide, face white.

Eleven soldiers watched for his command.

"Go," he said with a rasp. He cleared his throat. "Go!"

The soldiers cleared the lane.

Kravich waved them through.

As the roadblock shrank into the distance, Brian grinned at T.J. in the rearview mirror. "Damn, you really sold that...sir."

T.J. scrolled on his phone, muttering. "Fucking red-tape mouth-breather."

Nick put on his sunglasses, leaned to Brian, and whispered, "You know the secret to selling a lie? You have to actually believe it."

ELEVEN

"Brian, this thing is immaculate." Dana admired the Suburban's spotless interior as they rolled into the car wash. She had insisted on washing the exterior, given their exposure at the roadblock, and Nick had agreed.

Brian spun. "Oh yeah, I clean her every month, inside and out. Plus quarterly tune-ups and a weekly cruise, just to keep her fresh."

"Brian's Ark." Zoe grinned.

Tracy rolled her eyes. "I swear he's gonna leave me for this car."

Brian chuckled and shrugged.

They rolled out of the A-1 car wash and Brian guided them back onto the highway.

Even though it was sunny, the air was frigid. A light snow drifted down, dusting the road, swirling under the Ark as it cruised north.

"Kinda pretty, right?" Zoe said. "If you forget about the whole apocalypse thing."

T.J. chuckled without looking up from his phone.

Brian tapped the navigation display. "So, our travel time to Moose River is two and a half hours." He looked at Nick. "What are you thinking for lodging?"

Nick scrolled on his phone. "We're not going to Moose River."

"Oh…is that not our departure airport?"

"It is. But our flight doesn't leave until Friday night. We need a place to wait for forty-eight hours, and looking at this…" Nick gestured at his phone, "Moose River ain't it. There's nothing here. It's basically Canada."

"So where do we go?"

Nick tapped his phone, pinched a map, and looked at Brian. "Wolfeboro…we go to Wolfeboro. We need a house for six people that's isolated and vacant. Wolfeboro's a summer vacation town, a lakeside getaway for New England's richest families. But these places, they turn into ghost towns in the winter—just a few locals and hundreds of empty mansions. It has abundant freshwater, retail shops, a grocery store—it's the closest real town to Moose River, just ninety minutes south."

Brian changed their destination to Wolfeboro.

"What kinda grocery store are we talking about?" T.J. asked. "Because if they don't carry organic, we're gonna need to stop somewhere else."

"Ooh, can we get stuff for s'mores?" Zoe made an excited face at Dana.

"We're not stopping anywhere until we secure lodging," Nick said. "And then we're doing a focused supply run, not bouncing around town for everyone's favorite snack."

"Yikes…who made you mean dad for the trip?" T.J. said.

Everyone giggled.

"Look, that roadblock was a disaster," Nick said. "I don't ever want to be in that position again. So from now on, we need to follow a strict plan."

"Ehhh, but it all worked out fine, right?" T.J. smirked.

"Fine?" Nick pulled off his sunglasses. "Did it work out fine? I used the name of a private client—a high-ranking government official—to bluff through a National Guard roadblock, which, by the way, makes him an accomplice to a felony. By now he's gotten the message and either denied clearance—in which case we're wanted on a half dozen charges—or approved, in which case he's going to expect a big favor...from me. That's *not* a position I want to be in right now."

Everyone was silent.

"Sooo, no s'mores?" T.J. asked, looking around for a laugh.

Nick unbuckled his seatbelt and faced the back. "Look, this isn't a vacation. Things are about to get very, very ugly. And it may not seem like it, but every choice we make is a life-or-death decision. We don't have time to sit around, and think, and debate, and make mistakes. We need to plan and execute with cold, hard precision."

Nick looked from face to face. "This is what I do. I'm not your friend, I'm not your tour guide, I'm not your babysitter...I'm the planner. So from now on, we follow my playbook. When we get to New Zealand, you're on your own—you can do whatever you want. But for the next forty-eight hours, it's my show." He paused. "And if you slow me down, if you put me in danger, I will leave you behind."

Silence.

Nick faced forward again, opened his mouth to soften his last words, then decided against it.

He turned to Brian. "Also, we need to discuss your pay. I'm covered under your existing contract, but T.J. is paying me directly, so I'll pay you for his fare. When we arrive safely in New Zealand, I'll wire you two hundred thousand dollars. Fair?"

Brian's eyes widened and he cleared his throat. "Yes...yes, sir."

Nick addressed the group. "Our only goal right now is to find a house in Wolfeboro. That's it. Then we'll work on supplies. Any questions?"

"I have a question." Dana leaned forward. "What about everybody else? If we know this virus has high transmission and high mortality, shouldn't we warn everyone?"

T.J.'s head snapped up from his phone. "I could post it on Zen. I have a hundred and twenty-five million followers—we could really get the word out."

"Absolutely not," Nick said. "First of all, ninety-five percent of people won't believe you and the other five percent will panic and hurt themselves or someone else. Second, you'll make us a top target for the FBI, National Guard, White House, and god knows how many other institutions that want to control the narrative."

"OK, so we tell the authorities," Dana said. "Call the CDC, or Washington, or the WHO—tell them everything we know."

Nick shook his head. "Anyone with the power to help is busy saving themselves. Why do you think the National Guard is saying it's a terrorist threat? To buy time for the power players to get out first. Right now the nation's top leaders—businessmen, congressmen, celebrities, scientists—they're all being escorted to safety while the virus spreads unchecked. I know, I booked them all.

"Besides, the president is going to tell everyone tomorrow. And anyone not living under a rock will figure it out before then. If we want to survive, we take care of ourselves—no one else. If you don't like it, we can part ways in Wolfeboro."

Nick put his sunglasses on.

They cruised north in silence.

* * *

An hour later, they arrived in Wolfeboro. After passing through the empty downtown, they headed to Lake Wentworth, a midsize lake with three hundred homes along her shores.

Nick toggled between his phone's map and a real-estate app and settled on their destination: Cradle Cove. Positioned at the southern point of Lake Wentworth, it was an isolated community of summer getaway mansions.

The sole entrance to Cradle Cove was a slim wooden bridge spanning a small tributary. Surrounded by thick woods, it was designed to look rustic and allowed to fall into disrepair. The bridge groaned as the Ark squeezed across, its loose planks drumming under the car's tires. Brian watched his side mirrors, monitoring their clearance through the narrow passage.

Between the fairy-tale bridge, the gentle tributary, and the drifting snow, it looked like they had crossed into a country snow globe. Brian cruised down a half-mile stretch of straight road that led from the bridge to the beginning of the Cradle Cove community.

"Fourteen miles per hour?" Zoe pointed to a speed-limit sign. "Kinda weird, right?"

"Huh, that's pretty clever," Nick said. "People ignore safety instructions. But if you make them memorable, compliance goes way up. Who's going to forget fourteen miles per hour?"

Brian eyed the speedometer and slowed to fourteen.

Nick turned to Brian. "OK, so there are twenty-three houses in this community, most of them summer mansions. We need something spacious that's clearly vacant. And it needs to be lakefront, with private beach access."

"Little cold for a swim, don't you think?" T.J. asked.

"Most of these houses rely on well water," Nick said, "so they have to install high-end filtration equipment to remove radon, arsenic, minerals, etc. But all that equipment runs on electricity, so if we lose power, we lose water—that's a big problem. If that happens, we need direct access to lake water."

"How do we know the lake water's safe to drink?" Dana asked.

"We purify it," Nick said. "Or there's always rainwater as a last resort."

They reached the start of Cradle Cove, where the road split left and right, leading to homes along both shores. They chose right.

The houses were spread far apart and surrounded by woods to ensure privacy from neighbors. The old road—cracked and potholed from harsh winters—conformed to the natural landscape, rising and falling like a roller coaster as it snaked around ancient trees and boulders. The snow had grown heavy and was beginning to accumulate, making the road even more treacherous. They crawled along, staring at each passing home like buyers with a blank check.

They cruised past the first three mansions, each one a sprawling, custom design accompanied by various guest houses, docks, gardens, and recreational facilities.

"Are these places really empty?" Tracy asked.

"Fifty weeks a year," Nick said. "Give or take."

Tracy shook her head. "What a waste, spending ten million dollars for fourteen days."

"Eh, these are more like five million," T.J. said. "And it's only a waste if you don't enjoy it."

Zoe jumped in before her mom could reply. "Ooh, what about this place?" She pointed to a resort-style home with a swimming pool, tennis court, and basketball court.

Nick stared straight ahead. "It has exterior security cameras. Last thing we want is some lawyer in Connecticut calling the local sheriff."

Brian leaned over and squinted out Nick's window as they cruised past the house and crested a steep hill. "How'd you spot those cameras? They're completely hidd—"

"Look out!" Nick pointed ahead.

Brian whipped his head straight and slammed the brakes. The anti-lock braking system thudded like a muted machine gun as the Ark fish-tailed through the snow to a crooked stop.

Everyone stared down at the teenage girl standing two feet beyond the Ark's rumbling hood. She stared back up, her frightened eyes glistening in the headlights. She broke away first, casting her eyes to the ground and shuffling to the side of the road.

As she emerged on Nick's side of the car, Dana gasped—the girl was pregnant.

She waddled toward the entrance to Cradle Cove, flashing a sheepish wave as she passed Nick's window.

Something was definitely wrong. She looked about sixteen, and was wearing a tattered sweatshirt, black leggings, a small knapsack, and sneakers, but no jacket, gloves, or hat. Her rosy cheeks, pink nose, and red fingertips suggested she'd been outside for a while. Nick traced her snowy footprints back to an overgrown gravel road up ahead.

"What do we do?" Brian asked Nick.

Tracy leaned forward from the far back row. "Brian Donahue…if you don't check on this half-dressed pregnant girl, wandering through the woods, alone in the snow, I will divorce you today, virus or no virus."

Nick rolled down his window. “Everything OK?”

The girl flashed a polite smile. “I’m good. Thanks.” She sped up.

Tracy tapped Dana’s shoulder. “Put your window down. All she can see is these two creeps.”

Dana lowered her window.

The girl’s eyes widened at Dana in her scrubs and white coat. She stopped and turned.

“Hi there, I’m Dana. This is my niece, Zoe, and my sister, Tracy.”

“Hi there.” Zoe gave a peppy wave.

“Hi, hun,” Tracy called.

“It’s so cold,” Dana said. “Could we give you a ride somewhere?”

“Dana!” Brian whispered.

“Brian!” Tracy whispered.

The girl hesitated. “Umm, I’m OK. I’m going to the bus station downtown. It’s not far.”

They had passed it on the way in—it was far, a five-mile walk, at least—brutal in this weather, probably lethal for a pregnant, half-dressed child.

“Can we give you a ride there?” Dana asked.

Nick turned halfway toward the back seat and gave Dana a subtle head shake.

The girl looked at the ground.

Dana pivoted. “Where are you traveling to?”

“Umm, Canada…somewhere in Canada.” Breath steamed from her shivering lips. “I’m still deciding.” She kicked at fresh snow.

“Ooh, Canada’s fun. We did a girls trip there a few years ago. So many moose,” Dana said in a chipper voice. “Hey, I didn’t catch your name.”

The girl hesitated. “Abby.”

“Nice to meet you, Abby. Listen, would you mind if I talked to my family for a minute? Would you hang here?”

Abby shrugged. “OK.”

Dana and Nick rolled up their windows.

“Let’s give her a ride to the bus station,” Dana said. “It’s a fifteen-minute drive.”

Nick stared straight ahead. "She's an unquantifiable risk. We don't know her situation, we don't know if she's infected, and in her condition, she'll slow us down. Our focus is shelter."

"She's just a kid, Nick," Dana said. "You're gonna leave her out here in the freezing cold? You know she won't make it downtown."

T.J. held a palm to his forehead. "Oh come *on*...we just cleaned the car and agreed Nick's the boss. Last thing we need is some preggo runaway. Let's roll."

Tracy lurched forward. "Excuse me, how about *you* get out and walk to the bus station, spare us your selfish attitude."

T.J. rolled his eyes and dove back into his phone.

"She doesn't look sick." Dana touched Nick's shoulder. "Come on, Nick—can't she stay with us until the storm passes? Then she can walk to the station."

Brian placed a hand on the gear shift and eyed his family in the rearview. "Your show, Nick."

Nick studied Abby. She was staring into the falling snow with glassy eyes, tugging at the straps on her knapsack, kicking streaks into the fresh powder. She did look like a runaway, probably was. God knows from what. These towns were paradise in the summer, but in the winter they turned dark. Locals, alone in the freezing woods, had nothing but booze, drugs, guns, and demons. Places like this were hard on kids.

Abby began murmuring to herself, her jaw chattering as she quietly argued with some invisible adversary. Pregnant, rosy-cheeked, admonishing the drifting snow, she looked like something innocent that had been broken again and again and again.

Nick shook his head, already regretting his decision. "Until the storm clears, then she walks."

"Yes, thank you." Dana lowered her window.

"And make sure she's not sick," Nick whispered.

"Hey, Abby, sorry about that. So, it's really starting to come down out here, and it's a long walk downtown—why don't you stay with us until the storm clears? We have a house just up the road."

Abby looked from Dana to Nick's tinted window and back. Her shivering had progressed to full-body shaking.

"I promise we're nice people." Dana gave a warm smile.

Abby looked down the hill, as if calculating her odds on foot. "I'm sorry, I can't. But thanks anyways." She flashed a quick wave and started toward the hill.

"Let's go." Nick pointed ahead.

Brian shifted into gear.

A car horn sounded in the distance.

Abby froze, peering into the snow, then spun back to Dana. "If I come, you can't call the cops, OK?"

Dana gazed into Abby's eyes and delivered a line that sounded both well-practiced and deeply genuine. "Abby, you're safe here. I promise. Let us help you."

Abby gave a quick nod.

Dana quickly confirmed she wasn't infected or exposed while Zoe scrambled into the way back with Tracy. Dana slid over and helped Abby into the Ark.

They continued up the road, searching for a suitable house.

"What about this place?" Brian said.

"Too far from the water," Nick said. "Keep going."

Dana leaned to Abby and whispered, "OK, so now you have to promise not to call the cops on *us*." She grinned and winked.

A shy smile crept across Abby's frozen face.

They approached a tiny cabin with smoke streaming from its chimney. The run-down house and accompanying shed were an eyesore in an otherwise pristine neighborhood. It must've belonged to a local.

As they passed the cabin, a large figure stepped out from behind the shed. It was an old Black man with short white hair. He was definitely a local—Nick could tell with one glance. His right eyelid sagged, the surrounding skin crisscrossed with scars. His nose was slightly flattened, and his big hands were stiff and knotted. Silhouetted against the falling snow, his head askew, he looked like a haunted scarecrow guarding the side of the road.

He glared at the Ark as it rolled past.

"Jesus Christ, next house please," T.J. said.

They continued up the road another half mile, Nick finding a flaw with every house they passed.

They approached a sprawling, modern colonial painted in forest greens and browns.

"This." Nick pointed. "This is it. Spacious, set back, waterfront access, no security cams, a generator, and a four-car garage for storage. Plus I see a jacuzzi in back."

Brian turned into the driveway. "Home sweet home."

TWELVE

Brian climbed back into the Ark and shut the door. "Cold out there."

They idled in the mansion's driveway, halfway between the front door and the garage.

Brian shivered. "OK, so I climbed through an unlocked window in the fitness center, and everything looks good. No security system, working electricity, water filtration in the basement, and plenty of beds. If you want to go inside, the door's open and I turned up the heat."

"Let's go." Nick opened his door.

"Hey Nick, would you mind if I chat with my family here a minute?" Brian asked. "Then I'll pull in the garage and unload the bags."

Nick nodded. He, T.J., and Abby headed into the house.

Brian turned to face Zoe, Dana, and Tracy in the back. "OK, family," he said with his stern dad voice, "we need to get on the same page. This is my job. My mission. It's my duty to get my clients to safety, and I can't do that if you're arguing with them, and goofing around, and distracting me, and second guessing every decision."

The windshield wipers scrubbed back and forth, clearing the falling snow and providing a steady beat to Brian's speech.

"I have thirty-seven days left on my contract…*thirty-seven days.*

And then, when the new year hits, ten years of escrow payments will be released. There's enough there to pay off the mortgage, the medical bills, the business loans—Zoe you can stop working at the nursing home and focus on school—and maybe, just maybe, I can think about retiring from this shit.

"Oh, plus the two-hundred-thousand-dollar direct payment for T.J." He gestured at Tracy. "Hun, you could take another shot at a restaurant."

Tracy crossed her arms.

"In thirty-seven days, we'll be free," Brian said. "But if we don't deliver our clients to New Zealand, if they get infected, if we piss them off and they call for a replacement, we lose *everything*. Ten years of hard work—*gone*." He snapped his thick fingers on the last word.

Tracy waited to make sure his speech was over. "Brian, I hear you, we all know how important the contract is. We've been planning your big New Year's Payout Party for, like, nine years. But the thing is, we have to survive to cash in." She pointed at the house. "These guys… they don't give a shit about us. Our lives mean nothing to them. I'm sorry, hun, but your loyalty only runs one way. To them, you're just another butler. And if this virus is as bad as they say, you need to focus on protecting our family, not serving these pricks."

Brian shook his head. "T.J. is…well yeah, he's a prick. But Nick, he's just doing his job, and he's damn good at it. They call him The Posh Prepper, and all the top guys use him. Honestly, we're lucky to have him. What else would we do? Head back home? Drive to Canada? Sail to New Zealand?" He scoffed. "The truth is, we need him as much as he needs us, maybe more. One phone call and he gets another pilot. Where are we gonna find another crisis planner? Right now, there's no safer place than with Nick Ritter."

"Brian, you're not hearing me," Tracy said. "I don't care if he's the greatest prepper that ever lived—his job doesn't include saving us. It's about him and T.J. We're all expendable pieces in his big brilliant escape plan. Can't you see that?"

"He could've left me at the hospital," Dana said quietly. "Or left Abby in the snow."

Brian pointed to Dana. "Right! And he could've left us at the house, but he didn't. Trace, we gotta trust him. He's the best chance we have to survive. Once we arrive in New Zealand, the company will put us up in housing and we'll collect our payout. Then we'll be done with them for good."

"I'm sorry about the s'mores thing, Dad." Zoe hung her head. "I was trying to be funny. I didn't mean to piss him off."

"Aww, you're good, Z-Bird." Brian smiled. "He wasn't mad at you."

Zoe looked at Tracy. "Mom, please. If we help Dad get through this, we'll get a fresh start in New Zealand."

Tracy took Zoe's hand and nodded. "OK, Zo."

"Thank you." Brian took a deep breath. "For the next forty-eight hours, let's follow Nick's lead so we can get out and get paid. OK?"

Everyone agreed.

"OK." Brian exhaled and his eyes softened. "Love you guys."

THIRTEEN

"WE'VE GOT a ton of prep to do if we want to survive."

Nick stood by the floor-to-ceiling windows that overlooked the lake. He held an uncapped red marker, with "Arrive," "Survive," and "Thrive" headlining the big center pane behind him. Everyone else was seated on couches and loveseats around the family room's crackling fireplace.

While Brian was talking to his family in the Ark, Nick had filled Abby in on the situation. She had seemed numb to it, and he wondered if she thought he was crazy or was just too cold to care.

Dana walked in, handed Abby a steaming cup of tea, and sat down. Everyone turned their attention to Nick.

He took a deep breath. "OK, so in any crisis there are three stages: Arrive, Survive, Thrive. Arrive is about getting to your destination safely. Survive is about outlasting the crisis. And Thrive is about building a life in the new world. Our goal for the next forty-eight hours is to Arrive in New Zealand."

He turned to the window and began adding bubbles with little symbols. "There are eight categories we need to prep for: Transportation. Food and water. Shelter. Health and medical. Safety and defense.

Currency and assets. Communication and continuity. Leisure and entertainment."

T.J. stood and cocked his head. "Wait, I thought we were leaving Friday? Why do we need all this stuff?"

Nick nodded. "We need to plan for two scenarios. Plan A is to wait here for forty-eight hours, then head to New Zealand. It's a good plan, and it should work. But if something goes wrong with Plan A, and we can't make it to New Zealand, we'll be stuck here without food or supplies. So we need a Plan B, which is to stay here and outlast the virus. Anything can happen, it could be weeks, months, even years. So we hope for Plan A, and prepare for Plan B."

"We're ready, Nick." Brian gave a thumbs up. "Just tell us what to do."

Nick gave an appreciative nod. "OK, let's start by taking inventory. I have a bug-out bag, and Brian, you should have one too."

"I do." Brian unzipped the two duffel bags on the floor.

Nick turned and raised his marker to the window. "Inventory?"

Brian began unpacking. "Umm five, no six, flashlights. Four sleeping bags. Four mylar blankets. Forty N95 masks. Two hundred surgical gloves. Two binoculars. Four butane torch lighters. Six packs of waterproof matches. Two flints. Six road flares. Two hatchets. Five permanent markers. Two gas masks. Two multitools. Six fishhooks with line. Two rolls of duct tape. Two first-aid kits. Two envelopes of cash."

"Should be ten thousand dollars in each." Nick scribbled.

"Two small bars of gold. Two dozen meal-ready-to-eat rations. Four water-filtration straws. A hundred water-purification tablets. Two camping stoves with six gas canisters. Two bottles of lighter fluid. Two hand-crank radios. Four walkie talkies. Two prepaid cell phones."

"Anddd..." Brian scraped the bottom of his bag. "A pink seahorse whistle."

Nick turned and tilted his head.

"I think Zoe added that when she was little." Brian chuckled.

"Oh my god, I'm sorry." Zoe's face turned red.

"No, that's good," Nick said. "We can use that." He turned and skimmed a finger down the list. "Good, everything's there. Anything else?"

"I have a company-issue defense kit." Brian gestured to a black hard-shell briefcase leaning against his chair. "Pistol, knife, and some other tactical toys."

Nick added it to the list. "Given we're dealing with a virus and we have a head start, hopefully we won't need any of that. But better to have it and not need it, than need it and not have it."

Nick stepped back and scanned the window. "OK, the bad news is we don't have enough supplies to last two days, never mind two months. And we have major category gaps."

He turned. "But the good news is, right now, we have a tiny window of opportunity to prep before everyone else finds out. Between the roadblocks, the hospitals, the news, social media, people will piece it together. But if we go now, we can get what we need before it's gone. But we need to move fast. Every second we spend outside this house increases our risk of infection or confrontation. So we should only gather things that we absolutely need to survive for, let's say, sixty days."

Nick pointed to T.J. "T.J., while we go through the categories, can you gather the latest intel? Local news, social media, whatever. We want to know exactly what's happening before we go out there."

T.J. began tapping his phone. "I can check private rooms on Zen. I'm thinking...Feds Anonymous, Hypocritic Oath, Washington Insiders, ooh, and Conspiracy Central, of course."

"Perfect." Nick started to turn back to the window, but stopped. "Wait, I thought Zen was a hundred percent secure?"

T.J. swiped. "Eh, more like ninety-nine point nine percent."

Nick shook his head and turned to the window. "OK, let's go through the categories. We'll start with the easy ones."

He moved to the airplane symbol. "Transportation. We're good with the Ark, but we need to refill her tank and get some extra gas in case there's a run on the stations. Plus we'll need gas for the generator." He sidestepped to a blank section of window and started a list. "If we want a second car, we can get one tomorrow, after we've secured the high-priority items."

"Shelter." His eyes swung around the million-dollar family room. He put a big check mark. "We're good."

He squatted. "Safety and defense. We've got the defense kit, and we're dealing with a virus, not a combat threat. So we're good." Big check.

"Currency and assets. Between the cash and the gold, we've got forty thousand dollars on hand. Plus we can max out credit cards. T.J., you'll want to transfer some money, at least ten million, to a New Zealand bank. I have a local banker you can use."

T.J. paced the side of the room, staring at his phone.

Nick turned to Brian. "Brian, we'll have your direct payment for T.J. when we arrive in New Zealand. You can take it via wire or cash or gold, whatever you prefer."

"What about the escrow money?" Brian asked.

Nick shook his head. "That's up to your employer."

He turned back to the window. "Leisure and entertainment…L&E will have to wait. It's crucial for long-term mental health, but it's not an immediate need. Plus Cradle Cove probably has enough books and board games to entertain us for a year." Check.

"Communication and continuity. I'll run the operation, so anyone who doesn't have my number, put it in your phone now." Nick wrote his number high on the window. "And text me right now with your name, so I can add you to my contacts. If phone lines go down, which they probably will, Brian and I have satellite backup on our phones. And there's always the walkie talkies."

Nick rested his hands atop his head and squinted at the window. "OK, that leaves us with two big categories. Food and water, and health and medical."

"Let's start with health and medical." Nick stepped to a blank section of window.

"Obviously, we need the basics. Toothbrush, toothpaste, floss, mouthwash, razors, shaving cream, deodorant." Nick scribbled down the window, his hand racing to keep up with his mind. "Shampoo, soap, hand sanitizer—*lots* of hand sanitizer—toilet paper, nail clippers—" He stopped and stepped back. "You know what? Just get it all. We'll go to CVS and shop like, well, like it's the end of the world."

He turned to the group. "We have the first aid kits. What else do we need?"

"Vitamins," Dana said. "If food runs low, we'll want multivitamins, vitamin C, vitamin B complex, vitamin D for the winter, etc. Abby, do you have prenatals? Iron? Fish oil?"

Abby stopped with her tea halfway to her mouth. "Umm, I did. But not anymore."

"Dana, can you make a vitamin and OTC shopping list?" Nick asked.

Dana grabbed a pen and notepad from the pile on the coffee table. "On it."

"Make sure to put potassium iodide on there," Nick said. "There's a nuclear facility in Seabrook, less than fifty miles from here."

Dana pointed her pen at Nick. "Right—to block thyroid radioiodine uptake in the event of radiation exposure."

Nick nodded.

"What about prescription meds?" Brian asked.

"I have asthma," T.J. blurted out, leaning against the wall, his phone inches from his face.

Nick ignored him. "Good call, Brian. I usually stockpile antibiotics, painkillers, anxiolytics, antidepressants, inhalers, antihistamines—modern medicine's greatest hits. But those are impossible to get in bulk on short notice."

"What about vet clinics? Or farms?" Brian said. "They'd have some stuff in bulk."

"Right," Nick pointed his marker, "there must be livestock farms around here. But we'd have to raid them, which—"

"I can write prescriptions." Dana looked up from her notepad.

A smile crept across Nick's face. "Good call, Doc. Can you do bulk?"

"Hmm, no. They'll only dispense a limited supply for one person."

"Hmm." Nick's smile faded.

They stared into space, racking their brains.

"What if you're a family of explorers..." Abby broke the silence, staring at the Donahues. "Returning from safari in Africa...and everyone got sick?"

Everyone stared at her, confused.

"Yes!" Dana's eyes lit up and she pointed at Abby. "They got *really* sick. The whole family." She scribbled. "I can write a three-month supply of three different antibiotics for each person, plus an antifungal and an antiviral. An opioid and anxiolytic for the pain. And inhalers for the asthma."

"And prednisone...for the inflammation," Abby said.

Dana tilted her head and smiled at Abby. "Right...prednisone for the inflammation. The pharmacist will take one look at this infectious-disease cocktail and want them out the door ASAP."

"If anyone has a specific medication they need, talk to Dana," Nick said.

"Asthma," T.J. blurted.

Nick looked at Dana. "Do you need a computer?"

Dana held up her phone. "The hospital has an app. I do everything from here."

Nick nodded and turned to the Donahues. "Wear masks and gloves when you go. A pharmacy is likely to attract sick people. Plus it'll sell your story."

Nick turned back to the window. "OK, last is food and water. Bare minimum, we need two gallons of water per person, per day. Half a gallon to cook, half to clean, and one to drink." Nick scribbled some math. "Two gallons per day, times six people, times sixty days...that's seven hundred and twenty gallons. Yikes.

"We've got filtered well water, which is great. But if power goes out, we're relying on the generator until it runs out of gas. Then it's purified lake water, or rain and snow collection as a last resort. Not ideal.

"Water is a top priority, and we want to give ourselves as much runway as possible. So we'll grab some large jugs for storing well water, plus we'll fill all the bathtubs, refreshing both every week. That way when the power goes out we'll have enough supply to get a purification system up and running."

Nick moved to a fresh patch of window. "Last is food." He took a deep breath and scanned the room. "We're gonna need a lot of food. Six people…a long, cold winter…we don't want to be hunting squirrel a month from now. We each need at least two thousand calories a day to survive, but we can get by on fifteen hundred for a stretch, if needed."

He scrawled a quick formula. "If we each eat only one can of Spam per meal—" he turned and held up his palms, "I'm just using Spam to do the math—with six of us, that's eighteen cans per day. We'd need over a thousand cans to last two months. Whatever we get, we're gonna need to buy in bulk.

"We'll target foods with a long shelf life—anything perishable will go bad in a week. Same with anything frozen, if we lose power. So we'll focus on nutritious canned foods and dry goods with high caloric density, durable containers, and easy prep—you know, canned salmon over potato chips. Variety is sanity. So we want rice, beans, lentils, canned veggies, canned meats, nut butters—"

"I can write a list," Tracy said, and reached for a pen and notepad.

"She's a chef." Zoe beamed.

Nick turned to Tracy. "I didn't know you were—"

"Organic," T.J. blurted out without looking up. "Get all organic."

"We'll get what's available," Nick said.

T.J. lowered his phone. "Do you have any idea how many pesticides they use? Big Food insiders did a huge document dump on Zen. That shit is pure poison—causes cancer, autism, Parkinson's, obesity, infertility—they've known for fifty years."

Nick sighed. "OK, we'll get organic."

T.J. dove back into his phone.

Nick gave Tracy a little head shake and eye roll.

She grinned.

"Also, Tracy," Nick said, "in the spring we can homestead—grow our own food—so if we come across seeds for carrots, potatoes, squash, whatever, we should grab them."

Tracy nodded as she scribbled.

"Oh, and if we can't find enough canned meat, get cat food," Nick said.

T.J.'s head shot up. "Cat food? Are you joking?"

"A week without food and you'll be begging for Meow Mix," Nick said, and turned back to the window. "Oh, and can openers—as many as you can find."

Tracy looked up. "Can we get food for a Thanksgiving dinner? It's perishable, but I'll cook it tomorrow."

Nick paused. It had been a long time since he shared a Thanksgiving dinner. He turned and gently nodded. "Yeah, sure. That'd be nice."

"Where are we going to get all this food?" Brian asked.

Nick looked at his watch. "It's four p.m. the day before Thanksgiving and there's a snowstorm. The grocery store will be picked over. Even if it's not, we couldn't buy that much food without raising questions. Plus, if locals are doing last-minute Thanksgiving shopping, the risk of virus exposure is too high."

"What about a church or shelter?" Brian asked. "They might have a pantry with canned goods."

Tracy shot him a death stare. She spoke carefully through a forced smile. "Brian, I'd strongly prefer we *not* rob a church or shelter the night before Thanksgiving."

Nick nodded.

"Right. What about a hotel?" Brian asked.

"Maybe," Nick said. "But they're all closed for the season, and they probably don't carry supplies through the winter. We could try a factory or farm, but again, we'd have to raid it. And while there might be quantity, variety would be limited."

Nick took a deep breath, studied his watch, and exhaled. "We're gonna have to solve this on the fly. We'll start by scouting the grocery store and reassess from there." He drew circles around the words "gas station," "CVS," and "grocery store."

"So we're just going to snatch up all these supplies and food and medicine?" Dana asked. "What about other people?"

Brian shot her a look.

"We have to prioritize our own survival," Nick said. "When Plan A works, the plane has strict weight limits, so we'll donate everything to a local shelter."

Dana nodded, satisfied.

Nick stepped back, capped the marker, and admired the window. It was a good plan. "T.J., what's the latest intel?"

T.J. looked up, his eyes red, face pale. "It's…it's everywhere… every major city in the U.S., London, Tokyo, Brazil, Shanghai, Moscow. They're small outbreaks, but governments are reacting and people are starting to panic." His eyes fell to a carousel of live images streaming across his phone. "The people…I can't…Jesus Christ, Nick, what are we gonna do?"

Nick raised his eyebrows and pointed to the window. "This. This is what we're gonna do."

T.J. stomped forward. "Wait, what? This is your plan? Cat food and bathwater? Are you serious? I thought you were the best. The Posh Prepper—escape in luxury. How the *fuck* is this worth two million dollars?"

Tracy's eyes widened and locked on Brian.

"There is no plan!" Nick threw the marker on the coffee table. "First of all, I *told* you to go your own way, but you forced me to bring you along. Second, I usually have weeks or months to prep a client, not minutes."

"I want an extraction." T.J. blurted.

"Sure, I can have an extraction team here in twenty minutes. Where do you want to go? Back to Boston? The cornfield in Idaho? Trust me, wherever they drop you will be a big step down from here."

"They can bring me to your ranch."

Nick scoffed. "They won't do that. Plus, everything from the front gate to the coffee maker is on a security system that requires my key and code. Nothing works without me there, so don't get any ideas."

"I thought you knew people, important people—senators, generals, VIPs—people who can help us."

"I know plenty of them. Problem is right now they're either locking down the country, fleeing on my escape plan, or blowing up my phone." Nick held up his phone, which was lit with an incoming call.

T.J. waved Nick down. "This is bullsh—"

"Listen to me," Nick stepped to T.J. and hardened his tone, "there's a deadly virus of unknown origin tearing across the world. Governments are panicking. Roads are closed. Escape routes are overwhelmed. And we're stuck in the middle of nowhere with zero supplies. And you know what? The real crisis hasn't even started. Know what happens next? Phones go down. Power goes out. Markets tank. Looters. Scavengers. Martial law. Military hospitals. Mass graves."

Everyone stared in horror.

Nick softened and addressed the room. "There is no magic plan. Even with the best plan, something will always go wrong. Prepping isn't about bunkers, or beans, or the perfect plan—it's about solving problems under pressure—reading the situation and maximizing your chance of survival. While everyone else is gawking and panicking, we focus on solving the problem in front of us, and then the next, then the next. That's all we can do."

He turned back to T.J. "But if you're unhappy, let's call an extraction." Nick unlocked his phone. "Or see if your private security guys will pick you up." He paused. "Or we can drop you at the bus station."

Tracy crossed her arms and smirked at T.J.

"Otherwise, let's get to work," Nick said. "With a little luck we'll be in New Zealand by Saturday. Then we'll talk about long-term survival."

"I thought that's when we part ways." Dana tilted her head.

Nick stared and blinked. "Right…exactly…that's when we part ways." He gave a stern nod.

Dana gave him a gentle smile and a slow blink.

Nick cleared his throat. "We need to go. Every second we wait means less food and more risk."

Dana stood. "Abby, we can drop you at the bus station, it's right by the grocery store…if that's still what you want?"

Abby hesitated, then stood. “Umm, yeah, definitely. I should get going.”

“OK, let’s go,” Nick said. “We can discuss details in the—”

Someone pounded on the front door—three deep, aggressive thuds.

Nick and Brian locked eyes.

Brian reached for his defense kit.

Nick gave a quick head shake.

Brian slid the case under the couch.

“Everyone stay here.” Nick headed for the door.

FOURTEEN

"Good afternoon, sir. I'm looking for my daughter, Abby Hunziker. Have you seen her?"

Nick squinted through the cracked door at two men in green-camo fatigues.

The speaker looked late forties, tall and strong, with dog tags around his neck. There were patches on his uniform: an upside-down American flag, a matchstick bursting into flame, and a name tag that read, "General Kurt Hunziker." He had the insignia of a five-star general on his shoulders.

Behind him stood an old man with tired eyes and a wispy, gray beard. He had the same upside-down American flag and matchstick patches, plus a New Hampshire state-flag patch and a name tag that read, "Lieutenant Neal Dobbins—Old Glory." Below the patches hung three faded medals: a silver star, a purple heart, and a distinguished service medal.

Nick scanned the hodgepodge of patches and medals.

They're not Army, not private military, not cops—they look like local idiots.

If it's really her father, I should just hand her over.

But these guys seem off, and they could be infected.

Better not get involved.

"Haven't seen her," Nick said, and closed the door.

It stopped hard on Hunziker's boot. "You sure? Pretty girl, knocked up, kinda cranky. No? Nothin'?"

His accent was southern, definitely not local.

Nick shook his head. "Doesn't ring a bell."

Hunziker peered past Nick into the house. "What brings you up here? Little late in the season for leaf peeping, huh?"

"Here with my family. Thanksgiving tradition." Nick offered a fake smile.

Hunziker returned a skeptical nod.

"Listen, if I see your daughter, I'll be sure—"

Zoe screamed.

Nick turned and saw a giant face pressed against a side window.

A radio on Hunziker's belt crackled. "She's inside, sir. By the fireplace."

Hunziker flashed a big gotcha grin and shoved the door open. "Mind if I come in?"

The soldiers brushed past Nick. He followed them into the family room, studying their tactical belts—zip ties, radio, knife, sidearm pistol.

Brian had moved to the corner of the room, near the exit to the kitchen, Zoe and Tracy behind him. T.J. leaned against a wall, looking annoyed. Abby and Dana stood by the couch.

"Hiya, honey. There you are. Oh, we were so worried. Won't you come on home?" Hunziker said with maximum sarcasm. He had the air of a natural-born asshole, the kind of guy who tied firecrackers to cats.

Abby glared. "You're *not* my father."

A dickish grin spread across Hunziker's face. He reached inside his shirt, pulled out a folded paper, and handed it to Nick.

Nick opened the wrinkled paper—it was a certificate of adoption, dated two years earlier. It looked legitimate.

"I love what you've done with the place," Hunziker said, pointing to the prep plan scrawled across the window.

Nick held the certificate up to Abby. "Is this real?"

She crossed her arms and scowled.

An enormous soldier stumbled into the room, startling everyone. It was the face from the window. The young man was obese, with a pit-stained uniform and skinny jeans that hugged his massive thighs. His torso was perfectly round, and he was wearing a tight brown beanie, which made his head perfectly round, giving him the shape of a volleyball resting on a beach ball, supported by two upside-down bowling pins. Below the upside-down American flag and flaming-match patches, he wore a Maine state flag and a name tag, "Corporal Ronald Stubbs—Big Ron."

Panting and red-faced, Big Ron rested his hands on his tactical belt, which was crammed with a jumble of gear, including two sidearm pistols.

Hunziker clapped. "OK, Crabby—time to go. Let these nice people get back to…" he gestured at the marked-up window and emptied bug-out bags, "whatever the hell this is."

Abby plopped on the couch, crossed her arms, and stared at the ground.

Hunziker raised his eyebrows. "Abigail, do we need to call Sheriff Thompkins again? That didn't go too well last time."

Hunziker squatted to Abby's level and softened his tone. "Look, honey, I know you're trying to look strong for your friends here, but one way or another, you're coming home. If you come now, I'll put in a good word and you won't get in any trouble. But if you're a headache, you can say goodbye to your iPad, and your school, and all your special privileges."

An angry flush crept up Abby's neck and face. She raised her eyes, sharp and hot, and locked on Hunziker. "You don't own me. Go find someone else to make you feel strong…you arrogant prick."

"Mind your tongue, young lady!" Old Glory shook a finger.

"Shut up, Neal, you fraud," Abby said. "How many of those medals are actually yours? Oh yeah, none. You served two days, like, a hundred years ago, then broke a toe. Yeah, that's right, everybody knows."

Old Glory's jaw dropped with a wet smack.

Abby's eyes shot back to Hunziker. "Do us both a favor and say I left town. You can play general with your stupid army, and I don't have to live with a bunch of ignorant hicks."

Everyone stared at Abby. That was more than she'd spoken since they met her.

Hunziker stalked at her, stabbing a finger. "Listen up, you bitter *bitch*—no one cares about you. You're rude and selfish and fuckin' *weird.* If I hadn't scooped you outta that shithole, you'd be just another orphan frozen under a bridge. How about some goddamn gratitude?" He towered over her as she fumed at the ground. "You coulda been part of something special, but in two weeks, say goodbye, Princess Preggo, because no one's gonna want you."

"Hey!" Dana extended a hand toward Hunziker. "Take it easy."

"Dana!" Brian whispered and shook his head.

Abby stood up, eyes shimmering. "If I had known—"

"Oh, enough already!" T.J. exploded off the wall. "Can't you just go? Finish your tantrum somewhere else? We've got things to do here."

"Ha! See?" Hunziker chuckled. "Even the Arab doesn't want you."

"The fuck you say?" T.J. cocked his head. "I'm Indian, and I'm from Queens, you fuckin' dunce."

Hunziker turned to T.J. His face darkened.

Old Glory wobbled forward, pointing at T.J. "How dare you speak to a war hero like that? If you're gonna come here, show some respect for this great country."

Nick fired T.J. a warning look, but it was too late.

"Listen, gramps, I was born in New York. I went to Stanford, interned with a senator, got an MBA from MIT, and founded a Fortune 500 company with two thousand employees. I pay ten million dollars a year in taxes, own property in eighteen states, and take selfies with the president." He thumbed at Hunziker. "I'm more American than G.I. Joke will ever be."

Hunziker pulled his pistol with lightning speed and aimed at T.J.'s head.

T.J. raised his hands. "Nick!"

Brian locked eyes on Nick, ready for a command.

Nick gave a subtle head shake. Do not engage.

Hunziker glared down the barrel. "OK, debate time's over. Abby, you're coming home." He snapped his fingers and pointed. "Ronnie, escort Miss Hunziker to the truck."

Big Ron lumbered toward Abby, yanked a stun gun from his belt, and lit it up.

Everyone protested in unison. Dana jumped in front of Abby.

"Woah woah woah!" Hunziker extended his hand in a stop signal. "Ronnie, what the hell are you doing? She's a kid, and she's pregnant. God almighty, son." He shook his head. "Old Glory, you do it."

Big Ron holstered his stun gun and skulked behind Hunziker.

Old Glory shuffled to Abby and spoke with a wheeze. "Let's go, young lady. You've caused quite enough trouble for one day."

He put a pasty hand on her elbow.

She yanked it away and crossed her arms.

Hunziker stalked toward T.J., gun extended.

T.J. backed into the wall, squeezed his eyes shut, and turned his face sideways.

Hunziker pressed the muzzle to T.J.'s temple and cocked the hammer. "If you're not in that truck in thirty seconds, Mr. America is gonna paint the wall red, white, and brown."

The angry double-crack of a racking shotgun echoed through the room.

Everyone froze.

Behind them stood an old Black man with a rusty 12-gauge shotgun leveled directly at Hunziker's head.

Nick squinted at the man's busted eye—it was the haunted scarecrow.

Old Glory and Big Ron raised their hands high.

"Whatcha bothering these people for, Hunziker?" The old man spoke in a gruff grumble, with a faded southern drawl.

Hunziker squeezed his pistol grip. "Just bringing my runaway daughter back home, Herman."

Herman scoffed. "Thatta girl. If I was stuck with you hillbillies, I'd run away too." He gestured toward the door with the shotgun. "Time to go."

"That thing looks older than you, old man. Does it even work?"

"Wanna find out?"

Hunziker clenched his jaw. "OK, Herman, have it your way." He carefully holstered his pistol, raised his hands, and walked toward the door.

Herman tracked him with the shotgun. "Leave your pistol. All ya."

Hunziker took a long pause, then unholstered his gun and placed it on the floor. Big Ron and Old Glory followed suit. They all headed to the door, hands high.

Hunziker stopped in the doorway and turned his head. "Sleep with your good eye open, old man. We're comin' for you."

FIFTEEN

"THAT FELLA'S TROUBLE," Herman said, peeking out the window to confirm Hunziker was gone. "Ain't the first time we've nearly come to blows."

In his dirty jeans and faded red-checkered flannel, Herman looked like an old-timey farmer. Even though he was tall and strong, with a commanding physical presence, every part of him looked damaged or worn, like an old gladiator who'd been stooped by time.

Herman leaned his shotgun against the wall and turned to the group. "Now, what are y'all doing at the Gifford's place?" He crossed his arms like a grumpy grandpa.

Everyone looked at Nick.

Nick was about to respond when something caught his eye. Sneaking up behind the old man was a boy with Down syndrome. He looked about eighteen, with tanned white skin and a wide-eyed, curious expression.

Herman swiveled from one person to the next. "What? No one's gonna speak up?"

The boy was standing by his damaged eye now, but Herman didn't see him.

"What? Why y'all look like I have ten heads?"

Herman followed Nick's gaze and jumped. "Goddammit, boy! What'd I tell you about sneaking up on me? Damn near gave me a heart attack."

The boy stepped out from Herman's side, his eyes dancing across the new faces. "Hi, I'm Mikey," he stammered, then grinned. He was wearing dirty jeans, work boots, and a torn-up Carhartt jacket with a giant grease stain on one shoulder and a sloppy patch on the other. He pulled off his Boston University beanie and stuffed it in his jacket.

Herman shook his head. "I'm Herman Reed. This is my grandson, Mikey. He helps me with the handy work around town."

Nick looked from Herman—who was tall, dark, wrinkled, and frowning—to Mikey—who was short, white, tan, and grinning.

"I see the resemblance," T.J. said, smirking.

Herman glared at T.J.

Mikey laughed and clapped Herman on the back.

Zoe gave a friendly wave. "Hi, Mikey, my name is Zoe, and this is my dad, Brian, my mom, Tracy, and my Aunt, Dana. Nice to meet you."

Mikey smiled and waved, and a graying German Shepherd trotted in and sat by his side.

"You let the dog out, too?" Herman said.

"This is my brother, Cadillac." Mikey stroked the shepherd.

"Alright, now we all know each other." Herman looked at Nick. "Now, aside from avoiding Hunziker, what are you doing—"

"We stand up to bullies," Mikey said, raising a fist.

Herman's face softened, and he rested a hand on Mikey's shoulder. "That's right, Mikey. We stand up to bullies. Now, let's help these nice people get where they're going." Herman raised an eyebrow at Nick.

Nick walked them through the situation as clearly and quickly as he could. He explained the virus, everyone's role, and their intention to stock up and camp out at Cradle Cove until the flight on Friday. No point in bluffing. Whatever got them shopping soonest was best, and the truth usually saved time.

When Nick finished, Herman stared at the floor with a finger pressed to his lips.

"I know it's a lot to process," Nick said, "but we have to get shopping. We can talk more when we get back."

"We can help you, Nick." Mikey outstretched a confident thumbs up. "Herman can fix anything, and I'm his manager."

Herman snapped from his daze and squinted down at Mikey. "Now hold on just a minute, boy. Before you go committing us, we got responsibilities—salt, sand, shovel, winterize half the cove. Plus, they ain't even invited us. These folks don't want a half-blind old man and a smart-mouth busybody."

Mikey glared back up. "Herman...*attitude*. We talked about this after church. You need to be *positive* if we wanna make friends. Nobody likes a Gloomy Gus." He surveyed the room with mock disbelief and added an exasperated eye roll.

Everyone smirked.

Herman crossed his arms and scowled.

"Can you help us find a new house?" Nick asked. "We'll need a solid place to land after our big shop, and we can't stay here. It's only a matter of time until they come back."

Mikey thrust a big thumbs up. "We know all the cove houses, Nick. No problem."

Herman sighed. "We maintain most of the places around here, make sure they're just right when the owners arrive in summer. I can't have you breaking into all my houses, making a mess for us to clean up. What do you need?"

"Something spacious and vacant with private beach access, well water treatment equipment, and no security system. And, of course, someplace they can't find us."

"How *did* they find me?" Abby broke her silence.

Nick and Brian exchanged shrugs. "Honestly, I don't know," Nick said.

"Tracks." Herman scoffed. "Fresh snow on an abandoned street—might as well put up a billboard."

"Can we approach the next house by boat?" Nick asked.

"You could, but no need." Herman thumbed out the window.

"Snow's stopped. In this sun, it'll melt in a few hours. That said, if you want isolation, the Conroy place is on Bass Island."

"Islands are too risky, only one way out," Nick said. "What else is there?"

"The Kennebec house has everything you're looking for. It's on the other side of the cove. They have a security system, but I can turn it off."

"Any risk they show up?"

"Nah. In sixteen years they've never set foot on that property outside of July Fourth weekend. I've been in that house a hundred times more than they have."

"OK, let's do it."

"Should we check it out before we shop?" Brian asked.

Nick shook his head. "The house will still be there in two hours. The food might not be."

Nick stepped to the window and addressed the group. "Obviously, what just happened was disturbing, but it doesn't change our plan. We still need to get gas, hit the pharmacy, stock up on food, and find a new house. Except now we have less time and more risk. So we need to be fast and focused."

Nick pointed at Dana. "Dana, can you put in the prescriptions now?"

"Should only take a few minutes," Dana said, and picked up her phone.

"Brian, can you pack the car and prepare your family for the pharmacy?"

Brian was instantly in motion. "On it."

Herman cleared his throat. "You know…you could, uh, use my truck too—shop more quickly, cover twice the ground."

"You don't need it?" Nick asked.

"Nah. Mikey and I will walk up the road and prep the Kennebec place."

"That'd be great." Nick nodded. "So it'll be the Donahues in Herman's truck, shopping the pharmacy and gas station. Me, Dana, T.J., and Abby in the Ark, shopping the grocery store, and maybe elsewhere, depending what we find. And Herman and Mikey will set up the Kennebec place. Good?"

"Good." Brian gave an enthusiastic nod.

"Alright." Nick clapped. "Let's get going before they come back. Oh, and Zoe, can you erase the window? Last thing we need is them tracing our steps."

Zoe saluted and spun toward the kitchen.

Nick stood back and watched the group buzz around the house, preparing for departure.

T.J. appeared next to him, eager for a sidebar conversation. "Hey Nick, this is insane," he whispered. "I almost got my head blown off by the Gestapo and now we're partnering with the guys from Deliverance? Did anyone ask them the virus questions? I mean, how do we know they're not infected?"

"We don't. But at this point, we've been in a room with them. If they have it, we have it. Besides, they don't exactly look like commuters. Something tells me they haven't left this town, maybe even this street, in months."

"So that's it?" T.J. raised his hands in frustration. "They're just along for the ride now?"

Nick turned and snapped. "Look, I don't want the risk any more than you do, but this is what we're stuck with. They know the area and can help us survive the next couple days. Just focus on New Zealand. By Saturday this will all be a bad dream. I gotta check the window." Nick clapped T.J. on the shoulder and brushed past before he could protest.

Zoe, Tracy, and Abby were scrubbing the window with Clorox wipes, paper towels, and dish rags.

"Good for you, hun," Tracy said to Abby. "If my dad spoke to me like that, my mom would've slapped him across the face."

Nick leaned in and interrupted. "Abby, we can drop you at the bus station, get you out of town before they come back."

Abby turned, surprised. "Umm, yeah, sure, that works." She looked slightly hurt.

Nick squinted at the window. Despite three sets of hands, the marker wasn't scrubbing off. Their plan had smudged in a few places, but it was still clearly visible.

Zoe gave him a nervous grin. "I think, maybe, you might've used permanent marker?"

"We don't have time for this." Nick scanned the room, then stomped to a golf bag in the corner.

"We can try and find some Windex," Zoe said, "or maybe—"

"Step back." Nick drew the biggest club.

"What?" Zoe said.

Nick gave a slow practice swing. "Step. Back."

The women realized what was coming and scrambled from the window.

Nick swung and struck a bottom corner—the window shattered into a line of jagged glass.

Everyone startled and stared at Nick.

"You outta your mind, boy?" Herman gestured. "Now I gotta clean that up. Art Gifford is gonna have my head."

"He won't." Nick handed Herman the club as he brushed past. "He's never coming back."

Everyone watched in silence as Nick strode out the front door.

Nick jumped into the driver's seat of the Ark, which was idling in the driveway, facing the front door. He fingered his necklace and stared as they emerged, one by one.

Half-blind old man.

Downs kid.

Preggo runaway.

Asshole CEO.

Washed-up soldier.

Cranky chef.

Goody-two-shoes teen.

Bleeding-heart doctor.

Nick slid on his sunglasses. "We're screwed."

SIXTEEN

KURT HUNZIKER SLIPPED into the classroom and eased the door shut.

Dr. Teddy Monroe scrawled across the whiteboard as he lectured. He looked unnaturally young for his mid-fifties, with stylish thick-frame glasses, a black turtleneck under a doctor's coat, and overcaffeinated energy.

He turned to the class. "Now, when we talk about gene editing *in vivo*, what is our number one tool for cheap, easy, accurate genetic modification?"

Seven girls were seated in the seminar room—all 16–19 years old, all dressed casually, all nine months pregnant.

Monroe scanned the class, then pointed. "Yes, Sarah Jean."

"CRISPR?"

Monroe pumped a fist and spun to the board. "Exactly right." He scribbled her answer and circled it, then spotted Hunziker by the door.

"Girls, will you allow me a moment with General Hunziker? While you're waiting, consider CRISPR's real-world applications." He pointed to a girl in front as he strode to the door. "Aaliyah, I'll be coming to you."

Monroe huddled with Hunziker. "Is she back?" he whispered.

"Not quite…she's OK, still here in Wolfeboro, but she took up with some vacationers. We had her, but we ran into some…resistance."

Monroe's face darkened and he blinked rapidly.

"It's not a problem," Hunziker said. "Nothing we can't handle."

"Where is she now?"

"Right now, I'm not sure. But I know where she's gonna be."

Monroe leaned in, his snarled lip trembling inches from Hunziker's ear. "Get. Her. Back. Whatever you have to do, I want her back home…*immediately*."

"You got it, Doc." Hunziker opened the door and pulled a radio from his belt.

Monroe swung back into the classroom, his face cheerful. "Alright then." He rubbed his hands together and pointed. "Aaliyah, bring us back. What are the human applications for genetic engineering?"

SEVENTEEN

THE ARK RUMBLED in the Shop'n Save parking lot as last-minute shoppers rushed in and out.

Nick studied the building. "It's smaller than I—"

"There's a bus to Montreal that leaves tonight." Abby browsed schedules on Dana's phone in the rear driver-side seat. "It's four and a half hours. Should I take it?"

Dana leaned over from the rear passenger side and checked the details. "Yeah, that would work."

Abby added a ticket to her cart and checked out. "It's sixty-eight dollars."

"Good deal," Dana said, then realized Abby was staring at her. "Oh! Here, use my credit card."

"I'm sorry, I can pay you back later, I just don't have any—"

"Please, don't worry about it for a second. Honestly, Abby, I'm happy to help with your fresh start."

Nick pointed to the store. "It's smaller than I—"

"Fucking sell!" T.J. hammered at his phone in the front passenger seat. "Ohhh god, it's a bloodbath, everything's crashing. I've lost fifty million dollars in the last five minutes and my goddamn sell orders won't go through. Zen insiders are saying the big banks are dumping everything and overloading the exchanges."

"Money isn't our focus right now," Nick said. "Let's figure out food, then we'll plan assets."

T.J. ignored him.

"Sorry, Nick, we're listening now," Dana said.

Nick took a deep breath. "It's smaller than I hoped, and the place is packed. There are too many people to shop safely, the risk of infection is too high."

Dana stared out the window, watching shoppers pass. "So many people…and they have no idea what's coming. All they're worried about is whether there's any cranberry sauce left. We should warn them."

"We've been over this," Nick said.

"How can you sit there and say nothing?"

"Because I'm focused on saving *us*. Plus, they wouldn't listen anyway."

"But don't you want to try? Don't you want to at least—"

"You want to try? Fine." Nick rolled down Dana's window as a young husband and wife strolled past. A little redhead girl was holding their hands and swinging between them. "Go ahead. Warn them."

Dana hesitated, then leaned out the window. "Hi, hello there."

The family stopped and turned.

"Listen, I know this is going to sound strange, but I'm Dr. Dana Foster and I work at the Mercy Community Hospital ER clinic in Boston. I just wanted to warn you that there's a dangerous virus spreading and you should go home."

The family stared.

"It's highly contagious and I'd recommend—"

"Stay away from us." The mother scooped up the girl. "Stay away or I'll call the police." They rushed into the store.

Dana collapsed back into her seat.

Nick rolled up her window and studied her in the rearview. She looked genuinely hurt, and he felt responsible. "Look, it's not your fault. When everything's a lie, nobody knows what's real anymore. But

I'm sure they'll be fine. The president's going to tell everyone tomorrow, so they'll find out soon enough. And people this far north should be safe until then, especially with the roadblock."

He paused, then turned to face her. "But, Dana, even then, people won't listen. When the shit hits the fan, the government lies. Everybody knows they lie, so people don't listen. The government sees people don't listen, so they lie. It's a vicious cycle."

"What do you mean they lie?" Dana said.

"You know, doublespeak, white lies, half-truths. The president will say, 'it's an ongoing situation,' or 'we have a plan,' or 'we'll know more in the next twenty-four hours,' but it's all bullshit. He's just buying time so they can spin the narrative and give the power players a head start. All they care about is stability and control. They'll lie until they're forced to tell the truth, and by then it's too late. I tell my clients, 'when the government gets involved, yoyo: You're on your own.'"

Dana shook her head, staring into the busy parking lot. "It can't be…how can they just…"

"Right now, all we can control is the food situation," Nick said. "That's the problem in front of us. So let's focus and talk it out." He cleared his throat. "OK, it's small and it's packed, which means it's too risky and the food is probably picked over. Should we try someplace else?"

There was silence.

T.J. swiped his phone.

Dana stared out the window.

Abby played with her knapsack.

Nick pulled off his sunglasses, closed his eyes, and rubbed his throbbing forehead.

As usual, it all falls on me. Nobody's focused, everybody's selfish, and I'm the only one who—

"This is the biggest grocery store for fifty miles," Abby said, clear and confident.

Nick startled and opened his eyes.

"There are bigger ones in Portsmouth and Manchester," she said, "but they'll be shopped out too, and much more crowded. Plus, a delivery truck just pulled up."

His eyes shot to an eighteen-wheeler reversing into the loading area.

Abby shrugged. "There's enough food here, we just have to get it."

Nick met her eyes in the rearview. "OK, yes…that's good. Sure, we could get enough supply if we hit here, Portsmouth, and Manchester, but it's too much road time and—"

"It triples exposure risk," Abby said, "maybe more, given those are the biggest Mass border towns."

"Exactly right." Nick nodded. "So we stick here. We find a way to make this work."

Abby returned a quick nod.

Nick straightened in his seat. "OK, we have two problems to solve: First, how do we shop without getting infected? And second, how do we get enough food? I mean, ideally, we'd want to pick this place clean."

Abby scooted forward in her seat. "What if we wear masks and gloves?"

"We could, but assuming that doesn't freak the employees out, they wouldn't let us buy up the whole store—best case is one or two carts each. And we wouldn't have access to the delivery-truck stuff. It's not enough."

Nick pointed at the loading area, where two men in green aprons carried boxes inside through an open garage door. "What if we just take the truck?"

Abby swayed her head as she considered. "Well, we don't know what's in it—could be all perishable stuff, which you said to avoid. And someone would definitely call the sheriff. Plus, can any of us drive an eighteen-wheeler?"

"Hmm, good call." Nick tapped the steering wheel with his fist. "We just need the place to ourselves for an hour. Could we call in a bomb threat or something?"

Abby shrugged. "That would empty it out, but we'd only get ten minutes inside before they arrest us, or, more likely, shoot us."

T.J. smacked the dashboard. "Jesus, Nick, it's a massacre. My trusts are down, stock options won't load, even my fake charitable foundation is frozen. We gotta call my banker ASAP."

Nick slowly turned to face Abby, a mischievous grin spreading across his face. His excited eyes locked on hers. "I've got an idea."

* * *

A BELL atop the front door jingled as Nick and T.J. stepped inside the Shop'n Save. The place looked like it hadn't been updated in fifty years. The floor was checkered with scuffed-white and vomit-brown tiles, long fluorescent lights buzzed on rusty chains, and country music crackled from tinny overhead speakers.

Just inside the door, a boy with pocked skin and a green apron restocked apples. He looked up and froze.

"Excuse me," Nick said, adjusting his N95 mask, "we're from the state health department. Is the owner here?"

The boy pointed across the checkout lanes to the other side of the store. "Lady at the lotto counter."

"Thank you."

They walked over, keeping a healthy distance from the busy checkout lanes. Looking ahead, they spotted a rotund, gray-haired woman wearing a tie-dye t-shirt of a wolf howling at the moon. She was scratching a lottery ticket while a video blared on her propped-up phone.

T.J. leaned to Nick and whispered, "How do we know she's not sick?"

"That woman hasn't left New Hampshire in…maybe forever. Just don't touch anything."

They pulled off their masks.

As they approached the counter, the woman raised her droopy eyes and barked a raspy smoker's cough. "What can I getcha?"

T.J. flashed a salesman smile. "Hi ma'am, I don't know if—"

"Ohhh, you're famous." Her eyes shot open. "I seen you in People

Magazine. Umm…umm…J.T. Curry!" She spoke with a wheezy, thick New Hampshire accent.

T.J. stretched his smile a notch further, cocked his head, and raised his hands. "Ahhh, you got it—that's me! I'm looking for the owner of this fine establishment. I have a very exciting opportunity to discuss."

"That's me!" She sprung to her feet. "Oh my gawd, I told Cindy this was gonna happen."

"It's happening!" T.J. raised his eyebrows. "So listen, Miss…?"

"Hornbuckle. Pat Hornbuckle."

"So listen, Pat, every year I do a TV holiday special for my fans. As you probably know, I have a hundred and twenty-five million followers on Zencryptic."

"Oh my gawd."

"The show is called T.J.'s—sorry, J.T.'s Thanksgiving Shopathon Special. Do you see those two women out there?" T.J. pointed out the window to Abby and Dana, who were standing by the front door in a tattered sweatshirt and scrubs, looking cold and sad. "They're a mother and daughter from Laconia. Dana is a nurse who had her hours cut at the hospital, and her daughter, Abby, is pregnant from some deadbeat guy who skipped town."

He clutched his hands together and dialed up the sappiness. "These poor local heroes don't have enough money to buy Thanksgiving dinner. So they wrote to me, and I simply *had* to pick them for my Thanksgiving Shopathon."

Pat placed a hand over her heart. "Those poor dears."

"Have you seen my show before?"

"Umm, I mighta? I watch a lotta internet videos." She burst into a hoarse cackle.

"Well, here's how it works—we clear out the store, and those two women shop for anything and everything they need to make their holiday special. They run around, fill up as many carts as they can, and we film the whole thing."

"Oh my gawd, are you filming right now? Am I on?" Pat straightened her greasy, thinning hair as her eyes darted around in search of cameras.

"I do all the filming with my phone, that's part of the show," T.J. said, holding up his phone. "But here's the best part—I love to support small businesses, so in addition to paying for everything they buy, I give the owner of the store…that's you, Pat…a check for one hundred thousand dollars."

Pat clutched her heart and grabbed the counter for stability.

"What do you think, Pat? Should we do this?"

She nodded and smacked her mouth like a fish. "Sorry, J.T., I'm outta breath. Yes, I want in."

"Excellent! Come on out here."

Pat hobbled out from behind the counter and stood next to T.J. He held up his phone in a selfie pose so they both fit on screen. "Ready? We're live in three, two, one… Hey fans, this is J.T. Curry. Happy Thanksgiving! I'm here with Pat Hornbuckle, proud owner of Shop'n Save in Wolfeboro, New Hampshire. Pat, are you ready to play my Thanksgiving Shopathon Special?"

Pat flipped her hair back and shouted at the phone. "Yeah, J.T., sign me up for the win. Whewwwww. Number one, baby!"

T.J. winced behind his forced smile. "Alright, guys, you heard it here—lucky winner Pat is going home with a hundred thousand dollars. Next up, we follow our shoppers as they go wild in Wolfeboro. Stay tuned!"

T.J. lowered the phone. "Congratulations, Pat. So excited to meet a true winner."

She grabbed his hand in a two-handed shake. "Oh my gawd, thank you, J.T. You changed my life. So how does, like, the finances work? Do you do cash?"

T.J. waved his hand dismissively. "My people do all the paperwork."

Nick stepped forward and, for the first time, Pat looked at him. "I'm Mr. Curry's attorney. I handle all the paperwork. We like to present winners with a big check autographed by Mr. Curry. Would you be available tomorrow morning for a photoshoot in front of the store? Say, eight a.m.?"

"Uhh, yeah." She gave a sarcastic cackle.

"Excellent," Nick said. "Then all you have to do is announce the store is closing and ask everyone to leave. That includes all your staff. We can't have anyone in the background. It's a liability thing."

"Gimme a minute." Pat scurried across the checkout lanes and began chattering at a skinny old man with a "Manager" tag.

T.J. extended his palm.

Nick stepped in and squirted hand sanitizer.

"More."

Nick gave another squirt.

"*More.*"

Nick drained half the bottle. "Did you really broadcast that?"

"Ew, of course not. I just took a video." T.J. played a few seconds of the video, then deleted it.

Pat's voice came over the loudspeaker with a rusty cough. "Attention shoppers. Attention please. The store is closing due to an emergency. Please leave immediately."

She wobbled to the front door and ushered everyone out. The staff left first, eager to get off early, and within five minutes she had chased out the last few shoppers.

Pat stepped outside and held the door for Abby and Dana. "Good luck, hun."

"Thank you." Dana smiled.

Abby grinned and gave a double thumbs up.

Nick locked the door and flipped the sign to CLOSED. He pulled everyone into an aisle and they huddled up. "First of all, I can't believe that worked. We bought ourselves at least an hour before she comes back with questions. With any luck, she'll be gone until tomorrow."

"She's gonna be pissed when she figures it out," T.J. said.

Nick shrugged. "I'll wire her the money from New Zealand. And we'll tell her where to find the food—that'll be worth more than the money." He straightened and scanned the aisle. "You were right, Abby, there's enough here. It'll work."

Dana gave Abby a playful nudge. Abby returned a shy smile.

"OK, let's do this," Nick said. "Put on your gloves. Fill up a shopping cart, drop it in the loading area, then grab a new cart from the front and do it again. Hit every aisle, and don't forget to check the supply rooms and the delivery truck. Stick to Tracy's list—I don't want to see any organic grapes or artisanal waters in there."

"Why are you looking at me?" T.J. said.

"Oh, and remember, two is one, and one is none," Nick said. "When it comes to can openers, electric lighters, other tools, assume something will go wrong and you'll need a backup. Everyone good?"

Everyone nodded.

"Then let the Thanksgiving Shopathon begin." Nick clapped and gave a cheesy smile.

Dana rolled her eyes and patted him on the shoulder as she brushed past.

Nick confirmed the staff had left the parking lot, then backed the Ark into the loading area. Pat must have convinced the truck driver to leave too, because the cab was empty and the back was wide open.

Nick walked into the loading area to find three carts already lined up, all overflowing with canned meats. He smiled, jogged inside the store, and grabbed an empty cart.

He started in a center aisle and filled the cart with an assortment of pastas. As he exited the aisle, Dana careened around a corner with a cart full of canned veggies and playfully bumped his cart. "Watch where you're going!" she said.

Nick smiled and bumped her back. "You drive like a Bostonian."

As they dropped off their carts, Dana gave Nick a sassy smile. "Bet I can get all the rice before you can get all the beans."

"Oh, you're on."

They jogged back inside.

They passed Abby, who was straining to push an overflowing cart in front while pulling another behind.

Nick stopped and took the rear cart. "Where's T.J.?"

"He's reading the soup labels."

Nick shook his head. "God help us." He pulled up alongside her and cleared his throat. "Hey, Abby, thanks for doing this with us. It's a big help."

"Yeah, no problem. I mean, what better way to indulge my food cravings." She raised a half-eaten cucumber and chomped down.

Nick smiled.

A half hour later, they had finished Tracy's list and picked through the supply rooms and delivery truck.

Nick huddled everyone by the front entrance. "OK, there are only four empty carts left. And even though we finished the list, there's still something very important left." Nick put on his most serious tone. "We need...junk food."

Abby and Dana laughed.

T.J. twisted his face in confusion.

"Obviously, it's not nutritious," Nick said. "But we need something fun to break up all the rice and beans. So everyone grab your last cart and fill it with whatever your heart desires."

"Wait, really?" Dana said. "Go nuts?"

"Go nuts." Nick smiled.

"I call the candy!" Abby grabbed a cart and took off.

Dana wheeled after her. "Don't touch my chocolate!"

Nick and T.J. lined up all four carts down the center of the junk food aisle. It was a feeding frenzy—chips, soda, candy, chocolate, donuts, popcorn, cookies—raining down into the carts.

Nick tossed a giant bag of Swedish Fish like a fadeaway three-pointer.

Dana tucked a tube of cinnamon rolls into Nick's chest like a quarterback handoff...he passed it to Abby...she dunked it and raised her arms. "Touchdown!"

Nick gave her a high five and, for the first time in a long time, he laughed. A deep, hearty, genuine laugh. It felt like he stretched muscles he hadn't used in years. It felt good.

* * *

THEY STOOD in the loading area, tired and dirty, and admired their Shopathon spoils by the light of the setting sun. They'd gathered forty-seven carts, checking every item on Tracy's list, and more.

Nick cruised the double-thick line of carts overflowing with cans, bags, boxes, and a smattering of fresh produce. "Nicely done, nicely done. There's enough here to last us six months, at least."

"Wait, I've got one more thing." Abby turned her back and slipped something over her head. She spun around for a big reveal. "Ta-da!" She was wearing a dull-yellow apron that said, "Bun in the oven!" above a bright-yellow cartoon bun that looked like an excited-face emoji who'd had way too much coffee.

Everyone burst out laughing.

"Tracy's in trouble," Nick said, "looks like we've got a new head chef."

Abby giggled and gave a playful curtsy with her apron.

T.J.'s phone rang. "Oh shit, it's my banker. Nick, I gotta take this." Nick nodded and T.J. marched back into the store. "Talk to me, Orlando, I'm dying here."

Nick checked his watch, then turned to Dana. "I'm going to walk to the pharmacy and check on the Donahues. I'll ride back with them. Are you good loading up here with T.J.?"

"Yeah, no problem."

"Great. It won't all fit in the Ark, so I'll meet you at the house, and we'll come back for more trips."

Nick turned to Abby. "Thank you again, Abby. We couldn't have done it without you."

A proud smile crept across her face. She straightened and nodded. "Any time."

"And done in plenty of time to catch your bus," Nick said. "Need any snacks for the road?" He gestured at the overflowing carts and laughed.

Abby's smile faded and her lip quivered, her eyes softening with hurt. She pulled off the apron and threw it on the ground, then turned and rushed into the store.

A pang radiated in Nick's chest as he watched her go. He looked at Dana. "What...what did I say? I don't get it."

Dana picked up the apron, folded it, and hung it on a cart handle.

She stepped to Nick and spoke softly, "Come on, Nick…she wants you to ask her to stay." She brushed past and followed Abby inside.

Nick started to follow, then stopped and looked at his watch. A wave of frustration washed over him.

How is this my fault? How am I the bad guy? I'm supposed to plan the escape, run the prep, and hold everyone's hand?

He shivered, as if shaking off a spell. "We don't have time for this shit."

Nick pulled out his phone and headed for the pharmacy.

EIGHTEEN

NICK LOOKED both ways as he crossed the empty street, the phone pressed to his ear.

It rang once. “Operator.”

“This is Nick Ritter. Passphrase, Wantabo Lake.”

“Thank you, Mr. Ritter. I’ve got you fully verified. What’s your situation?”

“I’m in New Hampshire with my passenger and the pilot. He brought his family. We’ve secured shelter and we’re doing a prep, in case there’s trouble with the flight.”

“Roger that, sir. How can I help?”

“Any change in the flight status?”

“No, sir. You’re still scheduled for Friday at five p.m., departing from Moose River, Brian Donahue as pilot.”

“What about the priority waitlist? Any chance we can get out earlier?”

She punched a few keys. “It’s quite long, sir. We’ve seen significant demand in the last four hours—but you’re in the top half.”

“Top half, huh?” Nick rolled his eyes. “Thanks. Keep me posted.”

“Yes, sir.”

He hung up. “There goes a hundred grand.”

Nick stepped into the far corner of the parking lot and spotted Herman's truck in front of CVS. He strode toward the entrance.

OK, I want to make sure they got the prescriptions, the OTC drugs, the vitamins, and—

A pickup truck screeched to a stop in front of Nick, almost hitting him as he pulled up on his toes. The red Ford F-150 growled for a moment, then the driver's window rolled down. Kurt Hunziker smirked behind the wheel.

"Hiya, Nick. Wanna go for a ride?"

Nick weighed his words. "Is the invitation optional?"

"Ehh, not really."

The back door opened and a young soldier in a camo uniform hopped out, stood uncomfortably close behind Nick, and extended a stiff arm toward the open door.

Nick looked toward the pharmacy. Brian wasn't there.

No point trying to run or fight...

Nick stepped into the truck and slid to the middle seat, next to a soldier seated on his right. The young soldier hopped in on his left and slammed the door.

Hunziker shifted into drive and headed for the exit.

"I wanna apologize, Nick, I think we got off on the wrong foot. Let's start over. I'm General Kurt Hunziker, on your right is Private Burt Winkler, and on your left is Private Tanner Ratliff."

Private Winkler wore a full military uniform with thick glasses and a camo boonie hat. His shoulder-length hair and patchy beard would never fly in a real military unit. He was too busy jumping between apps on a large tablet to look up at Nick.

Private Ratliff had a young, plump face with rosy cheeks and a cocky, wet-lipped grin. He eyed Nick and played with the safety on an assault rifle resting between his legs.

Both men wore the same patches at Hunziker, an upside-down American flag and a matchstick bursting into flame.

Winkler had a California state flag and the nickname, "Wiretap."

Ratliff wore Ohio and the nickname, "Blitzkrieg."

Hunziker pointed to the passenger seat. "And this is my blushing bride, Lieutenant Tammy Hunziker."

A woman turned and curled her thin, snappy lips into a fake smile. "Pleased to meet you." Same southern accent as Hunziker. She wore a camo baseball cap and a tight ponytail that pulled back her entire face, freezing it into an unsettling mix of stern and surprised. Her nickname was "Stormy."

"Nice to meet you, ma'am," Nick said.

Hunziker guided them onto the highway. "We'll hold on to your phone."

Wiretap extended a hand.

Nick paused, then handed it over.

"So, here's the thing, Nick, my wife and I are awful worried about our daughter, Abby. She hasn't been herself lately. I think the pregnancy hormones are messing with her head." Hunziker twirled a finger by his head. "Can you help us find her, so we can get her the care she needs?"

This guy's full of shit.

"Where's she at, Nick?" Tammy turned and beamed a plastic smile.

"I don't know," Nick said in a measured tone. "I found her walking on the road two hours ago. After you left, she made a phone call from the house and then someone picked her up. Beyond that, she's a stranger to me."

"Someone picked her up, huh?" Hunziker said. "Where was she going?"

"I didn't care to ask."

"What kind of car?"

"Some kind of old sedan…I really wasn't looking."

"OK, well, we'll look into that." Hunziker took the next exit—they'd been on the highway less than a mile.

There was a long silence.

Let's change the subject, chew up airtime so they can't corner me on details.

Nick cleared his throat. "Back at the house, Lieutenant Dobbins—I think that was his name—he mentioned you served in the military. Are you a group of veterans?"

"Some of us are veterans," Hunziker said, "but all of us are patriots. We're a group of concerned citizens banding together for real change."

I can work with that.

Nick leaned forward. "I work in crisis management, and I'll tell you, this country has truly lost its way. It's just one catastrophe after another. The American Dream has become a waking nightmare."

Hunziker pointed to his chest. "Flag code uses an upside-down American flag as a signal of dire distress in extreme danger. That's what we got in this country today—dire distress, extreme danger."

Bingo. Bet you'll like this one...

"It's sad, but true." Nick shook his head. "For starters, there's a silent civil war—economic sanctions, states attacking each other, citizens disappearing on U.S. soil—the founding fathers would be appalled."

Wiretap looked up from his tablet. "Well, what do you expect? The federal government collapsed eight years ago," he said in a rushed and nasal tone. "They defaulted on their debt, so, following the protocol of the *original* Constitution, foreign bondholders held a secret bankruptcy proceeding and installed their own political leaders. Ever wonder why all of a sudden Washington got so...colorful?"

Haven't heard that classic in a while.

"And you know how they're repaying all that debt?" Tammy squeezed Kurt's shoulder. "By stripping veterans of their benefits and sending the money overseas. It's pure treason."

Interesting...that's a new one. Let's see where it goes.

Nick sighed. "You know, I work with a lot of veterans, and what they come home to, the way they're treated, it's a disgrace. There's no respect."

"Goddamn right." Hunziker straightened. "I served two years in the Eurozone Liberation and four years in Egypt and came home to zero respect. *Zero.*" He flipped up the truck's sun visor with a bang.

There it is. There's the nerve. Let's dig.

"First of all, thank you for your service," Nick said. "People don't even say that anymore. I guess I'm just old fashioned. But how is that possible, General? What happened?"

"I was unfairly discharged from the Navy as a, kinda, political statement. Some judge who wasn't even born here needed a scapegoat for a mission gone wrong. She stripped my veteran benefits, my right to vote, my gun license…my fuckin' *honor*."

Deeper…gentle…gentle…

Nick shook his head. "That's how they do it—they make a mess from a desk in Washington, send you to some shithole to clean it up, then blame you when you get dirty. I've seen it a thousand times. When you came back, what did you do?"

They turned onto a well-lit, perfectly paved, two-lane road leading directly into the woods.

What the hell? Who puts a road like this in the middle of nowhere?

"Well, I did a little private security work in Houston," Hunziker said, "then a few years as a cop outside Atlanta. But there was a political situation there too."

"Law and order ain't what it used to be," Nick said.

Blitzkrieg turned, his big eyes bulging, and snickered like a sneering cherub. "My old man was a cop. When thugs got rowdy, he'd crack skulls—no problem. Now? You get suspended for hurting someone's feelings. It's the pussification of America."

This guy's a loaded gun.

"Truth is, Nick, it's all corrupt," Hunziker said with a touch of sadness. "Military, police, government, business—all rotten to the core."

What are you up to?

"In my line of work, I see greed, corruption, abuse, every single day," Nick said. "The whole system is rotten from top to bottom. But what can you do? The machine is too big, too powerful…you can't change it."

Hunziker raised his chin with reverence. "'For true patriots to be silent is dangerous.' Samuel Adams, 1776. We refuse to be silent. Before this, I was in the Georgia Militia—good guys with their hearts in the right place, but mostly just sat around complaining. So, me and some other guys, we split off and formed our own nationwide group… the Matchstick Militia."

Blitzkrieg puffed out his matchstick patch and stared down Nick.

"We're committed to *real* change," Hunziker said, "and change starts with *action.* The time for talk, for steady progress, for small wins…it's over. We're past that. The people, the institutions, the soul of this country…it's too far gone. We need a hard restart."

Oh shit, he's one of those guys?

Nick leaned forward. "You're talking about Year Zero…The New Dawn…blow it up and start over?"

"Goddamn right." Hunziker's face darkened. "A house corrupted cannot stand. Mold, rats, termites, caved roof, rotten foundation, every fuckin' thing—it's beyond repair and needs to be torn down. The good news is she's already soaked in gas and ready to burn. All we have to do is light the match.

"We don't pick sides. We no longer care about this politician or that bill—we're past all that. Our only job is to accelerate the inevitable collapse—to provide the spark that lights the fire—to get it over quickly and mercifully, so we can start to rebuild.

"We started small, the eight-day Hanukkah Riots, that was us. So was the Seattle Panic—well, not the blackout, obviously, but the panic part, that was us. But we realized we needed something bigger, much bigger, so we—"

"That's enough, Kurt." Tammy crossed her arms. "How do you know he ain't a sympathizer?"

Hunziker studied Nick in the rearview. "Fair question. Your house was kinda…multicultural."

Nick leaned forward and steadied his tone. "I'll be honest with you, General, I'm not here for Thanksgiving. But you already knew that. The truth is, I'm a professional prepper. There's a deadly outbreak in Boston, the government is locking down the city, and I fled here to hide out. I got a head start because of a tip from a corrupt politician. The Indian forced me to bring him along, the Black man showed up at my door, even Abby guilted her way in. Frankly, the only person I actually invited was Brian. He's my business partner, and a decorated veteran. All the rest are freeloaders."

"Yeah, we heard about that virus." Hunziker nodded. "Sounds real bad. You and Brian should lay low for a while."

The truck slowed as they approached the road's end, a giant chain-link gate protecting a sprawling office park. Hunziker lowered his window and gave a little wave to two guards in military fatigues. They wheeled back the gate and saluted as he drove through.

They passed a large entry sign that read, "Monroe Sciences," and parked in front of an impressive steel-and-glass building.

Hunziker killed the engine, turned to the back, and beamed a dickish grin. "Alright, Nick, the doc will see you now."

NINETEEN

ABBY WATCHED as Dana folded down the Ark's back seats, leaving just the rear passenger seat up for the drive home. Inside the store, T.J. paced the aisles, yelling at his banker.

"There we go, plenty of space, especially if we pack tightly," Dana said, dusting off her hands. "Ready?"

They each wheeled a heaping cart to the Ark and began loading groceries into the empty trunk.

"Hey, it's like a giant game of Tetris, right?" Dana laughed.

Abby nodded a weak smile as she stacked bags of oats.

I shouldn't have made a scene back there. Now she's being extra chipper.

Whatever...at least she's trying.

"So, Montreal...do you have anyone up there?" Dana asked and gestured at Abby's belly. "Is the father in the picture?"

"He's a self-centered asshole." Abby slammed down a bag of oats. "I want nothing to do with him."

Dana winced. "Got it." She pivoted. "Hey, so, prednisone for inflammation...that was brilliant. How did you know that?"

"Umm, well, I'm studying medicine. Not in school or anything, just on my own."

"That's awesome. What are you studying?"

"All kinds of stuff. Where I live there's a medical library and a lab. I study there a lot. And at night I watch lectures on my iPad."

"Good for you, Abby. That's really impressive."

Does she actually care? Or is she just being nice?

They wheeled the two empty carts to the garage door and grabbed two more full carts. T.J. popped his head out and covered his phone's microphone. "Hey," he whispered, "are we ready yet?"

"Ten minutes," Dana said curtly.

T.J. disappeared back into the store, and Dana shot him a dirty look.

She grabbed a case of canned cat food. "I wish I had started studying at your age, it would've made med school applications sooo much easier." She slid the cat food snug to the rear passenger seat.

"Well, I've been taking practice MCATs," Abby said. "I got a 490 on one. I know that's not great, but I'm still studying. I can do better."

"Are you kidding me? That's really good! Honestly, better than some of my med-school classmates. And you're still in high school, right?"

"Yeah. Well, I was. But I don't go anymore."

Dana nodded and stacked on another case of cat food. "So, what type of medicine are you interested in?"

"I want to be a cancer researcher, get some big grants and do famous research. Harvard Medical School has the best MD-PhD program in the world. I know it's impossible to get in, but if I can get my MCATs up," Abby shrugged, "I don't know…maybe someday."

"It's a wonderful school." Dana smiled. "I had amazing professors and classmates there. You've got a big head start, you can do it."

Abby's eyes snapped to Dana. "You went to Harvard?"

"I did, I took their MD pathway, with a focus on emergency care."

"Did you ever see Dr. Billings around campus?"

"Martha? Sure, she was my thesis advisor."

Abby's eyes widened and sparkled. "She was the first to use CRISPR to program immune cells to fight cancer. Her paper was, like, world famous. What…what was she like?"

Dana stood back and admired the floor-to-ceiling tower of cat food leaning into the rear passenger seat. She turned and gave Abby a warm smile. "Brilliant, passionate, eloquent, and very kind. She still calls me just to check in."

Abby stared, spellbound.

"If you want, when your MCATs are ready, I can introduce you. She'd love to meet you."

Abby raised a hand to steady herself and knocked over a tower of canned chicken. Cans clattered across the ground.

"Sorry. I'm sorry."

"It's OK," Dana said, crouching with Abby to gather the cans.

Stupid! Nice job, idiot. Dr. Billings would be so impressed. Real Harvard material. I'd probably destroy her entire lab. Say something. Say something!

Abby pivoted. "So, do you like being a doctor?"

Dana took a deep breath. "Yeah, I love it. The ER is crazy, always a new challenge, an interesting case. It keeps me busy…really busy, which is good."

Hmm, there's something more there.

"Do you ever think about moving from the ER to something less…crazy?"

Dana sighed. "Yeah, all the time. To be honest, it's not like I thought it would be. You see things, hard things. There's a lot of suffering…a lot of broken, forgotten people. But I get to be there for them during their darkest moments, and that's really rewarding."

Dana grabbed a case of soup. "What about you? What made you want to be a cancer researcher?"

Abby placed a hand on her belly and watched a bus drive past, toward the highway. "My mom…*not* Tammy, Kurt Hunziker's stupid wife, but my biological mom. When I was young, she worked two jobs. One was finishing wood in a furniture factory—applying flame retardants, sealants, stains, stuff like that. She would get these headaches and bloody noses…when she started seeing double, she went to a clinic. The doctor said it was allergies and gave her an antihistamine."

Dana stopped stacking and faced Abby.

"It kept getting worse, and by the time they figured it out, it was too late. She was diagnosed with sinonasal undifferentiated carcinoma. It's a rare nasal cancer, from years of breathing furniture chemicals. It had spread to her lymph nodes and lungs, and there was nothing they could do. When she couldn't work anymore, couldn't take care of herself, the money dried up and the state put me in a foster home."

"Abby, I'm so sorry. They should've caught it earlier," Dana said, genuine pain in her eyes.

"Yeah, so I want to be a rare-cancer researcher. Nobody cares about the rare cancers. They're forgotten."

"Well, I can see the headline now." Dana waved a headline across the air. "Harvard Dedicates New Lab to Leading Cancer Researcher, Doctor Abby…" Dana winced. "Sorry, what's your last name?"

Abby's eyes sparkled. "Blackwell."

"Ah, there you go!" Dana pointed at Abby. "You've got the perfect name for your dream. Elizabeth Blackwell was the first woman in America to become a doctor."

"I know." Abby grinned. "That's why I chose it."

"You chose it?"

"Yeah." Abby started stacking boxes of rice. "After my mom died, I was placed with a bunch of different foster families and group homes. I was even adopted, twice…but it didn't work out. Every couple years was a different town, different school. I was always the new kid and never really fit in. The kids thought I was too serious and weird. The teachers did too. So I spent a lot of time alone in the library.

"But every new family, they kept changing my last name. And right before the Hunzikers, I lived with this old lady, Mrs. Glenfield. She was half blind and had thirteen cats." Abby held her belly and laughed. "But she was really nice. She just, like, let me be myself. She drove me to the Harvard library, bought me an iPad for my birthday, and paid for a science camp. Before she died, she helped me change my last name. She said, 'Abby, today you choose your own name. And from now on, you decide who you are. No one else.' So yeah, Blackwell seemed pretty cool."

Abby looked up and smiled. Dana was staring at her with tears streaming down her face.

Shit! You said too much. Nobody wants to hear your sob story.

Abby winced. "I'm sorry, I shouldn't have—"

"No, please, don't apologize." Dana wiped her tears. "I'm glad you shared. I'm just sensitive—I cry at everything. I'm sorry, Abby. You deserved better."

Abby looked down and kicked at a price tag stuck to the asphalt.

Dana put a hand on her shoulder. "Come on."

They wheeled their empty carts toward the collection by the garage door.

Dana dabbed the corner of her eye. "Hey, how about a joke? It's the only one I know, so you have to laugh. Ready? What do you call the person who graduates last in their class from medical school?"

Abby shrugged.

"Doctor!"

Abby forced a half-hearted laugh.

They grabbed two full carts and started toward the Ark. Dana leaned over and added, "Actually, Larry Muzbino graduated last in my class and he was a *total* jackass."

Abby burst into a full laugh.

Dana admired the packed Ark. "Perfect. Just enough room for two more carts."

You need to say something. This is it. Now or never.

Abby's smile faded. "Hey Dana, can I ask you something?"

"Of course. Anything."

"This virus you're running from…what if—"

A cart slammed against the brick wall behind them.

They spun around.

T.J. was pushing through the tangle of empty carts, staring down at his phone. "Hey what's up? We done yet? I need to see if the new place has a computer."

Dana's face reddened. "We're ready. Get in."

T.J. reached for the front passenger door.

"No." Dana pointed. "In the back."

T.J. got in back and shut the door.

Dana turned to Abby. “I’m sorry, you were saying? About the virus?”

Abby watched another bus pass, headed for the station up the road. “Never mind. It doesn’t matter.”

TWENTY

NICK SAT in front of the doctor's big mahogany desk, scanning the office walls while he waited.

To the left were more honorary diplomas than one person could earn in ten lifetimes.

To the right were dozens of awards, framed articles, and magazine covers, including a New York Times special edition titled, "Dr. Teddy Saves the World," and a series of five separate Time Magazine covers declaring the doctor, "Person of the Year."

By the door was a small collection of photos featuring the doctor hugging people in wheelchairs, high-fiving children in hospital gowns, and cutting ribbons with smiling patients.

Behind the desk towered a mahogany bookshelf crammed with thick medical volumes, history books, and famous literature. Peppered across its shelves were pictures of the doctor with various celebrities, including one of him strolling the White House lawn with the president.

How does a hick like Hunziker know a legend like Dr. Teddy Monroe? What could they—

The door opened.

Nick stood and turned.

The doctor strode in with an eager grin on his face. "Nick Ritter, thanks so much for waiting." He thrust out a hand. "Dr. Teddy Monroe, pleasure to meet you."

Why is he wearing a doctor's coat and stethoscope? He doesn't see patients, he's a researcher and CEO.

"Pleasure to meet you, Doctor."

"Please, have a seat." Monroe gestured.

"This is a very impressive campus," Nick said.

"Ah yes, thank you. Are you familiar with what we do here?"

"Just the headlines—genetic engineering, the five cures."

"Yes, of course. We've since moved into the promising area of cognitive adaptation, the science of shaping the human brain for optimal performance. As revolutionary as the five cures were, I believe our new therapies hold infinitely more potential." He waved a dismissive hand and smiled. "But that's not why you're here."

Nick cleared his throat. "Yes, Abby…as I told General Hunziker, I bumped into her on the road just a few hours ago. We barely spoke, she made a phone call, and someone picked her up. I wish I could be of more help, Doctor, but that's all I know."

"Yes, General Hunziker filled me in. He's checking local acquaintances, shelters, hotels, the taxi company, the bus station, etc. I'm sure we'll find her."

Shit.

"But just in case she returns to you, or contacts a member of your family, would you please let me know?"

"Of course."

Monroe leaned back in his leather chair. "You're probably wondering what's happening here and how Abby's involved. I'm sure it all seems a bit strange, right?"

Nick shrugged and nodded.

"It's really quite simple. Kurt and Tammy Hunziker are Abby's adoptive parents. She's lived with them happily for the last two years. However, recently, about nine months ago, in fact, she became pregnant under…unusual circumstances. They came to me because her pregnancy was a complicated, high-risk case, and since then she's been under my care.

"Now, Abby is very bright and very willful." He forced a laugh. "At times, her pregnancy and treatment program have been challenging for her, both physically and emotionally. But I want to assure you that Abby is receiving the absolute best care here at our facility."

Monroe leaned in and lowered his voice. "Nick, she's due in the next two weeks, and it is absolutely *critical* that she's back here for her delivery. A public hospital is *not* equipped to treat her and would put both her and her baby at great risk."

His face softened with rehearsed concern. "So, you can see why we're so insistent on her return. We're all just terribly worried about Abby and want to ensure she gets the care and support she needs at this critical time."

Monroe leaned a notch closer and stared. "So, are you sure you can't think of *anything* that might help us find her?"

Maybe she really is just a troubled kid who ran away. Maybe she's overwhelmed with the pregnancy, afraid of motherhood. Maybe she'd be better off here. I mean, this guy's one of the smartest doctors in the world. Plus, if the virus isn't already in Montreal, it will be soon.

Monroe cocked his head and squinted. "Nick?"

But...this guy reeks of bullshit worse than my clients.

Nick shook his head. "I'm sorry, Doctor. If I think of anything, I'll let you know."

Monroe stared for a moment, then tapped the desk and stood with a grin. "Alright then, Nick. Thank you for your time." He breezed around the desk and extended a hand.

* * *

NICK STARED out the window of Hunziker's truck as they cruised toward the front gate. Tammy sat perfectly still in the passenger seat, her hands folded on her lap. Without Wiretap and Blitzkrieg breathing down his neck, Nick could focus on his surroundings.

He spotted a large field at the edge of the complex, and noticed something he hadn't seen on the way in: a grid of stadium lights had been switched on, illuminating rows and rows of luxury mobile homes.

They rolled to a stop as soldiers wheeled open the front gate.

Nick looked at the opposite side of the complex and spotted a similar field, except with rows of long grassy mounds. Each mound was roughly the size and shape of a buried fifty-foot shipping container, with a pipe on top and a single steel door carved into a concrete front. They were underground bunkers.

Nick squinted. "Are those the Millenium 2200s?"

"Yessir!" Hunziker said. "Best subsurface survival shelter on the market, other than the OmniTerra with the greenhouse modification. But those were backordered forever. How'd you know?"

"Like I said, I'm a professional prepper."

At the far end of the bunker field stood a gun range and a tactical training course made of plywood and corrugated steel. It was riddled with bullet holes and blast marks.

Why are there mobile homes, bunkers, and a gun range on a Fortune 500 medical campus?

As they drove through the gate, Nick's eyes locked on something strange at the head of the bunker field: a mobile decontamination chamber. It was the size of a small party tent and made of white and clear medical-grade plastic.

When planning for clients, Nick considered a wide range of decontamination chambers available on the market. Some tailored to chemical, or biological, or radiological, or nuclear contaminants, and the popular CBRN models covered all four. Judging by its size and design, this was almost certainly a top-of-the-line Kaneko SteriSafe Community model. That particular unit was manufactured in Japan, took six weeks to deliver, and performed only a single function: removing 99.99 percent of viral particles from the human exterior.

Why buy a top-of-the-line, biological-only model, when you can get a full-coverage CBRN model for less? Obviously budget isn't an issue. And it's not a mistake, he knows his prep tech. It can't be a coincidence...

Hunziker flicked on the radio and country twang blasted through the speakers. "Love this song!" He cranked the volume and drummed the steering wheel.

Nick watched him bob and hum, and for the first time since he met the man, Nick felt a real visceral fear for General Hunziker.

Hunziker rocked to Country 104.1 all the way back to CVS, then parked crooked in a handicapped spot by the entrance. "Sure I can't give you a ride home?"

Not a chance.

"I'm good, but I appreciate the offer, General."

Hunziker handed Nick his phone back with a white card. "If you see Abby, let us know. My number and the doc's number are on the card."

"I absolutely will."

Tammy turned to face Nick, and he was surprised to see tears in her eyes. "If you see my Abby, please tell her that her mama is worried sick about her." Her voice trembled as she placed a small backpack on her lap and fumbled items out. "This is her lab notebook…and her medicine textbooks…and her iPad for her classes…and her prenatal vitamins, she needs four of these every day, two in the morning and… oh, and her favorite sweatshirt." She refolded a worn Harvard Medical School sweatshirt, then carefully repacked the bag and handed it to Nick.

"Ma'am, I can't take this," Nick said, "I don't think I'm going to see her again."

Tammy started to sob.

Hunziker rested a hand on her shoulder and gave Nick a stern look. "Can you take it, Nick? Please? Just in case?" He nodded toward his sniffling wife and flashed his eyebrows.

"Of course." Nick nodded. "If I see her, I'll make sure she gets it. And I'll call." Nick stepped out. "Have a good night, ma'am." He closed the door and headed for the road.

The Hunzikers sat in silence as they watched Nick walk away.

Tammy dabbed her eye with a camo bandana. "When we find her, I'm gonna thrash that little bitch."

TWENTY-ONE

NICK WALKED AS QUICKLY as he could without looking alarmed. As he crossed the street from CVS to the town park, he powered on his phone —nine missed calls from Brian, two from Dana, plus a dozen clients. He dialed Brian.

One ring. "Nick, you OK? Where are you?"

"I'm alright. I'm downtown."

"Oh, thank god. Dana thought you rode home with us, and I thought you were with them. I looked everywhere for you. What happened?"

"Hunziker picked me up. It's a long story. I'll fill you in when I get back."

"I'll come get—"

"Where's Abby?"

"Abby? Uhh, she was helping Dana unload the groceries. I think they're heading to the bus station soon. Why?"

"Don't let her go."

Brian hushed his voice. "Wait, I thought we decided—"

"Just make something up—tell her we'll buy her another ticket, or drive her halfway, or...or just take away the keys. I don't care, but don't let her leave. I think she knows who's behind the virus. Plus, Hunziker's guys are waiting for her at the station."

"Yes, sir. She stays here," Brian said, like he was speaking to a commanding officer.

"How's the prep?"

"Good. We got everything on our lists and it's all unloaded and secure in the new house. Herman found a solid spot—private, spacious—you'll like it. Only trouble is T.J. and the old man have been at each other for the last two hours, bickering and posturing and such. I had to put them in separate rooms."

"My money's on the old man," Nick said as he switched to speakerphone and opened the map app. "Listen, I need you to come pick me up. Right now I'm crossing through the park, into the town forest that borders its west side. In about twelve minutes I'll come out of the woods on the side of 93 North. I'll drop you a pin, come get me there."

"I can just come to the park, it's a short drive."

"Hunziker's here, and he's probably got guys on me. If I cut through the woods, they can't follow by vehicle. Maybe on foot, but I'll jump in the Ark and we'll speed off."

Keys jingled, Brian's breath quickened. "I'm on the move."

"Hurry. We need to talk."

* * *

A HALF HOUR LATER, Nick followed Brian into the theater room of their new house.

"Look who I found wandering the highway." Brian thumbed back at Nick.

Dana turned from the giant projection screen and smiled. "Heyyy, did you get lost on the way to CVS?" Behind her smirk, he could see genuine relief.

She was seated at one of two low-top pub tables located at the front of the theater, ahead of three rows of plush recliners. Nick swung Tammy's backpack off his shoulder and placed it under a table.

Herman gave a grunt and a nod from a recliner in the first row, where he was whittling a little wooden loon.

T.J. lowered his phone from a recliner on the opposite side of the room. "Oh, thank god, Nick. Where the hell were you? We've been busting ass here unpacking all your precious cat food."

"We?" Herman glowered at T.J.

Nick was about to answer when Zoe walked in balancing two platters of sliced cheese and deli meat. Mikey followed close behind, arms full of condiments and utensils. Abby emerged a few steps later holding bread and chips, Cadillac glued to her side. When she saw Nick, her eyes dropped to the floor. Tracy trailed after, carrying drinks and cups. They spread dinner across a bar on the side of the theater.

"Finally, I'm starving," T.J. said. "I'll have tofu and tomato on whole grain. Lettuce and mustard. No cheese. Sliced diagonally."

Tracy's eyebrows jumped. "You want a sandwich? Make it yourself."

Brian closed his eyes.

Zoe jumped in with an infomercial voice. "What our head chef meant to say is that tonight's meal is a deluxe, one-of-a-kind, build-your-own sandwich bar. Choose from dozens of combinations with a delicious side of salad, chips, or pickles. Dinner is served!" She swept her hand across the bar like a dramatic magician.

"Dinner is served!" Mikey grinned.

Zoe laughed and they exchanged a high five.

T.J. sprung up and snatched a plate off the bar, cutting off Abby as she reached out to take a plate.

Herman exploded out of his recliner, spraying wood shavings across the floor. "Are you outta your mind, boy? You contributed exactly nothing to this meal, and now you're gonna cut off a pregnant young lady who worked up an appetite making your dinner? Not a chance." He stepped to T.J. and lowered his voice. "What's a matter with you? You raised by wolves? Ain't you got a care for anyone else?"

T.J. slid his plate back onto the bar and turned to Herman. "Listen, old man, I know you haven't left the woods in fifty years, but in the real world, you can't just spout off every time your blood sugar gets low. So how about you grab an apple juice, settle into your recliner, and take a nice long nap."

Brian positioned his intimidating frame over the two men, making it clear the argument was over. "Alright, alright, that's enough, gentlemen." He looked down at T.J. "Cook always goes first. Donahue house rule." He extended his arm, inviting Abby to start.

T.J. scowled.

Once everyone was seated with their dinner, Dana turned to Nick. "So, what happened, Nick? Where did you go?"

Nick filled them in on the Hunzikers, the Matchstick Militia, his conversation with Monroe, and the strange medical complex. When he was done, the group was silent.

"Dr. Teddy Monroe? The five cures guy?" T.J. asked.

"Exactly," Nick said.

"Who the hell is that?" Herman asked.

"Dr. Teddy is the founder of a genetics research company," Dana said. "Over the last decade, he's cured five of the top ten deadliest diseases in the world. Most people think he's a genius, or a saint, depending who you ask...but that was before his controversial new treatment. Now he's basically a silent mascot for the company."

"What do you mean?" Nick asked.

"Haven't you heard of ACE? The Harvard meltdown?" Dana said.

Nick shook his head.

Dana picked up the tablet remote control for the theater and started tapping. "Oh, you gotta see this. He was invited to speak at Harvard Medical School to debut his new treatment and, umm...he, umm..." She swiped and jabbed at the remote as the big screen opened and closed random apps. "How the hell do you play this thing?"

T.J. grabbed the tablet. "Let me see." He tapped twice and the big screen streamed a dark stage with two crimson seats under a spotlight. The video's title faded in, "Dr. Teddy ACE meltdown at Harvard Medical School." It had 660 million views.

The crowd hushed as a woman walked across the stage and sat down. She had shoulder-length gray hair and glasses that hung from a faded crimson strap around her neck. She placed her glasses at the end of her nose and thumbed through a stack of notes while the audience watched. Then she dropped the glasses onto her chest and looked up at the crowd.

"Good evening. Thank you for coming. For those of you that don't know me, I'm Dr. Susan Wan-Geller, Dean of Medical Ethics and a professor of healthcare policy here at Harvard Medical School." She spoke quickly, with a touch of boredom, like she had given her intro a thousand times.

She squinted into the packed crowd. "I see we have quite a turnout tonight. I didn't realize my paper on the ethical considerations of murine enrichment models was so popular."

The crowd laughed.

"Today we welcome back one of our own. A graduate of the class of 2008, a man who needs no introduction, please welcome Dr. Edward Monroe."

The crowd erupted as Monroe strode across the stage in a black turtleneck, waving enthusiastically. He shook hands with Dr. Wan-Geller and plopped down in the opposite seat.

The crowd continued to roar, and the camera zoomed out to show a standing ovation.

Monroe gave them prayer hands and a little bow, then waved them down as they kept cheering for just a little too long.

Finally the applause faded, and Wan-Geller glared at the audience. "My goodness."

A little laugh from the crowd.

She turned to Monroe. "Welcome, Dr. Monroe. Or should I call you Dr. Teddy?"

Monroe shifted excitedly in his seat. "Of course! Even the mailman calls me that now."

Big audience laugh.

No smile from Wan-Geller. "Can you tell us where that name came from?"

"Well, there was a young boy named Ben who was suffering from severe type 1 diabetes and receiving my protocol at one of my clinics. I stopped in to meet him, and at one point his mother asked him a casual question, something like, 'Do you want some water, Beanie?' And he said, 'Mom! Don't call me that.' He turned red and got quiet, so I told him that my mom used to call me Teddy when I was his age, because it's short for Edward, and that really embarrassed me too.

"That made him feel better and we had a nice visit, talked about his treatment, and his favorite restaurants, and all the sugary foods he was going to eat when he got out. And when I stood up to leave, I think with so many doctors coming and going, he forgot my name, so he said, 'Thank you for saving my life, Dr. Teddy.'"

A huge "awww" from the crowd.

Monroe put a hand over his heart. "And they happened to be filming for our website, so they caught the moment on video, and it was watched, I think, over fifty million times. Then other kids, and later adults, started calling me Dr. Teddy." Monroe gave a cute shrug.

"Isn't that wonderful," Dr. Wan-Geller said as she scanned her notes. "So, let's start with your five cures. Over the last decade, you and your company, Monroe Sciences, have effectively cured five of the deadliest diseases on the planet: heart disease, stroke, chronic obstructive pulmonary disease, diabetes, and Alzheimer's. How did—"

The crowd interrupted with a swell of applause.

Wan-Geller stared ahead with a slight frown until they quieted.

"Tell us, Dr. Teddy, how did you do it?"

Monroe leaned back and crossed his legs, like an elder about to impart wisdom. "For each disease, we conducted epidemiological surveys to identify patients who had experienced either unusual resistance or anomalous resolution. We sequenced thousands of their genomes and identified common genetic variations, looking for outlier patterns that might confer an advantageous response to the disease. Then we took those genetic variations and recreated them using CRISPR technology in newly diagnosed patients. That led to rapid disease resolution, driven by the patient's own biological response, without the need for further medical interventions."

"So it was a cross-functional solution that combined epidemiological surveys with individualized genetic engineering," Wan-Geller said.

"Exactly right, Doctor."

She pointed at the camera. "Can you summarize for anyone watching at home without a medical background?"

"Sure—think of it like a DNA transplant. You see, for every disease there are people who are completely immune. They get HIV, but they don't get sick. They smoke for seventy years, but they never get lung cancer. Now, imagine you're diagnosed with a deadly disease. Well, we go out and find the one-in-a-million people who are immune to your disease, we study their miraculous DNA, and then we update your DNA to look like theirs. And just like that," he snapped fingers, "you're immune too."

Wan-Geller flipped through her notes. "The National Institutes of Health estimates that your treatments have saved more than ten million lives worldwide. You were awarded five Nobel prizes, named Time's Person of the Year five times, and Pope Gregory said your 'five miracles' qualified you for consideration as a saint. So where do you go from here?"

A grin flickered at the corner of Monroe's mouth. "I'm working on a top-secret nanotechnology that will stop your cereal from getting soggy."

Big audience laugh.

Wan-Geller's expression was blank. "You do have a new technology. You recently described it as, 'a once-in-a-species discovery' that was bigger than your five cures. That's hard to imagine, Doctor. Tell us more."

Monroe turned serious. "Dr. Wan-Geller, this is the greatest medical breakthrough in the history of mankind. It's going to transform billions of lives and change the course of humanity. It's called Adaptive Cognitive Expression, or ACE. It's a simple genetic alteration, just like my five cures, but ACE increases expression of certain desirable parts of the human brain—such as logic, reasoning, problem solving, language—and decreases expression of undesirable parts of the brain —such as fear, anxiety, aggression, and impulsiveness. It's like an instant upgrade for your mind."

"So the idea is to remove our emotions and dial up our logic. Is that right?" Wan-Geller used the skeptical, disinterested tone of a woman who'd spent a lifetime being the smartest person in the room.

Monroe shifted uncomfortably. "Most people don't know that we actually have several layers to our brain. The oldest, core layer is called the reptilian brain because it was formed hundreds of millions of years ago in birds and reptiles. It focuses on basic instincts and survival. It's very primitive and very flawed. And if you look at the worst of human behavior, it all stems from reptilian thinking. Now, the newest part of our brain, called the neomammalian brain, emerged much more recently in higher mammals, and was evolved to the extreme by human beings. It focuses on logic and higher thinking. It's very advanced and very effective. If you look at our greatest achievements as human beings, they all stem from neomammalian thinking.

"Now, you can think of ACE as a brain upgrade—a long-overdue operating-system update for an ancient brain still running five-hundred-million-year-old buggy software. It will downregulate your reptilian brain and upregulate your neomammalian brain. It will forever transform your life, literally overnight." He scooted forward and faced the audience. "And I'm excited to announce that I'm in discussions with the FDA to make it freely available to every man, woman, and child in the country, and eventually, the world!"

There was a smattering of applause.

"What's the goal here?" Wan-Geller squinted. "Does it make you smarter?"

"In a way, yes. It doesn't directly increase cognitive performance, but by reducing emotion-driven thinking and increasing logic-driven thinking, ACE will help you make smarter decisions. It will eliminate foolish biases, unreasonable fears, and instinctive reactions, and allow you to think clearly and objectively."

Monroe leaned in, his eyes sparkling. "Dr. Wan-Geller, this is powerful at the individual level, absolutely. But it's the *collective* impact that will be transformative. As a country—no, as a *species*—we will think, communicate, decide, and live on a whole new level."

Wan-Geller dropped her glasses to her chest. "Some people have expressed concern that ACE is unethical because it removes our emotions and replaces them with hard logic. The New York Times called your ACE technology, 'a cure for being human.' Doctor, are you erasing what makes us human?"

"Not at all. Just the opposite, in fact. We have a chance here to upgrade our humanity. It's our logic, our *reason*, that has driven all our greatest breakthroughs. ACE will bring out the best in humanity, and leave behind the traits that no longer suit us."

Wan-Geller flipped a page and raised her glasses. "The American Medical Association published a letter this morning, signed by three hundred leading doctors, including myself and several others from this institution, criticizing your ACE technology, saying it is, 'a form of modern eugenics that carries tremendous unknown risks, not just to individual patients, but to humanity as a whole.'" She lowered her glasses and locked on him. "Dr. Monroe, is ACE eugenics?"

Monroe shook his head and chuckled.

Wan-Geller raised her eyebrows.

He took a deep breath. "'Eugenics' is a very loaded word. It carries a lot of baggage from the Nazis and the Holocaust, which, of course, was awful. But the underlying concept of eugenics is a sound one. Technically, ACE is a form of non-coercive new eugenics, but let's not get hung up on the terminology. Why shouldn't we upgrade our collective genetics using our technology? Why shouldn't we choose to amplify our best human traits and suppress our worst?"

Wan-Geller stared.

The crowd stirred.

Monroe reddened and shifted in his seat. "Look, you're not following. Let me try and simplify with an example everyone can understand. We all know that person who makes good, smart decisions—he's balanced, he's successful, he contributes to society—because he's driven by his logic. Let's call him Logical Larry. But then we also know that person who makes bad, irrational decisions—she's difficult, she's always struggling, she's a drain on the world around her—because she's driven by whatever emotion rules her at the moment. Let's call her Emotional Emily. Now, why wouldn't we want more

Logical Larrys in the world and fewer Emotional Emilys? Wouldn't we all be better off?"

Complete silence.

Wan-Geller leaned forward. "Are you saying we should systematically purge emotional people, Doctor?"

Monroe pressed a palm to his forehead. "Susan, you're not listening—"

"It's Dr. Wan-Geller." She crossed her arms.

"Oh, come on—look at our world! Our species is headed in the wrong direction. Eighty-five percent of Americans are obese, half the U.S. budget is dedicated to war, lifespans have declined every year for the past two decades...oh, and twenty million people think the president is an alien."

Monroe lowered his tone. "Did you know, since I cured COPD, smoking rates have increased tenfold? It's all because people are irrational. We're ruled by our base impulses. Unless we change course, it will be our undoing."

Dana paused the video on a red-faced Monroe. "After another five minutes, he storms off the stage. He used to lecture at Harvard all the time when I was there. But after this, he was never invited back. And he hasn't talked about ACE or given an unscripted interview since."

The room was silent as everyone absorbed the video.

"You went to Harvard?" T.J. raised his tofu and tomato sandwich.

"Yeah, MD pathway," Dana said.

"Why are you at a cut clinic? Couldn't you get into private care?" He took a giant bite and a chunk of lettuce dropped on the floor.

Dana tilted her head. "What is that supposed to mean? Public patients don't deserve the best care?"

T.J. shrugged and worked his overstuffed mouth like a cow.

Dana wound up and Nick jumped in. "Abby, what's going on? Hunziker wants to restart the world, Monroe's got trailers and bunkers on his campus...what's happening?"

Abby stared at the empty tabletop in front of her.

Dana moved and sat next to her. "Abby, if you know something, please tell us. It could help us survive."

Nick placed the backpack on the table in front of Abby and sat down opposite. "Tammy gave me this. She said she's worried about you, and to come home."

Abby opened the bag and pulled out the folded Harvard Medical School sweatshirt. She stared and gently traced the lettering with her finger.

"Abby, please," Nick said, "we need—"

"It's his," she whispered.

"What?" Nick said. "What's his?"

Abby looked up and locked Nick's eyes. "The virus."

Dana gasped.

"He made it, and Kurt released it," Abby said. "They want to erase mankind."

"How does it work? How does it spread?" Nick said.

Abby took a deep breath. "He designed it to maximize transmission. In the air, it spreads like any other respiratory infection—cough, sneeze, talk, etc. But it also spreads through touch—the virus concentrates in the sweat glands and blood vessels of the hands, and multiplies. Once infected, you lose all feeling in your palms—no hot, cold, pressure, pain—nothing. It's all replaced by an overpowering, insatiable itch. You scratch your palms raw trying to get at it, leaving contagious blood and sweat on everything you touch. And when the itching starts, you get a wave of energy so you spread it as far as possible."

Dana grabbed a napkin and started scribbling notes.

"He thought of everything," Abby said, "tested and refined it until it was perfect. It has a narrow host range to prevent it from jumping to animals, a short incubation period to increase transmission speed, and genetic stability to prevent mutation."

"How confident are you about all this?" Nick asked.

"One hundred percent. He gave us this big TED Talk on his brilliant design." Abby rolled her eyes.

A little grin spread across her face. "At the end, Kurt made a joke, he called it 'Scratch 'n Sniff.' Dr. Teddy *hated* that. So that's what I call it now."

"How could he do this?" Dana said. "He's saved more lives than any person who's ever lived. Now he wants to wipe them all out?"

"Not the first time," T.J. said.

"What are you talking about?" Dana said.

"Well, AIDS, for one. The CIA created the virus to wipe out the gays and the Blacks, which they almost did. And then there was the Tuskegee Study, when the CDC experimented on poor, Black syphilis patients for over forty years without telling them there was a simple cure. Should I go on?"

"Please don't," Nick said.

"But I don't get it," Brian said. "Why does a brilliant scientist need the Matchstick Militia?"

"Protection, I guess," Abby said. "Kurt loves to play the General, and Dr. Teddy gets a bunch of idiots to do his dirty work. I mean, Kurt's guys were the ones who released the virus. They infected themselves, spread it all over Logan Airport, then flew to eleven different cities. Monroe would never ask his brilliant medical staff to do that."

"It makes sense." Nick nodded. "Hunziker's an accelerationist. He just wants his hard restart, he doesn't care how he gets it."

"Exactly," Abby said. "Dr. Teddy called it a 'temporary symbiosis.' They were working on something else too, but after I ran away, they cut me out."

"So that's it?" Herman said. "This celebrity doc got his feelings hurt because no one liked his new techno-bio thing, so now he's gonna end mankind?"

Abby looked confused. "Not end it. Just the opposite—he's going to repopulate the earth."

"Repopulate?" Nick scoffed. "With who? Tammy? Big Ron?"

Abby placed a hand on her belly. "Me."

Dana's eyes widened, she covered her mouth.

"What do you mean?" Nick said.

Abby began drawing items from the backpack and arranging them in front of her.

"He calls us his Mothers of Mankind. There are thirty-three of us, all teen girls, all nine months pregnant. He used a corrupt adoption agency to pull us from foster homes and place us with parents in his compound. I was lucky enough to land with the Hunzikers."

T.J. pointed. "A Zen insider did an expose on those adoption agencies. Rich families buy kids as housekeepers or sex—"

"Shut up," Nick said, then looked at Abby. "Keep going."

"The father's DNA is from the smartest men he could find—scientists, mathematicians, engineers. His company has access to millions of sperm samples. Plus he used the top doctors from his compound."

"The mothers, he found us through his foundation. He offered a free STEM summer camp for bright girls from troubled backgrounds. To apply we had to submit an entrance exam and an essay about our home life. Our first project was to analyze our own DNA. We gave him everything he needed to pick his mothers. From there, he arranged the adoptions."

This poor girl. That camp was probably the best thing that ever happened to her, and he turned it into a nightmare.

"But thirty-three girls, that's not enough to repopulate humanity," Dana said. "He must know that."

"He's got this whole big plan," Abby said. "He chose young girls because we're the healthiest, most likely to carry to term, and have the longest fertility timeline. He implanted us with healthy embryos, all prescreened for genetic and racial diversity. The babies have a seventy-thirty female-to-male ratio—'more second-generation mothers,' as he put it. He's gonna get us pregnant every two years and have his nursing staff raise the babies at the compound. He said we can grow to five hundred people in fifteen years, and by then the second-generation girls will be ready to conceive." She shrugged. "I don't know...he drew this big chart, it looked right."

"Jesus," Brian said. "What kind of a doctor holds thirty-three pregnant girls hostage?"

"Nah, they're not hostages," Abby said, "they love it there—organic smoothies, luxury beds, prenatal massages. Before Dr. Teddy, these girls were living a nightmare—abused, neglected, passed around the system. Now they're the most important people in the history of the world. What's not to love?"

"How…" Nick rubbed his forehead. "How do we avoid infection?"

Abby sighed. "You can't."

"There has to be a way," Nick said. "What about—"

"He has a vaccine," Dana said, staring down at the table. She looked up at Abby. "He has to, right? A virus will always find a fresh host—he knows that. Eventually his virus will find him. He wouldn't risk losing the mothers or the babies. And no way he'd bring Nick into the compound unless the girls were protected—he's smarter than that. So he has a vaccine, doesn't he?"

Abby looked at the floor and gave a little nod. "We're all vaccinated…one hundred percent effective…the only vaccine in history created before its disease."

"So there's a cure?" T.J. said. "Why didn't you say anything?"

Abby stared at the floor.

"Hey." T.J. snapped his fingers at Abby. "Wake up."

"Alright, take it easy," Herman said, "can't you see she's been through hell?"

"Fuck that," T.J. said. "She's known about a cure this whole time. She could've saved us. Why didn't you say something? Hey, I'm talking to you."

Herman started toward T.J. "That's enough. One more word and—"

"Because you're all gonna die and there's nothing I can do about it," Abby blurted out.

Herman froze. The room went silent.

Abby looked from face to face. "Dr. Teddy…he's a genius. He's ten steps ahead of you. You'll never get the vaccine in time. A month from now you'll all be gone and I'll still be here, alone. So what was the point in telling you?"

She's worried about us—refusing a ride in the snow, the strange behavior, the bus to Canada. This whole time, she's been protecting us.

Abby started stuffing items back into her backpack. "Look, I told you everything I know. Just take me to the bus station and he'll leave you alone."

Dana touched her shoulder. "Abby—"

"Run as far away as you can. Run to New Zealand. Maybe you can wait it out." Abby zipped up the bag.

Nick leaned in, trying to catch her eyes. "Abby, wait—"

"I'm sorry!" Abby slammed the backpack on the table. Her eyes shimmered. "I never wanted this. I ran away because I didn't want to be part of their fucked-up plan. I tried to convince the other girls, but… whatever, they're all stupid and brainwashed." A tear streamed down her cheek, she smudged it away. "I didn't know they'd track me to you. I *told* you to leave me on the road. I'm sorry, I did everything I could. I helped you plan, and shop, and unpack, and cook, and—"

Dana placed a hand on Abby's shaking wrist. "Abby, it'll be OK. We can get you someplace safe."

Abby sniffled and looked up at Dana. "You don't get it. You can't hide from him. I'll be fine. The Mothers of Mankind, we're his precious flock…and I'm his favorite sheep."

"Why you?" Nick said.

Abby touched her belly. "Because they're his."

"They?" Dana's eyes widened. "You're having twins?"

"Of course." Abby shrugged. "We all are."

TWENTY-TWO

"HOLY SHIT, CHECK THIS OUT." T.J. grabbed the remote control and unmuted the sound.

On the massive screen, the president was seated behind his desk in the oval office. "My fellow Americans, I come to you tonight with a somber message."

"He's early…" Nick whispered.

"An hour ago, I was briefed on an urgent health situation. There is a virus of significant concern that has begun infecting people across the United States. We believe it is of natural origin, not a terrorist attack, and we are working as quickly as possible to identify the source and method of infection. I have assembled an emergency task force of leaders from the CDC, FDA, FEMA, and National Guard, and we are finalizing a plan. Because this is an ongoing situation, I am asking that, effective immediately, all non-emergency workers avoid public spaces and shelter at home. However, if you feel an unusual illness, go to your nearest hospital. We will know more in the next twenty-four hours, and I will address the nation again as soon as I have an update. Stay safe, have a happy Thanksgiving, and God bless the United States of America."

The feed cut back to the studio, where two dumbfounded newscasters stared into the camera. T.J. muted the sound.

"What does it mean?" Brian looked at Nick.

"It's smoke, as usual." Nick cleared Abby's backpack off the table. "He was supposed to speak tomorrow. They moved it up, which means it's worse than they thought. They're buying time."

Nick reached back and fished in the pockets of his jacket, which was hanging on the back of his chair. He pulled out a red permanent marker.

"We've still got major gaps." Nick uncapped the marker.

Herman reached out. "Oh no, wait wait!"

Nick drew two big vertical lines on the table, dividing it into three sections.

Herman rubbed his face and groaned.

"There's gonna be mass panic…" T.J. stared at the silent news stream, "looting, riots, a run on the banks, grocery stores…do we have enough food? People are gonna lose their minds."

"They won't…" Nick scrawled on the table, "not yet."

"What? Why not?" T.J. said.

Nick stopped writing. "It's called the disaster myth, the idea that people instantly panic when disaster strikes. It's the opposite—people underreact, not overreact."

"What do you mean, underreact?" Brian asked.

"People in hurricane paths wait until they see the storm. People in sinking planes climb past exits to grab their bags. People in burning restaurants finish their dinner. People don't panic, they deny and deliberate and wait to see what happens next."

"How can that be?" Dana asked. "It makes no sense."

"Because people are irrational," Nick said. "They fear what they dread, not what's actually dangerous. They ignore facts and hyperfocus on emotional imagery and memorable anecdotes."

Everyone stared at him, confused.

He took a deep breath. "OK, when my clients need to escape by yacht, I worry about a lot of things—running out of fuel, bad weather, losing course, pirates, spoiled food—all extremely high risk and deadly. You know what they worry about? Sharks. They're obsessed. Sharks kill five people a year, but it's the imagery, the deep visceral dread of a shark attack, that makes it scarier than a hundred other risks."

Nick circled a word on the table and started adding spokes. "The president was vague and boring, by design. Until people see the infected tearing their hands off, they won't panic."

"So if they won't panic, what will they do?" Tracy asked.

"They'll watch what happens next, wait for instructions, and follow social norms."

"Social norms?" T.J. asked.

Nick sat back. "When the Titanic sank, the escape was perfectly proper. The first-class passengers had the highest survival rate because they were offered the lifeboats first. The second-class passengers had a lower survival rate, followed by the third-class passengers. Women and children were three times more likely to survive than men. There was no panic, it was as calm as when they boarded—perfect social harmony."

"But what about yelling 'fire' in a crowded theater?" Abby asked. "Doesn't that cause panic?"

"Yes, it does." Nick gave her a little smile. "Because there's one *big* exception to the disaster myth: When people are facing an immediate deadly threat and their exit routes are closing, *then* they will panic. When the Lusitania sank, healthy young men had the highest survival rate, regardless of social class. Why? The Titanic took nearly three hours to sink, but the Lusitania went down in eighteen minutes. Facing imminent death and closing exits, the passengers panicked, and the strongest survived."

Nick declined an incoming call and continued writing. "There's a phrase preppers use: 'seventy-two hours to animal.' It means we're never far from anarchy. We're not there yet. But once people realize how bad this virus is, that there's no cure, that basic necessities are disappearing—once they see the exits closing—chaos won't be far behind."

"Oh shit shit shit." T.J. ran his hands through his hair. "What do we do, Nick? We gotta get outta here."

Nick capped the marker and placed it on the table. "We stay the course, keep working the prep. Yes, we thought we had more time. But we knew this was coming. This is why we prepped the essentials first."

"I didn't think it was gonna happen this fast." T.J. fumbled out his phone and started scrolling through his contacts. "I gotta get outta here."

Nick stood up and calmly plucked away T.J.'s phone. He turned to the group. "Look, the next week is going to be very ugly and very hard. We're about to see a biblical flood of pain, suffering, and death. These situations, they bring out the worst in humanity. All we can do is stay focused and take care of ourselves. If we can make it to New Zealand, maybe we can wait this thing out. If we're stuck here, we've got shelter and two months of food, water, and medicine."

Nick looked at T.J. "We're in a good position. I wouldn't want to be out there starting over right now. But we've still got work to do. Supplies are dwindling, the virus is spreading, and people are starting to see the full horror—the countdown to panic has begun."

Nick pulled on his jacket and looked across their faces. "Clear your mind and harden your heart—hell is coming."

He threaded through the stunned group, toward the door.

As he brushed past T.J., he thumped the phone into T.J.'s chest. "Still think the cat food was a stupid idea?"

TWENTY-THREE

For the third time in ten minutes, Nick rolled over and groped his phone off the nightstand.

He tapped a note into his planning app: "Plan lake-water purification system."

He checked the time, 1:19 a.m.

We should've prepped for more than sixty days. What was I thinking? Is it too late to go back to the store? It's probably empty, but someone might call the police this late at night.

Nick sat up and rubbed his aching temples.

We're short on medicine. Dana's prescriptions were a good start, but not nearly enough for a group this size.

A faint smell of gasoline drifted in.

Currency and assets are a mess—forty thousand in cash and gold is a joke. With markets crashing and banks frozen, we might as well be broke.

The gas smell grew stronger, laced with a sting of burnt rubber that watered his eyes. He pulled the necklace from under his shirt—a long, deep smell of lavender and his vision cleared.

"Not tonight." Nick turned on the light and got dressed.

He decided to go through the food and medicine to make sure

everything was stored correctly. He wandered downstairs, through the dark and silent house, then stopped—a warm light danced on the wall opposite the family room door.

Is somebody up?

He crept down the hall and peeked inside. Herman was sitting in a high-back upholstered chair, whittling a baby loon by a crackling fire.

"Can't sleep?" Herman said without looking up.

How did he hear me?

Nick stepped into the doorway and cleared his throat. "Too much to do."

Herman grunted. "Have a seat."

Nick looked at his watch.

If it's a lecture, I'm leaving.

He lowered into the chair opposite Herman, inhaled the woodsy-sweet smell of burning cedar, and relaxed.

The old man whittled in silence.

Nick pulled out his phone and opened his email.

"You spent time in New Hampshire before?" Herman carefully carved the loon's eye.

Nick looked up. "Uhh, not really. A few client meetings, but never more than a day."

Herman grunted.

"What brought you to Cradle Cove?" Nick asked.

"Ohh, I moved here a while ago, before all these McMansions went up. Every couple years they try to get me to sell, but nah, I like it here. You know, my neighbor offered me a million dollars so he could put a pool where my house is—a pool! Why do you need a pool on a lake? Never mind he's only up here two weeks a year." Herman shook his head. "Downright foolish."

Nick watched as Herman shaped the loon's beak and noticed for the first time the old man was wearing a scratched and tarnished wedding band.

"So is it just you and Mikey up here?" Nick asked.

Herman examined the beak for a long moment. "You asking about the ring?"

"I, uhh…yeah, I guess I was."

Herman grunted. "I was married a long time ago, but my wife, she passed on."

"I'm sorry to hear that." Nick shifted. "I didn't mean to—"

"That's alright. She's been on my mind today, actually, on account of the dust up with Hunziker."

"Why's that?"

"Well, cause I spent a lifetime tangling with guys like that. Years ago, me and Clara and our son, Luke, we lived up in northern Maine, in a little town called Dwyer. The winters were hostile, and so were the people, but rent was cheap and there was factory work nearby. Luke and I, we had the same birthday, December nineteenth. When I turned forty and he turned ten, Clara treated us to dinner at the town pub.

"We were finishing up with a slice of pumpkin pie, and some fellas at the bar started bothering us. I recognized 'em, couple of young packers from the factory. And I recognized they were having the type of night where you drink until something breaks. They were throwing peanuts at us, making animal noises. Didn't really bother me, to be honest—you get used to it. But my wife and son…well, they were of a gentler nature, and they were near tears.

"So I sat there and thought about what to do—peanuts bouncing off the table, hollering and such. I knew I should let it go, they'd move on soon enough."

Herman stared into the fire, his lip twitched a slight snarl. "But…it ain't really in my nature to let a bully gather speed. Guys like that, guys like Hunziker, they got no conscience—they'll go until you make 'em stop.

"So, when a peanut bounced off Luke's face, I walked over and made those boys an offer. We stepped outside and, well, I didn't count on there being three of them…but they didn't count on me being a boxer." Herman grinned. "I knocked two of them out cold, and the third one ran."

He rotated the loon in front of the fire, admiring the details.

"Well, the next night we were driving home from Clara's church choir and a rusted-out pickup pulled up behind us, blasted the high beams, rammed us off the road." He stared into the flames, running a thumb over the loon. "Clara hung on a few minutes…" He paused, steadying himself. "Luke was rushed to the clinic down in Bangor. He joined her two days later."

Herman blew wood dust off the baby loon and placed it next to its parents on the fireplace.

"Chief of police said they couldn't find the truck, but they knew who it was, they just didn't care. A week later I moved here."

"Herman, I'm so sorry. I hope you were able to find some peace here."

Herman scoffed. "I spent a lot of time alone in these woods. Most nights I drank until they joined me in the room. Next morning I'd wake up on the floor with an empty bottle and a loaded pistol.

"I used to be a boxer, but Clara made me quit when Luke was born. Well, there was no work up here, and winters were long, so I went back to fighting. Not the gentleman's sport I used to love, but nasty brawls in fields and barns and basements—spectacles that went on too long, which was the whole point. I'd drink, and fight, and come home broken. Only way I could get up and fight again was to drink more, so…I did a lot of damage in a short time."

He nudged the loons until they were all perfectly aligned. "Anyways, at some point I met Mikey and decided on more respectable work. We've been here ever since."

"How did you meet Mikey?" Nick asked.

"He lived with his mom in a trailer across town. His father was a vagabond who only showed up when he needed money. He didn't care for the boy, couldn't get comfortable with his condition, I suspect.

"When Mikey was eight, his mother died of a stroke and his father came back to live with him. But that deadbeat kept coming and going, leaving Mikey alone in the trailer for days on end. Then one day, he didn't come back.

"Well, Mikey got hungry, walked eight miles up the highway to the grocery store, and filled a backpack with food. I walked in to buy a bottle, and I saw this skinny, dirty kid trying to leave without paying. Everyone was yelling at him. The manager called the police. Poor boy was crying, scared, confused—like a cornered animal. So I told them I was his grandfather and paid the bill.

"I gave him a ride back home, and the trailer was a pit—covered in trash and bugs. I asked Mikey if he wanted to stay with me a few days, and we never went back there again. That was nine years ago."

Herman sighed. "Honestly, Nick, I don't know what to tell him. He still talks about his mom like she's alive, thinks his dad is away with the army and coming back soon. I explained it a few times, but I can't tell if he doesn't understand or doesn't want to. He calls me 'grandpa' and I just let it go."

"Can't the teachers help? Isn't there some kind of program?" Nick asked.

"He didn't do too good in school. Between the teachers and the bullies, it wasn't the right place for him. He works with me now. The houses keep us busy—maintenance, repairs, what have you. Mikey helps me keep track of the projects, steps in when my hands and vision fall short." Herman nodded with a little smile. "He's a good helper. He's a good boy."

"Well, he's lucky to have you, Herman."

"Nah, other way around. Boy keeps me straight, keeps my mind from wandering to the past." He shrugged with a big sigh. "Anyways, point is, we don't always choose our family, but you need someone to show you the good in the world. Otherwise, the darkness…it'll drag you under."

Herman cleared his throat. "Hand me that toothbrush." He pointed to a worn-out toothbrush lying next to a dirty rag, two bottles of paint, and a thin paintbrush. Nick passed it over and Herman started scrubbing one of the parent loons.

"Can I ask you something?" Herman said.

"Yeah, sure."

"What have you got in New Zealand that you don't have here?"

Nick tilted his head. "Well…uh…everything. Solar, wind, crops, livestock, hydroponics, aquaculture, vehicles, security, and enough supplies to last a decade. Here we've got—" He looked back to make sure no one was in the doorway, then leaned in and whispered, "We've got almost nothing."

"Is that so?" Herman nodded as he processed. "OK then, I'm gonna get some sleep." He stood up and brushed dust off his lap.

Did I say something wrong? Does he want an invite to New Zealand?

Herman aligned his loon family, then straightened and stared down at them. "You know, these people trust you, Nick. Don't give them hope unless you plan to see it through. They need you. And, well..." He looked at Nick. "Maybe you need them too."

Herman grunted and walked out.

TWENTY-FOUR

ABBY SAT up in bed with a big stretch.

She must've slept in, because she could hear everyone downstairs: muted voices, clinking plates, music, and what sounded like a blender.

Sooo now that I spilled my guts to everyone, what's next?

Maybe they bought me a bus ticket for today? Or tomorrow?

Or maybe Nick will ask me to stay?

She looked out the window at the beautiful fall morning. Light filtered through a wispy mist that drifted across the lake and into the woods. Birds called with extra cheer, as if they knew it was Thanksgiving.

Yeah right. If anything, last night scared them off.

'You're all gonna die!' Great way to make friends.

No one wants a runaway with two babies and a bunch of baggage. I'll just take the bus. Montreal will be cool—it's far from Kurt and Dr. Teddy, and I can focus on studying for the MCATs. I'm better off on my own anyways.

Abby got ready and threw on a pair of yoga pants and her Harvard Medical School sweatshirt. She opened her bedroom door and nearly tripped over Cadillac, who was laying across the threshold. He looked up at her, tilted his head, and gave a little whine.

"Good morning, Cadillac."

He sprung up and waited for her to lead downstairs.

She took a deep breath.

Whatever. Here we go.

Abby walked downstairs, Cadillac by her side, and turned down the hallway toward the kitchen. As she passed the dining room, she slowed —Nick had turned it into a war room. Spread across the table were papers, pens, two laptops, and a half-eaten breakfast. Nick was running his finger down a notebook and talking on the phone.

"Hold on one second, Maia." Nick covered the phone. "Good morning, Abby."

She stopped in the doorway. "Good morning, Nick."

"I've got something for you—an idea. I'll grab you later."

"Cool." She gave an awkward wave and headed for the kitchen.

OK sooo…that's a good sign, right?

Abby tried to hide her smile as she approached the kitchen. The smell of home cooking, delicious and comforting, stirred up an old feeling.

"Hey, there she is." Tracy looked up from chopping carrots.

"Good morning." Zoe turned from rinsing potatoes.

"Love the sweatshirt. How'd you sleep?" Dana slid a giant bowl of cranberry sauce into the fridge.

"Umm, really well, actually," Abby said. "The bed was super comfy."

"Mine too," Dana said.

Tracy wiped both sides of her hands on her apron. "D, can she have coffee?"

Dana leaned out from reorganizing the overstuffed fridge. "Yep, she's good."

Tracy handed Abby a steaming mug of coffee. "Mikey was looking for you. They're in the garage. Go ahead, we'll bring out breakfast."

"Oh wow, thanks." Abby started down the hallway to the garage, then turned back toward the kitchen. "Oh, and thanks for the coffee."

Tracy gave her an it-was-nothing wave. "You got it, hun."

Abby stepped into the four-car garage and spotted Herman and T.J.

by a jacked-up car in the farthest parking spot. She walked past the stacks of food they'd unpacked the night before.

Looks like someone reorganized—probably Nick.

She slipped past Herman's truck, then the Ark, and emerged in the fourth parking spot.

T.J. was sitting on a stool by a workbench, browsing on his phone.

"Hey, morning," T.J. said.

"Morning." Abby nodded.

Herman cleared his throat and T.J. looked at him, confused. "Oh, sorry. Here." T.J. jumped off the stool and slid it toward Abby, then went back to browsing his phone.

"Oh, thanks." She took a seat and sipped her coffee.

"She's a 1981 Chevy El Camino," Herman said. "Walter Kennebec bought her online, asked us to fix her up for his next visit."

It looked like an old muscle car, with a front like a station wagon and a back like a pickup truck. It was painted black with two mean red stripes down the hood.

Mikey popped out from underneath wearing a black sweatshirt with a big H&M-brand logo. He wiped grease across his forehead and grinned. "Hi, Abby!"

"Hi, Mikey."

"Did you know Cadillac slept at your door? He likes you."

She looked down, the dog was curled up at the base of her stool. "Yeah, I guess he does. What are you working on?"

"We're fixing the transmission for Mr. Kennebec. I can fix anything. I love cars. Did you know Cadillac is my favorite car?"

Abby gave a warm smile. "My grandmother used to drive an old white Cadillac. It was cool."

"Wowww," Mikey said with genuine awe. "That's so cool. One time, my dad drove me in a black Cadillac. We're gonna go again when he comes home from the army."

"Alright, that's enough gabbin'," Herman said. "Back to work."

They both slid under the car.

"Alright, Mikey, this piece right here is stuck," Herman said. "I'm gonna count to three, and you give it a good bang with the hammer while I pull down, see if we can't knock her loose. Got it?"

"Got it."

"One…two…"

BANG.

"Goddammit, boy! You hit my thumb! Jesus, Mary, and Joseph—I said *after* three!"

"You said *on* three, Herman."

"I can't afford to lose fingers, they barely work as it is."

"Herman, please, I barely even hit it. Count to three and the pain will go away." Mikey squirmed out from under the car and whispered to Abby, "What a big baby."

"I heard that!" Herman said.

Abby covered her mouth and giggled.

"Hand me that open-ended wrench," Herman said from under the car.

Mikey fished around the toolbox and placed a wrench in Herman's extended hand.

There was a bang, then the wrench clanged on the garage floor.

"Goddammit, Mikey! This is a ring-end wrench, boy. I said open-ended."

"Herman! It's a combination wrench—turn it around."

There was a beat of silence.

"Oh. So it is."

Mikey put his hands on his hips and rolled his eyes at Abby. "Oh, brother." He turned back to the car. "Herman, can you *please* take a deep breath. You know the rule—no grumps in the garage."

There was a big sigh under the car.

Brian emerged from behind the Ark holding a cup of fruit, his hair wet, like he'd just showered. "Hey Abby, good morning. I have orders to hand-deliver this to you."

She took the fruit and spoon. "Thank you."

"My pleasure." He smiled and started back toward the house.

"Hey, Brian?"

He turned. "Yeah, what's up?"

"Is the plan…do you know…is Nick going to buy me another bus ticket, or…"

"Uhhh, I don't think so? He told me to wait, said you didn't need a ticket. Do you want me to go ask him?"

"No no, that's OK. Thanks, Brian."

He nodded and headed inside.

She smiled and chomped a big scoop of blueberries.

No bus ticket...that has to mean New Zealand, right? What else could it be? They're going to ask me to come—I knew it.

A clang drew her attention to the car. Mikey and Herman were back underneath.

"This thing keeps slipping out of my hands," Herman said. "Goddamn—" He stopped himself and took a deep breath. "Mikey, could you please turn this for me? Between my old fingers and the grease, it's troublesome."

"Of course, Herman. I'd be happy to help," Mikey said with exaggerated politeness.

Abby giggled, took a bite of berries, and enjoyed the comedy routine.

Ten minutes later, Zoe strode out from behind the Ark carrying a steaming plate and a glass of orange juice. She put the juice on the workbench and handed Abby the plate.

Zoe straightened and gestured to each item like a proud chef. "Today's breakfast special is an everything bagel with local cream cheese, goat-cheese scrambled eggs with blistered tomatoes, a free-range maple chicken sausage, and…sliced cucumber? Nick said you were having a craving?"

Abby grinned and nodded. "I was chomping one at the grocery store."

Zoe laughed and clapped. "Love it! Who says you can't have cucumber for breakfast?"

Zoe handed her fresh utensils and a napkin. "Can I grab you anything else?"

"No, this is amazing. Thank you so much."

"No problem. If you need anything, just holler. Maybe we'll hear you over the sound of these two." She gestured toward the car and rolled her eyes.

They laughed and Zoe headed back to the house.

Mikey emerged from under the car and cleaned his hands with a rag.

Herman called out from underneath. "Hey T.J., hand me that big Phillips-head screwdriver on the workbench."

T.J. stared at the bench, then grabbed a screwdriver and placed it in Herman's extended hand.

There was a scraping sound, then a clang. "Goddammit!" Herman squirmed out from under the car and glared at T.J. "This is a flathead. I said Phillips. Turn off your phone and listen for once."

"Hey, do I look like a friggin' carpenter?" T.J. lowered his phone. "I don't know what these things are."

"Herman!" Mikey stomped a foot and crossed his arms. "You need to be patient. T.J. doesn't know our tools. Now try again...*nicely* this time."

Herman stood up and huffed. "I'm sorry for being short." He walked to T.J. and softened his tone. "Look, this is called a flathead screwdriver, because of the flat head. You see? This here, with the little cross, it's called a Phillips head. They do different things. Does that make sense, son?"

T.J. nodded. "Yeah, makes sense." He picked up the Phillips head and offered it to Herman. "The big Phillips head."

Herman gave a wink and a grin. "Thatta boy."

T.J. smiled.

Dana peeked out from behind the Ark. "Hey, Abby, can I steal you for a minute? I need your help with something."

"Oh, yeah sure." Abby sprung up, put her plate on the workbench, and followed Dana to the house.

As soon as they stepped inside, Dana turned. "Hey, I wanted to chat about your trip," she said softly, trying to stop a grin sneaking across her face. "So I talked to Nick, and he said you should stay with us for Thanksgiving dinner tonight. Do you want to?"

Yes! Here it comes.

"Um, yeah." Abby smiled. "I'd love that."

"Great. And then tomorrow, forget the bus, you should ride with us to Moose River..."

I knew it! I knew it! I knew it!

"...and from there you can cross straight into Canada. Nick got you a luxury fallout shelter in Montreal, and Herman and Mikey offered to drive, help you settle in."

Wait, what? No New Zealand? He still wants to dump me in Montreal?

Dana grinned. "Well, what do you think?"

Abby forced her best fake smile. "Yeah, that would be great. Thank you so much."

"Oh, and the best part? Your place is right next to McGill University—it's basically the Harvard Medical School of Canada. Perfect, right?"

"Wow, yeah, that's perfect." Abby clasped her hands behind her back and dug a nail into her palm to stop from crying.

"Are you sure?" Dana's eyes shifted to concern. "Listen, Abby, if you don't want to go to Montreal, you can tell me. I'll talk to Nick, maybe convince him to—"

"No, it's OK, Montreal's good. Tell Nick I appreciate it."

"Are you sure?"

"Totally."

"OK...I'll let him know."

Abby flashed a quick smile and stepped back into the garage. As she walked toward the clanging tools, her eyes started to tear, and the garage blurred.

Why did you even hope? You're such a fool.

It always ends the same, nobody cares, nobody wants you. Why would they be any different?

She passed Herman's truck and stopped beside the Ark. She didn't want the guys to see her cry. She could go back inside, but she'd never make it through the kitchen without the women stopping her. And she couldn't step outside because Kurt's soldiers might be around. Abby quietly opened the Ark's rear passenger door, climbed inside, and eased it shut.

Whatever. I'll just do my own thing. Get my MCATs up, get into McGill, become famous for my rare-cancer research. I don't need anyone else. I'm better off alone.

Cadillac pawed the door and whined.

Abby covered her mouth and tears spilled down her face.

It's a lie and you know it.

McGill, Harvard, medicine…they're history now. You'll never become a doctor.

Nick, Dana…they're already gone.

A month from now there won't be anyone left. Just you and two cursed babies alone in Montreal.

Abby buried her mouth in her elbow and sobbed silently in the back of the Ark.

TWENTY-FIVE

"ALRIGHT, CHEFS, LISTEN UP!" Tracy clapped her hands like a head coach. "Everyone has a station in our pie assembly line."

Nick stood with the rest of the group and admired the neat assembly line laid out across the kitchen island.

Tracy pointed to the first station. "OK, D, you're first, cutting applies."

Dana sprung to her station and clasped her hands behind her back.

"Zoe, you're in charge of the filling. You've got sugar, brown sugar, flour, cinnamon, nutmeg, and lemon juice. You know what to do."

Zoe took her station and saluted.

Mikey shuffled up next to her.

"Mikey, leave that poor girl alone." Herman shook his head.

"It's OK," Zoe said, "I need a buddy to help with the mix."

Mikey stuck out his tongue at Herman.

Herman scowled and grunted.

"Herman, you're lining the pie crust into the dish."

Herman took his station.

"Then, Nick, you're bringing it all together, combining the apples and the filling inside the dish."

Nick smiled politely. "Tracy, I'm not a very good cook. I'll watch and offer encouragement."

"Oh no no no, Mr. Prepper." Tracy took Nick by the arm and dragged him to his station. "My kitchen, my rules. Rule number one is no idle hands in my kitchen. If you can prep out there, you can prep in here."

Everyone laughed.

Nick smiled and manned his station with a nod.

"OK, next up is Brian. You're laying the pie crust on top and folding over the edges. You know how I like it."

"Yes, ma'am."

"Then, Abby, come here, my dear. You're painting the top of the pie with this egg wash and sprinkling sugar. Be generous with the sugar.

"And lastly, T.J., you're taking this foil and making a pie shield around the crust. Then into the oven."

Tracy stood back and admired her fully staffed assembly line. "We're going to make four pies so we have leftovers, then we'll eat dinner, and they'll be ready just in time for dessert. Any questions? OK, get to work!"

The group buzzed as everyone dug into their station. After a few minutes, Tracy strolled behind her line of workers and inspected each station like a factory boss.

"Nicely done, D. Not too thin."

"Come on, Aunty D," Zoe mock scolded, "not too thin."

Dana gave Zoe a playful scowl and a gentle hip-check.

"Looking good, Zoe and Mikey."

Mikey lowered a hand by his side and plopped a giant dollop of pie mix onto the floor. Cadillac lapped it up.

Herman looked down. "Boy, you better not be feeding that dog again."

"Herman," Mikey pointed to Herman's station, "eyes on your own station." He looked at Zoe and gave a mischievous wink.

Tracy rested a hand on Herman's shoulder. "Is this OK for your hands, Herman?"

He nodded. "I'll make do."

She gave a squeeze and moved on to Nick. "Well look at that, not such a bad cook after all." She gave him a wink and stepped to Brian, who was squatting and carefully folding the edges of a pie.

"OK, Brian, let's pick up the pace. They don't need to be perfect—they're going in the oven, not the museum."

Brian squinted and kept folding. "We had a saying back in the SEALs…"

"Oh boy, here we go." Tracy and Zoe rolled their eyes at each other.

"'Slow is smooth and smooth is fast,'" Brian said. "There are two ways to do something—the right way, and again."

"OK, Hell Frog." Tracy patted his head. "As long as my pies are ready sometime today."

She moved on to Abby. "Beautiful coat, even sprinkle—perfect, my dear. Keep it up."

Abby gave a weak smile.

Tracy stepped to the last station, where there was a backup of pies surrounded by crumpled and shredded aluminum foil. "T.J., my friend, what's going on here?"

"I can't…there's no…how the hell do you get it to tear straight?" T.J. crumpled a sheet of foil and threw it down.

"Haven't you ever used tin foil before?" Tracy smirked. "Maybe to make a hat or something like that?"

Everyone laughed.

T.J. crossed his arms. "Plenty of times, but it was pre-cut sheets, not this homemade shit."

"I'm kidding, I'm kidding." Tracy put a hand on his shoulder and softened her tone. "It's OK, cooking is the art of adjustment. If you look here, the dispenser has a serrated blade. You just pull a sheet, fold it down, and tear along the blade like this."

"Yeah, but it's not straight." T.J. pointed to Tracy's foil.

Tracy looked down at her near-perfect sheet, bewildered. "It doesn't have to be perfect. This is good enough."

He cast his eyes to the floor and nodded. "Yeah, OK, fine."

Ten minutes later, T.J. slid the last pie into the oven.

Tracy applauded. "Nicely done, nicely done. OK, my little sous-chefs, wash up and head to the dining room—dinner is served."

Nick stood at the back of the wash line for the kitchen sink. Up ahead, Abby finished washing her hands and walked past him toward the dining room.

"Hey." Nick stopped her. "Did Dana fill you in on my plan?"

"Umm, yeah." Abby looked down as she dried her hands.

"Great prep, right? The place is a high-end loft right by McGill—jacuzzi, fireplace, smart home, the works. You're gonna love it."

Abby looked up and glared. "Yeah, great prep." She walked to the dining room.

What the hell was that? Is she moody? A pregnancy thing? Did she change her mind about Montreal?

"Wash up, Nick." Tracy clapped. "Everyone's waiting on you."

* * *

Nick sat down and admired the steaming spread of turkey, stuffing, gravy, cranberry sauce, mashed potatoes, green beans, sweet corn, and biscuits.

"Trace, this looks incredible," Dana said.

Everyone echoed the sentiment.

"Should somebody, you know, say something?" T.J. asked.

"Zo, you want to say grace?" Brian asked, then turned to the group. "Would that be OK?"

Everyone nodded.

"Geez, Dad, don't put me on the spot or anything," Zoe said. "OK, everybody take hands and bow your heads."

Nick held hands with Dana and Abby and closed his eyes.

"Tonight we think of—"

A chair screeched back.

Nick's eyes shot open.

Mikey hopped out of his chair, sauntered around to Zoe, inserted himself between her and T.J., and clasped their hands.

Herman put a palm to his face and shook his head.

Zoe closed her eyes, and Nick followed. "Tonight we think of all the good people in the world who are suffering, alone, afraid. Our hearts are with them, and we pray that you watch over them, Lord, and protect them in this moment of darkness. We're grateful to be prepped and safe, with shelter and money and resources to survive this awful plague."

Zoe took a deep breath. "Please don't give up on us, Lord. Don't let this be the end." Her voice trembled. "We know we are deeply flawed, hopelessly drawn to evil, but look past our shortcomings, our sins, and see that there is still good in this world, still good in us. Soften our hearts, so that we may see the good in each other."

Dana squeezed Nick's hand.

"Whatever tomorrow may bring, tonight we're grateful to have each other. Tonight we're a family, and that's good enough. Amen."

"Amen," everyone echoed.

Abby pulled her hand away.

Nick opened his eyes, and everyone sat in silence.

"Jesus, kid," T.J. said with glassy eyes.

"Was it too much?" Zoe looked at Brian.

He gave her a loving smile. "Just right, Z-Bird."

Tracy dabbed her eye with a napkin. "Alright, everyone dig in before it gets cold."

After a flurry of passing and scooping, everyone faced a full steaming plate. They took a first bite, buzzed about the flavors, and complimented the chef at the head of the table.

As everyone dined, Brian leaned over to Tracy. "Almost feels like Salt of the Earth, doesn't it?"

Tracy took a big bite of potatoes, closed her eyes, and nodded.

"What's Salt of the Earth?" T.J. asked.

Tracy, her mouth full of potatoes, looked at Brian to answer.

"Salt of the Earth was a restaurant we opened. Well, Tracy opened it, really. She was executive chef and designed the whole menu as a fun, elevated take on comfort food. It was incredible—lobster mac and cheese, ginger chicken-noodle soup, the Million Dollar Meatloaf—

mmm, everything was to die for. People traveled from across the state, across New England, to try it. We were always packed, line out the door. And in the three years she ran it, not a single staff member left. That place…it was magical."

"Anddd," Dana said, "she won Boston Magazine's Restaurant of the Year award two years in a row."

"You never told me that, mom," Zoe said.

"Oh yeah," Brian said, "they did a big feature on her—Tracy Donahue, 'Boston's Queen of Comfort.'"

"Place sounds great, what happened?" T.J. asked.

Brian opened his mouth, then stopped and looked at Tracy.

"I got breast cancer," Tracy said.

The room went silent.

Tracy folded her napkin. "The chemo was rough, which kept me from the restaurant. Plus it was expensive, and Brian's VA benefits didn't cover it all. So we took on medical debt, on top of the loan to start the restaurant, and the mortgage…we lasted eight months, then we shut it down."

Tracy placed her napkin on the table and forced a smile. "But I'm still here, so that's good. And I was able to go back to work a year later."

"Do you still cook?" Herman asked.

"Kind of. I work at corporate cafeterias as a station chef—baked potatoes, grilled chicken, that sort of thing. Actually, I worked at Zencryptic last year." She gave T.J. a humbled look. "At night I do the same thing for corporate events, fundraisers, stuff like that. Plus the occasional shift at the diner up the street. And weekends I cook for the church soup kitchen."

Zoe watched her mom, her eyebrows scrunched with concern.

Tracy stared at the Thanksgiving spread, lost in a bittersweet memory. "We get by, it's good work…but I forgot what it's like to cook with love."

"Well, on the bright side, now all your debt is gone." T.J. smiled.

Tracy laughed, then turned serious as the thought sunk in. She looked at Nick. "Do you think so?"

Nick shrugged. "Could be. If this goes how we think…debt, wealth, it won't matter."

Tracy took Zoe's hand and looked at Brian and Dana. "Well, we have each other, that's all the wealth we need."

Zoe squeezed Tracy's hand.

"You know, my dad was a chef," T.J. said, and wound up into pitch mode. "After my parents moved to Queens from the slums of Mumbai, my father opened his own Indian restaurant. He didn't run that restaurant for profit, because, trust me, there was none. He ran it to provide jobs for his employees and food for his community."

T.J. looked around the table at the annoyed, skeptical faces. He deflated.

"Actually, it was more like a soup kitchen," he said quietly, looking down at the table. "All kinds of people coming and going, only some paying. He never turned anyone away though, he treated everyone like family."

T.J. sighed. "Everyone loved Tushar from Big Table. I was never charming like he was, but I was smart. I worked hard, did well in school. When I got a scholarship to Sterling Academy, my dad scrimped and saved to cover the remaining two thousand dollars of tuition. Then when I got into Stanford, well, I think that was the proudest moment of his life. He got up on a chair and told the whole restaurant Tushar Junior was going to become president someday. Then he comped everyone's meal." T.J. laughed at the memory.

"That's wonderful," Tracy said. "Does he still run Big Table?"

T.J. shook his head. "Six years later, when I was at MIT for my MBA, I started Zencryptic on the side and it really took off. So I decided to leave school and focus on Zen, and my dad…he was devastated, said I was 'throwing everything away for an evil website.'"

The words left a bitter taste in T.J.'s mouth.

"By then he was in financial trouble, partially because he gave away too much food and partially because the neighborhood had gone to shit. The restaurant used to attract good people who were down on their luck, but by then it was mostly riffraff. I asked him…I *begged* him to move Big Table to a better neighborhood. I gave him a check to cover it. But he refused, tore it up, said he didn't want my 'blood money.' We had a blowout fight and something changed for him. He never looked at me the same again."

Herman tilted his head and studied T.J.'s face.

"Two years later, he was killed in a robbery. They took twenty-three dollars from the register." T.J. shook his head. "He would've emptied the whole safe if they'd just asked."

T.J. stared at the table with misty eyes. "If he wasn't so goddamn stubborn…if he wasn't so *disappointed*…he would've accepted the money. He'd still be here."

"Anyways." T.J. shook off his spell and looked at Tracy. "He would've loved this. Not just the food, but, you know…" He gestured around the table. "Just his kinda thing."

"Well, I wish he could've joined us." Tracy gazed at T.J. "Given me notes on my little tandoori turkey experiment."

T.J. laughed and nodded. "Speaking of, pass some of that my way before Brian eats it all."

* * *

THEY DINED and talked and laughed for another hour, happy and present, forgetting the world around them, until the smell of apple pie called them to dessert.

"Well, should we clean up? Get some dessert?" Tracy said.

"I thought you'd never ask," Dana said.

Everyone started up.

"Oh no no no." Brian wagged a finger at Tracy. "The cook doesn't clean. You know the rule."

"Sounds good to me." Tracy leaned back and beamed at the head of the table. "I'll just sit here and watch my little sous-chefs clean up."

T.J. stacked a few plates and headed for the kitchen. As he passed Tracy, he paused. "Incredible meal. Thank you, Chef Tracy."

She gave a polite nod.

Herman followed behind with silverware and napkins. He smiled as he passed Tracy. "Thank you for the meal, and the company, Chef."

She gave a mock bow.

Mikey followed. "You're the best, Chef Tracy."

Then Zoe. "Go, Chef Mom. Proud of you."

Next Dana. "Amazing, as always, Chef Tracy."

Tracy covered her mouth, her eyes shimmering.

Next Abby. "Best Thanksgiving in…well, ever. Thank you, Chef Tracy."

Finally Nick. "Thank you, Chef Tracy." He lingered. "We're lucky to have you."

Brian, the last in the room, stepped to Tracy with a loving smile. "My Queen of Comfort." He stooped down and kissed her forehead. "I love you, Chef Tracy."

TWENTY-SIX

THEY SAT around the family-room fireplace and watched as Mikey blew on crackling kindling. The flame grew and spread. He turned to the group with a proud smile.

"Nicely done, Mikey." Herman clapped a hand on his shoulder. "Nicely done."

Abby sat at the end of the couch, next to the fire, Cadillac curled at her feet.

How long until I can excuse myself for bed? I'm done playing house. Let's just get to Montreal and get it over with.

"Herman, can we read the new book?" Mikey asked.

"No no no, these folks don't wanna hear that."

"Oh yes we do." Tracy grinned.

Herman was working up an excuse when Zoe popped into the doorway. "Look what I foundddd." She held up a faded board game called Cranium.

"Yay!" Dana started clearing the coffee table.

Forty-five minutes later, the girls team and the boys team were tied in overtime.

"OK, next unanswered point wins." Dana rolled the colorful dice, it landed on blue. "Ooo, Storytime!"

"What are these again?" T.J. asked.

"I pick someone on my team to draw a Storytime card," Dana said, "if I can guess their answer before they give it, we get a point. Everybody ready? OK, I choose…Abby."

Ughh, leave me alone, lady. I just wanna go to bed.

Abby drew a card from the stack and read aloud. "What does your dream career look like, and why?"

"Ahh perfect." Dana did a little dance in her seat and scribbled her guess on a scrap of paper. "OK, Abby, go."

"I'd be a doctor."

Dana raised her arms in victory.

"Woah woah woah, wait a minute—you have to say more than that," T.J. said. "It's not 'What job do you want?', it's 'What does your dream career look like?'"

Abby gave him an annoyed look. "OK, well, I'd go to Harvard Medical School, graduate top of my class, join a big research company, cure a bunch of rare-cancers, become world famous, speak at conferences, sit on boards, then finish my career as a professor at Harvard."

Everyone was dumbstruck. Dana grinned.

"Oh wow," T.J. said, "I thought you were gonna say pediatrician or something."

Dana displayed her scrap of paper to the group: "HMS + rare-cancer researcher."

"That's a point for us," Tracy said. "We take the lead. You're up."

"Hold on," T.J. said. "And why?"

"Why? Because I guessed right." Dana gave him an annoyed look.

"No, the question was, 'What does your dream career look like, *and why?*'. You didn't put the *why* on there. No point."

"Alright, then I'll do it now." Dana scribbled on the paper.

Everyone turned to Abby.

Abby stared at the group. "Why? I don't know…umm…for the money."

"Wait no, come on, give your real answer," Dana said.

"I don't know why." Abby shrugged.

"Come on," Dana said, "we talked about it at the grocery store. Tell us."

Abby stared into the fire.

Whatever. I'll never see these people again.

"If I'm a world-famous doctor, I'll always have someplace to belong," she said softly. "I'll always have a home."

The room went silent.

Dana slid the scrap of paper into her pocket.

Abby felt Nick staring at her.

T.J. cleared his throat and looked at Herman. "OK, OK, we'll give you that one. Our turn." He rolled the dice. "Here we go, boys. A point here ties it back up. A miss, and the girls get the win."

The dice landed on green. "Scribble," T.J. said. "Herman, you take it."

Herman cocked his head. "Scribble? The hell is that?"

Mikey slapped a palm to his forehead. "The one where you draw what's on the card and we guess. We've done it five times. Come on, Herman, this is for all the marbles."

Herman grunted and drew a card. "Oh OK, this is an easy one."

T.J. started the timer. "Ready, go."

Herman gripped the stubby golf pencil in his stiff fingers and started to draw.

"Cloud!" Brian shouted.

"Snowman!" Mikey pointed.

"Tree! Forest! Bush!" T.J. said.

"Uhhh…uhhh…weightlifter?" Brian said. "No, basketball player?"

"Ghost? Bigfoot?" Nick said.

Herman dropped the pencil. "Goddammit!" He snatched it up and kept drawing.

"Superman? King Kong?" Brian said, losing steam.

"What the hell *is* that?" T.J. said.

"Time's up! Girls win!" Tracy exchanged high-fives with Dana and Zoe.

T.J. blinked at Herman. "What was it?"

"A bear."

"A bear?! What the hell? I don't know what kind of wildlife you get up here, but I've never, ever seen a bear that looks like that."

"Herman, that's not a bear." Mikey frowned and shook his head. "Where are its feet? It looks like a worm."

"Right here!" Herman pointed. "How can you not see that?"

"What is he doing?" Brian squinted.

"He's stealin' some honey," Herman said matter-of-factly.

Everyone burst out laughing.

"Alright, good game." Zoe clapped. "How about another round?"

Everyone buzzed in agreement.

Abby stood up. "I'm going to bed. I'm tired…feet hurt…you know."

"Can I get you anything?" Tracy asked.

"No, I'm good, thanks. Goodnight."

Abby turned and walked out.

* * *

ABBY SAT in bed watching a med-school lecture on her iPad. She tried to finish one per night to stay on schedule with her MCAT prep. Plus it helped her relax before bed. She turned up the volume as Harvard's Chair of Dermatology strolled across a packed auditorium. "Following last week's discussion on contact dermatitis, today we're going to deep dive into allergic dermatitis. As you can see here, the exponential increase in disease prevalence is, frankly, astounding. There are a range of theories, but the latest research suggests—"

There was a gentle knock at her door.

Ugh, what is wrong with you people? Just leave me alone.

She paused the video and sighed. "Come in."

The door opened halfway, and Nick peeked in. "Hey, sorry to bother you, I brought you something." He held up a steaming mug.

Abby nodded and he entered.

"It's raspberry leaf and chamomile tea," he said. "Mrs. Kennebec must be British or something, because she's got like fifty different flavors in there." He laughed.

She stared and blinked.

"Anyway, Dana said it would help with sleep." He placed a coaster on her nightstand and lowered the mug.

"Thanks," Abby said with a tone that asked, "Are we done here?"

"Yeah, no problem." Nick smiled awkwardly and started to leave. He stopped and turned. "Oh, I was going through our food earlier and I found this." He reached into his back pocket and pulled out the yellow "Bun in the oven!" apron. He shook it out and held it up. "I thought you might want it."

Abby stared. "OK."

Nick gazed down at the manic cartoon bun and chuckled. Then his smile faded. "Abby…" He looked up and met her cold stare. "Come with us to New Zealand."

An uncomfortable thrill surged through her body.

He lowered the apron. "I don't know what we'll do, or how long this will last, but it's better than Canada. Come with us."

Abby shifted and studied his face. "Dana made you ask."

"No. This is me." He stepped closer. "Back at the grocery store, I couldn't have done it without you. You're smart and resourceful and analytical…I need your help. We all do."

Don't play games with me.

She crossed her arms. "I already told you everything about the virus. I don't know any—"

"I know," he said gently. "I know."

She held his stare. "I'm gonna have twins, you know…like, two hungry, screaming, needy babies."

"I know," he said with a little smile.

"What if I say no?"

"Then I'll ask again."

"And if I still won't?"

Nick sighed and dropped his gaze. "Then I'll just have to bring the apron instead." He dropped the apron's neck strap over his head and began to tie the waist.

She scoffed. "Oh my god, take that off."

"What?" He smirked with mock innocence, turning like a model. "You don't like it?"

"You look like a banana." She pulled the comforter up and buried her face.

"I think it looks good. I'll wear it. Try me."

Abby peeked over the comforter and burst out laughing.

Nick did a slow spin. "See? You're into it, I can tell. It's OK, you can admit it."

She giggled and waved him off. "OK, OK."

Nick stopped. "OK?"

Abby dabbed her eyes. She turned serious. "You promise?"

"I promise."

"OK, I'll come."

Nick took off the apron and laid it on the back of the chair facing her bed. He shrugged. "I thought it looked good, but if you feel that strongly…"

Their eyes met and they burst into a final laugh.

"Goodnight, Abby."

"Goodnight, Nick."

Nick pulled the door shut behind him as he left.

Abby put away her iPad, she was done with medicine for tonight. She turned off the light, nuzzled into the comforter, and whispered a happy little squeal.

TWENTY-SEVEN

Nick swung into the family room with a spring in his step. He rubbed his hands together. "Alright guys, what'd I miss? Hit me with a Scribble, I'm feeling hot."

He stopped short.

They looked like someone had died.

"It's happening," T.J. said quietly, "the panic is starting."

"What?"

T.J. gestured at his phone. "Riots at grocery stores, quarantine zones in China, soldiers opening fire at E.U. borders—it's chaos."

Nick's eyes darted back and forth as he calculated.

"Tell him the rest," Brian said.

"It's in New Zealand, Nick…bad." T.J. shook his head. "They activated the military and locked down the borders."

Nick brushed it off with a decisive wave. "Doesn't matter, I'm a citizen. And this is why we use private airports."

Dana was alternating between calculating on her phone and scribbling on scraps of Cranium paper. She murmured, "It shouldn't be this fast, there's no precedent." She looked up. "Can the R-naught really be that high?"

She flipped through scraps. "And the growth rate…it's unheard of."

Her eyes darted between two notes, then shot up to Nick. "If this is right, we're quickly approaching a tipping point."

"Tipping point?" T.J. asked. "What does that mean? Then what?"

Dana gathered her notes. "Then what? That's it, the end—there's nobody left to save."

"What about vaccines?" Tracy asked. "If Dr. Teddy made one, then maybe other doctors can make one too?"

Dana scoffed. "Maybe. With full staff and functional facilities, best-case scenario, we're talking twelve to eighteen months." She tossed the notes on the table. "It'll be over long before that."

Nick looked down at his watch, then up at Dana. "Twenty-one hours…we just have to make it twenty-one hours, then we're in the air."

TWENTY-EIGHT

Nick sat by the patio fire pit and skimmed the latest news. It was bad, worse than the others realized. He flipped through pictures of grocery store riots and fought the urge to go recheck their supplies.

The patio door opened. Dana stepped out wearing an oversized purple sweatsuit that said, "I Love Wolfeboro." Mrs. Kennebec's closet must be a sight.

"Can't sleep," Dana said, "mind if I join you?"

"Of course." He put his phone on the next seat.

She curled into a chair on the opposite side of the circle and held out her palms to the crackling fire. "Ooo, nice and warm."

"Herman made it for me. I don't think that guy sleeps."

Dana laughed and watched the fire's hypnotic dance with a sleepy gaze. "I can't believe it's real," she said softly, "like…this could be the end."

"It won't be. If we can make it there, we can buy a whole lotta time."

"Yeah, but what about—"

Nick's phone lit up as a silenced call came in, casting a bright beam into the night. He frowned and clicked a button to decline the call.

"It's OK, you can answer," she said.

"Nah, it's a client."

"You don't answer your clients?"

"I'm the planner. I don't do live support. They know that."

She nodded for a moment. "Do you like what you do, Nick?"

He shifted. "I guess I used to. But now, these last few years..." He shook his head. "Not anymore."

"Why not?"

Nick reached to the seat next to him. "Marshmallow?" He held up a bag of white puffs. "Tracy dropped them off on her way to bed."

Dana chuckled. "No thanks, I'm good."

He shrugged, skewered a marshmallow on a twig, and picked up a butane torch lighter. It was the type of kitchen blowtorch chefs used to finish creme brulee, but Nick liked it as a survival lighter and included two in all his clients' bug-out bags. He squeezed the trigger and a blue flame hissed. He started to brown the marshmallow. "So, clients hire me for one of two reasons—"

"Hold on." Dana pointed. "That's cheating."

Nick looked down at the torch then back up at Dana.

"We're in the woods, you have to use the fire."

He shrugged. "Oh, sorry, I didn't know there were marshmallow rules."

"Yeah, there are," she said with a sassy grin. "And that's a big one."

"Yes, ma'am, won't happen again." He lowered the stick over the fire. "So, clients hire me for one of two reasons. Most see me as a cheap insurance policy against losing everything they have. For just a few million dollars, they can sleep well at night knowing they're protected from a wide range of low-probability, high-impact events. The rest, they want to fantasize about the end of the world and all the wonderful change it will bring."

"Fantasize? What do you mean?"

"Well, they know something's coming. They see behind the curtain —hell, they built the curtain. Someway, somehow, they're pulling the strings in this giant mess." He gestured around them, as if surrounded by an obvious tragedy. "They're smart, they know how the story ends, and they want a free pass when it all comes crashing down. But more importantly, they want to release their guilt by imagining a fresh start —a better, happier world."

Dana curled her lip in disgust.

Nick changed course. "Point is, planning for these guys, it wears on you. I consider *everything*—everything they want, everything they need, everything that could happen—days and nights dreaming up everything that could possibly go wrong. Every horror, every variation —rewind, pause, slow motion—scrutinizing every detail, again and again and again. Most people never imagine the apocalypse…I replay it a hundred times before noon."

He withdrew his stick and inspected the marshmallow's crispy exterior. "The thing is…that shit seeps in. It doesn't shut off. All that time alone, dreaming of tragedy, dissecting our worst moments…it changes you."

He chuckled. "I mean, try getting a good night's sleep after fourteen hours prepping the rise of the lizard people." He nodded Dana a look and laughed. "Yeah, seriously."

Nick plucked the marshmallow and popped it in his mouth. "So, to answer your question," he said with a gooey mouthful, "no, I don't like what I do."

"Wow, Nick. How did you even find this line of work? I can't imagine your school offered a major in Apocalypse Planning for Rich Assholes."

He laughed. "No, definitely not."

"Pass me a marshmallow," she said, and nodded at the bag. "Just put it on your stick. We'll share."

He skewered a fresh marshmallow and passed it over. "Well, I *did* major in Social Psychology and International Relations at Georgetown. After graduation I moved to Boston and joined Thorne Global, a big crisis-management firm—basically what I do now, but for large corporate and government assholes instead of millionaire assholes."

He dropped a fresh log on the fire. "Anyway, I was there over a decade, and then there was…an incident. So I left and started my own practice."

"What kind of incident? Like a disagreement?"

"Nah…more of an accident."

"What happened?"

He shifted uncomfortably. "It's not a happy story."

"Tell me."

"Dana, you don't wanna hear it. Trust me."

"Nick, you know what I do for work every day? I can handle it." She plucked her marshmallow and popped it in her mouth with attitude. "Trust me."

Nick nodded. "OK." He picked up a twig, snapped off a little side branch, and tossed it in the fire. "Thorne sent me to a cobalt mine in Congo—standard disaster planning with a bunch of checked-out managers, nothing unusual. But at the end of the day, the client asked me to inspect some equipment in the mine. It was strange, but they were a big client, so I agreed."

Nick stared into the flames. "These African mines…they're hell on earth. I mean, the locals believe they're an *actual* gateway to hell. You can't even imagine—cold, dark, damp, appalling working conditions. Kids…kids as young as five, starving, drugged, slaving away day and night. I knew it was bad, but not like this…a fucking horror."

He cracked off another little branch and threw it in.

"Well, I'm down there and there's a collapse—actually, a fire and then two collapses. We're trapped. The place is filling with smoke and fumes and dust, and we're all gonna die."

He leaned in, and the flames danced across his face for a long, silent moment.

"I found a way out, an old sealed-off shaft. I got as many out as I could, and I was halfway up when I saw this little girl. She was blind, no more than six years old, and she was all alone, groping along a wall, trying to find the way out. Everyone had left her behind. So I went back in, which you never do in a disaster, and there was a collapse, and I passed out. I woke up in a Congo hospital two days later."

He blinked out of his daze and tossed the whole stick in the fire.

"Twenty-three people died, including thirteen kids. Sixteen people got out."

"So you saved sixteen people," Dana said. "You were a hero."

He laughed. "Just the opposite, I was a villain."

"What do you mean?"

"An American businessman, a tragic mine collapse, dead African kids…it drew international headlines, and these guys *hate* headlines. So, the local government blamed me, spun up stories about negligence or sabotage or whatever. They held me in a Katanga prison camp for six weeks while the local media smeared me as a white devil. It was a nightmare. Finally some high-level U.S. officials got involved and they let me go. When I got back home, Thorne offered me a big promotion…and I quit, started my own thing."

He stood up and grabbed another log. "Anyways, I'm getting out, retiring. I don't sleep right—flashbacks, nightmares, phantom burning smells—I know enough to know what it is."

He tossed the log and a burst of sparks swirled into the sky. "I was headed to New Zealand anyway, before all this. Monroe just started my retirement a few weeks early."

He plopped back into his chair and smiled. "Once we get there, it'll be a nice, quiet, easy life. No prepping. No clients. Just rest and fresh air."

The new log caught fire and a stream of smoke drifted across Nick's face. He squinted and wafted it away, then stood and moved over two chairs. He looked up, Dana was scowling.

"So that's it?" she said. "You help rich and powerful assholes escape catastrophe for ten-plus years, then you go through one yourself and now you're done?"

He sat back, caught off guard.

"I'm serious," she said. "You have skills, money, connections… why don't you help?"

"Help? What do you mean?"

"I mean instead of running off to your island paradise, how about you help clean up this giant mess your clients made."

He scoffed. "It's not that simple."

"It seems pretty simple to me. You wake up, you find someone who needs help, and you help them. What's so hard about that?"

He stood up and raised his palms defensively. "Look, I tried—trust me, for years I tried—but you don't understand, you can't fix this…it's too wide, too deep."

"What? What kind of excuse is that? You can't stand up and say something? Or push back? Or—"

"I did push back," Nick snapped, "and they tried to kill me for it."

Dana stopped.

Nick sighed. "At Thorne, we made money by helping clients handle disaster. A catastrophe would happen, there'd be public outrage, and leaders would bring us in to clean up the mess and prep for the next one. That was our sales cycle. Riot plans for Disney Parks, terrorism prep for UNICEF, mass shooter scenarios for the Department of Education. Governments, NGOs, corporations—they spent billions on crisis consulting.

"It was the second great Doom Boom, with the Kennedy nuke era being the first. The world kept getting worse, and business kept getting better. Every day was a new catastrophe and a new multi-million-dollar project.

"I rose up quickly. I was smart, hardworking, good with social psychology, and great with scenario planning. Plus I was good with clients. Soon I was a Junior Partner overseeing multiple projects."

He sat down and exhaled a painful memory. "I wanted to save the world, Dana. I really did. I felt like a first responder, in my own way. I'd show up and ask, 'How do we fix this? How do we make sure this never happens again? How do we help more people survive next time?'

"The more projects I took, the harder I worked, the more lives I saved. I was traveling or working a hundred hours a week. No time for family or friends. Every new project was someone calling out for help, and I couldn't say no. Plus, I was happy because I was making a difference. I was preventing the next big disaster, helping people survive. I was saving lives."

He leaned back and scrutinized the flames. "But once I made Junior Partner, I started to see it, little oddities here and there. At first I thought I was imagining it, maybe it was just coincidence. But soon I saw the whole thing."

"Saw what?"

He looked up. "We were starting work *before* the disasters."

"What do you mean, before?"

"This one Senior Partner, he wanted to enter Argentina, pitched it as a huge untapped opportunity. He started ramping up staff, consulting local leaders, vetting suppliers. Six months later, farmers in Buenos Aires lost forty percent of their soybeans to a mutant species of aphids. Guess who they called—hundred-and-thirty-million-dollar contract.

"I started seeing it everywhere. The playbook was simple: Something awful happens, we give leaders talking points, they push our 'never again' soundbites, public support swells, budgets appear, we lock in a mega contract.

"In Qatar, our largest banking client moved their executive suite across town one week before terrorists flew kamikaze drones into their building. We closed a forty-five-million-dollar contract with the government's new Aerial Security Force, and a twenty-million-dollar contract with the bank.

"In Madagascar, one of our defense contractors delivered two thousand military coffins to a rural village twenty-four hours before a lead factory contaminated their water supply, killing eighteen hundred people—twenty-five-million-dollar contract.

"Leaders gained popularity, suppliers got contracts, citizens felt safe, and every step of the way Thorne raked in millions. How we were involved, I don't know. But I couldn't unsee it, a giant disaster machine—death goes in and money comes out."

"How is that possible? How could anyone do that?"

Nick sighed. "People have been planning disasters for profit since...well, since Moses brought the ten plagues. There was the Great Chinese Famine—fifty million people died to cement Mao's power, the Chernobyl nuclear disaster—orchestrated by the KGB to scare Europe into sticking with Russian oil, and, of course, J.P. Morgan and the Titanic."

"The Titanic?"

"Sure. When the Titanic sank, J.P. Morgan's three biggest millionaire rivals were on board: Jacob Astor, Isidor Straus, and Benjamin Guggenheim. All three opposed the creation of the Federal Reserve, something Morgan desperately needed. He canceled his ticket last minute, all three rivals drowned, and the Fed opened a year later."

She shook her head, dumbfounded. "When you saw it at Thorne, why didn't you tell someone?"

"Oh I did. I told a Senior Partner at the firm, someone I considered a friend and mentor, and he told me I was imagining things, to let it go. Two months later I brought him specifics, and he promised he would look into it. The next day they sent me to Congo, down into a mine with a deadly fire…and a broken fan, a jammed elevator, and a missing ladder. Twenty-three people died because I asked the wrong question.

"Sitting in that work camp, I realized something. My entire career I thought I was saving lives, but I was just a cog in a giant killing machine."

He sat back and looked up at the stars. "When I got home, I was numb. I took on as many clients as I could, filled every waking moment with work, and I never looked back."

He met her gaze. "I tried helping, Dana. I really did. But it's just too…broken."

She gazed with her gentle doctor eyes. "I'm sorry, Nick, I know how broken everything is. Trust me, I see it every day. But you can't quit. There are still good people out there, and they're worth fighting for."

He gave a frustrated little scoff. "You don't understand. I've seen behind the curtain, and everything's broken by design. The greed, the corruption, the hate…it's a cancer…and it's everywhere. Companies, governments, churches, *people*… You can't fight it. We're too far gone —all you can do is take care of yourself."

She looked hurt. "What about us? What about Abby? What about me? Are we too far gone?"

"That's not what I meant. You're the good ones. That's why I got you at the hospital. And that's why I'm bringing Abby to New Zealand."

Dana's eyes widened. "You are? I thought you were sending her to Montreal."

Nick cleared his throat and avoided her intense stare. "I guess I changed my mind. I asked her an hour ago, practically had to beg, but she said yes."

He looked back up. Dana was studying him with probing eyes and a little grin.

"What?" he said defensively.

"Nothing. I just didn't expect that."

"Yeah, well…anyways, what about you—"

Smoke drifted into his face. He coughed and waved it away. "Are you getting any of this? Or is it just following me?"

She laughed. "Nope. None at all."

He moved to the other side of the circle.

"What about you?" he said. "How do you do it?"

"Do what?"

"You know…how do you do what you do and not…give up?"

Dana crossed her arms defensively. "What do you mean?"

"Working in a cut clinic—the people, the politics—I don't think I'd last a day."

She sighed. "I don't know…I try not to look at the bigger picture. I just focus on the patient in front of me, then the next one, then the next."

He let her answer hang, hoping for more.

"But yeah, sure, it wears on me," she said, "the poverty, the desperation, the ignorance. Every day is like being down in that mine, in its own way. It's a carousel of pain and suffering, round and round, day after day. Honestly, I don't know if I make any difference at all. The same people come in again and again, and all you can do is slap on a band-aid and tell them everything will be OK." She forced a smile. "But you stay positive, for the patients and the families and the staff…step into the cry closet if you need to…then put on a smile and get back to work."

Nick steered her to a lighter subject. "What about outside of work? What do you do with your free time?"

"Outside of work? Umm, let's see...well between the hospital and the shelter I work ninety hours a week, so there's not a lot of free time. But, I don't know, I jog around Crystal Lake, read books halfway through, bake more cookies than I can possibly eat, bug the Donahues, rewatch my favorite movies, drink too much wine and pass out on the couch...I don't know, I guess I'm boring."

"I heard about the cookies—Gobbles, right? What are they—"

She was crying.

"It wasn't always like this..." She sniffled and wiped away tears. "So *depressing*. I was a happy kid—a dreamer, a feeler, a fighter." She shook a fist and laughed. "I always wanted to be a doctor, but the world I dreamed of saving died somewhere along the way.

"I didn't see it until my parents got sick. I was interning at Boston General, this amazing pediatric oncology rotation, and one morning my mom called and said they weren't feeling well, they had the flu. I was between patients, and they were at a clinic nearby, so I figured they'd be fine.

"It was pneumonia—how do you miss that, Nick? Especially in two elderly patients. I would've found it in thirty seconds. But...the next day my dad called and said my mom had passed. He went two days later."

She rubbed the inscribed heart on her bracelet. "It was just so... sudden. They were here one day and gone the next. My heart broke and Tracy's heart hardened. I quit my rotation, decided on public ER, and never looked back. As long as I'm working, I'm OK."

Nick waited to see if there was more, but she just stared into the fire. "You're making a difference, Dana. Every day, for all those people. You can't save everyone. You can't stop the carousel."

She sighed and dabbed her eyes with her sleeve. "Maybe you're right, Nick. Maybe it is too far gone."

"Maybe. But...maybe there's still some good left." He smiled. "Speaking of, we've got a lottt of marshmallows left." He held up the bag and grinned. "Better get to work."

A cloud of black smoke puffed into his face. "Ugh!" He winced. "I swear it's following me."

She burst out laughing. "Nick, just come sit here, there's no smoke." She patted the chair next to her.

He hesitated, then moved over.

She sat up and leaned toward him, her eyes sparkling. "OK, I'll have a marshmallow, medium-char, crispy on the outside, gooey on the inside, with just a touch of burn."

Nick laughed. "I'm a terrible cook. You're the baker, you should make it." He handed her the bag and leaned into her gaze.

He saw it in her eyes now, clearer than before—she wanted him. And he realized he felt the same. They leaned closer.

A looming, misshapen figure stumbled from the shadows behind them. "You folks need any wood up here?" Herman cradled an enormous stack of firewood.

Dana leaned back and crossed her arms.

Herman shook his head. "Mikey was supposed to bring it up, but that potato head left it in a pile on the beach. Now, what good is firewood soaking in a lake? Goddamn it, boy."

"Uh, no," Nick said, "I think we're all set here. But thanks."

Herman squinted at them, grunted, and dropped the firewood with a loud clatter. "Alright then, goodnight." He trudged back into the darkness.

They looked at each other and snickered.

Dana stood up and stretched. "Well, I should probably head up. Long day tomorrow." She gave him a flirty smile. "But you owe me a marshmallow."

"You know it." He returned her sweet gaze. "Goodnight, Dana."

"Goodnight, Nick."

She headed toward the house, and he tossed another log on the fire. She grasped the door handle, paused for a long moment, then turned.

"Hey Nick…"

He looked up. "Yeah?"

"What happened to her?"

He tilted his head, confused. "Who?"

"The girl…the girl in the mine?"

His chest tightened at the sting of burning rubber. He peered through the flames and saw her there, groping, stumbling, disappearing into dust…darkness…a whisper.

When he finally spoke, his voice was haunted and gravelly. "I don't know."

He swallowed his soul and met Dana's eyes. "I don't know."

TWENTY-NINE

NICK SAT OUTSIDE for another hour, poking the fire and replaying his conversation with Dana.

A carousel of pain and suffering…round and round…day after day.

Just look at Monroe, restarting mankind. He'd be right at home in my client book—another rich asshole gracing us with his better, happier world.

Nick rested his throbbing head in his hands.

Stay focused. If I can get to the ranch, none of it matters.

But what am I gonna do with all these people? They're not moving in, that's for sure. Do Herman and Mikey think they're coming? No way there's space on the plane.

The fire had faded to glowing embers, and the night air was starting to bite. He checked his watch, 1:02 a.m.

Sixteen hours and we're home free.

His phone lit up with an incoming call, a beam of light in the darkness.

Ugh…these guys never listen. I don't do live—

It was the operator. Nick snatched his phone.

"Nick Ritter. Passphrase, Wantabo Lake."

"Fully verified, Mr. Ritter," she said. "Confirming GPS, are you still in Wolfeboro, New Hampshire with your passenger?"

"Yes."

"Sir, I'm calling because ten minutes ago a client missed his rendezvous at Moose River. He's unreachable. I've dropped him off the list and reopened his flight. You're next on the waitlist—do you want his spot?"

Nick stood up. "Now?"

"Yes, sir. You're roughly ninety minutes away. We'll allow a twenty-minute buffer, so takeoff is in one hundred and ten minutes. Can you make that work?"

Move and confirm.

Nick started toward the house. "Yes, yes we can."

"OK sir, just a moment." She started typing.

He stepped inside and whispered, "Can you take seven passengers?"

The typing stopped. "Say again, sir."

Nick cupped the phone as he crept up the stairs. "Seven passengers. Can you take seven?"

"Seven?" The typing was slower this time. "No, sir, this is a small aircraft. Based on weight capacity, the limit is two passengers, both under two hundred and fifty pounds, and no bags."

Shit.

He moved down the hallway toward T.J.'s room. "What about my pilot?"

She paused. "Your pilot is waiting at the airfield, sir. He's ready to depart as soon as you arrive."

"No, my current pilot…Brian Donahue."

"We'll assign him another client."

"When would they fly out? How much longer?"

"For security reasons I can't discuss other client details."

Nick snapped as best he could while still whispering. "Come on, whoever you assign, I probably did his escape plan. Now I need to know when my pilot would fly out."

She paused. "We'll assign the next client on the waitlist to your original flight, leaving today at five p.m. I'll contact Mr. Donahue shortly with details."

Nick reached T.J.'s door and stopped.

"Sir, do you want this flight? If you decline, you forfeit your spot and your deposit. If you accept, you'll be at your ranch within a day. But I need to know in the next ten seconds or I'm required to move down the waitlist."

I can't just leave them...in the middle of the night...

His hand hovered over the door handle as his eyes darted back and forth in the dark, speeding through the scenarios.

"Sir?"

They'll be right behind us. If we go ahead, we can make sure it's safe. Plus we'll free up capacity for Abby on the second flight, maybe even Herman and Mikey if—

"OK sir, I'm declining the flight."

"We'll take it."

"Are you sure?"

"A hundred and ten minutes. We'll be there."

Nick twisted the handle and silently burst in.

* * *

NICK AND T.J. crept down the hall toward the kitchen.

"Hey," T.J. whispered, "what about the—"

"We'll talk in the car," Nick said.

The kitchen still smelled like apple pie. When they reached the island, there was a loud *click*, and overhead lights flooded the room. They flinched and looked around. Herman was leaning against a counter, scowling.

Aww shit.

They must've been a guilty sight, tiptoeing through the house at one a.m., Nick carrying his bug-out bag, T.J. half awake with sleep-mask lines across his face.

"Herman, listen," Nick said, "a flight just opened up. We're leaving now to free up capacity on the next flight, that way Abby can come, maybe you and Mikey too."

Herman raised a palm and grunted. "Save it—I heard you on the phone." He tossed car keys to Nick. "Take my truck. If you're gonna abandon these people, at least leave 'em the good car."

"Herman, I'm not abandoning anybody. There's limited capacity—"

"You don't have to sell me, Nick. It's better if you go. These people trust you, they'll follow you anywhere, but, son…you're lost." He extended an arm toward the door. "You wanna go? Go."

"I'm going to call Brian, fill him in and coordinate."

"Mm-hmm," Herman said.

"Nick, we gotta go," T.J. whispered, and headed down the hall to the garage.

Nick backed toward the door. "Listen, I'll call you from the road, we'll figure it out." He turned and followed T.J.

"Hey Nick?" Herman said.

Nick stopped in the doorway, his back to Herman.

"What's the point of surviving if there's no one worth living for?"

Nick hung his head and walked out.

* * *

HERMAN'S TRUCK groaned along Cradle Cove's winding, pitch-black road.

"Hey," T.J. said, "so I was gonna ask, not that I'm complaining, but…what about Brian and the gang? Do they…I mean…they'll be good, right?"

"We'll call them from the highway. I would've woken them, but we don't have time for a debate." Nick glanced at his watch. "It's gonna be tight as it is. They'll be half a day behind us, and if they get stuck, they've got the supplies and two fewer mouths to feed."

Nick turned onto the long straightaway that led to the little wooden bridge and accelerated. Their headlights shimmered off a truck parked in the middle of the road just ahead.

Nick squinted. "Is that—"

The truck's high beams exploded with light, blinding him.

"Oh shit!" T.J. yelled.

Nick slammed on the brakes. They skidded to a crooked stop in the middle of the road.

The truck crept to within a few yards of their bumper and idled.

"What the hell?" T.J. said.

Nick shaded his eyes from the blinding light. Suddenly it went black, revealing a big red pickup truck. Two smaller pickups pulled alongside, and a white Mercedes sedan rolled to a stop behind the three-car roadblock.

Kurt Hunziker hopped out of the red pickup. "Hiya, Nick. Nice ride."

"Shit." Nick cracked his door. "Stay in the car."

He met Hunziker between their trucks.

"Now, where are you and Mohammed headed in the middle of the night?"

"We're leaving town. Called away on business."

"That so?" Hunziker gestured and two heavily armed soldiers began inspecting Herman's truck.

Dr. Teddy Monroe strolled from the shadows behind pickups. "Good evening, Nick."

"Dr. Monroe."

"Look, Nick, I think you know why…" Monroe squinted at Herman's truck. "Is that…T.J. Chandra?"

"Who?" Hunziker said.

Monroe approached the truck, and T.J. stepped out with an awkward wave.

"T.J.! Good to see you. We met briefly at the Innovator Awards." Monroe extended a hand. "Dr. Teddy Monroe. A pleasure. I'm a big fan of Zen."

T.J. smiled and nodded, then glanced nervously at Nick.

"How do you two..." Monroe pointed back and forth between them.

"He's a client," Nick said.

"Fantastic." Monroe clapped. "Well, listen gentleman, I'm sorry to disrupt your evening, but I think you know why we're here. Can you help us locate Abby? Just point us in the right direction and you can be on your way."

Hunziker stepped toward Nick. "Is she in the fourth house down, on the left?"

Wiretap strolled up, pinching and zooming on his giant tablet. "Looks like it's...eleven Cradle Cove."

Nick raced through the options in his head.

"Is she there, Nick?" Hunziker moved closer.

Nick swallowed his nausea and chose a path. "Yes, she is."

"We gonna meet with any resistance?" Hunziker rested a hand on his sidearm.

"It's the same group as before."

Hunziker grinned. "Alright boys," he yelled over his shoulder, "we got a live situation. Gear up!"

A dozen soldiers spilled out of the pickups and began strapping on gear and loading assault rifles. Hunziker jogged back to his truck and pulled to the side of the road.

"You're doing the right thing, Nick." Monroe patted his shoulder. "She'll be safe in our care, I promise." He turned to T.J. and extended a hand. "T.J., it was a pleasure. Keep up the great work with Zen."

T.J. shook with a stiff smile.

Monroe walked toward Hunziker's truck.

Nick and T.J. headed for Herman's pickup.

"Oh, and T.J.," Monroe called as he spun, "I'm sure you've been following this crazy virus situation, but there's a lot of speculation on Zen that...well, just take care of yourself, stay safe, OK?"

T.J. gave a thumbs up and a pale smile. "Got it. Good tip." He hustled into the passenger seat and buckled up.

Nick cracked the driver-side door and scanned the scene one last time.

Hunziker and Monroe stood by the red pickup, chatting and gesturing toward the house. Tammy sat shotgun, arms crossed, scowling like an angry witch.

On the other side of the road, the soldiers circled up—a zoo of men in mismatched tactical gear, their bodies a strange mix of malnourished thin and junk-food fat.

Blitzkrieg carefully handed out flashbang grenades one by one, then flipped the last one at Big Ron. "Rise and shine!"

Ron juggled the grenade and pulled it to his chest.

Everyone burst out laughing.

Blitzkrieg tossed back an energy shot and flicked the bottle into the woods. "Alright ladies, it's Hiroshima time."

"Nick!" T.J. whispered. "Let's get the hell outta here."

Nick looked down to respond and startled at his reflection in the window. His face, backlit by Hunziker's headlights, was a veil of shadows—grave, tired, worn—a dark, broken stranger.

He squinted ahead at the lamplit bridge that led out of Cradle Cove…to the highway, to Moose River, to New Zealand.

He looked back toward the house, where everyone was sound asleep, resting up for their big trip—Dana snuggled in her "I Love Wolfeboro" sweatsuit, Abby passed out with her iPad.

"Nick." T.J. snapped his fingers. "Let's go. We're gonna miss—"

BANG.

A gunshot cracked and echoed through the woods.

Everyone flinched and ducked.

"Jesus fucking Christ, Ron!" Hunziker stomped across the road. "How many times I gotta tell you? Finger off the *fuckin'* trigger. Now we gotta go in hard. Load up!" He clapped at the soldiers, and they scrambled to their trucks. "Go go go!"

T.J. banged the dashboard. "Let's—"

Nick slammed his door and strode directly at Monroe. "I'll get her."

Monroe looked up and cocked his head, half confused, half interested.

Nick pointed at the trucks. "If they go in, someone's gonna get hurt, maybe Abby. Let me do it, I'll bring her out safely."

Hunziker jogged in. "No need, Doc. We got it covered. We'll go in graceful."

"Please, Dr. Monroe. She trusts me. She'll follow me."

Hunziker glared down at Nick.

"Alright, Nick." Monroe grinned. "We'll do it your way."

THIRTY

NICK ROLLED up to the dark house—motion-sensor lights flooded the driveway.

Monroe's convoy pulled in behind, blocking him in.

Nick unzipped his bug-out bag and dug through.

"What are you gonna do?" T.J. asked.

"Bring her out."

"And then?"

"And then we're going to make our flight." Nick pulled out a prepaid cell phone and slipped it into his back pocket as he stepped out of the truck.

Hunziker's men were gathering at the front steps, preparing to storm the house.

"Two minutes, Nick," Monroe called from his car. "If she's not out in two minutes, I send in the cavalry."

Blitzkrieg spat dip toward Nick and flashed a shit-eating grin.

"Lay on the horn," Nick said to T.J.

"What?"

"Do it now." He slammed the truck door and bounded up the steps.

The horn blasted.

Nick burst through the front door and closed it behind him.

Brian crouched beside a front window in gym shorts and a tank top, delicately peeling back the curtain with one hand and gripping a semi-automatic pistol with the other.

"Abby!" Nick yelled as loud as he could. He moved into the house and called back to Brian, "Put the gun away."

Dana, Zoe, and Tracy huddled on the living-room couch.

"Where's Abby?" Nick said.

A bedroom door opened above them, and he looked up. Abby stepped to the banister in pajamas, her face a mix of dread and terror.

"Come down. Now."

She rushed downstairs—one hand on her belly, the other gripping the handrail—and faced Nick in the center of the room.

"Abby, listen to me carefully. They're going to take you—"

"Like hell they are!" Herman stormed into the room and racked his shotgun.

Brian answered the battle call and racked the slide on his pistol. "Get in the basement," he said to his family.

"No," Nick said, "everybody stays here." He pointed to Herman. "Brian, take his gun."

"Over my dead body," Herman said.

"Goddamn it, Herman," Nick said, "there are fourteen soldiers out there, hopped up like some hillbilly SWAT team. In ninety seconds they're gonna toss flashbangs in here, shoot us all, and take her anyways. Put the gun away."

Herman bludgeoned Nick with a look-what-you've-done glare as Brian gently lifted away his shotgun. Brian slid both weapons under the couch and stepped back into the corner of the room. "Get behind me." He beckoned to his family.

Nick turned back to Abby.

She glared at him, fists clenched at her side, chest heaving, her face a mix of deep hurt and boiling rage.

"They're going to take you—"

"You *promised*," she said through gritted teeth.

"I know, I'm sorry. Listen carefully because we don't have much time. I got moved to an earlier flight and I'm leaving now. Brian is leaving today at five p.m. with a new client. You can still come with us. Escape from Monroe and go back to the road where we first found you. Brian will stash a cell phone there. Call him and he'll pick you up and drive directly to the airport. If phone lines go down, send a text. If that doesn't work, just wait there—he'll stop by at three p.m. on his way to the airport."

Nick tossed the prepaid phone to Brian, who caught it effortlessly. "Put everyone's number in the phone and stash it on the road. There should be an extra seat on your flight. If you bring her to New Zealand, I'll pay you two hundred thousand dollars on top of your existing contract."

Brian slid the phone under the couch and looked offended. "I'll bring her, Nick. You don't have to pay me."

Tracy glared at Brian.

Nick turned back to Abby. "You have fourteen hours to escape. Get to the road, and Brian will bring you to New Zealand. Do you understand the plan?"

"Oh, I understand." Her voice trembled.

Nick placed his hands on her shoulders. "Abby, I'm so sorry. I promise—"

The front door blasted open. Everyone flinched.

"Sweetheart! Daddy's home!" Hunziker sang.

Soldiers streamed into the room, guns raised, gloved fingers on triggers. Somewhere in the back of the house a door burst open and glass shattered. Seconds later, five soldiers poured in through the hallway door.

Hunziker stepped into the living room. Everyone had their hands in the air, except for Abby. "There's my little angel. Your mama's been worried sick. Time to come home."

Abby looked at Nick for direction.

He took a deep breath and nodded for her to go.

Big Ron lumbered to Abby and grabbed her by the elbow. "Let's go, princess." He dragged her toward the door, and she tripped on the corner of the coffee table, falling to her knees.

"Get your hands off her." Herman two-hand shoved Big Ron

square in the chest, sending him stumbling backward. The coffee table took out his legs, and he crumpled into a wedged heap between the table and the couch.

"Fuckin' coon!" Blitzkrieg rushed in from Herman's blind side and sucker-punched him with an arching left hook. Herman reeled into the wall, then recovered and raised his hands with the instincts of a boxer.

A bald soldier rushed in, and Herman buried an uppercut in his chin, crumpling him into a limp ball. A gorilla-like soldier roared and swung a meaty fist at Herman, who dodged effortlessly and returned two quick jabs that KO'd the ape into a stiffened face plant.

Herman turned to Blitzkrieg and beckoned for him to advance. Blitzkrieg returned a wicked grin as Big Ron raised the butt of his rifle high above the back of Herman's head and rammed it down with a sickening thud.

Herman went down and soldiers swarmed, raining down a vengeful storm of punches and kicks.

"Fuckin' spook!"

"Fuck you!"

"Hit him in his good eye!" Blitzkrieg shrieked and raised the butt of his rifle. "Hold his hands!"

Brian locked on Nick with wild eyes and glanced down at the couch, his fingers outstretched, ready to strike.

Nick gave a firm head shake. Do not engage.

Brian clenched his fingers into a fist and glared at Nick.

"Stop!" Dana cried. "You're gonna kill him!"

Tracy clutched Zoe to her chest and turned away.

Abby watched wide-eyed, frozen in horror.

"Hold his fuckin' hands!"

Mikey charged in from the hallway with a full-throated battle cry and leapt onto Blitzkrieg's back, wrapping him in a rear choke. Cadillac skidded in, snarling, and sank his teeth into Blitzkrieg's calf. The soldier shrieked and spun and clawed at Mikey.

Three soldiers tried to pry Mikey off, but his grip was too tight. They started pummeling him. Two soldiers kicked at Cadillac until he yelped, released, and struck again.

Blitzkrieg fumbled at his sidearm, drew the pistol, and fired a deafening shot into the wall.

Everyone froze.

He aimed the pistol down at Herman.

Mikey and Cadillac released and retreated.

Blitzkrieg—sweaty and heaving—stepped over Herman's body and aimed the gun in his face. He cocked the hammer with a trembling hand. "Any last words?"

The room went silent, everyone braced for the shot.

"I can't see, I'm going to faint." Abby stumbled, grabbing at the fireplace mantle, knocking off picture frames and porcelain bowls.

Dana rushed over and steadied her. "She needs a doctor!"

"Oh god, here we go." Hunziker rolled his eyes. "Alright, princess, the doc's outside. Let's go, before you get somebody killed." He turned to Blitzkrieg. "Let's roll out, Private."

Blitzkrieg towered over Herman, glaring with crazy eyes, his hand shaking.

"Private!" Hunziker barked. "Roll out. That's an order."

Blitzkrieg lowered his gun and stared down at Herman with fascination. He looked up at Big Ron and grinned. "Hiroshima, bitches!" They burst out laughing, and Blitzkrieg limped out the door.

Dana helped Abby walk out.

"Search the place," Hunziker said, and the remaining soldiers moved into the hall. He stopped and squinted at Brian, who was standing in front of Zoe and Tracy. "You a Navy man?"

Brian's tank top exposed a patchwork of scars and burns, plus three tattoos: on his right shoulder was a faded green Celtic cross, and on his left shoulder was a SEAL trident and a frog skeleton, signature marks of the Navy SEALs.

"Yes, sir," Brian said cautiously. "SEAL Team Six. Served in the Eurozone and briefly in Egypt."

Hunziker's face lit up. "SEAL Team Six? The Hell Frogs? The guys that took out Captain Cairo? Oh man, you boys are legends! I was Navy, mostly Egypt, a little Eurozone. Hooyah!"

"Hooyah!" Brian said.

"Listen, you should come join us, I could use a guy like you. Bring the whole family—not the mouthy Arab and the other riffraff, but the girls can come."

Tracy stepped in front of Zoe.

"Thank you, General," Brian said. "That's very generous, and we'd love to, but we're headed out of town today."

Old Glory poked his head into the room. "General, you gotta see this."

Hunziker started after Old Glory, smiling at Brian as he passed. "Offer stands if you change your mind, soldier."

Brian returned a grateful nod.

They were alone. Nick exhaled.

"Brian, I'm sorry." Nick started backing toward the door. "T.J. and I have to go. We're gonna miss our flight. Follow the original plan with your new client. Plant the phone and pick up the package." He nodded toward Abby outside. "I'll call you from the road."

Tracy pushed Brian aside. "Are you kidding me? Abby's abducted, Herman's beat half to death, and you're worried about your flight?"

Herman pulled himself up behind the couch, his face a bloody mess, and teetered. Mikey steadied him, and Tracy rushed over to help.

"Brian, please," Nick said, "this is the only way everyone gets out safely. You see that, right?"

Brian pulled down the neckline of his tank top, exposing a tattoo above his heart: "NO MAN LEFT BEHIND." He shook his head like a disappointed father and followed Tracy.

"Herman, I'm sorry." Nick reached the living-room door. "Come with Brian tonight. If there's no room, I'll find you another flight. I promise."

Herman spat blood at Nick's feet.

Nick turned to the doorway and bumped into Dana as she rushed in. "Is Herman OK?" She froze. "Where are you going?"

"I have to leave right now, or we're going to miss the flight. I'll be waiting for you in—"

Her eyes widened, and she threw up her hands and brushed past him into the room.

He watched her go, took a step to follow, then turned and walked out the door.

Nick swung open the truck's driver-side door and stopped—he spotted Abby sitting in the back of Monroe's Mercedes. A nurse sat beside her, monitoring her blood-oxygen level while Monroe squatted outside, checking her blood pressure with a stethoscope and cuff. Tammy hovered near the open door, arms crossed, glaring at Abby. Hunziker stood in front of the scene, directing his men as they loaded up Nick's food and medical supplies.

Abby looked up and locked eyes with Nick.

I'm so sorry. Get free, I know you can. I'll wait for you in New Zealand.

She stared back with wounded eyes, and her voice whispered in his head. "You *promised*."

Zoe walked past and broke his stare. She handed Hunziker Abby's backpack. "Here's her stuff, General Hunziker."

Monroe removed his stethoscope and smiled at her. "Thank you, sweetheart. How thoughtful."

Zoe flashed a polite smile and rushed back to the house.

Hunziker unzipped the backpack, pulled out the Harvard Medical School sweatshirt, and flung the bag into his truck bed with a *bang*. He looked at the sweatshirt's logo with disgust and tossed it to Wiretap. Wiretap flipped open a knife, plunged it through the hood and shredded up. He reached in and removed a small GPS tracker. He flipped the tracker to Hunziker, who dangled it at Nick with a giant fuck-you grin.

Monroe shut Abby's door and opened the front passenger door. "Thank you, Nick." He smiled and waved. "Appreciate your help. Safe travels."

Nick climbed into Herman's truck and watched the Mercedes drive away in his rearview mirror.

"We're not gonna make it," T.J. said.

Nick watched the soldiers wander in and out of the garage. "Oh, we're gonna make it." He stepped out of the car and approached a soldier smoking a cigarette, leaning against the pickup directly behind them. "Private, could you please make a path? We have to go."

"Woah woah woah, where's the fire?" Hunziker strolled over. "Relax, boss. We're almost done."

"General Hunziker, sir, we have a flight to catch. If you could please take just a moment—"

T.J. blasted the horn and gestured impatiently.

Hunziker flipped him off with both hands and backed away.

Nick climbed back into the pickup. "How was that helpful? He was about to move."

They sat in silence another five minutes, watching the soldiers load.

"Come on, come on…we're not gonna make it," T.J. said.

Nick squinted at his phone. "It's mostly highway. If we do a hundred the whole way, we can make it."

The soldiers finished loading and climbed into their trucks.

Nick started the engine and shifted into reverse. "OK, here we go."

The convoy backed out slowly, with Hunziker leaving last. As he reached the road, he put his truck in park, stepped out onto the running board, and leaned over the open door. "Have a nice flight, asshole!" He aimed his pistol and cracked off a single shot.

Their rear tire popped and hissed.

The truck sank as Nick gripped the steering wheel and watched Hunziker disappear in his rearview mirror.

* * *

"We can take the other car, the Ark." T.J. pointed at the garage. "Let's go!"

"We can't leave them with nothing," Nick said quietly, "they'll miss their flight."

"No, listen, we take the Ark, and they fix the tire for tomorrow."

"This truck can't fit them all."

"Shit, well…ugh…they can find another car. There's plenty of time to look." T.J. glared. "Nick, come on!"

"We're not gonna make it." Nick dialed the operator. "We need more time."

"Operator."

"Nick Ritter. Passphrase, Wantabo Lake," he said, his tone tired and defeated.

"Fully verified, sir. What's your status?"

"We ran into a conflict situation. We're through it, but we need more time. Can you delay the flight?"

"Unfortunately, sir, I cannot. If you miss the flight, you forfeit your deposit and you're off the waitlist."

"Please, we just need another hour."

"Respectfully, sir, you know how this works, you wrote most of the rules. Right now I've got nine clients within twenty minutes of Moose River, all begging for a call. I'm sorry, sir, I can try to find you something else, but you're at the bottom of a very long list."

Nick rubbed his face and sighed. "Fine. We'll just stick with the original flight plan, today at five p.m."

"Sir…we've given your spot to another client. He's en route to your pilot now."

Nick's head whipped up. "What? Already? How much space is on that flight?"

Silence.

"*Please,* help me."

Slow typing.

"Look, you know I can't share this," she whispered, "but it looks like a single client and a midsize aircraft—so after Mr. Donahue and his family, there are three open seats. Officially, you're at the bottom of my list. But if you can convince everyone to let you join, that's up to you. That's all I can say. Good luck, sir."

Nick lowered his phone and looked up at the house. His stomach turned. He wondered how long it would take to swim to New Zealand.

* * *

THEY STEPPED out of the car in silence, and T.J. trudged toward the house. Brian and Tracy stood on the front porch, drawn outside by Hunziker's gunshot.

"What happened?" Brian asked as T.J. plodded up the steps.

"We missed our flight." T.J. brushed past them and walked inside. "And now we have no ride," he added over his shoulder.

Tracy gave a satisfied little scoff and followed him inside. Brian looked down at Nick for a moment, then turned inside and shut the door behind him.

Nick lowered the tailgate on Herman's truck, sat down, and stared into the woods. His breath drifted away in misty puffs, backlit by the driveway's motion floodlights.

What a complete and total catastrophe.

Herman, Mikey, Cadillac...all hurt, who knows how badly.

Abby's gone.

We lost our food, our medicine.

We're down a car.

We need a new house.

I have no flight and I'm banned from the waitlist.

There aren't enough spots for everyone on tonight's flight.

And panic is spreading as a deadly virus erases mankind.

He lowered his head into his hands and squeezed hard.

Oh, and everyone hates me. They should...this is my fault.

I can't go back in there. I can't face these people. I never should have—

"Hey there."

He looked up.

Dana stood by the truck, wrapped in an oversized winter jacket.

"Hey." He cast his eyes to the ground.

"Mikey has a concussion, some bruising, but he'll be OK. Herman will survive, but he may lose vision in his left eye, which would leave him effectively blind. I won't know until the swelling comes down. I need to stitch up some lacerations, but they took all our medical supplies."

"There's a surgical kit in my bug-out bag." He thumbed behind him. "On the seat."

She paused, waiting to see if he'd say more. Then she grabbed the bag and started back toward the house.

"She knows, right?" His voice was rough and pained. "They were going to tear through and take her anyway. She knows that, right?"

Dana stopped and turned.

"Dana…I can't…" He looked up at her with haunted eyes. "I can't keep these people safe. What am I supposed to do?"

She placed down the bag, walked back to Nick, and sat on the truck bed beside him. "In my first year as a doctor, I had a patient, a little boy with cystic fibrosis. It's a nasty disease in kids, and he had it bad. His lungs were always filled with fluid and he couldn't breathe. I was the new, bright-eyed doctor and I insisted on taking his case, because, you know, I love the broken ones." She rolled her eyes.

"His treatments were awful—nebulizers, horse pills, vest therapy—every day was torture for this poor kid. Honestly, I couldn't have done it. But he never complained. I mean, he literally never said one bad thing. The way he was, quiet and kind and grateful, it just got to me, it got under my skin. And I decided that no matter what happened, I was going to save this boy.

"So I told his parents, 'There's a breakthrough gene-therapy trial starting early next year. Whatever it takes, we will make it to that trial—I promise. Your son is going to be OK. You're going to take him home.'" She chuckled and shook her head. "As a doctor, you never, *ever* say that. But I made Christopher my personal mission, my obsession. I attended to him seven days a week—holidays, days off, didn't matter—I oversaw every treatment. I called or texted his parents every night. And, amazingly, I got him a match off the double-lung transplant list, which would buy us enough time to join the trial. The transplant was a success, Christopher got better and better, and he was on track to be one of the first children ever cured of cystic fibrosis."

She raised her arms in triumph. "I was the hero doctor I always wanted to be. The nurses baked him a cake with two big blue lungs, and his parents got him this little black bunny. He named it Dana." She laughed. "Nick, you haven't seen real, true joy until you've seen a child given a second life." She basked in the happy memory for a long moment.

"At five forty-one a.m., the morning of his release, an unlicensed orderly administered a massive dose of the wrong medication, and Christopher went into cardiac arrest."

Nick looked up, eyes wide.

Tears streamed down Dana's cheeks, her gaze lost deep in the woods. "It happened fast, I don't think he suffered." Her voice wavered. "I did ninety the entire way to the hospital, straight through three red lights, but by the time I arrived, he was gone."

She exhaled and wiped away tears.

"Dana, that's not your fault—"

"Of course it's my fault. It happens all the time." She shook her head. "I should've been there. It never would've happened if I was there."

She paused and gathered herself. "His family showed up in a limo an hour later, overjoyed to bring their little boy home. And I had to sit them down in my office and explain how I failed...how I lost Christopher...an hour ago.

"The father was inconsolable. He raged and cursed and tore up my office and stormed out. Christopher's mother, she just stared up at the wall, at this cheesy poster with two turtles hugging above the phrase, 'Hope is the last thing ever lost.' I kept crying and apologizing. 'I'm so sorry, Lucy. I'm so sorry. I don't know what happened. I lost him. I should've been there. I lost him.' And she took my hand, looked into my eyes, and said, 'Thank you, Dana. You were our light in the darkness.' And then she walked out."

Dana's words hung in the frigid air.

She took Nick's shivering hand and gazed into his eyes, her expression as warm and comforting as her gentle grip. "We need you, Nick. I need you. Without you, there's nothing but darkness."

"Dana...I can't...I can't save everyone."

She squeezed his hand and leaned in. "So save the good ones."

THIRTY-ONE

"Where were you, Nick?" Tracy crossed her arms and glared.

They were seated in the wrecked living room, the Donahues on one couch, everyone else on the opposite couch. Muddy boot prints crisscrossed the white rug, broken pictures and bowls covered the fireplace, blood streaked the hardwood floor, and cold air drifted in from a shattered window somewhere in the back of the house. Two bug-out bags sat open on the coffee table.

"Yeah, Nick, where were you?" Mikey crossed his arms.

Herman grunted in support, a bag of frozen peas pressed against his eye.

Nick panned across the jury of angry faces.

He took a deep breath. "Look, I'll explain it again. Before I met you, T.J. and I paid to be put on a priority waitlist. If a faster escape route became available, we'd have a chance to upgrade. The operator called me an hour ago and gave us twenty minutes to get on the road. I asked if you guys could come, but there wasn't space, and she assured me you'd be right behind on the original flight at five p.m. So I took the new flight to open up spots on your flight, that way Abby could come, maybe even Herman and Mikey. I didn't have time to wake everyone and discuss, so I was going to call you from the highway… but we never made it past the bridge."

"You were going to call and say what, exactly?" Tracy asked. "'Good luck with your new client, I'll send you a postcard from my private ranch.'"

"You shouldn't have left, Nick," Mikey said while stroking Cadillac. "That's really bad."

Nick rubbed his temples and sighed. "Look, what's done is—"

"We didn't have to come back, you know," T.J. said. "They let us go, but he offered to play hostage negotiator so you wouldn't get blasted to pieces."

Everyone looked at Nick.

"That's right," T.J. said, "without Nick, you're starring in Herman's Last Stand while we sip champagne over the Atlantic."

"Look, what's done is done," Nick said. "When we're tanning on a beach in The Catlins, we can debate the details as long as you like. But right now the clock is ticking and we have life-or-death decisions to make." He finally had their attention. "OK, first we need a new house. We have a few options—"

"Wait, I'm sorry, did I miss something?" Tracy looked around with attitude. "Who is this 'we'? *We* don't work for you anymore. You left. Our contract is done."

Brian nodded. "Sorry, Nick, I gotta take care of the new guy. You know that."

"Brian, forget the new guy," Tracy said, "we're just gonna trade one asshole for another. The money's not worth dying for. We've made it this far without it, let's just walk away and find someplace to wait things out."

"And lose my contract payout?" Brian blinked in disbelief. "All we have to do is get the new guy to New Zealand and we're set for life. I've been working ten years for this, I'm not about to blow it with a few hours left."

"Mom, if we stay here we might catch the virus," Zoe said. "We know it started in Boston, how long until it's here? New Zealand is safer for us anyway, right?"

"Great point, Zo." Brian took Tracy's hand. "Honey, if we leave for New Zealand tonight, we'll be there by tomorrow. Then we can relax in free company housing and collect my payout—hell, we can even throw my big New Year's Payout Party early. We'll be home free."

"Brian, it's not that simple," Nick said gently. "When—"

"Fine," Tracy said. "We take the new client and then we're *done*. And we're not helping these two anymore." She pointed at Nick and T.J. like a disapproving mother.

T.J. turned to Nick with prayer hands. "Nick? Nick? Can I have a sidebar please?" He forced a frustrated grin. "We are wasting time here. I have, like, infinity money, and while I've had a great time flying coach, I'm ready to upgrade to first class now. Call the operator and get us moved up, whatever the cost. Thank you."

Herman scoffed and shook his head.

Nick took a deep breath and addressed the room. "Guys—"

"Oh, I'm sorry, T.J., are we below you?" Tracy slid to the edge of her seat. "Why don't you offer infinity money to your infinity followers and see who comes to help you. Oh, right, they're both imaginary, and no one gives a shit about you. If it wasn't for my husband, you'd be hiding under your bed posting crying videos on your precious website. Honestly, I feel bad for you."

"Now hold on…" Nick held out a hand.

T.J. threw back his head in a maniacal laugh and clapped sarcastically. "OK, honey, as much as I appreciate everything you've done, I'm sure there are plenty of escape plans that don't come with a broken G.I. Joe and a miserable nag."

Brian launched to his feet and aimed a finger at T.J. "Use that tone with my wife again and you're gonna redefine the word broken."

"Dad!" Zoe tugged him back down.

Herman and Dana joined the fray, and the room devolved into shouting.

Nick stood, calmly reached into Brian's bug-out bag, and fished around until he found what he was looking for. He moved in front of the fireplace, at the head of the group.

"How dare you?" Tracy fumed and pointed at T.J. "You think—"

Nick blasted Zoe's pink seahorse whistle as hard as he could.

Everyone jumped and stared up in shock.

Nick tossed the whistle to Zoe. "Look, we don't have a lot of time, so let me simplify the situation. Brian, we need you to give us a ride to New Zealand. Otherwise, we're stuck here, at the bottom of a long list of rich and powerful people trying to buy their way to safety."

Brian crossed his arms, unimpressed.

"But here's the thing," Nick said, "you need us too. See, when you arrive in New Zealand tomorrow, one of two things is gonna happen. One, the company tells you to turn right back around for another rescue mission. They fly you all around the world, picking up rich assholes in deadly places until 12:01 a.m. on New Year's Day. Meanwhile, your family's waiting in a mobile home by the airport, living on military rations and praying you survive your world tour of the apocalypse."

Brian slowly uncrossed his arms.

"Or two, you get lucky, and the company lets you wait out the rest of your contract in New Zealand. They put your entire family in a one-bedroom shithole in downtown Auckland for thirty days—that's all they're required to do, so, trust me, it's bad. If the virus isn't there already, it's coming soon. And you're trapped in the most overcrowded square mile in the entire country.

"Either way, will they pay out your contract in January? Probably? Assuming their financial operations aren't disrupted, which they definitely are. And if they do pay out, will that money even matter if this is an extinction-level event?"

Brian slumped, pale and speechless.

Nick turned to a smirking T.J. "That goes for you too. As much as I appreciate your offer for infinity money, right now the only real currency is food, water, and medicine. And last I checked, our bank account is empty. Welcome to poverty."

T.J.'s smile faded.

Nick turned back to Brian. "My ranch has 277 acres, 5,225 feet of lakefront access, eight bedrooms, two independent energy sources, three fresh water supplies, crops, livestock, hydroponics, aquaculture, recreation, and enough stockpiled food, water, and medicine to last a decade."

Brian's jaw dropped.

Nick took a deep breath and stepped in. "If you get me there, I will give you and your family a safe place to stay for as long as you like. If you have to break your contract, and money still matters, between T.J. and I, we'll make you whole.

"But here's the thing—we all need this new client. Without him, we have no plane. Airport security won't let anyone board without verifying the client. Pray that he's a single client and not a family, otherwise we won't have enough seats. And pray that he'll let us join, otherwise I'm screwed here, and you're screwed there."

Everyone stared up at Nick.

He returned to the couch and dropped into his seat. "Look, I fucked up. I'm sorry, I truly am. But I can still get us through. If we burn all our time and energy fighting, trust me, we won't survive. We have to work together."

He raised his hands defensively. "But it's up to you. We can still go our separate ways. You roll the dice with the client and the company, I work the flight list, and we wish each other good luck."

He scanned the group. "But if you're willing to trust me, I will try and get us through...*all of us.*"

Silence.

Tracy was grasping Zoe's sweatshirt and fighting back tears. Zoe had her arms wrapped around her dad's bicep, her face buried in his shoulder.

Brian looked at Tracy, and she nodded.

Zoe sniffled and nodded into his shoulder.

Brian looked up, his face a mix of fear and gratitude. "OK, Nick, we're in. We get you to the ranch, you give us a spot."

Nick returned a solemn, binding nod. He looked at Dana. "Dana?"

She gave a sweet, admiring smile. "Just tell me what to do."

He turned to T.J., who looked defeated.

"What?" T.J. said. "Are you asking me? Goddamn right I'm in, that's what I'm paying you for."

Mikey stepped in and extended a hand. "I'm in, Nick."

"Thank you, Mikey." He shook and turned to Herman. "Herman?"

Herman turned and slowly lowered the frozen peas. He looked at Nick, and it was clear that despite the damage, he could still see through both eyes. "It's about goddamn time."

* * *

"LET'S GET TO WORK." Nick sprung up and retook his position at the fireplace. "Most of our supplies are gone, but if we leave tonight that won't matter. If we get stuck here, well, then we're in trouble. We still have both bug-out bags, plus the defense kit, which is something. We'll gather our remaining supplies, including any food in the fridge, and load everything into the Ark."

Nick looked at Herman. "We're going to want two cars, just in case. Do you have a spare tire?"

"Of course, in my garage."

"Good. Could you change out the tire and load up any food and supplies from your house?"

"We got it, Nick. No problem." Mikey gave a thumbs up.

Nick paused. "Herman, you feel up to it?"

"What? Oh please, I've taken beatings far worse than this."

Dana smiled and nodded her doctor's approval.

"Priority one is safety." Nick looked at his watch. "We just have to last thirteen hours and then we're on the road to Moose River. Priority two is this new client. We need to take care of this guy, convince him to support our plan."

Nick took a deep breath. "Herman, Mikey, there probably won't be enough space for you on tonight's flight. It may take some time, but I'll find a way. Once we settle in New Zealand, Brian and I can find a plane and come get you, cut the company out completely."

Herman grunted. "We ain't going to your Disneyland Down Under. Lake Wentworth is good enough for us."

Mikey hung his head.

"OK, well, we'll come back to that. Last thing…" Nick looked around the battle-scarred room. "We need a new house. We leave in thirteen hours and we can't afford another run-in with Hunziker, so let's optimize for safety over comfort."

"Herman, what about your place?" Brian asked.

"Too small. Plus, they know where I live. Trust me."

Nick rubbed his chin. "What about—"

"I got an idea, but you ain't gonna like it," Herman said. "There's an old hunting cabin not far from here—deep in the woods, unpaved road, not on any maps. Nobody knows about it but us and the owner, and he ain't been up in nine years."

"Perfect," Nick said.

"Yeah, well, prepare yourself…it ain't the Hotel Infinity." Herman cackled and nudged T.J., who forced a miserable smile.

"Alright, we've got a plan," Nick said. "Herman and Mikey, back to your house to change the tire and load supplies. The rest of us, gather everything here. We'll meet at the cabin. Brian, we'll call the operator from the Ark and game plan your new client. Sounds like he's already on the way.

"Oh, and remember, everyone knows about the virus now, and panic is setting in, so public spaces are strictly off limits. Keep it simple—we just need to hold out until three p.m."

Nick clapped to break the huddle. "Ready? Let's go."

Everyone started up.

"Wait, what about Abby?" Dana said. "We can't just leave her there."

Everyone stopped and looked at Nick.

"We'll plant the phone for her," he said. "If she gets out before three p.m., we'll pick her up and head straight to Moose River."

"And if she doesn't? Then what—she's just stuck there? Forever? With those pigs?"

"What else can we do?" Nick said. "We can't delay the flight. We can't cancel and wait around for her next escape. We can't go get her. She's in a militarized compound guarded by a hundred heavily armed, mentally unstable soldiers just begging for a reason to kill. We have a pistol and a rusty shotgun, one person with combat experience, and no idea where she is. I care about Abby, I do…but going in there, it's not possible."

"He's right, Dana," Brian said. "The odds of success on a mission like that are near zero."

"OK, so let me get this straight," Dana channeled her sister's sass, "it's far too dangerous for a professional prepper and a Navy SEAL to break in, but somehow it's much safer for a sixteen-year-old pregnant girl to break out? How does that make sense?"

Nick softened his tone. "She'll make it out. I know she will, she's a fighter. And if she doesn't, we'll resupply in New Zealand and come back, and we'll keep coming back until she's free. I promise."

Dana sat back and crossed her arms, unhappy but outnumbered.

"Anything else?" Nick asked the group. "OK, let's roll."

Everyone sprung into action except for T.J., who slumped in his seat, closing and reopening his frozen banking app. Herman leaned over from behind the couch. "Welcome to poverty. Don't worry, you get used to it." He clapped T.J. on the shoulder and burst out laughing.

T.J. tossed his phone on the coffee table and put his face in his hands.

Herman's laugh faded, and he placed a hand on T.J.'s shoulder. "It's alright, son. Better to be a good man than a rich man. Your father knew that…I think you do too."

Herman gave T.J. a comforting pat and headed for the door.

* * *

NICK SCANNED his bedroom for anything he might've left behind. He scooped up a phone charger, sweatpants, and a box of protein bars, and stuffed them in his bug-out bag. As he hustled back toward the stairs, he passed Abby's open door, and something caught his eye.

He stopped and backed up.

The "Bun in the oven!" apron was exactly where he'd left it a few hours ago, hanging on the chair, its giddy face beaming up at him. He walked over, gently folded it, and placed it in his bag.

"I promise," Nick whispered.

THIRTY-TWO

THE ARK CRAWLED along Cradle Cove's winding road, Nick and Brian squinting into the dark, looking for the path to the cabin. T.J., Dana, Tracy, and Zoe searched from the back seats.

"Let's hope this guy is easy to work with," Nick said.

"It's just one guy?" Brian asked.

"That's what the operator said. Better be, we need all three seats."

"How do we convince him?"

"Money, information, connections, maybe the ranch…I'll know when I meet him."

"And what if—"

"There!" Nick pointed to an overgrown gap between two huge pine trees.

"Man, Herman was right, no one will ever find this place." Brian turned down the dirt path.

"Alright, I'm calling." Nick dialed the operator from Brian's phone. It rang through the car's Bluetooth system.

"Operator."

"Brian Donahue. Passphrase, Superman."

"OK, Mr. Donahue, I've got you voice verified."

"I'm checking in for instructions on a new client."

"Yes, I was about to call you. The client has been medically cleared and is en route, but running into some resistance. We're working through it. Are you ready to receive?"

"Yes, but at a new location. We had a security breach."

"This is Nick Ritter, I'm with Brian. I'll text you the latitude-longitude coordinates as soon as we arrive. Should be within two minutes."

"Roger that, Nick. I'll update his destination."

"Call me if anything changes," Brian said. "Over and out."

Nick reached out to end the call.

"Oh, one more thing," the operator said. "Nick, I'm sending you an intelligence briefing. We're getting reports of a cure."

"A cure?"

"It's unverified, but we're seeing a wave of signals across our intelligence network—mostly social and alternative media, but also some official sources."

Nick turned and looked back at Dana. "Yeah, send that over right away. We'll take a look."

"Roger that. Over and out."

They crept along the pitch-dark path, hanging branches and dense overgrowth forming a tight tunnel through the woods.

"This better not scratch up my baby." Brian patted the Ark's dashboard.

"Umm, I thought I was your baby?" Zoe crossed her arms.

"Of course, baby." He winked in the rearview mirror. "That's what I meant."

Tracy rolled her eyes and gave gloating Zoe a playful shove.

"T.J., can you check the latest intel on this cure?" Nick said. "Zen or local news or whatever."

T.J. stared out the window into the dark.

"T.J.?" Nick turned around. "T.J.? You with us?"

"Huh?" He looked at Nick, startled and confused.

"Can you check the latest intel on the cure?"

"Cure?"

"Yeah." Nick gestured. "On your phone…do your thing."

"My phone stopped working an hour ago—no internet, no phone, nothing loads all the way, it just stops and starts." He turned back to the window as they exited the tunnel into a large clearing.

Nick looked down and compared his and Brian's phones. "Oh yeah, we've fallen back to satellite. Lines must be down. Man, this thing is moving fast."

"Is that it?" Tracy said. They slowed to a stop, their headlights spotlighting a mossy, dilapidated cabin. "Tell me that's not it."

"Herman wasn't kidding," Brian said, "it ain't the Hotel Infinity."

* * *

THEY SWUNG flashlights around the cabin's gloomy interior. It was small, one main room and a single bedroom in the back. The ceiling shimmered with spiderwebs, the wood-burning stove vomited wet leaves, and the walls sweated a musty rotting-wood smell.

"Welp, good thing it's only fourteen hours," Brian said.

"Thirteen and a half." Nick frowned at the filthy kitchenette.

"This place is *disgusting*." Tracy gagged. "Ladies, let's get to work."

"Dana, I need you on cure research," Nick said.

"You just want out of cleanup duty." Tracy mock-scowled at Dana.

Dana returned a self-important hair flip.

"T.J., I need you too." Nick handed him Brian's phone. "Check social, local, Zen…you know the drill."

They sat around a dusty dining table and researched in silence for five minutes, Nick and T.J. browsing while Brian and Dana chatted softly.

T.J. looked up. "I mean, yeah, it's everywhere. Alternative media is pushing it hard, there's some local coverage, but most of it's on social."

"What are they saying?" Nick asked.

T.J. scrolled and read aloud.

"Penicillin is the cure. The original miracle is back."

"Don't wait until you're sick, get penna-sealin for early prevention."

"My ninety-three-year-old grandma got last rites this morning.

Now she's singing Fly Me to the Moon karaoke on my coffee table. Penicillin is real!"

"Insider tip: Grab your Panasullen before the rich stockpile it all."

T.J. looked up "Stuff like that. They're saying you can take it before or after infection, it works either way. And there are a bunch of hashtags. #Penicillin, #Curicillin, #Miracillin, #BigP, #FreeThePen, #OriginalMiracle, #ThePenIsMightier, etc."

"Is that it?" Nick asked.

"Pretty much. Some tips on how to take it, and a big list of where to find it, but mostly it's people confirming it works."

"My intelligence reports say the same thing." Nick nodded. "Plus there are a few studies out. A research lab in San Francisco gave fifty rats penicillin—the ones who encountered the virus didn't get infected and the ones who were already infected recovered within hours. Two additional labs replicated the results. Some doctors are already endorsing it. Seems like it could be real."

Nick turned to Dana, who was staring into space with a furrowed brow. "Dana, what are you thinking?"

She sighed. "I don't know…it sounds promising, but…it doesn't make sense."

"What do you mean?"

"Well, for starters, antibiotics don't work on viruses. A virus has a completely different structure and replication method than bacteria. Sure, an antibiotic could help with a secondary infection, but it should be ineffective against the virus.

"Also, penicillin is an entire class of antibiotics, it's not even a specific drug. There are over a dozen types of penicillin. So unless they're talking about penicillin G, which is given by injection, or penicillin V, which is taken orally, it's not clear which drug they're actually referring to. Penicillin V would be my best guess, but it's not even the most popular penicillin. Amoxicillin is far more commonly used and should have the same therapeutic effect as the other penicillins because they share the same mechanism of action." She took a breath. "I don't know, it just seems…weird."

Nick processed, then turned back to T.J. "Where is the social content coming from?"

"Mostly Zen, but it's on every social network."

"Can you see who's posting it on Zen?"

"Not really, it's all anonymous user-generated content, maybe a little from our content partners."

"Who are they?"

"I don't know. We have hundreds of them. I don't scrutinize every deal."

Dana leaned toward Nick. "What are you thinking?"

Nick took a deep breath. "Well, it's the same message, everywhere, all at once. Either penicillin really works, or it's a TDC."

"TDC?" Brian asked.

"Targeted disinformation campaign. If it's not real, the only way disinformation spreads this far this fast is when it's a well-funded campaign. Your garden-variety grassroots conspiracy theory is much slower and it tends to stop with a certain demographic or burn itself out. This looks like it's being pushed."

"By who?" Brian asked.

"Could be anyone—foreign governments, terrorist groups, NGOs. Could even come from here—the Feds, maybe the White House or the FDA, even the NSA. Wouldn't be the first time."

"Could be Big Pharma," T.J. said. "They never miss a chance to profit from a disaster."

Nick nodded. "Could be."

"But what about the studies?" Brian asked. "I mean, Monroe made this thing in a lab, right? So maybe it doesn't work like other viruses. Maybe penicillin kills it."

"Yeah." Dana shrugged. "I guess that's possible."

"Sooo...should we get some penicillin?" T.J. asked.

Nick considered. "I have some in New Zealand, but if we get stuck here we'll grab some when we resupply."

"It's incredibly common," Dana said. "It won't be hard to find."

"Can't you just write a prescription?" T.J. asked Dana. "Do the whole pharmacy thing again?"

Nick shook his head. “No public spaces. Right now, our only goal is—”

“Shhh—what’s that?” Brian held out a hand, his head cocked like a hunting dog.

Nick paused, then heard it: The sound of a helicopter approaching.

Brian stood and tensed. “Could it be Hunziker?”

Nick shook his head. “I doubt those idiots can fly. And why would they? It’s probably the client—he must’ve called for an extraction.”

Nick and Brian stepped outside and watched from the front porch.

A black military helicopter with no markings touched down in the field in front of the cabin. Three soldiers in black tactical gear jumped out, scouring the perimeter with rifle-mounted flashlights. A fourth soldier emerged and helped a man in a gray suit step to the ground. The helicopter aimed a floodlight down the front path, and the soldiers formed a diamond around their client, raised their weapons, and glided along the beam of light toward the cabin.

Nick squinted and whispered, “Oh shit.”

Marty Kettenbach stepped onto the porch, his smooth gray hair somehow unruffled by the helicopter. “Nick Ritter.” He leaned in with a cocky gotcha grin. “Looks like you’ll be my live support after all.”

THIRTY-THREE

"WHERE WOULD you like the bags, sir?" A young extraction soldier with a bushy black beard stood in the cabin doorway, his burly frame supporting five overstuffed bags and a wooden case.

"Over there." Marty pointed from the dusty table. "Careful with the case, they're antiques."

An older soldier with neat gray hair stepped inside. "Sir, we're departing shortly. Is there anything—" He spotted Brian and burst into a wide grin. "Heyyy, what's up, Hell Frog!"

Brian lit up and stepped to the soldier. "Hey, Ramirez. Long time, brother."

They exchanged a warm bro hug.

"Guys! Look who's here," Ramirez called outside. Three soldiers stepped in and traded enthusiastic hugs and back slaps with Brian.

Tracy and Zoe watched and smiled.

"So, they still let you fly, old man?" Ramirez said.

"Retirement's coming up in a month." Brian shrugged. "Good time to get out, right?"

"Oh man," the young soldier said as he gently lowered the bags, "I got seven years left—no way I'm getting out alive."

"That's their plan, bro." A short soldier shook his head. "Cheaper to *take you out* than *pay you out*. Know what I'm saying?"

"Seriously, how you been?" Ramirez smiled at Brian.

"Can't complain. Staying busy, family's good, the job…you know."

They grumbled a chorus of agreement.

"Well, it's good to see you, frogman." Ramirez put a hand on Brian's shoulder. "Next time you're anywhere near Virginia you better give me a call. I owe you a beer—actually, more like ten beers."

"Will do, frogman." Brian nodded modestly. "Will do."

"You lucked out, sir," Ramirez called across the room to Marty. "You got a living legend here."

"Alright alright." Brian waved them out the door. "Isn't there a cat in a tree somewhere that needs an extraction?"

They laughed and filed out the door.

Ramirez stopped in the doorway and hugged Brian again. "Stay safe, brother." As he let go, he nodded toward Marty and whispered, "Good luck with this one."

* * *

"I'M FUCKIN' starving." Marty glared across the table at Nick.

Brian and T.J. stared ahead, hands clasped on the table, like schoolboys on their best behavior.

"Marty, this is Brian's wife, Tracy," Nick said calmly.

Tracy stepped to the table and forced a smile.

"She'd be happy to make you something," Nick said. "Right now our supplies are—"

"So housewives come with your package too, huh? Real nice, Nick." Marty barked in Tracy's direction, "Turkey sandwich. Lettuce, tomato, mayo. No cheese."

Tracy's face reddened, and Zoe hugged her and walked her backward to the freshly cleaned kitchenette. "Coming right up!" Zoe said.

Do I smell alcohol? Is he drunk? Oh, right, I required in his contract that extract teams have scotch on board. "Steadies my nerves"—that's what he said.

Marty turned to T.J. and clapped. "So, T.J., how's the digital anarchy business?"

T.J. returned a slow, tired blink.

"Relax, kid, I'm kidding. I love what you're doing. So does Ray, by the way. Says you're 'leading the next generation of Boston big shots.' Didn't realize I was on my way out." He leaned in with a sly smile. "I ain't done just yet, kid." He winked.

T.J. forced a smile.

"Anyway, did Nick put you up in this dump?" Marty looked around the cabin and shook his head. "I hope he's giving you a discount. But hey, at least he answers your phone calls." He glared at Nick.

Zoe lowered a sandwich with a side of chips and a sliced apple. "Bon appetit."

Marty stared at the plate. "The fuck is this? This is ham, honey. I said turkey."

"Unfortunately, we're out of turkey right now, Mr. Kettenbach. All we have is ham and roast beef. Is there a drink I could get you? Water? Sparkling water? Orange juice?"

He stared at the plate with disgust.

"This is what we have, Marty," Nick said.

Marty shooed Zoe away and turned to Nick. "Your phone broken, big shot? I've been calling you for forty-eight hours straight. Nothing."

Nick steadied his tone. "Marty, I don't do live support. I've been trying to get to New Zealand myself. Now let's talk about your situation. Your—"

"My situation? My situation's *fucked*, Nick. That smooth escape plan you promised? Yeah, well, that's the real disaster. My family's in a hotel in New Zealand, I'm stuck here, I don't know what's going on, I'm making all kinds of mistakes—this is why I wanted you on call." He chomped an apple slice.

"I'm sorry it hasn't gone smoothly, these situations rarely do. But I can help you get back on track. Your flight tonight—"

"I'm not your only unhappy customer, by the way. Ray is *pissed.* He's been trying to reach you too—something about using his name at a roadblock."

Nick closed his eyes and sighed.

Marty scoffed. "Yeah, well, you should call him—he wants that paradise in the French Riviera you promised." He grabbed a handful of chips. "I talked to Carlton, he got out no problem. And Landry activated early, he was on one of the first flights. Most of my executive team is still waiting. Everyone else, well, obviously they're fucked." He tossed a chip in his mouth and shrugged.

"Marty." Nick placed his hands flat on the table. "We need to talk about your flight."

"Oh, now we need to talk? Now you're in a hurry?" He leaned back and snapped his fingers at the ladies in the kitchenette. "Honey? Honey? This won't do. Ham is for the plebs. Take it away and bring me a roast beef."

"We're trying to ration for ten people here." Nick felt his calm starting to crack. "We can't afford to waste—"

Marty slammed the table. "I don't give a fuck, Nick! I'm hangry because I've been stuck in my house alone for two days, calling you on a loop, while my wife and kids enjoy Thanksgiving dinner halfway across the world. Pick up your phone! Fix my plan!" He glared at Nick. "And make me a goddamn roast beef sandwich."

Tracy started toward them, ready to unleash.

T.J. stood and calmly picked up the plate. "I gotcha, Marty. No worries." He placed a hand on Tracy's shoulder and gently turned her around. "Come on, Tracy, I'll show you the secret behind my dad's famous roast beef sandwich."

* * *

Fifteen minutes later, Marty slid his empty plate across the table, burped, and wiped his mouth with a party napkin. "Delicious."

Tracy fired a dirty look from the kitchen.

"Can we please talk about your plan?" Nick asked.

Marty beamed a satisfied grin. "Sure, Nick. Let's talk."

"Your flight leaves tonight at five p.m. Brian is your pilot. His family is coming with, that's allowed in his contract. Now the plane has space and weight capacity for three additional passengers. I'd like to propose bringing me and T.J. and one other passenger."

Marty straightened and grinned. "Ohhh, I see...you've got no flight. Is that it, Nick? The Posh Prepper, down here scrambling for the exits with the rest of us poor schmucks?"

Nick took a deep breath. "It's a long story. If you're interested, I'll tell you on the flight. But if you agree to let us join, I will do everything in my power to get you and your family set up exactly how you want."

Marty stared and blinked. "That's it? That's your offer?"

"Yes—oh, and for weight capacity reasons, you'll have to leave your bags."

"I'm not leaving the watches." Marty jabbed a finger at Nick. "It's my great-grandfather's antique collection. He spent—"

"You can bring the watches," Nick said calmly. "No problem."

"Well, Nick, now that I have a flight, I don't know what you can really do for me." He shrugged. "Besides, one of the seats is already taken."

"Taken? By who?"

Marty flashed his eyebrows in a suggestive you-know-who look.

"Marty, I don't follow."

"Come on, Nick, don't be an asshole. You know...what we talked about...at the club."

"Marty, I'm sorry, I don't—"

Marty huffed. "I asked if we could add someone...a *friend...* discreetly. And you said, 'Sure, Marty. Anything for my number one client, Marty. I'll get right on it, Marty.'"

Shit. I completely forgot. He wanted a plan for a girlfriend.

Nick nodded. "OK, yes, now I remember."

"Yeah, well, when I called the operator they had no idea what I was talking about, treated me like an asshole. So my family went ahead, and I said my flight was delayed so I could work with my trusted prepper to make sure my friend got out." He glared at Nick.

"I didn't have time to add her. Creating a new plan, it takes months. I have to line up contracts, stress test scenarios—I mean, you know, Marty, you went through it—it's not an overnight process."

"Yeah, well, maybe you should've said that at the club. Or, I don't know, picked up your phone." He scowled and took a sip of sparkling water. "Anyways, here we are, so, we gotta get her and then, *only then*, can we talk about the two extra seats."

Nick glanced at his watch, 3:53 a.m.

Thirteen hours to departure…it's possible, depending where she is.

But only two seats, that's a problem.

"OK, Marty, let's talk it out. Where is she now?"

"Where do you think? Downtown Boston."

"Boston?" Nick's eyes widened. "That's literally the last place we want to go—it's ground zero for the outbreak. No way. Out of the question."

"No shit, Sherlock. Am I being charged for these brilliant insights? That's why I wanted to bring her out with me. I explained, I begged, I threatened, but everyone just pointed to your stupid contract. So now, how about you fix it?"

"I'll get her a separate flight. It may take a few days, but I can find something. We can extract her today and move her to a secure location with plenty of supplies."

"Oh yeah?" Marty gestured around the cabin. "Secure…with plenty of supplies…like this shithole?" He leaned in and snarled. "I don't wanna wait. I'm done waiting. She says it's getting bad in there, my family's wondering where the hell I am, and I want the new life you promised…*now*."

"Marty, I understand, but—"

Marty threw up his hands. "Why am I even talking to you, Nick? I don't need you." He turned to Brian. "We gotta get her out, pal. I'll give you her location, you bring her up here, and we'll fly out tonight. Good?"

"Respectfully, sir, I'm just the pilot. I'm not trained or equipped for a high-risk rescue. Can we send in an extraction team?"

"Tried that. She's not in the contract. Were you paying attention?" He leaned toward Brian with a condescending look. "Listen, I'm gonna make this very simple—if you want my seats, then pick up my friend. Otherwise, I call the operator and report you as non-compliant—no flight, no payday, no future." He leaned back with a smug grin. "Do your job or find a new one."

Tracy launched a handful of silverware into the sink with a violent clatter and started toward the table.

"Now hold on." Nick stepped in her path and pointed at Marty. "You can't do that. His contract requires him to fly, not go on whatever suicide mission you dream up."

Marty stood and jammed a finger in Nick's face. "'Push them hard.' That's what you told me, remember? 'Push them hard and they'll do whatever you need, or they won't get their payday.'"

Nick lowered his finger as the Donahues all looked at him.

Marty turned and loomed over Brian. "Pick up my girlfriend or make this cabin your forever home. What's it gonna be...*Hell Frog?*"

Brian looked up at Tracy—her eyes raging, chest heaving—she shook her head.

He looked at Zoe—her lip trembling, hands clutched to her heart—she shook her head.

He looked at Nick—his fists clenched, face pale—he shook his head.

He looked around the rotting cabin.

Brian slid back his chair and stepped face to face with Marty. "I'll do it."

Tracy threw up her hands and stormed back to the kitchenette. Zoe and Dana followed.

"Brian." Nick stepped to him. "You don't have to—"

"What choice do I have, Nick? Huh? You *screwed* me. Now what choice do I have?"

Nick shook his head, out of words.

"I'll load up the Ark." Brian grabbed the defense kit and headed for the door, his limp noticeably worse.

"Brian," Nick called.

Brian turned in the doorway.

"I'm coming with you."

THIRTY-FOUR

"BETWEEN THE ROADBLOCK and the traffic we'll never make it in and out of Boston alive, never mind make the flight," Nick said as Brian guided the Ark over Cradle Cove's little wooden bridge.

"Yeah, the roads are a mess," Marty said from the back seat. "That's why I called for the extraction."

Nick had convinced Marty to come by telling him they might find an earlier flight out of Boston. The truth was if Marty was present he'd hesitate to go into a dangerous situation—they were safer if Marty had skin in the game. Also, if they left him behind, there was a non-zero chance Tracy would kill him.

"A helicopter would be perfect, but we'll never find one on such short notice," Nick said. "Rail is out of the question—probably out of service and definitely infected. That leaves us with backroads. We could try to find a route that—"

"What about a boat?" Brian said.

Nick and Marty looked at him.

"We drop in from New Hampshire or Maine, follow the coast south, and pull right into Boston harbor."

"Good call." Nick tapped on his phone. "The company has escape vessels in every major port. We'll want something out of New

Hampshire so we don't have to cross state lines, risk another roadblock."

Nick held up his phone. "Portsmouth Yacht Club. It's an hour drive, no state lines, and they've got two boats available."

Brian tapped the destination into the Ark.

"How do we navigate in the dark? Won't we get lost?" Marty asked. "I mean, can you even drive a boat at night?"

Brian tried not to laugh as he looked in the rearview. "Hooyah…sir."

* * *

THE TRIP to Boston was a smooth two-hour cruise in a high-end pontoon boat. Nick and Marty spent most of the ride wrapped in beach towels, shivering in the pre-dawn drizzle. As they approached Boston Harbor, the first rays of light painted Brian behind the wheel. He looked like a younger man—happy and strong—oblivious to the frigid gusts rippling across his windbreaker, lost in an old feeling.

They cruised up the Charles River and tied at a small community dock as close to downtown Boston as possible. Wearing N95 masks and surgical gloves, they crept into the city. Nick carried his phone, Brian carried his pistol, and Marty carried a pair of binoculars.

"It's a short walk, maybe half a mile to the Charles River Plaza," Nick said.

Cambridge Street was strangely quiet without the morning commute. Its lanes were scattered with abandoned cars and lighted emergency vehicles. Its shops were closed and undisturbed, except for the restaurants and grocery stores, which were all smashed and stripped.

"Try calling her." Nick handed Marty his phone.

"It's not ringing," Marty said. "Just beeping."

"Phone lines are down here too. She better be here, and she better be ready."

"She was ready when I talked to her yesterday."

"That's good. But let's just get this out of the way right now, just in case—if she's not here, we're leaving. No searching the city, no checking her mom's friend's neighbor's aunt's place…we go straight back to the boat, straight back to Wolfeboro. Agreed?"

"Raina will be there, Nick. She's got nowhere else to go."

"Right, but what if she's—"

"Good morning!" A shirtless man in dirty jeans and work boots jogged up the road with a cheerful smile. His eyes were blood red, his hands scratched raw. He gave a friendly wave and headed up Cambridge Street.

Marty stared, his eyes wide with horror.

"Mask and gloves on tight," Nick whispered, "we're almost there."

They passed a huge sign written in orange spray paint, "FREE CLINIC—1/2 MILE AHEAD." It pointed toward the Boston Garden arena, which was up the road from the Charles River Plaza.

"Do you hear music?" Brian asked.

Nick nodded. "Up ahead. Go slow and be ready to run."

They approached a public basketball court and stopped and stared. At center court, thirty homeless people danced around a barrel fire to Bruce Springsteen's "Born in the U.S.A." A young man in a leather jacket windmilled an air guitar, a blind man in a wheelchair banged air drums, and the others skipped and twirled around a circle of dried blood. Between their wild eyes, pulpy hands, and spasmic sneezes and coughs, they looked like zombies conducting a tribal ceremony.

"Methadone Mile, the homeless encampment," Nick whispered. "They probably came here for the free clinic."

"Comin' through, boys!" A pack of homeless women sprinted past, dribbling a trail of blood behind them.

"Keep moving." Nick pushed Marty along. "Into the parking garage up ahead."

As they reached the garage, Marty looked down a side alley and froze. It was scattered with bodies, some sleeping, nested in cardboard and trash, others dead, stiff and covered in rats. An enormous homeless man with faded overalls and bare feet stood facing a white brick wall. He slapped both hands high on the wall, then dragged them down two bloody streaks. He shivered, raised his hands, and did it again.

Marty dropped the binoculars. "Oh my god oh my god oh my god."

The man slowly turned his head and nodded a toothy grin.

"Get inside!" Nick pulled Marty into the parking garage and snatched the binoculars.

They made their way upstairs to the corner of the roof that overlooked the plaza.

"You can lower your masks," Nick said, "get some air."

He looked down at the plaza. It was a perfect square of buildings enclosing a large parking lot in the middle. The only way in was a vehicle entrance with a parking gate and a few small alleys and walking paths between the buildings.

Nick raised the binoculars. "OK, we've got a Market Basket, thoroughly looted. A bakery and a Dunkin', both destroyed. A bank and a dry cleaners, untouched. And…there it is, Charles River Condominiums, six stories high, one main entrance—looks untouched."

"Alright, let's go," Marty said.

Nick peered through the binoculars for a long moment. "There's something else."

"What is it, Nick?" Brian asked.

"There's a small cut clinic with a long line of sick waiting on the sidewalk, like at Dana's hospital—maybe a hundred people. But they're starting to leave the line and walk across the parking lot to the other side of the plaza, to the CVS. There's a crowd gathering there. And there are others, not everyone looks sick."

Nick followed a group of infected as they left the plaza and crossed Cambridge Street to a fire station on the other side. A crowd was forming by the garage door, mostly sick and homeless, but some looked healthy, wearing masks, gloves, and duct-taped homemade gowns. The healthy were in small groups, many carrying pistols or rifles.

Nick swung back to the clinic and followed an old woman walking out, carrying a pill bottle in her gauze-wrapped hands. As she crossed the parking lot, three healthy-looking subway workers jumped out of a city truck and surrounded her. The one wearing a conductor's hat flashed a gun under his jacket. She tried to run, but they grabbed her and snatched the bottle. She screeched and spit on them, and the conductor pistol-whipped her to the ground. A group of homeless men moved in to intervene, and the conductor raised his gun as the subway workers backed into their truck. The sound of shattering glass echoed across the plaza, and the homeless men turned and rushed toward CVS as a crowd spilled through the broken front window.

More glass shattered, and Nick swung to see a healthy-looking man in a tracksuit clearing the front window of the cut clinic with the butt of his rifle.

All at once, the long hospital line dissolved into two groups, half rushing the clinic and half sprinting across the parking lot to CVS.

Nick lowered the binoculars, his eyes dancing across the horizon as he processed.

Then it clicked.

He grabbed his phone, opened the latest intelligence report, and tossed it to Marty. "At the bottom, there's a list...a list that's circulating on social media. You see it?" He raised the binoculars and studied the plaza.

"Uhh, yeah, here it is."

"Read it out loud."

"It says, 'Here is THE definitive list of where to find your penicillin. Make sure to check them ALL before it's too late.'" Marty looked up. "Then it's a long list of places."

"Read it."

Marty took a deep breath. "Hospitals. Pharmacies. Cut clinics. Doctor's offices. Ambulances. Pharma warehouses. Medical delivery trucks. Police stations. Fire stations. Vet clinics. Government buildings. Public offices. Town halls. Military bases. Roadblocks. National Guard medical tents. FEMA medical tents. 911 phone centers. Private homes of high-ranking government and military officials."

Nick slowly lowered the binoculars. "Most of those places don't stockpile penicillin." He looked at Brian. "It's a TDC...designed to overwhelm and destabilize health and safety systems."

"What's a TDC?" Marty asked.

"Targeted disinformation campaign." Nick took his phone back.

"Someone's tapping into public fear and promoting penicillin as a wonder cure, available at select locations while supplies last. If the virus is a fire in a crowded theater, they're funneling everyone toward a dead-end exit."

"Meaning penicillin doesn't really work?" Brian asked.

"Exactly." Nick skimmed the list again.

"But if it doesn't work, what's the point?" Brian said. "After a day or two everyone will figure it out, and those places will be fine, right?"

Nick pocketed his phone and pointed at the plaza. "Yeah, but look at all the damage—shattered windows, ravaged supplies, injuries, and..." His eyes went wide. "Oh my god...it's a superspreader attack."

"A what?" Marty's eyes darted around the roof.

Nick gazed down into the plaza, lost in the chaos. "Concentrated anarchy...a burst of destruction designed to spread the virus farther and faster. Get the sick to descend on local health and safety systems, disrupting service for a few days, and in the process, they mix with the healthy, specifically doctors, nurses, cops, firefighters, soldiers, politicians—all the essential workers. Disrupt the response and spread the virus—kill two birds with one stone." He turned and locked on Brian. "Someone orchestrated panic into one giant superspreader event."

"Who...who would do that?" Marty asked.

"There's a long list, but I have a pretty good idea who's on top."

THIRTY-FIVE

KURT STOPPED at the lab door with the blacked-out windows. "Now listen, the doc's got a lot on his mind, so try not to be so…" He looked Abby up and down. "You know."

She crossed her arms and gave an ice-cold stare.

"OK." He shrugged. "Have it your way, Crabby, 'cause that's been working so well for you lately." He swiped his security badge, and the door unlocked. He pulled it open and extended his arm with a sarcastic smile. "After you, princess."

Kurt and Dr. Teddy had been in this lab a lot recently. She didn't have access. After her second runaway, her badge stopped working on a lot of doors.

Abby stepped inside. It took a minute for her eyes to adjust to the dim light, and her brain to process the strange scene. The room contained ten long tables, each with ten computer stations complete with monitor, keyboard, mouse, and chair. A third of the stations were manned by Kurt's soldiers, posting and commenting on a range of social networks. Spanning the rear wall was a long wooden board with three shelves, each holding at least a hundred cell phones. A dozen militia members strolled along the shelves, refreshing, browsing, and liking social media posts. It was a click farm. She'd watched a medical-ethics lecture on how they were used to distort information and manipulate public opinion.

Dr. Teddy stood at the head of the room in his white doctor's coat, studying a small tablet.

"Let's go." Kurt gave her a firm nudge, and they moved toward Dr. Teddy.

"She's good, Doc." Kurt called ahead.

Dr. Teddy looked up.

"All checked and cleared by your staff." Kurt gave a thumbs up.

"Excellent." Dr. Teddy smiled. "Do you feel better, Abby?"

I'll feel a lot better in a few hours...

"Much better. Thank you, Dr. Teddy." She forced a smile.

Dr. Teddy lowered his tablet. "Listen, Abby, I know this is difficult. It's normal to have big feelings so close to your due date. You see, your hormones are—"

"Sorry, Doctor T, I was soothing a cranky spam filter." Wiretap strolled up, tapping and swiping his tablet like an orchestra conductor. "All good now. You wanted to see me?"

"Not a problem, Private Winkler. I just wanted to check in, see how we're doing."

Wiretap stared down at his tablet. "Uhhh, well, put simply...we're doing great. We're running in thirty-four languages across two hundred and twenty-five cities, promoting over ten thousand pieces of content, and trending on every platform. Alternative media is all in, and mainstream is starting to nibble—we've got your docs hitting the big networks. Honestly, promotion has shifted mostly organic—users have taken over pushing the message, which is why I've got us half-staffed right now." He gestured at the room behind him. "When do you want to release the next batch of studies? Oh, and the monkey video?"

Dr. Teddy looked at his watch. "Oh, I don't know...ten a.m.? Is that too early?"

"Feels right." Wiretap gave two decisive taps.

"Yeah—feels right." Dr. Teddy winked at Abby. "Well, Private

Winkler, excellent work. If you need anything from me, please inform the General."

"You got it, Doc." He strolled away without looking up.

Dr. Teddy turned back to Abby. "As I was saying, I know this is a challenging time, but the next few weeks are going to be critical. Not just for our big project, but for your little project." He made a playful little pinching gesture at her belly.

Ew—don't touch me.

She must've made a face because his tone shifted. "Please, Abby, no more acting out, we're all quite tired of it. No drama with the other girls, no agitating the General's men, and absolutely no running away. Your reckless expeditions distract the militia and upset the mothers, and I won't tolerate it. From this point on, any bad behavior will be met with *severe* consequences. Am I clear?"

Don't worry, asshole, I'll be out of your hair very, very soon.

"I understand, Dr. Teddy. I'm sorry. I think the hormones got to me." She cast her eyes to the floor.

"No need to apologize, dear. You're doing a big job." He beamed a condescending smile. "And soon you'll get to meet your…*our* babies. I'm so excited!"

I'll send you a postcard from New Zealand.

She did a little excited dance.

"If you need anything, please let me know." He squeezed her shoulder and nodded to Kurt that they were finished.

"Let's go." Kurt gripped her arm and turned her toward the door.

She spun away from his grasp. "There is one thing."

"Yes, dear?"

"Could I have access to the labs again? I just love doing research and experiments, and it keeps my mind off…" She twirled a finger by her head. "You know."

He hesitated, then smiled. "Of course. I'll have Private Winkler restore your access right away."

"Thank you, Dr. Teddy. You're the best." She gave her best daddy's-girl smile and bounced toward the door.

"Oh, Kurt?" he called.

They both turned.

"Let's put a man on her…just in case she needs something."

Abby and Dr. Teddy exchanged fake smiles, and she turned to the door.

No no no, not now! I only need a few hours.

THIRTY-SIX

"We need to leave. It's a death trap." Nick shook his head.

"Are you crazy? She's right there." Marty pointed down at the plaza from the parking-lot roof.

Nick thumped the binoculars into Marty's chest. "Do you need another look? The place is overrun with scratchers and looters. And people are just waking up—once they check the news, read their feed, watch their videos...more will come. Trust me, this doesn't end well."

Marty looked at Brian. "Come on, pal. Can't you just do your army thing? Sneak in there, grab her, bring her out."

"Well, sir, I could try and—"

"We don't even know if she's in there," Nick said. "Last time you talked to her was, when, yesterday? She could've left. Or gotten infected. Or gotten..."

Marty glared at Nick.

"Look," Nick said, "if we go in that plaza, in that building, we risk getting trapped. I've spent the last decade training people to get *out* of a crisis, the last thing we want to do is go *in*."

"Sir," Brian said to Marty, "where in the building is she located? If I can—"

"Brian, you don't have to do this," Nick said.

"Actually, yeah I do, Nick," Brian snapped. "I can't just buy another flight or call my favorite CEO. If I lose this contract, I've got nothing—no food, no shelter, no money, no flight...*nothing*. My family's not starving in that cabin. For us, it's now or never."

"Exactly." Marty pointed and nodded in support. "Let's get you in and out, right now, so you can get back to your family."

Nick threw up his hands. "This is a huge mistake. Sorry, Marty, but I'm not dying for your girlfriend." He stormed away, leaned against a wall, and started browsing his phone.

Marty shot him a sour look and turned to Brian. "OK, buddy, what's the plan?"

"Well, sir, it looks like there's an alley between CVS and the condos. If I can enter the plaza through there, I should be able to reach the front door with minimal exposure."

Marty gave a half-impressed head sway. "Yeah, maybe...but then you gotta take Raina back through some dark alley, and god knows who, or what, is waiting in there." He shuddered. "I think it'd be better if you use the main entrance on the other side, by the Dunkin'...then creep along the perimeter, past the bank, the dry cleaners, and the Market Basket...and then sneak into the condo building. All the activity is on the other side of the plaza, so you should be fine."

Marty gave Brian a big slap on the shoulder and a well-practiced grin. "Ready, chief?"

Brian returned a hesitant nod and pulled up his mask.

"I'll be watching the whole time," Marty said. "Any trouble, just signal."

"Yes, sir." As Brian walked toward the stairwell, he took a final look at Nick, who was absorbed in his phone.

Brian started down the stairs.

"Stop," Nick commanded.

Brian stopped and looked up.

"That is the worst, most dangerous, most ill-conceived plan I can possibly think of." Nick pushed off the wall and started stalking toward Brian. "Really, Brian? Ten years as an escape pilot, a dozen more as a Navy SEAL, and you're good with that plan? You might as well shoot yourself in the leg and join the Springsteen dance party—same outcome, way faster."

Nick veered toward Marty. "First of all, you want to stay as far away from the plaza interior as possible. One touch could be the end. Hell, one wrong breath and you're exposed. If you get confronted down there, you're instantly cornered with limited escape routes." He pointed to the road below them, where a steady trickle of people moved toward the plaza. "Plus you run the risk of getting trapped by a crowd."

Nick stopped at Marty and put his hands on his hips. "Also, you're assuming the Dunkin', the bank, the dry cleaners, and the Market Basket are all empty because you can't see any activity from here—big mistake. It was near freezing last night, I guarantee there are infected squatters inside." He turned to Brian, who was returning from the stairwell. "What's your plan when one of them pops out for a high five?"

Brian opened his mouth to respond, but Nick turned back to Marty and continued. "Also, do you need a key to enter the building? Did you think of that?"

Marty's face sank.

"Yeah, I thought so. When you're surrounded by scratchers and looters, and the door won't open, what's your plan then?"

"Shoot out the glass." Brian gave a confident nod.

"Exactly. And then what happens?" Nick crossed his arms.

Brian and Marty looked at each other and shrugged.

"Everyone thinks you found penicillin. Even if you manage to get inside before they surround you, you just choked off your one way out."

Brian raised a finger. "Yeah, but—"

Nick raised a hand. "Those are just the problems I can see from here, and we've got huge gaps in visibility. What can't we see? How many sick? How many looters? How many guns?"

He glared from Brian to Marty and back like a father scolding his sons. "Under no circumstances should you set foot inside that plaza."

They waited to make sure he was done.

"OK…so…what do you suggest?" Marty asked.

Nick pointed to the condos. "Go wide, around the plaza, and approach the back of the building from Staniford Street. There's a walking path that ends there, which means the building has a rear entrance. Even if it doesn't, there has to be a staff door or a maintenance dock of some kind. If it's open, great. If not, break in...*quietly*... out of sight. Go upstairs, grab Raina, and exit out the back. Never enter the plaza. Never make a peep. In and out."

A big satisfied grin spread across Marty's face. "There's my Posh Prepper. See, Nick? Live support ain't so bad after all." He nodded at Brian. "Do it his way."

"Yeah, well, nothing ever goes according to plan." Nick looked at Brian. "I'm coming with."

Marty nodded in stern agreement. "Absolutely, yes, good idea. Better to have backup, just in case."

Nick glared. "Oh, you're coming too."

* * *

NICK'S PLAN WORKED PERFECTLY. Someone had propped open the rear door with a magazine, and they crept inside undetected and made their way to the third floor, Unit 303.

Marty knocked on the door.

Paws skittered across the floor inside, and a little dog yapped.

Marty squatted and whispered, "Marty, shhhh. Marty, it's me. Quiet."

Nick and Brian looked at each other, then down at Marty.

"Yes, she named the dog Marty Jr. Get over it."

The dog barked for another twenty seconds as Marty tried to talk him down.

Nick and Brian scanned the hallway.

"She must've left," Nick said. "Let's go."

Marty shook his head. "Where would she go? And she'd never leave the dog." He leaned into the door. "Raina! Raina, it's Marty. Open the door."

The dog snarled and bumped the door.

"Let's go."

"Shouldn't we at least look inside?" Brian asked. "Confirm either way?"

"We have no idea what's in there," Nick said. "And every second we spend here is added risk. Marty, I'm sorry, but we need to go."

Marty opened his mouth to protest, but the dog went silent. The door's deadbolt clicked back.

"Get back." Nick stepped away. "Everyone back ten feet."

Nick pressed his back against the wall and watched the door.

Brian posted on the other side of the door, his pistol half raised.

Marty hid behind him.

The door creaked open. A woman peeked out, the bottom half of her face covered by a stack of coffee filters tied with a red necktie. A pair of pink dishwashing gloves reached out and gripped the door frame.

"Raina?" Marty peeked around Brian and cocked his head.

"Marty?" she said in an eastern European accent.

"It's me, baby. I'm here to get you out. These men are soldiers who work for me. Follow their instructions, OK?"

Nick stepped off the wall. "Raina? My name is Nick. I'm going to ask you a few questions. When was the last time you left the apartment?"

"Umm…one week. Dinner with Marty at Ostra."

"Are you feeling sick?"

"No."

"Has anyone visited that was sick?"

"No."

"When was the last time you saw another person?"

"One week. Dinner with Marty at Ostra."

Nick looked at Marty and nodded.

"OK, baby, we're coming in." Marty led them inside and closed the door.

It was dark, with the only light coming from a flickering TV in the next room. Nick peeked around the corner and saw the curtains were all drawn and duct-taped shut. The TV was muted with subtitles, streaming a news station with a split-screen view of a celebrity doctor opposite cell-phone footage of infected children dancing in the street.

Marty flicked on a light in the entryway, and Raina winced as her eyes adjusted. She was wearing a blue sequined cocktail dress and high heels, which paired strangely with the dishwashing gloves, coffee-filter mask, and scowling rat-dog under her arm.

Nick pulled off his mask. "Raina, you can take off your mask and gloves. We brought you fresh ones." He handed them to her, and she looked at Marty.

"It's OK," Marty said, "you can take them off."

She placed the dog on the floor and began removing her mask and gloves.

Marty Jr. scampered to Nick's feet and growled.

She was stunning, with full lips, rosy cheeks, and big innocent eyes. She'd clearly had some plastic surgery done, which looked strange on someone so young and naturally beautiful.

Jesus, Marty, she's barely twenty-one.

"I'm ready to go, Marty," she said. "Packed, just like you said."

Nick squinted down at a six-piece luggage set, the bags overstuffed and lined up perfectly from smallest to largest.

"Great job, baby. The pilot will take it."

She turned to Nick. "Do you have any pen? The doctors say it's the cure."

Nick was about to answer when he noticed her hand. She was counting, gently tapping each finger to her thumb in a repeating pattern.

Obsessive-compulsive disorder? These last few days must've been hell.

Marty saw Nick's gaze and batted at Raina's hand. "Stop. Remember what Dr. Pasternak said."

"Do you have any penicillin?" she asked.

"No." Nick looked up. "It doesn't work anyways."

She squinted at him like he was a liar. Marty Jr. started barking.

"OK." Nick took a deep breath and waved over the luggage. "None of this is coming. We can't carry it back to the harbor, and even if we could, it won't fit on the plane without displacing seats."

"Now hold on," Marty said. "You told me you could bring luggage. 'I'll save the family china, your rock collection, the kids' hamster.' That was your pitch, Nick."

The dog nipped at Nick's pants.

"First of all, shut the dog up," Nick said. "*Now,* before someone comes to check on it."

Raina dropped her fresh mask and gloves on the floor and scooped up Marty Jr.

"Second of all, property preservation requires pre-planning—it's too late for that now. And third, we agreed to rescue Raina in exchange for your other two seats—that was the deal. So the bags stay, or Brian and I walk. No one else will bring her out, you know that, and you may not get another chance. So the four of us walk out together, right now, and head to New Zealand, or none of us go." He glared at Marty.

"OK, Nick." Marty threw up his hands. "You're the planner."

"Marty Jr. is coming," Raina said in a hurt tone.

"Fine," Nick said. "But you carry him, and he has to stay quiet."

She kissed the dog and nodded.

"Do you have shoes you can run in?" Nick pointed to her high heels. "Can you run in that dress?"

She unzipped a bag of shoes and pulled out a pair of white sneakers. "Dress is good."

"OK." Nick moved to the door. "Here's the plan: we go out the door, left down the hall, down the stairs, through the lobby, out the back door, and onto Staniford—just like we came in. From there, it's ten minutes to the boat and we're home free. Ready?"

"Wait, we should get penicillin from CVS," Raina said. "They open in forty-two minutes."

Nick scoffed. "We're not waiting forty-two minutes. Plus, they're already open and sold out."

"What you mean?"

"The store is being looted. Even if there were any penicillin left, we can't go in there, it's too dangerous. Plus, penicillin is a TDC...it's a hoax, not real."

"No no no." She wagged a finger at Nick. "Not a hoax. Real. Doctor Gold said on news to take it. Works for dogs too." She gave Marty Jr. a little head scratch, and he beamed a death stare at Nick.

"The virus doesn't spread to animals, we know that. And penicillin, it doesn't—" Nick huffed. "Look, we don't have time for this. The situation outside is a ticking time bomb. The good news is I have plenty of penicillin back at the cabin. You and Marty Jr. can take it as soon as we get there. But we need to go *now.*"

Her eyes brightened and she nodded.

"OK. Put your sneakers on. Everybody, mask and gloves on. Remember—"

There was a loud crash outside the TV-room window, then a screech and yelling.

"Stay here." Nick strode to the window and peeled back a tiny corner of the curtain. Three Army National Guard humvees had smashed through the entrance gate and skidded to a stop in the middle of the parking lot. Soldiers in N95 masks and black medical gloves poured out, pointing and shouting, automatic weapons raised. They formed two units—one advanced on CVS and the other moved on the clinic.

The giant homeless man from the alley hopped down from the shattered CVS window, a pill bottle in his hamburger hand. He grinned from ear to ear and strolled toward the soldiers.

All guns aimed at him. "Hands up! Get on the ground!"

He opened the pill bottle and continued his leisurely advance.

They backed up in a chorus of frantic shouts. "Stop right there! On the ground now! Down down down!"

He swallowed a handful of pills, laughed, and tossed the bottle at them. Everyone opened fire, sending him reeling backward through the CVS window.

"M4 carbine," Brian whispered from the entryway, down on one knee, pistol drawn.

Nick extended his arm in a hold signal. "We need to—"

Wild pistol shots cracked from a ground-level condo at the other end of the building, echoing across the plaza. A nearby soldier crumpled to the ground. All the soldiers in the plaza raced to the condo and opened fire.

Three more humvees tore in and spilled soldiers. A commander with flushed cheeks and bulging veins leapt out and strode up behind the firing line, waving his hand and screaming in a hoarse voice. "Cease fire! Cease fire!" He pointed. "Clear that building—*now*."

Nick squinted. It was the CO from the roadblock—Captain Kravich.

Soldiers streamed into the lobby below.

"Shit." Nick scrambled back to the entryway and whispered, "Listen to me, there are soldiers downstairs. We need to get out of this building and away from the plaza right now, or get infected, arrested, or shot—which all end the same way." He pulled Brian up from kneeling. "In the next thirty seconds, we're going to come up with three escape plans, choose the best one, and go. If you have an idea, shout it out."

"Uhh…uhh…break the window." Marty pointed into the TV room. "Lower down with a rope or bed sheets."

Nick gave him an impatient look. "No rope, no time to tie sheets. Even if we could lower four people and a dog down three floors, we'd be easily visible, and we'd land right in the parking lot. What else?"

"Hide out and wait for them to leave," Brian said. "They won't occupy the building, they'll clear it and move on."

Nick swayed his head as he considered. "Could work. But hiding four people is tough. There's a risk they leave a post here, or set up a command center, or lock down the entire plaza. And time isn't on our side—if we miss the flight tonight, we're screwed. Better to get out now, while we still can."

A thud resonated directly below them, then shouting.

"Oh my god, they're breaking down doors," Marty said. "Enough brainstorming. You're the planner, Nick. What do we do?"

Nick took a deep breath. "Down is no longer an option. So we go up…up to the roof. There are three ways off a roof: Up, via aircraft…

not gonna happen. Over, to a neighboring roof…maybe, but high risk. Or down, via fire escape…that's our move."

"I watch stars on roof," Raina whispered. "No fire escape."

"There's a fire escape." Nick nodded confidently.

"How can you be sure?" Marty asked.

"There has to be. State building code requires it. Plus I saw it when we scouted the plaza. It lowers down the side of the building, into the alley between here and CVS."

"How do we know it works?" Brian asked.

"They're inspected every five years. On a building this new, it works." Nick panned across the group. "Ready?" He moved to the door.

"I want to stay." Raina clutched Marty Jr. and backed toward the TV room. She pointed at Brian. "His plan is better. We hide here. It's safe, no virus."

"It's not safe here," Nick said. "It just feels safe because it's familiar."

"Are you sure they're coming up?" Marty said.

Nick stared at Marty. "Trust me, they're coming up."

"Well, can't we just explain that we're not sick? That we're leaving?"

Nick opened his mouth to respond when shouting erupted in the unit below, followed by automatic gunfire and shattering glass.

Nick raised his eyebrows at Marty. "We need to go in the next thirty seconds, or Plan A is off the table." He looked at Brian. "Move and confirm. If the conditions change, if we get new info, we'll adapt on the fly. Gloves on, mask on."

He strode to Raina, who had backed into the hallway bathroom and shut the door halfway. "Raina? Raina? Listen to me. We're leaving now. If you come with us, we'll take you and Marty Jr. to a safe place far away from here where we have plenty of penicillin. Or you can stay here, all alone, and hope the infected soldiers don't find you."

Her eyes went wide and she threw open the door. "OK, I come." She brushed past Nick toward the TV room. "I need to turn off TV—"

Nick grabbed her arm and guided her to the entryway. "Leave the

TV. Give Marty the dog. Here, step into your sneakers. Good. Now hold your mask and gloves, we'll put them on when we reach the roof."

She stuffed the mask and gloves down the top of her cocktail dress and tried to lift three pieces of luggage at once.

Nick gently squeezed her hands. "Raina, we're leaving the bags. Follow Brian outside now. He'll make sure it's safe."

Brian stepped out and cleared the hallway.

Nick ushered Raina out behind him.

"The hell is wrong with her?" Marty whispered to Nick.

"Nothing. It's too much to process. She's cognitively and emotionally overwhelmed—happens to most people. Let's go." He pushed Marty out.

Nick quietly shut the door behind him and pointed toward the stairwell. "Me and Raina lead, then Marty, then Brian in the rear—hide your pistol."

"Why I in front?" Raina said as Nick took her arm.

"Because they won't fire on a woman…especially one dressed like you."

They crept down the hallway to the stairwell. Nick eased the door open, listened, then stepped inside. He held the door for everyone then closed it softly. He started up the stairs and beckoned with a shhh gesture.

A door below them screeched open and clanged against the brick wall.

"Lombardi, Romero, Hunt—you guys come with me." A soldier's gruff voice echoed up the stairs. "What? No, just leave it. Clean-up crew will come through after. What?"

Nick winced and rushed up the stairs, pulling Raina with him. They reached the top floor and eased the roof door open. The bright morning sun reflected off the all-white roof, temporarily blinding him.

"This way." Nick pulled Raina toward the side of the building. "Put on your mask and gloves."

Gunshots erupted in the plaza below, a heated exchange of disciplined automatic fire and crazed single shots.

"Keep your head down," Nick whispered as they reached the shiny fire escape. One by one, they climbed down the ladder and dropped into the alley.

"We're almost there." Nick took Raina's hand and put it in Marty's hand, then gestured for everyone to follow him down the alley. They crept away from the yelling and shooting inside the plaza, toward the quiet of Staniford Street. Nick squatted behind a dumpster at the end of the alley and nodded back at Brian. "We're home free."

He started forward—a humvee screeched to a stop ten yards away —soldiers jumped out. They positioned behind the humvee, their backs to Nick, and aimed out onto the road. An Army supply truck rolled up —soldiers leapt out and started unloading wooden crowd-control barriers.

Nick watched as two more trucks and a half-dozen humvees rolled in. "No no no, they're securing the plaza. They're going to seal us in." He waved for everyone to fall back.

Keeping low, he rushed halfway back down the alley to a side staff entrance to CVS. The steel door was ajar, jammed with empty cardboard boxes. Nick eased it open and peeked inside. To the right, the pharmacy in back was wrecked—smashed shelves, scattered bottles, bullet-riddled walls, dead pharmacists. To the left, looters crawled the aisles and huddled behind displays, exchanging gunfire through the blown-out front window.

Nick backed out and turned to the group. "We're not getting out that way."

He looked toward the plaza parking lot as two more humvees and a humvee ambulance skidded to a stop ten yards from the alley—soldiers spilled into the fray.

They were trapped.

Nick squeezed his eyes shut and rubbed his temples.

"Come on, Nick. Wake up." Marty tugged his shirt. "What do we do?"

"What's the play here, Nick?" Brian said.

Nick took a deep breath and started to run through the options.

Both ends of the alley are blocked. CVS is a firefight. We could go back to the roof, try and—

Marty Jr.'s shrill bark pierced Nick's focus—his eyes shot open. "Shut that goddamn dog up."

Marty and Brian were staring into the plaza in disbelief. Raina was crawling on all fours into the parking lot, her blue sequin dress sparkling in the morning light.

"Oh my god." Nick scrambled to the end of the alley.

Brian and Marty followed.

They called her back as firmly as they could while keeping a whisper.

She kept crawling, eyes locked on the humvee ambulance just ahead. Somehow she reached it without being spotted and crawled up the open back, disappearing inside.

The dog shot out of Marty's grasp and raced to the ambulance, leaping and yapping at the back.

"What the hell is she doing?" Marty said.

Raina appeared in the back of the ambulance and held up a gallon-sized pill bottle. She pulled down her mask, revealing a big smile, and popped two pills in her mouth, then scooped up Marty Jr. and pushed a pill down his throat. She closed her eyes, and a blissful calm swept across her face.

"Come back!" Nick whispered as he looked both ways. "Come now, you can make it."

She scooted to the end of the ambulance, dog in one hand, bottle in the other. As her feet touched the ground, the front window of the dry cleaners blew out, and a gang of twenty infected vagrants spilled toward her like a horde of hungry zombies. Terror filled her eyes, and she scrambled back into the ambulance.

Marty grabbed Brian's jacket. "Go get her. And bring back the pills." He started pushing Brian toward the plaza. "Do your job! That's an order!"

"Do *not* go in there." Nick yanked Marty's hand off Brian. "She can still make it back." He turned to the plaza. "Raina, run back. Come right now."

She shook her head and clutched the pill bottle, frozen in fear.

As the infected horde closed in, soldiers repositioned to protect their ambulance. They opened fire on the vagrants, sending them scrambling.

"Raina!" Nick beckoned between gunfire. "Leave the pills and—"

Marty rushed past him into the plaza.

"Marty, no!" Nick grabbed and missed.

Marty leapt into the ambulance, pulled down his mask, and popped two pills. He grabbed Raina's hand and they stepped out.

A gang of looters inside the clinic opened fire on the soldier's flank, drawing them away from the ambulance.

The dry-cleaner vagrants re-emerged and rushed the ambulance.

Marty and Raina scrambled back up and pulled the doors shut. Two old vagrants with wild eyes and oozing hands ripped the doors open and climbed inside. The open bottle came tumbling through the air and landed on the asphalt, spraying pills everywhere. The vagrants descended like chickens attacking fresh feed.

Nick pulled himself away from the scene. It was time to make a hard choice, before there were no choices left. He scanned his surroundings in silent slow-motion.

In the plaza, soldiers mowed down the sick. Looters fired recklessly, some trying to get in, others trying to get out.

On Staniford Street, outnumbered soldiers tried to disperse a gathering crowd.

In the ambulance, Marty and Raina, blood-smudged and frantic, waved for help.

By his side, Brian squatted like a sprinter on starting blocks, gripping his pistol, picking his moment to charge into the fray.

And then it hit: burning gas and melting rubber. Nick closed his eyes and took a deep breath.

The plaza interior is a death trap. If we can find a way through the perimeter, we'll be free in sixty seconds. But how?

Bluff our way out?

As National Guard soldiers? Too complex, too risky.

As looters? Or infected? That's a sure way to get shot.

As law-abiding citizens trapped inside? Might work. Also might get us shot.

Sneak past the perimeter undetected? That's the only way. But we have to move fast—in thirty minutes they'll have this place locked down.

So how do we sneak out, right now, past fifty yards of soldiers and scratchers and looters, without being seen?

An idea clicked into place.

Nick's eyes shot open—Brian was advancing into the plaza. Nick grabbed his jacket and pulled back hard. "One more step and you'll never see your family again."

Brian turned with shock.

"I can get us out," Nick said, "but you have to trust me, and we have to move now."

Brian turned back to the ambulance. "I'm going in."

Nick grabbed his jacket. "We need to leave them—they're exposed. If you go in there, you can't go back to your family, you can't go to New Zealand."

Brian swiveled and got in Nick's face. "This is the mission, Nick! You don't choose the mission, you get it done. If I don't go in there I lose my payday, I lose my flight, I lose my honor."

Nick stared back. "Brian, if you go in there, you're going to lose a lot more than that. Who's going to take care of your family when you're gone? Not the company. Not the government. Me? Herman? T.J.? They need you."

Brian turned back, white-knuckling his pistol.

"You're a warrior." Nick put a hand on his shoulder. "Your honor, your loyalty—they're beyond question. But these people…they will get you killed, and they won't even notice. Trust me, I know. How about loyalty to your family? How about loyalty to the people who deserve it most?"

Brian spun around, his face tortured. "Get us out of here."

* * *

NICK RAN Brian through the plan in twenty seconds. Brian looked skeptical.

"Just follow me." Nick rushed back down the alley to the side door of CVS and peeked inside. Soldiers had taken out most of the looters, but a half-dozen holdouts still snuck through the aisles, firing bursts into the plaza.

"Stay low." Nick crawled inside, toward the destroyed pharmacy, Brian right behind. They got behind the pharmacy counter, and Nick pulled a cardboard box off a shelf.

"Fill it with pill bottles," he whispered, and snatched a bottle off the floor. "Like this—small or medium size, amber plastic bottle, white top."

They scrambled around the pharmacy on all fours, wincing at every gunshot, until the box was filled. Nick gave a satisfied nod. "Let's go."

They crawled back to the side door, Brian leading the way, Nick pushing the box across the floor. As Nick reached the door, his eyes fell on a dead pharmacist sitting in a nearby aisle. He crept over, pulled off the man's white coat, and placed it in the box. He glanced up at the shelves and spotted stethoscopes on sale. He placed one in the box.

Nick crawled back into the alley and squatted next to Brian. "We won't have much time, so be ready to run."

"Is this gonna work?"

Nick wavered. "It's the best chance we've got, so…just be ready."

He started up the fire escape to the CVS roof. The ladder was old and rusted, and he was unsteady with the box hanging from one hand. He crept across the roof to the far corner, peeked over the wall, and surveyed the exterior of the plaza: The army had set up a wide perimeter around the entire plaza, a ring of wooden barricades with humvees and soldiers positioned inside. People were gathering at the barricades—some sick, some healthy, some armed. Soldiers were ordering them to disburse. Directly off Nick's corner of the roof, a restless crowd of fifty scratchers paced and swayed at the barricade like caged animals.

Nick sat with his back against the wall, removed his mask, and stuffed it in his pocket. He pulled on the white pharmacy coat and draped the stethoscope around his neck.

"Alright…here we go." He took a deep breath.

Nick popped up facing the perimeter and waved his hands.

The scratchers pointed and smiled and waved back.

He lifted the box above his head and yelled as loud as he could. "The last penicillin! Save yourself!" He poured the box over the side. A waterfall of pill bottles clattered on the concrete below, spraying pills and rolling around the sidewalk.

There was a strange, silent pause that felt like an eternity. The sick and the soldiers stared up in confusion. Nick held his breath and waited for the reaction.

A bone-thin woman in a tank top leapt over the barricade and sprinted for the pills. Two men followed, and the rest flipped the barricade and flooded in.

Nick turned and sprinted across the roof in a low run.

Gunfire erupted below, and the corner of the roof disintegrated. He raced down the fire escape, dropped into the alley, pulled off his coat and stethoscope, and secured his mask.

"Brian!" he whispered and scanned the alley. "Brian!"

Brian was gone.

"Goddammit."

Nick ran to the Staniford end of the alley and squatted behind the dumpster. Soldiers sprinted past. A burst of undisciplined gunfire rang out and was answered by a roar of automatic fire.

"Secure that breach! Now!" More soldiers streaked past.

Nick crawled to the end of the alley and peeked both ways. Everyone was focused on the breach. The barrier was fifty yards away. The path was clear. This was it.

Nick sprinted from the alley and ducked behind an empty humvee. He positioned to run for the barricade, but a pack of armed looters rushed up and flipped it. Soldiers engaged, driving them back. Now he'd have to move up the line of humvees until he found another stretch of open barricade.

Nick eyed the next humvee up the line—all clear.

He scrambled and crouched behind it.

He checked the next humvee—all clear.

He sprinted ahead.

A huge green blur blindsided him, sending him crashing into the humvee. Nick got to his hands and knees, shook away the stars, and stood up. Two enormous soldiers grabbed him and threw him back against the humvee. He slid to the ground, hands raised.

"This is the guy, sir. He threw the pills. I saw it."

Captain Kravich marched up between the soldiers and sized up Nick. "You a real doctor?"

Kravich didn't recognize him. Thank god they were all wearing masks.

Nick cowered and disguised his voice. "I'm a doctor. Just trying to help, sir."

Kravich squinted. "Take off your mask."

"I can't…I'm sick."

The soldiers took a big step back. Kravich drew his sidearm. "Take off your mask, or I'll put you out of your misery."

Nick held his breath and quickly pulled down and replaced his mask.

Kravich's eyes went wide. "*You.*"

"Now hold on—"

Kravich raised his pistol and stepped forward. "I got chewed out by the governor in front of my entire company. I've been a soldier for twenty-six years, and that was the most fucked-up, humiliating, ass-backwards moment of my entire career."

"I'm sorry." Nick raised his hands. "I didn't think Ray would—"

"Yeah? Well he did, asshole." Kravich cocked the pistol.

"Sir?" One of the soldiers looked around nervously.

"What?" Kravich said. "He's sick and he interfered with a state of emergency—*twice*. You know the orders."

Kravich looked both ways and steadied his aim. "Welcome to the losing end."

Nick winced and waited for the shot.

A blur rammed Kravich from behind, sending him tumbling head-first into the humvee. Brian grabbed a stunned soldier by the lapels and body slammed him into unconsciousness. The other soldier charged, and Brian booted him square in the chest, crumpling him into a wheezing ball.

Nick gazed up at the mighty warrior.

Brian extended a hand. "Come on."

They scrambled to the next humvee. More soldiers sprinted past. Brian squeezed Nick's shoulder. "Wait…wait…go!"

They rushed behind the next humvee and eyed an open stretch of barricade.

"This is it, here we go." Brian positioned for a sprint.

Two soldiers jogged over and took up guard at the barricade.

"Shit!" Nick whispered. He looked at Brian and they both nodded, each man intuitively knowing the plan. Brian crept away and Nick stood up, hands held high, and walked toward the soldiers.

"Captain Kravich!" Nick yelled.

They spun and raised their weapons.

"Captain Kravich, he's down, right back there." Nick pointed. "He needs help. He said to get you."

They looked at each other.

Brian stepped out from behind a supply truck, pistol leveled at the side of their heads. "Guns down, boys. Nice and easy."

They placed their guns on the ground and raised their hands.

Nick and Brian ducked under the barricade and started backing down the street, away from the plaza.

"Close your eyes and count to thirty, boys." Brian locked his gun on them as he backed away. "Open them early, and I'll be standing there. I promise."

Nick and Brian turned and sprinted toward the harbor.

* * *

THEY REVERSED AWAY from the dock into the misty Charles River. Nick stripped off his gloves and mask and took a deep breath of crisp, clean ocean air.

Brian shifted into drive and did the same.

They cruised toward the open ocean, gazing back at the city. Gunfire crackled in the distance, columns of smoke snaked into the sky, Army helicopters converged from all sides.

"Well, I hope you've got a good plan," Brian said, "because we're all-in now."

THIRTY-SEVEN

"Sure you don't want me to drive? Grab an hour of sleep?" Nick said as Brian started the Ark in the yacht club parking lot. Nick had slept an hour on the boat ride back and was feeling refreshed. Brian looked tired and worn.

"Nah, I'm good. Sleep deprivation is part of the job. Honestly, I don't even feel it anymore. Plus, I can't sleep until we've got a plan."

They pulled onto the main road and headed for the highway. Brian sighed. "Alright, should we do it? Call the operator? Get it over with?"

"We're not gonna call."

"Wait…what?"

"If we call, they'll either terminate your contract or assign a new client—bad outcome either way. As for me, well, I'm never getting off that list. We're on our own."

"No client, no plane, no food, no shelter, no money." Brian scoffed. "Goddamn right we're on our own."

"Well, I've got an idea. It's risky, but if we can pull it off, it solves all our problems."

"Oh god…I'm already afraid." Brian took the highway on-ramp and accelerated. "Well, I'm listening."

Nick took a deep breath. "OK, we need a mid-size plane for seven to nine passengers, right? The likelihood of finding one lying around here is low. Sure, we might be able to secure something out of state, but with roads and railways closed we couldn't reach it."

"Mm-hmm."

"Now, what if we took a boat to New Zealand? If we left from the west coast, say Los Angeles, it's a twenty-day trip to Queenstown. But we have the same problem—how do we drive cross-country when we can't even cross the Massachusetts border? There are plenty of boats here, but it would take weeks to sail from the Atlantic to the Pacific. Under normal circumstances, we could use the Panama Canal, but who knows whether it's still open. The Magellan Route around South America is way too far, the Northwest Passage is impossible, never mind the fact we don't have enough supplies to last three days, never mind three to six weeks."

"All I'm hearing are dead ends."

"That's exactly my point—it has to be a local plane. That's the only way to avoid high-risk travel and get there fast enough to outlast our supplies. And the thing is, we already have the perfect plane, fueled and ready to leave in five hours. So our highest-probability path is to take our current flight."

"Umm, am I missing something, or didn't we just ditch our boarding pass in zombieland?"

"Right, that's the catch, we need the client to fly…so we bluff."

"Bluff?"

"Hear me out—Marty's the client, and airport security won't let us board without him, but they don't know what he looks like. So what if we sub in T.J. instead?"

"Yeah, but security has to ID the client. They do it for all my flights."

"Right, no one can board until the client validates with their passcode and photo ID. And that's the bluff. We dress T.J. up like he's an injured Marty—unconscious, bloody, face all bandaged up—he can't give the passcode. And I'm sure there's a license or passport somewhere in Marty's bags. So I play the planner and flash his ID, you play the pilot and say he was injured by looters, Dana plays the private doctor and rushes him through."

Brian looked skeptical as he passed a station wagon with a mountain of bags strapped to the roof.

"Look, I'm not saying it's a great plan," Nick said. "I mean, fifty-fifty chance it works. But those are far better odds than anything else. If we get caught, we don't get arrested or shot, they just kick us out and report us to the company. No worse off than we are now. So, what've we got to lose?"

"And what if the real Marty calls the operator before we arrive?"

"It's a risk." Nick nodded. "But assuming he's still alive and not in an Army detention center, he's stuck in Boston without working phone lines. I'm betting he can't call."

Brian chewed on the plan for a long moment. "Well, assuming the bluff works, and we make it to New Zealand, then what?"

"Once we reach New Zealand, it's smooth sailing. We fly into a private airport, hop in a luxury caravan, and take a scenic thirty-minute drive to Lake Wantabo. Swipe my key at the gate, punch the code, and enjoy the summer."

"So, my family…we can still stay there? Even though I lost our flight?"

Nick looked at Brian. "I meant what I said. You can stay as long as you like."

Brian gave a humble, grateful nod. He looked relieved, but also defeated.

"Brian, this is going to work. We can make it work."

Brian forced a smile. "Yeah, no, I'm sure you're right…we'll make it work." He changed lanes to make way for a speeding RV with dealer plates and a tarp across the back window.

Nick shifted in his seat so he could look at Brian. "You did the right thing back there, leaving them behind. You gotta put yourself first."

Brian gave a weary chuckle. "The old me…the Hell Frog…he'd kick my ass." He patted the "NO MAN LEFT BEHIND" tattoo above his heart. "But who knows…maybe he was a fool."

"Sounds like he was a warrior. The Captain Cairo mission…that made a real difference, saved a lot of lives."

"Yeah, maybe. You know, I used to believe in the mission—we thought we were saving the world from the bad guys. And if we did a good job—and we did a *damn* good job—we'd be taken care of back home. But it was a lie…no job, no money, busted knee, bad sleep, shitty healthcare…what was I supposed to do?

"So I became an escape pilot. Yeah, I needed the money, but it was more than that. It gave me a purpose, a mission…it made me feel like a Hell Frog again. And I told myself, 'If you're loyal to the company, if you do a good job, they'll take care of you and your family.'

"I started strong, but the missions, the clients…they kept getting harder, riskier, meaner, and I just felt too old, too slow." He shrugged and ran a hand over his hair. "I don't know, man, maybe it's me. Maybe I just lost heart."

"It's not you," Nick said. "At the end of the contract they put you on the hardest missions and clients, hoping you'll fail so they won't have to pay you out."

Brian chuckled and shook his head. "Goddamn."

"Yeah, it's a con…all of it. The military, the company, the clients…it's all one big empty promise."

Brian shifted in his seat, agitated. "Yeah, well, shit…*now* I see that, a day late and a dollar short. I put my family through this miserable life for ten years—shitty pay, shitty healthcare, no benefits, tied to a phone, deployed with no notice—and for what? What good came of that, Nick? I spent ten years rescuing rich assholes, and when the shit hit the fan, they dumped us in a rotting cabin—broke, scared, hungry, praying for a payday that was never gonna come."

Nick nodded and looked at his feet, feeling guilty for his part.

"You know, when you have kids, you try to look strong, powerful, so they always feel safe, so they stay happy and innocent as long as possible and don't worry about…all this shit. Do you know what it's like to watch your little girl work two jobs to put food on your table? Or spend her weekend sorting overdue bills? Or grocery shop because you can't leave the house for an hour?" He shook his head. "It's a disgrace, Nick."

Brian stared ahead, his jaw tight. Then he took a deep breath, and his face softened into a nostalgic daze. "You know, when she was a little girl, Zo had this bring-your-dad-to-school day. She introduced me to the class and told them, completely serious, that I was Superman." He grinned. "Well, apparently that caused quite a stir around the first grade. So the next day, Ms. Crumley—god, she was there when I was a kid—well, she sat the class down, all serious, and explained how Superman is a comic book character, he's not real, and Zoe's dad is *not* Superman. The other kids teased Zoe, but she stuck to her guns, wouldn't back down.

"Well, a week later, she made me dress up as Superman for Halloween, and her teacher lived one road over. We knock on the door, and I hear the old lady wailing inside." Brian fought back a smile. "So I rush inside, and the house is filled with smoke, and Crusty Crumley's there on the kitchen floor, crying and coughing and throwing a fit." He started to crack up. "She'd fallen asleep, and her Halloween muffins caught fire. She says she's too dizzy to walk, so I carry her out, and there, standing on the sidewalk, is half her first grade class, eyes wide, mouths open, watching in total disbelief as Superman carries Ms. Crumley out of a burning building."

Brian slapped his knee and laughed. "Zoe was standing right in front, arms crossed, proud as can be. The stare she gave old lady Crumley…man, Nick, if a six-year-old could say 'Told you so, bitch!' with a look, well, she did it."

Brian belly-laughed so hard his eyes teared up. Nick laughed too, not so much at the story, but at watching Brian.

"Oh, man." Brian's laugh faded to a nostalgic smile. "Sweet girl, I think she really believed it…you know? I'm glad she got her moment." He dabbed an eye and his smile faded. "They grow up so fast, Nick. And now…well, now all she sees is a broken old soldier who can't protect his family."

"No way." Nick shook his head. "The way she looks at you…she still sees a warrior, believe me. Maybe it's a different battle, but she sees you fighting."

Brian shook his head. "Nah…the warrior's gone, Nick. I left him in Egypt. And whatever was left died a slow, painful death over the last decade. What kind of warrior abandons his client in battle? Bails on a mission to save himself? Bluffs his fellow soldiers? Steals a plane from his employer? We had a name for that guy, and it sure as hell wasn't 'warrior.'"

Nick gazed out the window. "Yeah, well, I guess I look at it differently."

"Oh yeah? How's that?"

Nick turned to Brian. "They've been running you since the day you were born—but now, for the first time, you're fighting back."

THIRTY-EIGHT

Abby rotated her DNA double-helix on the electron microscope's big screen. No matter how many times she did the DNA self-analysis experiment, she always got a thrill from studying her own genes close up.

She peeked over the top of the monitor and spied on Old Glory in the corner. He was hunched on a lab stool reading a thick biography of Robert E. Lee. Thank god Kurt assigned him instead of heavy-breathing Ron or creepy Blitzkrieg. Even though Old Glory was the least-bad option, he was still an annoyance, an offensive pest in her beloved lab. Every time he read something interesting, he gave a little "huh" grunt, breaking her concentration. And every time he flipped a page, his cluster of unearned medals clinked. At least his farting was far away.

"You done yet?" he called without looking up. "I'm getting hungry."

"Almost done, Lieutenant Dobbins," Abby said in a sing-song voice. "Just cleaning up."

Let's do this.

She moved to the back sink and placed a glass beaker by the drain.

First she poured a base of 300 ml of water.

Then added her adhesive agent, 100 ml of petroleum jelly.

A splash of alcohol for solubility.

And finally, her contamination agent: 200 ml of pure sodium hypochlorite…a.k.a. bleach.

She mixed her proprietary concoction with a glass stirring rod, and it swirled into its final form: bleach jelly.

She glanced back at Old Glory. A grunt, then clinking medals. All clear.

Using a pair of stainless-steel tongs, she submerged a fresh sponge in the beaker, soaking up the thick liquid. She raised the sponge and drained the excess back into the beaker, the viscous stream reminding her of Elmer's glue, except yellow…and toxic. When the stream stopped, she lowered the sponge into a plastic Ziploc bag, sealed it, and slipped it into her sweatpants pocket.

She turned and chirped, "Lunchtime!"

* * *

ABBY STOOD in the middle of the crowded cafeteria holding a tray of scrambled eggs, surveying the scene. In the back, two tables of medical staff watched an animated Dr. Teddy deliver a grand story. In the front, ten tables of Matchstick Militia soldiers chowed and hollered like frat boys. In the middle, the Mothers of Mankind dined and giggled.

"I'm going to eat." Old Glory appeared next to her, salivating over a ham and cheese sandwich. "Come get me when you're done." He walked off.

Abby made her way to an empty table in the Mothers section and put down her tray.

Alright, this is it. Now or never.

She strode to the ice cream sundae bar, grabbed a bowl, and stared down at three big tubs of local, grass-fed, organic ice cream: vanilla, chocolate, strawberry.

Perfect.

She slipped a hand in her pocket, wiggled a finger through one end of the bag's zipper, and dragged across, unsealing the bag. She slid her hand inside and squeezed the sponge. Bleach jelly oozed through her fingers.

OK, let's do this.

She hesitated, eyes jumping around the crowded cafeteria.

Come on, do it now.

There were so many people: the Mothers, the Militia, Dr. Teddy, doctors, nurses, cafeteria staff, janitors…so many people.

Am I really doing this?

What if they catch me? Dr. Teddy will kill me…I mean, he might literally kill me.

What if Nick and Dana left already? What if they forgot—

A loud clap by her head snapped Abby back to the ice cream bar. "Hey! Let's go, Crabby," Kurt said, "you're already big as a house, might as well get all three."

The soldiers behind him burst out laughing. Kurt basked in his clever joke.

Yeah, I'm doing this.

Abby drew a gooey hand from her pocket and picked up the first ice cream scoop. The handle was cold, wet, and sticky—perfect. She dropped a big scoop of vanilla into her bowl, stepped down the bar, took a big scoop of chocolate, stepped down, and finished with a scoop of strawberry. She smirked at Kurt and walked away.

She stuffed the Ziploc bag into a trash can and returned to her empty table. She examined her hand—it was starting to tingle, with pink splotches spreading across the palm and between her fingers. She wet a napkin and wiped it clean.

Abby savored every bite of her ice cream as she watched Mothers, Militia, doctors, and nurses file across the sundae bar. By the time she finished, the bar was empty. She leaned back and peeked at the Mothers seated behind her.

"What are we doing after this?" Lucy asked.

"I don't know about you girls, but I'm needed in the spa all afternoon." Gabrielle giggled and flipped her hair back. "Prenatal massage, reflexology, Reiki, and, of course, finish with a facial." She stuffed a spoonful of ice cream in her mouth.

"Oh my god, Gabrielle, you literally take advantage." Kathleen rolled her eyes.

"What?" Gabrielle mocked innocence. "You heard Dr. T. We have one job—rest, relax, and prepare for our big day. I'm just doing my part. Besides—"

Lucy's spoon clattered across the table.

"What the hell?" Lucy stared down at her pink-spotted palm.

Taryn gave a little shriek and spun her hand. "I have it too."

Gabrielle slowly turned her hands over and gasped at her swollen red-speckled palm. "Oh my god. Oh my god. Oh my god."

And...go.

Abby spun around, fear in her eyes. "Oh my god, Gabrielle, it's on me too." She held up her burning hand. "You don't think...it couldn't be..." She lowered her voice. "Scratch 'n Sniff?"

Gabrielle's eyes went wide and she shoved away from the table, spraying her tray and tipping her chair over with a loud crack. "It's on me! Get it off! Get it off!" She reeled backward, brushing her hands down her sweatshirt.

The other Mothers scattered away from the table, spilling trays across the tile floor.

Dr. Teddy shot up in the back, eyes locked, face grave and intense.

Abby stood and watched the other end of the cafeteria—spooked soldiers were backing toward the door.

"Oh my god...look," Abby whispered, "they're going to lock us in."

Gabrielle launched toward the door and slipped on an overturned tray, crashing to her hands and knees. Abby helped her up as a mob of panicked Mothers started a rush toward the door.

Dr. Teddy was suddenly among them, waving and barking orders. "Stop stop stop! Everyone bury your mouth in your elbow and go directly outside to the courtyard. Slowly and carefully. Do *not* rush." He marched ahead and waved off a cluster of soldiers by the door. "Out of the way. Clear a path for the girls."

The soldiers hesitated.

"Now!" he roared.

Kurt gave the order and the soldiers moved aside.

Dr. Teddy held the door, and a single-file line of thirty-three pregnant teens with faces buried in their elbows streamed silently out of the cafeteria.

* * *

"MOTHERS LINE UP to my left, everyone else on the right," Dr. Teddy said.

A steady stream of soldiers flowed from the cafeteria into the long courtyard. Most were so busy examining their hands that they missed Dr. Teddy's orders and milled around the Mothers.

"General. General!" Dr. Teddy clapped at Kurt. "Control your men. Everyone away from the Mothers."

Kurt gave a half-annoyed look. "Alright, boys, everyone on this side." He beckoned with a napkin-wrapped hand. "Come on. Let's go."

They were too preoccupied to follow his order, and Dr. Teddy began shooing them away one by one.

Now. Go now.

Abby turned and threaded through the crowd of incoming soldiers. They brushed and bumped her as she fought to a side entrance to the courtyard. She reached the door and grabbed the handle.

A wrinkly hand shot out and grasped her wrist.

"There you are." Old Glory shivered and frowned. "Where are you going?"

"I'm…I'm getting jackets."

"No, I don't think so. Let's go line up with the other girls." He pulled at her wrist.

She gripped the handle. "Dr. Teddy asked me to go get jackets. He's extremely upset."

"Well, let's just go see about—"

Dr. Teddy erupted at a confused soldier, berating him to the other side of the courtyard, away from the Mothers.

Old Glory cast a nervous glance over his shoulder.

Abby leaned in. "You wanna explain to him why there are no

jackets when one of the girls collapses from hypothermic cardiac arrhythmia?"

He blinked as if she'd spoken another language. "Alrighty then, but I'm coming with you."

She stared at him. "OK, but don't get too close, I think I'm infected." She released the handle and spun her hand so her flaming, blistered palm was an inch from his grasp.

"Oh good heavens!" He shoved her hand away and stumbled back. "I think…I think I hear the General giving orders." He slowly backed away, eyes locked on her hand. "I better…why don't you…"

She cracked the door and gave him an impatient look.

He looked up. "Come right back."

"I'll be right back."

Abby slipped inside, eased the door shut, and sprinted down the empty hall.

THIRTY-NINE

MONROE HUDDLED at the end of the courtyard with his top medical team—six nurses and three doctors.

"OK, just to confirm, none of you are experiencing any symptoms?" he asked. They confirmed. "Alright, put on your gloves."

Monroe pulled on his surgical gloves and addressed his head nurse. "Nurse Vargas, we'll need some things from the clinic. First, PPE for the medical staff: N95 masks, gloves, isolation gowns, face shields, safety goggles. Then we're going to take vitals and clear every single mother, one by one, which means stethoscopes, pulse oximeters, blood pressure cuffs, and thermometers. Until we know differently, we're going to treat this as a BSL-3 infectious agent."

"Yes, Doctor." Vargas spun from the huddle and beckoned to a group of young nurses.

"Everyone ready?" Monroe asked. They confirmed.

Monroe turned and addressed the line of Mothers like a headmaster. "Ladies, I want you to spread the line out lengthwise, putting as much distance as possible between you and the girl on either side. Stretch all the way across the courtyard—yes, perfect."

Matchstick soldiers, medical staff, and facilities workers watched from the opposite side of the courtyard.

"Now, I'm going to come down and examine each of you, one by one. This may take some time, so please be patient. I promise I will get you inside, out of the cold, as quickly and safely as possible."

He stepped to the first girl in line, who was shivering in sweatpants and a tank top, her hands stiff at her side. His medical team scurried into place behind him.

"Lucy, my dear," he said with a gentle tone and a warm smile, "can you tell me what you're feeling right now?"

"Umm, just tingling on my hand, like a burning."

"I'm sorry to hear that. May I examine your hand?"

She extended her arm.

He gently cupped her upturned hand and leaned in close. "Localized irritation and inflammation on the palm of the right hand, but not on the back of the hand." He dictated in a flat, authoritative tone as his doctors tapped their tablets. "Presents like a rash or a burn that's affected the epidermis layer, but no deeper. The stratum lucidum appears to have protected the dermis layer."

He looked up at Lucy and returned to his gentle voice. "Are you experiencing any other symptoms?"

"No, just my hand."

He gave her a sympathetic nod and released her hand. "Thank you, Lucy. I'll work to address your discomfort as quickly as possible. I promise."

"Thank you, Dr. Teddy."

"Nurse Wagstaff here is going to record all your activities over the last hour. Please don't omit anything, OK?"

"Yes, Doctor."

"And if you need anything, please don't hesitate to call me." He stripped off his gloves and dropped them into a plastic bag held out by a nurse. He took a new pair presented by another nurse and pulled them on.

Monroe and his team stepped to the next girl in line. He gave a warm, admiring smile. "Aaliyah, hurt and freezing the day before your big Genetics final and you *still* have a smile on your face. You inspire me. Tell me, what symptoms are you experiencing?"

"My symptoms are the same as Lucy, Doctor."

Monroe cradled her hand and leaned in. "No accompanying symptoms?"

"No, Doctor. Otherwise, normal."

"Same presentation as Lucy," Monroe dictated, "except on the left hand instead of the right."

"Aaliyah, are you experiencing any itching?"

"No, just a light burning."

"And are you left-handed?"

"Yes."

He leaned back toward Lucy. "Lucy, are you right-handed or left-handed?"

"Right-handed."

Monroe took two big steps back and addressed the line of Mothers. "Is there anyone who has a rash on their non-dominant hand? For example, if you're right-handed, a rash on your left hand, and vice versa? Anyone?"

Silence.

Monroe nodded and stepped back to Aaliyah. "Nurse Wagstaff is going to record all your activities over the last hour. Please don't omit anything, OK?"

"Of course, Doctor."

"And if you need anything, just holler." He winked and smiled.

She grinned. "You know I will."

Monroe stripped off his gloves and pulled on a new pair. He stepped away from the line and huddled with his medical team.

"Let's review. To state the obvious, we're all vaccinated." He spoke in a hushed tone, like a quarterback drawing up a play. "Is a break-through infection possible? Theoretically, no. But let's assume it happened anyway, due to mutation or direct ingestion. Even then, the probability of everyone becoming symptomatic within the same ten-minute window is near zero. And why no pruritus of the palms? Only burning? Why irritation only on the dominant hand? And why no accompanying respiratory symptoms?" Monroe shook his head. "This isn't the virus. There's something else going on here."

The other doctors tapped notes and murmured support.

Monroe nodded. "Let's proceed."

The huddle broke and Monroe approached the next girl in line. "Chen, thank you for your patience, my friend. How are you feeling?"

"Same as Aaliyah. My hand burns, but otherwise OK." She presented her shivering hand for inspection.

Monroe leaned in. "Rash on the right hand only. Same presentation as Lucy and Aaliyah." He leaned closer and squinted for a long pause. "It looks like exposure to some kind of external irritant, almost like a chemical burn. Look, I can see the area of contact here." He pointed with a gloved pinky and traced around the red-raised sections of her palm. "It's definitely not from scratching."

He straightened. "Thank you for your trust and patience, Chen. You must be so uncomfortably cold. I'm going to get you warmed up as fast as possible, I promise." He stripped off his gloves and pulled on a new pair. "In the meantime, Nurse Wagstaff is going to record all your activities over the last hour. Please don't—"

"Dr. T!" A panicked shriek shattered the quiet and echoed through the courtyard. "It's on my face! It's spreading! Oh my god help!"

Monroe sprinted up the line, his team scrambling behind him. He skidded to a stop face to face with Gabrielle and gently guided her flailing hands to her side.

"It's alright, Gabrielle, I'm here," he said softly. He leaned in close, walking his gloved fingers across the left side of her face inch by inch. "I'm seeing fresh irritation on the left lower cheek and left temple. Gabrielle, is it possible that you touched your face? Perhaps your hair?"

"I don't know…" her voice trembled, "maybe…I don't know."

He carefully pushed her hair off her left shoulder, exposing her bare neck. His eyes widened and he zoomed in on a partial red handprint. "Oh my, here we are. We've got a secondary contact site on the left neck and shoulder," he dictated. "I can see an impression from the palm and fingers of the right hand."

"Dr. Teddy, please…" She sobbed. "I don't want to die."

Monroe leaned back, looked deep into her eyes, and spoke with the confidence of the world's best doctor. "Gabrielle, my dear, listen to me. You are completely safe here. I won't let anything happen to you—you know that, right? I'm going to get you cleaned up and warmed up very shortly, and you're going to be absolutely fine. OK?"

She nodded, her face relieved.

"Nurse Nguyen?" he said over his shoulder. "Could you stay and monitor Gabrielle? If her condition worsens in any way whatsoever, call me *immediately*."

He raised his eyebrows and spoke in his gentlest tone. "Would that be OK, Gabrielle?"

"Yes." She sniffled and smiled. "Thank you, Dr. Teddy."

"And when this is done, I'm ordering extra spa time for you." He winked and smiled.

She laughed and nodded.

He gave a loving smile, then spun into his medical huddle and whispered, "This isn't the virus. This is a chemical contact dermatitis. I'm sure of it."

He stripped off his gloves with purpose. "Nurse Greenwood, get buckets of warm water, soap, and washcloths from the linen closet. Gather burn cream, gauze, bandages, tape, and scissors from the medical supply room. We're going to treat this as a mass exposure to an unknown toxic agent and follow emergency decontamination protocol for hazardous chemical irritants. Once we're clean, we'll treat the palm burns as needed. The girls and medical staff first, then everyone else. Agreed?"

"Yes, Doctor," they said in a chorus.

Monroe marched through the huddle to two soldiers laughing and shoving on the other side of the courtyard. "You there—yes, you and you. Are your hands OK?"

They stiffened and nodded.

"Go to the infirmary and get enough clean towels and hospital gowns for everyone here."

They hesitated and looked at Hunziker.

"Now!" Monroe clapped in their faces.

They sprinted toward the exit.

He turned to two more soldiers. "Your hands OK? Good. Go to the armory and get enough clean uniforms for everyone in the militia. Hurry back."

They marched toward the exit.

Monroe backed to the end of the courtyard and waved a hand. "Could I have your attention please?" He waited as everyone hushed. "Thank you. Everyone keep your hands by your side. Do not touch anything or anywhere on your body." He straightened and spoke in a calm, firm voice. "I believe we've been exposed to a chemical irritant. I've consulted with my medical team and I want to assure you—we are confident this is *not* the virus. Put simply, some of us touched something that had a nasty chemical on it. I expect we're all going to be completely fine, but we're going to proceed with extreme caution until we know exactly what it was and where it came from. So, for now, we're going to assume the worst: that this is a hazardous agent, perhaps even a premeditated chemical attack."

Gasps and murmurs from the crowd.

Monroe quieted them. "In a few minutes, we're going to get cozy here. We're all going to remove and discard our clothes because they're contaminated. I want you to pull them down and away. Do *not* pull them over your head because you risk spreading the chemical to your eyes, nose, and mouth. If you're wearing something that can't be pulled down, we're going to cut it off and pull it away from your body. Then we're going to decontaminate, get dressed, and treat your burns."

Snow began to fall, light flakes drifting down and dusting the courtyard. He looked up, smiled, and switched to a casual tone. "Look, guys, I know it's cold. I know it's scary. But if we work together, we'll all be safe and warm in under an hour. I promise." He clasped his hands and raised his eyebrows. "OK? Excellent. Thank you."

Monroe returned to his medical huddle. "OK, we're going to need cleaning stations. One at either end of—" His eyes locked on a nurse across the huddle. She was crying. "Nurse Jacobs, are you hurt?" He looked down at her hands.

"No, I'm fine, Dr. Teddy," she said between sniffles.

"It's going to be alright," he said gently. "Everything's going to be alright."

She wiped away tears with the back of her gloved hands. "It's not me, Doctor. I just don't understand. Why would anyone…who could… who could do this to the girls?"

His eyes softened, as if addressing a frightened child. "We're just being extra cautious, Nurse Jacobs. I'm sure this was just an accident. No one would…"

His mind stumbled on a thought, and his eyes drifted past her, beyond the huddle, and danced across the falling snow. His warm expression faded to concern. He turned and squinted down the line of shivering Mothers.

"Dr. Teddy?" Nurse Jacobs said.

Monroe took two giant steps back from the huddle and craned his neck to see the far end of the line. Unsatisfied, he jogged down the line, checking the girls' faces as he went.

When he reached the end, he spun, his face panicked, and raced back, scanning the crowd of soldiers like a frantic parent searching for a lost child—peering into gaps, bouncing on tiptoes, stalking through their ranks, craning around bodies, shoving men out of the way.

Hunziker approached, his face concerned. "Doc?"

Monroe backed out of the crowd, panicked and oblivious.

"Doc, what is it?" Hunziker followed, spooked.

Monroe turned and leapt onto a stone bench in the center of the courtyard and slowly rotated a full circle, his gaze jumping wildly around the perimeter.

"Doc! What the hell is it?" Hunziker scanned the perimeter for some unknown invader. "Wiretap! Blitzkrieg! On me!" They rushed to his side.

Monroe stepped down and slowly turned—fists trembling, face flushed, mouth twisted in a quivering snarl—he locked his raging eyes on Hunziker.

Hunziker moved a hand to his sidearm.

Monroe spoke in a low growl. "Where's Abby?"

FORTY

ABBY TORE THROUGH THE WOODS—SPRINTING with wide, labored steps, weaving around trees, stumbling over stones—one hand cradling her bouncing belly, the other blocking her face from whipping branches. Every few steps she felt them, a pack of rabid wolves closing in, and glanced back with terrified eyes.

She leapt over a log and landed on a turned ankle—staggering diagonally, pushing off a tree, careening back on course, regaining speed.

It was snowing harder now, big flakes rushing down with purpose. She'd taken this path a dozen times before—some for practice, some for real—and she knew it well.

Abby skidded to the edge of the shallow brook and took aim at the flat stone she always used to hop across. As she leapt, a stick cracked behind her and she whipped her head around. She landed off center, tilting the stone up on its edge, slipping off, crashing to her hands and knees on a bed of pebbles. She winced as pain screamed up her aching joints, then gasped as freezing water soaked her hands and legs.

Get up. GET UP.

She slowly rose to her feet in the middle of the brook and looked down. Her gray sweats were soaked from the knees and elbows down, and her muddy palms were scraped and bleeding. She wiped them down her pant legs, painting big streaks of dirt and blood.

Abby looked up the hill at the overgrown gravel road. It was a big loop that ran from the back of the medical complex, along the lake, to Cradle Cove, and back. Through trial and error, she'd found a shortcut through the woods that joined the road right before it met Cradle Cove.

You can't stop—they're right behind you. Keep moving.

She stepped out of the brook with a chilly huff and forced herself forward, back into a run. She scrambled and clawed up the embankment, burst out of the woods onto the road, and swung into an exhausted, uneven gait—head down, glancing back, racing toward the finish line.

Abby stomped onto Cradle Cove, rested her hands on her knees, and glanced from side to side. "I'm here!" she cried in a whisper, then cupped her hands to her mouth. "Guys! I'm here!"

Silent snow.

Standing there shivering, she wondered if she'd imagined Nick's whole plan.

A phone! He said they'd leave a phone.

Her eyes jumped around the road, searching for anything out of place.

"A phone…a phone…a phone."

Nothing.

She sprinted across the road, dropped to her knees, and crawled on all fours, combing through the long drift of frosty leaves that lined the side of the road.

"A phone, a phone, a phone," she repeated, the driving beat to her search.

Nothing.

She stumbled across the road, dropped to her knees, and combed along the other side.

Nothing.

"Phone phone phone…"

She staggered into the woods and searched behind a thorny bush, around a boulder, under a fallen tree.

"Phonephonephone..."

Nothing.

She flipped a sparkly, flat rock. Nothing.

She strained to lift an old tire and peeked underneath. Nothing.

She rolled a rotten log. Nothing.

Panic bubbled up inside and mixed with adrenaline, pain, cold, frustration, anger—she started to shake.

"Phonephonephone no no no no no."

They forgot. You can't find it because it's not here...because they forgot.

Accept it—they forgot about you and they left.

She backed into the middle of the road, peered up into the trees, and spun a slow circle, her eyes darting around the low branches. Nothing.

This can't be happening. How could they forget? He promised.

Are you surprised? It always ends the same way—nobody cares.

Abby stood in the empty road—shivering, filthy, fists clenched with dirt and dried blood, heavy snow burying her alive—and let out an angry roar. It echoed back at her, and she started to cry. She slowly sank to her knees, buried her face in her hands, and sobbed as she felt something inside breaking...letting go...giving up.

I was so close. A few hours earlier and I'd be free...flying to New Zealand...starting a new life...with them.

Now that they were gone, she could admit how badly she wanted to be with them. Little moments rushed through her mind in a wave of bittersweet regret:

Tracy teasing Brian about his slow apple-pie station... *"OK, Brian, let's pick up the pace. They're going in the oven, not the museum."*

Mikey standing by the muscle car in his H&M sweatshirt, hands on his hips, rolling his eyes... *"Herman, you know the rule—no grumps in the garage."*

Nick raiding the junk-food aisle, passing a tube of cinnamon rolls, slapping a high-five... *"Touchdown!"*

Dana wheeling groceries toward the Ark... *"Larry Muzbino graduated last in my class and he was a total jackass."*

Nick modeling the "Bun in the oven!" apron… *"I think it looks good. I'll wear it. Try me."*

Zoe saying grace as Abby peeked at everyone around the Thanksgiving table… *"Whatever tomorrow may bring, tonight we're grateful to have each other. Tonight we're a family, and that's good enough."*

A violent gust of wind yanked Abby back to the road, and she hunched over, arms crossed, tears streaking down her dirty face. She shook uncontrollably as the cold stabbed through her—through her sopping clothes, her clammy skin, her frigid bones—and clawed at her soul.

Out of the corner of her eye, she saw something…a flicker at the base of a big tree by the edge of the road. She turned and squinted. Nothing.

You're seeing things…that's moderate hypothermia. You need to get inside.

Another gust of wind, a yellow flicker. *Something.*

The wind shoved her hard, and a big leaf tumbled away from the base of the tree. A face grinned up at her—a yellow cartoon bun, its crazy smile like a long-lost best friend.

Abby scrambled to the tree on her hands and knees like a wild animal. She grasped the tightly folded apron and shook it out. A Ziploc bag dropped onto the leaves—inside was a phone.

She gave a teary laugh, tore open the bag, and grabbed the phone with shaking hands. She opened contacts, dialed Brian, and raised the phone to her ear. Three beeps, then dead air.

No no no.

She tried again.

Three beeps, dead air.

"Come *on*."

She switched to text. "I'm here!" The message landed and just sat there, no way to tell if it went through. She glanced around the blinding snow and sent another. "Please come."

Come on, come on, come on.

No response.

A stick cracked behind her and she whipped around, squinting through the rushing snow. She suddenly felt very alone, very vulnerable—shivering on her knees, covered in dirt, every inch of her soaked, sore, or throbbing.

"Hurry!" she texted.

Another crack, then a rustle.

Closer this time? Behind? To the side? Her head spun, round and round, panicked eyes jumping from tree to bush to boulder to tree.

Don't leave me here.

They'll catch me. I'll freeze.

Please don't—

The phone dinged.

Her eyes shot down.

"We're coming."

FORTY-ONE

"AND FINALLY, you finish it in butter so the bread gets crispy on the outside and soft on the inside, almost like a pastry." T.J. flipped the ham sandwich in the sizzling skillet.

"I love it," Tracy said, stuffing another log in the wood-burning stove. "Plus you melt the cheese and warm the mayo. So tell me, how did an Indian chef learn so many great sandwich tricks?"

T.J. chuckled. "Well, my dad always said—"

"I'm checking on it, Herman. Don't get in a tizzy." Mikey huffed and walked in from the bedroom. He passed Cadillac, who was staring out the window into the driving snow.

"Come on, Caddy." Mikey clapped.

The dog whined and stayed glued to the window.

"Did you know Cadillac is my favorite car?" Mikey asked Zoe as she poured potato chips on a paper plate.

"That's cool," Zoe said. "You know, I don't think I've ever been in a Cadillac. What's it like?"

"Well one time, my dad drove me in a black Cadillac. We're gonna go again when he comes home from the army."

"I didn't know your dad was in the army." Zoe grinned. "Look at that, we're both military brats. Where is he serving?"

Mikey considered a moment and his smile faded. He leaned in and whispered, "Actually, he's not really in the army. He left when my mom died. I don't think he's coming back."

"Aww, I'm sorry to hear that, Mikey."

"It's OK, Zoe. Just don't tell Herman, OK? He pretends to be my grandpa. It makes him feel important."

Zoe gave a warm smile. "You got it. Your secret's safe with me. Pinky promise." She extended a pinky.

Mikey lit up and shook with his pinky. "Pinky promise."

"Mikey!" Herman barked from the bedroom. "Where's that aspirin? Downtown Boston?"

"Herman! Hold your horses." Mikey took the ham sandwich from Tracy and the aspirin from Dana, rolled his eyes, and whispered, "What a big baby."

Herman grumbled something and the mattress creaked.

"Don't you get up off that bed." Mikey marched toward the bedroom.

"Alright, Dana, you're next." T.J. pointed his spatula. "Ham or roast beef?"

Dana grinned. "Gee, I think I'll have—"

Ding ding ding. Brian's phone lit up on the center of the dining table. He had left it behind so each party had a satellite phone, and they could stay in contact if phone lines went down.

Cadillac skidded to the table and began barking at the phone.

Zoe rushed over and picked it up. She looked up with wild eyes. "She's there! She said to hurry."

"Alright, ladies, let's go," Tracy said.

They began pulling on jackets.

"I'll tell her we're coming." Zoe tapped a quick reply.

Tracy popped her head into the bedroom. "We're going to get Abby. Can you guys pack everything up? In case we need to leave in a hurry?"

Herman started to sit up in bed. "Well, hold on," he grumbled, "where exactly—"

"No problem, Tracy. We got it." Mikey gave a thumbs up.

Tracy returned a thumbs up and headed for the front door.

T.J. stood by the door in a dusty old hunting jacket. "I can come too…if that's OK?"

Tracy put a hand on his shoulder and smiled. "You got it, chef."

* * *

THEY CRUISED along Cradle Cove in Herman's pickup, Tracy behind the wheel in a pair of Brian's aviator sunglasses.

"Do we have a signal?" Tracy asked.

"Yeah, but it's on satellite." Zoe pulled up Brian's contact list.

"That'll work. Try them."

Zoe called Nick on speakerphone.

Brian answered. "Hey guys, what's up?" He sounded tired.

"We're just checking in," Tracy said. "Abby texted us. We're on our way to pick her up."

"Hey, that's great," Brain said.

"How'd you guys make out?" Tracy asked.

"We, uhh, well the mission went a little sideways, but we're alright. We have a plan. Everything's still on schedule."

"Hey Tracy?" Nick came on the line. "As soon as you have Abby, pack up everything at the cabin and get ready to go. We'll be back in twenty-five minutes, and then we'll all head north. Safer to wait somewhere near the airport than hang out in Monroe's back yard."

"Sounds good, Nick. Mikey and Herman are packing up now. We'll be ready to go when you get back."

"Perfect," Nick said. "We're almost there, guys. A few more hours and we're home free."

* * *

"WHERE IS SHE?" Dana asked as they crawled through the falling snow, everyone searching out the windows.

"It's so hard to see," T.J. said.

"What if she's not here?" Zoe asked. "I tried calling, but without satellite backup her phone isn't ringing."

"She has to be here somewhere," Tracy said. "We'll just keep driving until—"

"There she is!" Dana pointed straight ahead.

They squinted through the snow at a ghostly figure standing fifty yards ahead. Tracy accelerated and Abby came into view. She was shaking in the middle of the road, hunched and clutching herself, face streaked with dirt, her clothes stained and soggy. Her eyes were wide, and she was slowly shaking her head and blinking rapidly.

"Oh my god," Dana said, "she's freezing."

"What's wrong with her?" Zoe squinted. "What is she doing?"

They rolled to a stop a few yards away.

Abby didn't move. She kept blinking.

"Something's wrong…" Tracy said.

A black pickup tore out of the gravel road behind them and skidded onto Cradle Cove. It accelerated for a short stretch, then slammed on the brakes and drifted to a crooked stop behind their bumper.

A red pickup crept over the hill behind Abby and idled behind her.

"Oh shit shit shit," T.J. said, glancing forward and back.

Tracy whipped off her aviators, looked in the rearview, and gripped the gear selector. "Should I reverse through them?"

"No!" Dana grabbed Tracy's wrist. "Not with Abby in the road."

Soldiers jumped from the trucks and surrounded them, guns drawn. Blitzkrieg approached the driver's side, eyes bulging, and ripped open the door. "Out, ladies. Hands up. You too, Osama." He smirked and licked his lips as they got out.

Hunziker strolled up. "Sorry, ladies, Crabby's not gonna make it. She's got an appointment she just can't miss."

Abby teetered in the road—pale, lips blue, teeth chattering, eyes fluttering—defeated and half dead.

"General, please, she's hypothermic." Dana pulled off her jacket. "She needs care right away. I'm an ER doctor, can I look at her?"

"Oh, don't worry, sweetheart, Dr. T is eagerly awaiting her return." He nodded and Big Ron dragged Abby, stumbling, to Hunziker's truck.

"You folks are lucky I'm on a schedule," Hunziker said, "or we'd have a chat about your role in Abby's little stunt." He grinned at T.J. "Maybe another time."

Hunziker gave a signal, and everyone started back to their trucks.

"Leave her." T.J. stood tall against the falling snow.

Everyone turned except Hunziker, who froze at his truck with his back to them and his door half open.

"She's been one big headache for you," T.J. said. "The only reason you're here is because you're following orders."

T.J. took a cautious step forward. "I'll pay you ten million dollars to leave her with us. Forty thousand in cash and gold right now, and the rest in two days. You know I've got it. Just tell him you couldn't find her and you'll never see us again."

Hunziker gently closed his door and stared into the bed of his truck. The soldiers looked from T.J. to Hunziker, trying to get a read on their general.

T.J. stepped closer and took a familiar tone. "Look, don't be his errand boy—you're more than that. The General calls the shots, right? Does what's best for his men? So ditch the girl and take the money. Take what you *deserve*."

Hunziker reached into the bed of his truck and dragged something toward him with a metal clanging. He turned to T.J. and let Abby's backpack drop to his side, hanging from his hand by a broken strap. It sagged under the weight of the iPad and textbooks, swinging back and forth like a medieval flail.

Hunziker's eyes were dark. "You know what, Mr. America? I think I will."

FORTY-TWO

"OK OK, I GOT ONE." Brian chuckled as he parked the Ark next to Herman's pickup in front of the cabin. "This one time, the client was so worried about space bugs that he wore a bee suit the entire trip." He burst out laughing.

Nick grinned and shook his head.

"I mean, he couldn't even take a piss. He had to bring a plastic bag inside the suit." Brian clapped and roared.

Nick stared straight ahead and his smile faded. The snow had stopped falling, and the sun was high—he could see it clearly.

"What?" Brian looked at Nick. "Was he one of yours?"

"Why is the door open?"

"What?"

"It's thirty-eight degrees out—why is the front door open?"

Brian's head snapped forward. They stared at the wide-open door.

Both men sprung from the Ark and raced to the cabin—up the porch, through the door, into the dark inside.

They stood frozen, eyes adjusting, brains trying to process what was in front of them. T.J. was lying on the floor—pale, motionless, mouth hanging open—surrounded by a halo of bloody rags and first-aid supplies. Dana kneeled beside him, streaked with blood, gripping his hand. Herman and Mikey kneeled above his head.

"T.J., can you hear me?" Dana spoke with the poise of a veteran ER doctor.

His legs convulsed, contracting and releasing in a rhythmic pattern.

"Herman, stabilize his head." She pointed. "Put your hands on both sides and keep it straight with his spine. Mikey, apply pressure here." She pressed his hand to a clean rag on T.J.'s forehead. "When it's soaked, just add another on top."

She leaned in. "T.J., can you squeeze my hand?"

"What…" Nick stared with wide eyes. "What happ—"

"Tracy! Zoe!" Brian glanced around the cabin.

"In the bedroom." Dana pointed back. "Mikey, hand me that surgical kit."

Brian rushed into the bedroom.

Nick hung on T.J. another moment, unable to tear himself away, then followed Brian. He stepped inside the bedroom and froze.

Brian stood motionless by the door, staring at Tracy across the room. She stared back, eyes wide and red, cheek bruised purple, face ghost-white. Both hands covered her mouth, her knuckles scraped and bleeding.

Brian held his breath with the stillness of a tiger about to strike. He knew what was coming, but he needed her to say it.

Tracy slowly lowered her shaking hands. "Brian…they took Zoe."

In under a second, Brian had spun and brushed past Nick, heading toward the cabin door.

"Brian—" Nick turned to follow, but stopped. Something in Brian had changed, and Nick suddenly didn't recognize the man. His eyes were cold and dark, like a light had shut off inside. With his jaw clenched and head high, he held the posture of an apex predator advancing on its prey.

But mostly it was the way he moved—with intense confidence and laser-focused purpose, a battering ram with every muscle in his body rock-hard, yet perfectly relaxed—striding smoothly across the cabin with zero limp.

* * *

Brian slammed the defense kit onto the dining table.

"Brian, hold on." Nick turned to Tracy. "What happened?"

Brian snapped up the latches on the black hard-shell briefcase and flipped it open. A display of deadly weapons and tactical gear rested inside foam cutouts. Everything was brand new and jet black. Brian began removing and checking items with the determined focus and automatic speed of a man who'd done it a thousand times before.

"Tracy, what happened to T.J.?" Nick gestured to T.J., who was sleeping on the floor, Dana sitting cross-legged by his side, covered in blood, forehead resting on her palms. Herman kneeled by his other side, head lowered in prayer.

Brian pulled a tactical belt from the case and fastened it around his waist.

"Where's Abby?" Nick asked Tracy. "Why…what did they say?"

She watched Brian, lost in a daze.

Brian examined a long fixed-blade combat knife and strapped it to his belt. He fastened a medium tactical knife on the other side, then hung a small curved blade in a necklace sheath around his neck.

Nick stepped to Brian. "Listen, we can figure—"

The front door burst open and Mikey stormed in carrying Herman's rusty shotgun. "I'm coming with, Brian."

Brian pulled out a pair of binoculars and a spotting scope, oblivious to Mikey's entrance.

Herman hustled up off the floor and spoke softly. "Let's hold on just a second, son. Hear the plan before we jump in, OK?" He gently lifted the shotgun from Mikey's hands.

Brian examined a pair of fingerless tactical gloves with hardened knuckles.

"We stand up to bullies!" Mikey stomped, tears in his eyes. "You told me that, Herman. I'm going."

"We're gonna help, you know we will." Herman rested a hand on Mikey's shoulder and lowered the shotgun by his side. "Let's just see what they decide. OK?"

Brian rose, grabbed the shotgun, sat back down, and began unloading and examining it.

Herman stared, dumbstruck.

Nick sat next to Brian at the table. "Brian, listen, we need a plan. If you—"

Brian's head shot up—he stared at Nick with dead eyes. "This isn't your fight and you don't want to miss the flight. I know, I get it—spare me the speech." He slid his phone across the table. "Call the operator, tell her I ditched you and Marty. He's hurt bad and you need a replacement pilot. Then run the T.J. bluff." He gestured at T.J. on the ground. "Should be an easy sell now."

"What are you going to do?"

Brian raised his pistol and slammed home a clip.

"Brian, it's suicide." Nick leaned in. "One man against a heavily armed militia on a secure compound—you said it yourself, the odds of success are near zero. Let's just take a minute and work out a plan."

Brian stood and holstered the pistol. He pulled a silencer and three extra clips from the case and started securing them to his belt. "I'm done planning."

Nick stood to reply, but suddenly Tracy was in his face.

"This is *your* fault." She jabbed a finger. "You baited that poor girl into running away, then dragged my husband through hell so your buddy could pick up some whore. Meanwhile we're stuck here with a horde of angry hillbillies. T.J.'s half dead, my daughter's gone, and all you care about is your flight…you selfish prick."

Nick winced. "Now, wait a minute—"

She stepped closer and lowered her voice. "Since we followed you, things have gotten worse and worse. We're done talking. We're done planning. It's time for a real hero to step up and do something. So go buy yourself a new pilot and leave us the fuck alone." She stepped back and brushed him away with both hands.

"Now hold on," Nick said. "I want to get her back, I do…whatever it takes." He held a hand to his forehead. "I'm just trying to…I just need a minute to think."

"You wanna help?" Brian turned as he pulled on his gloves. "If I don't come back, promise me you'll keep our deal, give my family a place in New Zealand." He shoved his phone into Nick's chest. "Call Ramirez and offer him the same deal—life at the ranch for his family in exchange for a flight. Tell him I sent you. He'll get you there, I guarantee it."

Brian turned to Tracy and nodded. "Go time." He gave a sharp exhale, then a wave of sadness swept across his face. "Hug and a prayer?"

Tracy covered her trembling lip and nodded.

Brian started forward and Nick put a hand on his chest. "Goddamn it, Brian, stop!"

Brian froze. He looked down at Nick's hand, slowly lifted his gaze, and stared with murder in his eyes.

Nick glared back. "If you go charging in there like Superman, neither one of you is coming out. Is that what you want? To go down in a blaze of glory while Zoe becomes his new favorite Mother?"

Nick didn't see Brian move, he sensed a whoosh of energy, a hand on his chest, then a falling sensation—backward off his feet, balance swinging like a confused compass—he slammed to the floor with a chest-crushing thud.

Nick gasped for air.

Tracy stared down in shock.

Brian stepped over him and pointed a finger. "Get this through your head…I am not your pilot. Fuck your contract. Fuck your plan. If you ever step between me and my family again, I will put you down."

They stared at each other for a long moment, Brian towering, his arm steady as a rock, Nick glaring, his hands up in surrender.

Brian stepped off and strode to the bedroom. Tracy followed.

Nick coughed and slowly rolled onto his hands and knees. Herman reached down and helped him up.

"Never step in front of a charging bull, son." Herman shook his head.

Nick wheezed and dusted off his pants. "Yeah, I got that."

"Well?" Herman shrugged.

"Well what?" Nick held his side and winced.

"What's the plan?"

Nick looked at the cabin door with tired eyes. "There is no plan. I'm done."

FORTY-THREE

NICK LEANED with his elbows on the porch railing, watching as rain poured off the cabin roof and washed away the morning snowfall. He gripped his phone in one hand.

One phone call and I can walk away from everything.

Brian was right, if Nick called the operator and reported Brian as non-compliant, he could get a replacement pilot, run the T.J. bluff, and be in New Zealand by tomorrow.

Why not? Nobody wants me here. Brian and Tracy hate me. Dana and Herman are disappointed. And I'm sure Abby and Zoe aren't too happy.

He pressed a palm to the center of his throbbing forehead. On top of his usual headache, Brian's body slam had rattled something loose.

Tracy's right, I can't keep anyone safe. Marty and Raina are infected, T.J.'s dying on the floor, Brian's unhinged—an hour from now he'll be dead, and god knows what Monroe has planned for Zoe, or Abby after she gives birth.

His vision blurred, the rain going in and out of focus—could be a concussion, or could be a panic attack, since the rain stank like gasoline. He pulled out his lavender necklace, then shook his head and dropped it back down his shirt. What was the point?

Nick unlocked his phone.

You should call...what are you waiting for?

If Nick called, Brian would be screwed either way: he'd either die during his assault or he'd succeed and be stuck here with his family—broke, starving, and hopeless. Nick wouldn't just be ditching Brian and Tracy, he'd be giving up on Zoe, Dana, Herman, and Mikey. And Abby.

Nick hovered a finger over the operator's number.

We were so close. A few more hours and we would've been on our way.

If they hadn't tracked Abby...

If Marty hadn't dragged us to Boston...

If I hadn't—

"T.J. needs a hospital," Dana said.

Nick straightened and turned, surprised to find her standing in the doorway. She was drying her hands with a towel. "There's only so much I can do for him here."

"Will he be OK?"

"He's OK for now, resting comfortably. But head injuries are tough—sometimes they wake up an hour later cracking jokes, and sometimes..." She shrugged. "You know."

She tilted her head. "Are you OK?"

Nick gave a little cough and winced. "I'm fine." He leaned his elbows back onto the railing and stared out into the rain.

"That's not what I meant."

"Why hasn't he left yet?"

"Brian? He's talking to Tracy. I think she's having second thoughts."

Dana stepped from the doorway and joined Nick at the railing. "Look, Nick, I know you want to help Zoe. I know you tried. This isn't your fault." She sighed. "You can't save everyone, I see that now, it's too far gone. You have to take care of yourself and your family. I just...well, if you call for another pilot, I won't blame you. I understand. Really, I do."

She slid to his side and placed a hand on his arm. "But, Nick, whatever happens, I wish…I wish you would stay. When Brian gets back with Zoe, we'll need you. And if something happens to him, we'll really need you. I mean, what's in New Zealand? I know you don't have family…why can't we be your family? Stay, Nick. Don't give up on us."

He scoffed. "Yeah, right. Brian hates me. Tracy might kill me. Let's be honest…no one wants me here."

"You're wrong." She shook her head. "They *need* you, now more than ever. Family isn't supposed to be easy, but you stick together when things get tough, and you do what's best for those you love, even when they hate you for it."

Nick cast his eyes to the ground and shook his head.

"In this broken world, family is all we have…but it's enough." Dana's words hung in the air as she gazed at Nick, hoping for a reply.

An idea struck him and blazed through his body like an electric current, leaving a trail of goosebumps behind. He played it out in his head, watching the scenarios unfold with lightning speed.

Dana lowered her gaze, squeezed his arm, and walked toward the front door.

Nick swung his head up, and the world came into perfect focus. He drew a deep breath of clean air, and his headache disappeared. He saw the plan all laid out—its risks, its variables, its permutations—and he knew it would work. Something inside relaxed and surrendered, and he knew he was going to see it through, whatever the cost.

Nick turned. "Hey Dana?"

"Yeah?" She looked back from the doorway, her eyes hopeful.

"I've got it."

She tilted her head. "Got what?"

"I know how to get her out."

FORTY-FOUR

NICK STEPPED INSIDE to find Brian and Tracy locked in a deep embrace.

Shit—he's going.

Nick's eyes jumped around the room until he found what he was looking for on the dining table. He walked across the room and slipped it into his pocket.

Tracy stepped back, took Brian's hands, and closed her eyes. "Lord, protect my husband and—"

Mikey tapped her on the shoulder. She opened her eyes, and he joined the prayer circle.

"Lord, protect my husband and daughter on this journey and show them a peaceful path home."

Nick moved along the wall, reached down by Marty's bags, then moved away.

"Make him a gentle shepherd…umm…a gentle guardian. Make him strong as…uhh…strong as your stone…and…*goddammit!*" Tracy stomped her foot.

They opened their eyes.

"I can't…I can't remember. She always says it." Tracy took a deep breath and closed her eyes. "Look, we tried to take the peaceful path,

Lord, but today evil came for one of your children. So…" Her lip quivered into a snarl. "Brian's gonna send you some sinners, do with them what you will. Amen."

"Amen," they echoed.

Brian held her shoulders and gazed into her eyes. "I'll get her back. I promise."

Tracy nodded and covered her mouth, fighting back tears. Dana embraced her from behind, and Brian kissed her forehead.

Brian turned and moved to the dining table with purpose. He holstered a few final items, pulled on his tactical gloves, and paused. He looked around the table, confused. "Where is it…where's the key? To the Ark? It was right here."

He looked under the defense kit, under the table, around the floor. "Where the hell is it?" He patted his pockets. "I put it right—"

"I took it," Nick said calmly, standing by the door.

Brian's eyes swung up—he straightened and squinted, as if trying to decide if Nick had just said what he thought he said.

Nick stared back. Neither man moved as they held a long silence.

Brian drew his sidearm with smooth and decisive speed and strode at Nick like a seasoned executioner. He stopped a foot from Nick's face and towered.

Nick held his glare. "It's not on me. I hid it."

Brian aimed the pistol at Nick's knee. "In ten seconds, you never walk again. In twenty, you never breathe again. Where is the key?"

Nick stared up, unflinching.

Everyone watched in horror.

"Nick, come on," Dana said, hands on her head.

Brian pressed the gun to Nick's temple and leaned in. "If you think you know me, you don't. If you think I will hesitate for even a second, you're wrong. I will ask you one more time and then I will take you apart. Where is the key?" He cocked back the hammer.

Tracy covered her mouth.

"Be smart, Nick." Herman shook his head.

"Five minutes," Nick said in a low and steady tone. "Give me five minutes and I'll give you a way to bring Zoe out, right now, without anyone getting hurt…and we still make the flight. Five minutes, and if you don't like the plan, I'll hand you the key, and you'll never see me again."

Brian's jaw flexed, his eyes pummeling Nick, his body so tense it could kill with a twitch.

Nick glared back with unflinching resolve.

No one breathed.

Brian leaned in. "You have two minutes."

* * *

NICK STOOD at the head of the table, Brian at the opposite end, everyone else at a distance. He took a deep breath. "We can get—"

Beep beep…beep.

Brian set his digital watch and slammed it on the table next to his gun.

1:58…1:57…1:56…the tenths-of-seconds panel raced backward.

Brian crossed his arms and glared.

"We can get Zoe out, I know we can, but if you go in guns blazing, you won't make it past the front gate." Nick raised his hands defensively. "I've been there, I've been inside. They've got six heavily armed guards at the front—four men at the gate and two spotters in towers. Plus a small army of trigger-happy soldiers with radios, trucks, guns, grenades—all kinds of gear they don't know how to use—just looking for any reason to kill. I have no doubt you'd tear through them—there might be five real soldiers in there—but ninety-five idiots with guns are a special kind of dangerous."

Brian huffed and shifted his stance.

"But let's say you get through…then what?" Nick said. "You don't know where she is. The place is huge, they use trucks to get around. Even if you find her, getting out is just as hard as getting in, probably more so, because now you've got Zoe with you, they've regrouped, and—"

Nick looked down at the spinning countdown, straightened, and took a deep breath. "You don't need to beat them, Brian. You don't even need to fight them. It's faster, safer, and easier if you just make a deal."

"A deal?" Tracy squinted, her arms crossed.

Nick nodded. "Look, I'm guessing Monroe doesn't really want her, because she's not part of his grand plan. I'm guessing Hunziker took her on an impulse, because he's an asshole. And I'm guessing we can offer them something they'll want far more than Zoe."

Tracy scoffed. "Yeah? You're guessing? And what if they don't like your deal? What if Brian gets stuck in there, in a shootout, one against a hundred, Zoe caught in the middle? What do you *guess* happens then?"

Nick nodded and cast his eyes to the ground. He sighed and looked up at Brian with resolve. "If they don't take the deal, then we do it the hard way…unleash disaster. Believe me, in a crisis, two men with a plan outnumber a hundred panicked fools."

"Two?" Tracy said.

Nick shrugged, as if it were obvious. "Well yeah, I'm going too… and I'm not coming out without her."

Tracy and Brian read each other and softened slightly.

"Look, when we first met, the way I was…what I said…I'm sorry." Nick looked back and forth between them. "There are some things… well, if I could go back, I would. But Tracy, Brian, I care about Zoe…I do. I want her back. And if we work together, we can get her out and get to New Zealand. It's a good plan—I can see it, all laid out, ten steps in every direction—but you have to trust me. Let me help you…let me bring her home."

Brian and Tracy looked at each other, sadness in their eyes.

Beep-beep beep-beep beep-beep.

Everyone looked down at the watch. 00:00:00:00

Brian stiffened—as if snapping from a daze—strapped on his watch, and shoved the pistol in his holster. He raised his eyebrows at Nick.

Nick sighed and nodded. He walked to Marty's watch-collection case, fished out the key, and extended it to Brian.

Brian watched the key dangle from Nick's hand—squinting,

chewing the inside of his lip, wrestling with a thought. He looked up at Nick, then back down at the key. He shook his head with a sharp exhale, like an angry bull, snatched the key, and strode toward the door.

He stopped in the doorway, rested a hand on the frame, and hung his head. "What…"

Brian slowly turned and looked at Nick. "What do you mean… unleash disaster?"

* * *

EVERYONE HUDDLED OVER THE TABLETOP, staring down at Nick's plan scrawled in red marker. It looked like a coach's clipboard—saturated with arrows, circles, diagrams, a map, margin notes, lists, and a constellation of hub-and-spoke mind maps.

"Man, there's a lot to it." Brian scratched his head.

"We have to consider everything," Nick said. "Hopefully they cooperate and we can just run Plan A—in and out, quick and easy."

"What do you think?" Brian looked at Tracy.

She sighed and shrugged. "Well, it's a lot better than charging through the front gate, that's for sure."

Brian nodded. "It's a good plan, Nick."

Nick returned a quick nod. "Well, for it to work, we're going to need everybody."

"Just tell us what to do," Herman said.

"OK, Herman and Mikey, can you set up the radios?"

"No problem." Mikey gave a big thumbs up. "We'll get it ready and test the distance, just like you said. I'll stand on the porch, and Herman will walk down the road."

"Now hold on." Herman put his hands on his hips. "Why do I gotta go outside in the rain? How about you walk down the road?"

"Herman, please." Mikey held up a palm. "Don't start with the backsass." He pointed out the window as he headed for the door. "It stopped raining."

Herman watched him go, dumbfounded. "Backsass? What are you…how is that…now hold on a second." He marched after Mikey.

Nick smiled as they walked out the door, bickering like an old married couple.

Tracy stepped up. "How can I help?"

Nick pulled out his phone and started tapping. "Can you make this?" He handed her the phone.

She squinted and scrolled. "How many?"

"Six."

"What color?"

"Black. All black."

She held out the phone and nodded. "Coming right up." She spun off toward the kitchenette.

A hand squeezed his shoulder. "What can I do?" Dana said.

He turned and took a deep breath. "Well, you have the hardest job…you need to wake him up."

"Who?"

"T.J."

"Wait, what? Are you serious? I mean, are you sure? Does it have to be him, can't somebody else do it?"

Nick shook his head. "Has to be him."

They looked down at T.J. sleeping peacefully on the floor.

"He's gonna be pissed," Dana said softly.

"Yeah, thank god I won't be here." He patted her on the back.

She gave him a mock sneer and started toward the kitchen.

"Oh, Dana?"

She spun.

"Make sure it's exact." He tapped a dense corner of the planning table.

She walked backward with two thumbs up.

Across the table, Brian squinted down at the plan.

Nick stepped up, and they shared a determined look.

"Run it again?" Nick asked.

"Run it again." Brian nodded.

They huddled over the table.

* * *

"ALRIGHT, ALL LOADED UP." Nick closed the cabin door behind him and turned to Brian, who was studying the table. "Ready?"

"Ready." Brian tapped his fist on the tabletop.

Nick stepped to Dana to say goodbye. "If you don't hear from me, do it. Don't hesitate."

She nodded. "Be careful in there." She leaned in and whispered, "Remember, you still owe me a marshmallow." She leaned out and pointed in a mock scold. "And I fully intend to collect."

Nick grinned. "Oh, you can count on it."

Dana gave him a slow doe-eyed blink and a flirty smile.

Nick's smile faded, and he took her hand. "Listen, Dana…thank you…thank you for—"

She waved a hand and cut him off. "No goodbyes. Tell me when you get back."

He nodded and released her hand with a squeeze. He turned to Brian, who was saying goodbye to Tracy.

"Listen, hun, I love you. If anything happens—"

Tracy waved a hand. "Don't, Brian."

"OK, well, it's a good plan. But just in case…stay here with Herman and Mikey. They'll look after you."

Herman stepped up behind her and placed a hand on her shoulder. "You think we'd let a chef like this get away?"

"Yeah, you're stuck with us, Tracy." Mikey grinned. "Herman's food is yuk. Yuk!" He made a sour face and everyone laughed.

Herman slowly turned. "Boy, are you outta your mind? If you—"

"Herman, Herman, I'm kidding. It's a joke. Don't get upset." He made a calming gesture and rolled his eyes. "You know I love Herman's world-famous stuffed ham."

Herman nodded and turned forward again. Mikey shook his head from Herman's blind spot and silently mouthed to the group, "Yuk."

Tracy suppressed a laugh. "Alright, everybody gather round. Quick prayer."

They all took hands and closed their eyes.

Tracy took a deep breath. "Lord, protect our family on this journey and show us a peaceful path home. Make Nick your shepherd, a gentle guardian. Make Brian your stone, a pillar of strength. And if they don't take the deal, make us your storm, a swift and mighty force. Amen."

"Amen," everyone echoed, and dispersed.

Nick and Brian faced each other.

Brian clapped a strong hand on Nick's shoulder and gave a solemn nod, a special nod reserved for soldiers, brothers with battle-tested trust charging into impossible odds. "Go time."

Nick returned the nod. "Go time."

FORTY-FIVE

NICK ROLLED the Ark to a stop fifty yards from Monroe's front gate.

Two snipers took up firing positions in opposing towers.

Six soldiers strapped on tactical gear behind the gate.

Nick killed the engine and stepped out. He took a deep breath and watched his exhale smoke in the misty air.

The front gate rolled open and a sloppy formation of militiamen cruised toward him, automatic rifles up. He raised his hands and began to walk forward. Halfway to the gate, four soldiers crept out from the woods and followed behind.

Nick took a long, silent walk through the gate and stopped twenty yards inside, his hands held high. The soldiers formed a wide circle around him, guns trained at his head.

Hunziker's truck skidded to a stop, and he stormed out, waving a hand. "Stop stop stop! Jesus Christ, guys, crossfire! We've been over this. Everyone behind him, lower your weapon and move in front." The rear soldiers shuffled forward. "And fingers off triggers unless he moves."

Hunziker turned back toward his truck. "Old Glory, call the doc."

Old Glory teetered away as Big Ron raced in from the gate, face red, chest heaving. "I checked his car, sir." He gasped. "Nothing but some camping stuff and an old six-pack."

"Park it inside."

Big Ron spun and rushed back.

Hunziker looked Nick up and down, then signaled for the militiamen to lower their guns. He strolled up and Nick lowered his hands.

"You got a lotta nerve showing up here." Hunziker rested his hands on his tactical belt. "He's pissed."

"I bet," Nick said calmly. "Just wait until he finds out you beat his favorite CEO into a coma."

Hunziker smirked and held up his palms in a guilty-as-charged gesture. "Oops! Collateral damage." He scanned the laughing soldiers like a stand-up comedian gauging his audience.

"Egypt, Houston, Atlanta, Wolfeboro…one long trail of collateral damage," Nick said. "No wonder you became a fake general for a fake army."

The soldiers stiffened and let out a hostile "ooh."

"Fuck him up, sir!" Blitzkrieg shouted.

Hunziker stepped forward, fire in his eyes, and drew back a clenched fist.

A white Mercedes skidded up next to Hunziker's pickup, and Monroe stepped out of the passenger side in a doctor's coat. He pulled the stethoscope from his neck and tossed it on the seat, slammed the door, and strode toward them like a man who'd spent the last of his patience.

"Alright, Nick, I don't have time for games. What do you want?" He stopped at Hunziker's side and flashed his eyebrows.

"Dr. Monroe, I came to make a deal for Zoe."

Hunziker scoffed. "Uhh, unless I'm missing something, you forgot your chips." The soldiers chuckled, and Hunziker stood a little taller.

Nick ignored him and addressed Monroe. "You don't really want her. She doesn't belong here. Let me take her home, and we won't bother you again."

Monroe pulled a cloth from his pocket and began cleaning his glasses. "Actually, Nick, I think she likes it here. She's very bright. She's going to fit right in."

Nick smiled and nodded. "Yeah, I thought you might say that. Look, I don't want any trouble, I don't want anyone to get hurt…but if you don't give her up, right now, I'm going to have to…escalate."

Hunziker cackled. "Big talk for a one-man army."

Monroe replaced his glasses and flashed a palm at Hunziker. "What, exactly, is that supposed to mean?"

Nick sighed. "My brother is a U.S. senator from Massachusetts, Paul Ritter. If I don't call Zoe's dad, give a code word, and confirm we're both headed home, in the next…" Nick glanced down at his watch. "…seven minutes and thirty-six seconds, he's going to call my brother and tell him exactly where we are."

Monroe squinted.

"Wiretap!" Hunziker barked.

Wiretap strolled up, scrolling on his tablet. "Paul Ritter, U.S. senator from Massachusetts since 2030. Democrat, Army veteran, co-sponsored the cut-clinic bill, serves on a bunch of committees…" He gestured at Nick. "Looks like this guy, but fatter."

Monroe stroked his chin like a skeptical professor. "So, what…you cry for help and big brother sends the cavalry? Who's coming, exactly? The FBI? The Army? Will they send helicopters? Fighter jets? Tanks? Maybe a battleship off the coast?" He smirked as everyone laughed. "We're in the middle of a global crisis, and the government's more dysfunctional than ever. Right now your brother's huddled in an underground bunker in Washington arguing with his ninety-nine incompetent colleagues. They've got the whole world to worry about, they're not interested in saving some nobody." He dismissed Nick with a backhanded wave. "We're done here." Monroe started back toward the car.

Hunziker gestured and two soldiers pulled out zip-tie handcuffs and moved toward Nick.

"Pennsylvania," Nick called after Monroe.

Monroe stopped and turned halfway. "What?"

Hunziker held up a hand and the soldiers paused.

"As Chairman of the Senate Subcommittee on Emerging Threats

and Capabilities, my brother is huddled in an underground bunker in *Pennsylvania*. Raven Rock Mountain Complex, to be exact."

Monroe turned and gave Nick his full attention.

"Some people call it Site R, others call it the underground Pentagon, but basically it's a high-tech military installation that headquarters operations for the Army, Navy, Air Force, and Marines during a national emergency."

Monroe started walking back.

"But you're right, they're probably pretty busy right now, they wouldn't care about some nobody lost in the woods." Nick paused, then cocked his head. "But you know what they might care about… your vaccine."

Monroe shook his head. "What vaccine? What are you talking about?"

"Oh, come on, you don't expect me to believe the great Teddy Monroe unleashed an apocalyptic virus without crafting the perfect vaccine, do you? You've got thirty-three pregnant Mothers of Mankind here, a hundred Matchstick Militiamen, doctors, nurses, support staff, and, very soon, sixty-six newborn babies." He leaned in for a friendly aside. "Congratulations on the twins, by the way."

Monroe crossed his arms and shifted uncomfortably.

"Bottom line, there's no way you can reach five hundred people in fifteen years unless you have a vaccine that's one hundred percent effective against Scratch 'n Sniff."

Hunziker hid a smirk at the phrase "Scratch 'n Sniff" and shot a guilty-schoolboy look at his soldiers.

Monroe's face reddened. "Very clever, Nick. What else did she tell you? Did she tell you I saved her from an abusive foster home? That she signed the adoption papers enthusiastically? That she helped recruit half my Mothers? Huh?" He stalked toward Nick. "Did she tell you that I help her study for her MCATs? Give her full access to my facilities? Provide a dedicated therapist for her nightmares? Did she tell you that I'm the only one here…*anywhere*…who gives a shit about her?"

He reached Nick and his face darkened. "Did you help her poison the Mothers?"

"What?"

"Spreading bleach, making everyone think they're infected, creating panic. Was that your idea?"

"Hmm." Nick gave an impressed nod. "Fire in a crowded theater… clever girl."

Monroe opened his mouth to unload, but Wiretap interrupted. "Paul Ritter, Chairman of the Senate Subcommittee on Emerging Threats and Capabilities. The committee oversees terrorist and biological threats, homeland defense, and special operations. And Raven Rock is…well, it's like he said…badass."

"Thank you, Private Winkler," Monroe snapped.

Nick moved in for the kill. "Paul would jump at the chance to end this virus tonight—save the world, rescue thirty-three kidnapped minors, expose a genius CEO as a sociopathic fraud, break up a corrupt adoption ring—oh, and capture a bunch of domestic terrorists. All in time for the election…doesn't get much better than that."

That's it, that's your big punch. If he's gonna take the deal, now's the time.

Nick stepped back and raised his palms defensively. "But none of that has to happen. Just take the deal—give up Zoe and you'll never see us again."

Monroe glared, eyes raging.

Hunziker fumed by his side, like a mad dog on a tight leash.

Nick stared back, not giving an inch.

He's not gonna take it, he's too angry. I can see it in his eyes.

Nick glanced at his watch. "Three minutes and seventeen seconds, Doctor." He paused. "Go time."

Monroe took a deep breath, chuckled, and began to pace like a lecturing professor. "First of all, they won't come. They're lazy, dysfunctional bureaucrats. They're *actors*, they never actually *do* anything. It'll take them a month just to agree there's a virus. Regardless, you think you're the only one with friends in high places? The second your brother opens his mouth I'll have a dozen senators scrambling to defend me. One phone call and I'll clear up the whole misunderstanding with the president himself.

"But, OK, what if they do come? What if the cavalry comes crashing through my gate?" Monroe raised his shoulders in a dramatic shrug. "Then I'll just spin the vaccine as a new discovery…a miraculous breakthrough…a trial in progress. Bring it on, I'd love to add another Person of the Year cover to my wall."

Monroe stopped in front of Nick and shook his head with disappointment. "But, Nick, your biggest mistake is that even if I wanted to take your deal, how do I know you won't call him anyway? Or that you haven't called already?" He leaned in and delivered his big conclusion. "Your offer carries no weight because it's unenforceable. And that leaves me with only one option."

He looked Nick up and down with disgust. "It's a bluff and it's thin. Get rid of him."

Hunziker grinned and pulled on tactical gloves. "OK, big shot, let's take a ride."

Two soldiers grabbed Nick, slammed him to his knees, and zip-tied his hands behind his back.

Hunziker started to escort Monroe back to his car. "I'll take it from here, Doc. You don't need to stick—"

"General! He's got something on him!" one of the soldiers yelled.

Hunziker spun to see the soldier peeking inside Nick's jacket.

"It's a bunch of wires," the soldier said.

"Everybody back!" Hunziker signaled. "Guns up!"

Everyone scrambled back and ten guns fixed on Nick. He kneeled on the pavement, hands tied behind his back, an evil grin spreading across his face.

"Blitzkrieg! On me!"

Blitzkrieg rushed to Hunziker's side like a rabid dog.

"Put a gun on him. If he blinks wrong, take his head off."

Blitzkrieg raised his rifle, fingered the trigger, and licked his lips.

Hunziker pointed. "OK, Big Ron, you go check him…*carefully*."

Big Ron crept toward Nick, beads of sweat dotting his forehead. He pinched Nick's jacket with two quivering sausage fingers and peeked inside.

"Careful, Ronny…nice and easy…slowww…slow."

Nick grinned up at Hunziker.

"What you looking at, dead man?" Hunziker glared back.

"You shouldn't have taken her." Nick shook his head. "You're about to witness true collateral damage."

Hunziker placed a hand on his sidearm and glanced around the perimeter.

"General?" Monroe said as he backed away. "Should we—"

Hunziker raised a hand and silenced him.

Big Ron fished inside Nick's jacket. "It's…it's a walkie talkie, sir. But, like, taped down."

Hunziker relaxed and cocked his head. "What? A walkie talkie? What do you mean taped down?"

Big Ron turned, dangling the walkie talkie from its wired earpiece like it might bite. "The talk button…it's taped down."

Hunziker's gaze drifted into space as he connected the dots. "He's not alone…"

Hunziker spun to Monroe, eyes wide with panic. "He's here! The Hell Frog!"

FORTY-SIX

Brian pulled his earpiece and strode from the shadows with his pistol extended. He glided across the short parking lot toward a three-story brick building, advancing on a circle of four guards laughing at a cell phone video. He stalked straight at them—gun up, smooth and confident—an elite warrior with complete commitment and zero hesitation.

"Hands up!" Brian boomed.

They flinched and spun, eyes wide. The closest guard dropped his phone and went for his sidearm. Brian squeezed the trigger twice and the man crumpled. The others reached for their weapons.

Brian placed a steadying hand under his pistol butt and strafed sideways toward the building. Six shots rang out in tidy pairs. All three men were down before a single one returned fire.

Brian put his back to the building, ejected the magazine, and slammed a new one home. He looked back at the sprawling grid of luxury mobile homes he'd emerged from. They were laid out across a large field beside the main complex and bordered by a tall chain-link fence that surrounded the whole campus. No activity. He scanned the main complex. Nothing.

He replaced his earpiece and heard yelling.

"Get the girls!" Monroe said.

"Brian!" Nick shouted. "Eight men, heavily armed, coming in three trucks."

"Go go go!" Hunziker said. "Shut that fuckin' thing off! Get him outta here."

A rough dragging noise, then silence.

Brian glanced at his watch—even though he was in the back corner of the complex and they were at the front gate, he didn't have long. He dropped the earpiece and stepped off the wall, reaching behind him to unclip the walkie talkie from the back of his belt.

A red freight train rammed him from behind, sprawling him on the ground, sending the pistol spinning across the pavement.

Brian rolled onto his back, and a massive soldier leapt into a full mount on top. The soldier raised both hands above his head, exposing a red t-shirt with black Nazi Schutzstaffel "SS" lightning bolts, and swung down a double hammer fist.

Brian dodged the blow, pulled the man down by the back of the neck, and locked his head into a tight hug with one arm. With his free hand, Brian drew his combat knife and buried it in the soldier's leg. Schutzstaffel howled and rolled off, gripping the handle.

Brian got to his feet, and a muscle-bound skinhead with an iron cross tattoo on his neck grabbed him by the lapels and drove him backward into the brick wall, slamming the wind out of him. Brian pulled his tactical knife, Iron Cross kicked it away and punched him in the gut. Brian gasped and pulled the man in close, hanging the weight of his giant frame off his opponent's neck. Then, like releasing a coiled spring, Brian shoved him off hard, and Iron Cross reeled backward, spreading his hands for balance. Brian attacked the opening with a series of thunderous blows, then grabbed him by the lapels and delivered a wrecking-ball headbutt.

Behind them, Schutzstaffel had drawn his pistol and was aiming in their direction. Brian dragged a stunned Iron Cross between them just as Schutzstaffel fired, blocking the shot. He grabbed Iron Cross' sidearm and drew it with lightning speed as he let the man drop to the ground. Two shots and Schutzstaffel went limp.

Brian leaned against the wall, checked his surroundings, and began box breathing—four counts in, four counts full, four counts out, four counts empty. Repeat.

Suddenly he sensed eyes on him. Brian spun and aimed at a soldier frozen at the far corner of the building. The boy was scrawny with a patchy beard and pocked skin, like a mangy stray dog. He stood in a wide stance with his fly down—piss stains down his pant leg, arms limp at his sides—gawking with his mouth open.

Brian pulled the trigger. It clicked. Iron Cross' mag was empty.

Brian dropped the pistol and eyed his gun twenty yards away. Too far. He locked eyes with Mangy Dog.

The boy reached for his sidearm.

Brian started toward him—head down, breath steaming from his nostrils, snarling like a fearless lion advancing on a helpless gazelle.

Mangy Dog tugged at his pistol, but it was stuck in the holster. He fumbled for his knife, drew it and lost his grip, the blade flipping through the air. He pulled a stun gun, extended it straight out and squeezed sparks.

Brian raised his fists and gained speed. "Come on!"

Mangy Dog dropped the stun gun and yanked at his stuck pistol. It came loose with a loud crack as he accidentally pulled the trigger. The boy howled and crumpled to the ground, clutching his boot with both hands.

Brian picked up the gun, stood over him, and cocked the hammer. "The girls…are they inside?"

"Yes." He winced and rolled as blood oozed from a hole in his boot.

Brian reached down and snatched a white badge off Mangy Dog's belt. "Will this open the door?"

"Yes." He gasped.

Brian tossed the gun down a sewer and headed for the front door.

* * *

BRIAN ENTERED the lobby and crept to a set of double doors immediately ahead. He leaned against them and heard a muffled commotion inside—thumping, yelling, then a girl's scream—Zoe's scream.

He gripped the handle and cocked his pistol, then closed his eyes and took a deep breath. Brian burst through the door and aimed straight ahead.

Thirty-two pregnant teens stared up in shock.

Brian blinked, frozen at the strange sight.

They were casual and relaxed—wearing yoga pants and sweatshirts, lounging on plush couches, sipping tea, reading books, watching TV, stretching—like college girls hanging around the dorm common room. Zoe was seated in a chair in the middle with three girls gathered around her—one was braiding her hair, one was holding up a hand mirror, and one was applying the finishing touches to her elegant makeup.

"Dad!" Her face lit up and she rushed to him.

He holstered his pistol and scooped her up in a big leg-wrapping hug.

"Awww." The girls clicked and cooed.

He put her down, and she touched his forehead. "Oh my god, what happened to—"

He pulled her toward the door. "We gotta go."

"But wait—"

"*Now.*"

She waved as she stumbled out the door. "Bye girls!"

"Bye Zoe!" They waved back with bandaged hands.

* * *

Brian peeked out the front door. All clear.

He put a hand on Zoe's back. "Out the door, across the parking lot, into the mobile homes—as fast as you can. Ready?"

"Ready." She nodded.

"Stay behind me. Three, two, one…go!"

They burst into the parking lot and raced toward the mobile homes.

Brian scanned the horizon as he sprinted, then glanced back at Zoe and stopped short.

She was frozen, staring at the carnage in the parking lot—six dead, one wounded. "Dad…are they…did you—"

"Eyes up, focus on the mission." He grabbed her hand and pulled her forward.

She stumbled after him, down a long column of mobile homes. They raced ahead, row after row, past a soldier lying face down on the grass, another slumped against a mobile home, two more slashed and limp in a pickup truck.

He pulled her along. "Keep going. We're almost there."

Skidding tires and shouting men echoed from the parking lot behind them.

"Down!" Brian pulled her into a squat behind the last mobile home.

"Dad, wait," she whispered between breaths, "we have to go back."

"No chance." Brian peeked back at soldiers sprinting into the dorm.

"But they took Abby. Dr. Teddy…he's doing a C-section."

Brian winced. "Nick can get Abby. We're getting out of here."

"But they're going to—"

He grabbed her. "Listen, we have to move right now. Look there, see that hole in the fence? We're gonna run for it, fifty yards through the open field, fast and low. Duck through and go straight into the woods. Hike five minutes, cross the river, and there's an old gravel road. Herman's truck is waiting there. Jump in and drive like hell."

He drew his pistol. "If anything happens to me, you keep going. Do *not* stop."

"Dad, no!" She grabbed his arm.

He put a firm hand on her back. "Ready?"

She crouched and dug her toes like a sprinter on the blocks. "Ready."

He scanned the perimeter. "I'll be right behind you. Three, two, one…"

FORTY-SEVEN

NICK SAT in front of Monroe's mahogany desk, his zip-tied hands resting politely on his crossed legs, and watched the doctor pace.

"How could you do this?" Monroe said. "Unleash some savage on our peaceful community."

"I'm sorry, Doctor," Nick said calmly, "but you unleashed the savage the moment you took his daughter."

Monroe dropped into his chair.

Time...we need time...as much as possible.

"He was hellbent on blowing this place up," Nick said, "but I convinced him to let me negotiate. I tried to avoid this, Dr. Monroe, and I will do everything I can to bring it to a peaceful resolution."

Monroe picked up his phone.

I need to get him talking...

"Why are you doing this?" Nick gestured at the wall of framed articles and magazine covers. "You've helped more people than anyone. Hell, you saved the world, and now you want to end it? Why?"

Monroe ignored him, absorbed in his phone.

OK, let's try to find a nerve.

"Is it the money? Hey, I get it, I've worked with leaders at your level—sometimes you need a bold new strategy to drive growth."

Monroe scoffed without looking up.

"Is it fame? The five cures are old news? It's time to get back in the spotlight?"

"Pfft, please." Monroe scrolled.

"OK, legacy then. You're the genius who saved mankind. How do you move up from there? You play god, restart man in your own image."

Monroe looked up and glared.

Bingo.

"Legacy?" Monroe placed his phone face down. "You got it backwards. I doomed mankind…now I'm trying to undo the damage."

Nick leaned in, as if Monroe had said something shocking. "Doomed? You eliminated our worst diseases, saved ten million lives. You're a hero."

"No no no." Monroe shook his head like an impatient professor. "My cures, they reversed natural selection—now the least-fit survive just as long, if not longer, than the rest of us."

Fan that flame.

"What? How can that be?"

"The people who get heart disease, stroke, COPD, diabetes, Alzheimer's—nine out of ten times they're sick because of their own foolish choices. They drink, smoke, do drugs, eat junk…they're undisciplined, selfish, ignorant. These people used to have shorter lifespans—evolution in action—but now they're free to indulge with no consequences. I gave the worst of us a free pass."

Nick nodded. "And a longer lifespan means greater reproduction, which means they're shifting our evolution in their direction."

"Exactly." Monroe gestured at Nick, acknowledging the point as correct. "Since I cured heart disease, the average American has gained twenty-five pounds. Since I cured COPD, smoking rates in Europe have increased tenfold. Since I cured diabetes, global sugar consumption is up six hundred percent."

Monroe leaned back, wading through a bitter memory. "The night I accepted my Innovator Award, I was waiting outside for my car when a man came up to me. He thanked me for saving his life. Happens all the time." Monroe voiced the man in a mocking tone. "Oh, thank you, Dr. Teddy. I was dying of stage four COPD, got your treatment for free through the government, and now I'm better than ever. It's a miracle!" Monroe looked nauseated. "He was fat and greasy, reeked of liquor and marijuana, cigarette dangling from his mouth, sipping a Big Gulp through rotten teeth. Well, a week later, I'm doing my morning reading and I come across an article—the FBI broke up a cybercriminal ring that was using social media to deal knock-off Chinese cigarettes to underage kids. And there, at the top of the article, was this guy's disgusting mugshot, staring up at me. That was the moment I knew I'd made a mistake."

Monroe shrugged. "The world loves me because I cured our deadliest diseases, but I left one behind, our worst…evil."

Keep him going.

"Evil?" Nick shifted to counter. "OK, sure, so some people abuse it —maybe they don't deserve it—but surely you've helped good people too. I mean, on the whole, your cures have done a lot more good than harm, right?"

Monroe shook his head and pushed back from his desk. "You're missing the bigger picture." He began to pace. "For the last hundred years, man has been advancing at an astounding rate, unlocking a series of wonders in science and technology. But the human mind is regressing—returning to ignorance, tribalism, hostility—sliding back to the dark ages. It's not a speed bump, it's not a growing pain, our monkey minds are rejecting progress.

"The great astronomer Carl Sagan noted it first." Monroe pulled a book from his bookshelf and straightened to deliver the quote. "'I have a foreboding of an America in my children's or grandchildren's time when, clutching our crystals and nervously consulting our horoscopes, our critical faculties in decline, unable to distinguish between what feels good and what's true, we slide, almost without noticing, back into superstition and darkness.'" He looked up and closed the book. "He wrote that in 1995."

"So, what will happen to us?" Nick asked like an inquisitive student trying to keep up.

Monroe sat solemnly, like a doctor delivering a devastating prognosis. "We're regressing back to our base nature, Nick. And underneath it all, at our core...we are *monsters*...savages driven by violence, lust, and greed. Look back at history, it's a nightmare on a loop—war, rape, torture, slavery, labor camps, medical experiments—again and again and again, since the dawn of man."

Monroe began a count on his fingers. "The violence is hardwired. What other creature rounds up its peers to systematically murder them out of existence?"

"You're talking about the holocaust?"

"Am I? Or am I talking about Holodomor, Stalin's man-made Terror-Famine that killed ten *million* Ukrainians? Or the Cambodian genocide, where one third of the country was wiped out through labor, starvation, and torture? Or the Armenian genocide? Or the Rwandan genocide?

"We act as if these things are appalling anomalies, distant tragedies to be studied with solemn reflection. But the truth is they're routine throughout history. Eighteenth century, the Selk'nam people are exterminated using a hand-and-ear bounty system to free up their land for European ranchers—ten thousand years of history, gone in a decade.

"Seventeenth century, sixty thousand innocent people are tortured and executed in the European Witch Trials—a barbaric purge of women, the elderly, and non-conformers—which, by the way, is still happening *today* across Sub-Saharan Africa.

"Sixteenth century, the Diet of Augsburg decrees, 'whosoever kills a Gypsy will be guilty of no murder' and unleashes a horrifying purge —but, eleven years later, they realize they went a bit too far and outlaw the drowning of Romani women and children.

"On and on and on...all the way back to the first genocide, 149 BCE, the Third Punic War, when Rome marched through Carthage and slaughtered all five hundred thousand residents in seven days—men, women, children. Only the last fifty thousand were spared as slaves.

"Man's capacity for cruelty is limitless. No other animal does this. No other animal puts so much time and energy into inflicting pain on its peers. There are entire museums dedicated to the long and gruesome history of human torture. Not just one, but seventeen worldwide."

Let him run…

Nick's eyes widened, like a student spellbound by a brilliant professor.

Monroe counted two on his fingers. "The lust is hardwired. Did you know, over the last hundred years, the Catholic church has sexually abused nearly one million children worldwide? It's an incomprehensible number. If I told you that tonight one priest will rape one child, you would be sick, outraged. But a million…all you can do is shrug."

He counted three. "The greed is hardwired. Since the dawn of organized society, we've been putting profits over people—Big Tobacco, Big Pharma, Big Food, Big Agriculture, capitalism, imperialism, colonialism, slavery—it's all the same thing, an irresistible urge to subdue others and collect far more than we need."

Monroe leaned in and whispered. "When I released my fifth cure, the president called to congratulate me. Do you know what he said?"

Nick shook his head.

"'Slow down.' We were working on the next five big killers, but hospitals and drug companies were seeing profits plummet from the first five. It was a modern version of the Cancer Problem."

"The Cancer Problem?"

Monroe sat back and reacted like it was obvious. "We've had the cure for cancer since 1977. The medicine was easy, the economics were the problem. A cancer patient is worth two hundred and fifty thousand dollars—a cure would put drug companies, hospitals, doctors, and researchers out of business. They couldn't find a way to make it profitable, so why bring it to market?"

Monroe leaned in and his face darkened. "The endless tragedy… it's *us*. It's not an accident, it's not our environment, it's not a problem of government, or culture, or education. It happens again and again and again across time and space. It's an undeniable pattern. There's something evil in us, and there always has been."

"But if that's true, if the evil is hardwired, then how did it get there?" Nick asked.

Monroe stood up and grabbed a red dry-erase marker. "If we look back three hundred thousand years, there were nine different species of humans on earth." He circled areas on an erasable world map beside the bookshelf. "Neanderthals in Europe, Denisovans in Asia, Red Deer Cave People in China, etc. But by ten thousand years ago, eight of them were gone, extinct, replaced by one dominant species: homo sapiens. Why?" He crossed through each circle. "We weren't better hunters, that award goes to homo rhodesiensis in Africa. We weren't smarter, Neanderthals had much bigger brains. So what happened?"

He capped the marker and tossed it on his desk. "We were more savage…driven by violence, lust, and greed…masters of rape and murder. We killed all the men and raped all the women until there was no one left…eight extinctions…one giant accidental genocide." He sat down, face grave. "We are all descended from the original mass murderers."

He leaned in, and a sinister grin crept across his face. "You've felt it, haven't you? The desire to crush your enemies, the urge to take something that's not yours." He sat back. "We all have. It's part of being human."

He stood and turned to his bookshelf. "Or perhaps you're a religious man, prefer creation over evolution." He plucked a bible from the top shelf and wielded it like a preacher. "Just look at Christianity. The largest religion in the world says that an almighty god—a big daddy in the sky—impregnated a twelve-year-old girl with a son who grew up to be the divine messiah. He was murdered by greedy Jews—a vilified minority group—after they drove thorns through his skull, whipped him to pieces, nailed him to a board, and stabbed a spear through his side. Now his followers worship a magical effigy of his tortured body on a cross. Every week they gather to eat his corpse and drink his blood as a reminder that we're all born into original sin, our souls stained with inherent wickedness." He dropped the bible on his desk with a thud. "It's the same story."

He sighed and delivered his conclusion. "The evil is within us, hardwired deep in our brain. And I'm going to tear it out."

"By replacing the savage masses with enlightened thinkers..." Nick prompted.

"Exactly. We are two species in one: the thoughtful man and the genocidal monkey. It's time to leave the monkey behind, to liberate the best of the human mind—logic, reasoning, problem solving, language—from the monkey's endless rage, lust, fear, and greed."

"Like your ACE therapy..."

Monroe grinned. "Indeed, just like that. I'm going to end our infinite loop of pain and suffering, and the only way to break the cycle is a complete genetic reset...a new beginning, a fresh start. Yes, it will be painful in the short term. But within one generation we'll be an entirely new, and exponentially better, species, thriving in a peaceful paradise."

Nick leaned back, digesting, pondering.

Monroe lowered into his chair. "If I'm wrong, Nick, point it out. But you agree, I can tell."

Keep him going...we need more time.

"Well, I follow your logic, I see the bigger picture, but...well, what makes you any different? I mean, aren't you killing more people than anyone who ever lived?"

"What's different? Oh, come on...everything! Both the intention and the result. This isn't an act of cruelty, or greed, or lust...it's an act of *mercy*. We are racing toward extinction. How long until we wipe ourselves out? I mean, do you really think we'll still be here in a thousand years?" He shook a finger. "Nature is coming—she may be fast, she may be slow, but she's coming. Our bill is long past due, and she *always* collects."

He looked Nick up and down. "What about you? Helping the powerful avoid disaster—is that not its own form of artificial selection? Survival of the richest? Extending the lifespan of some of the most violent, greedy, lustful people on earth?"

He did his research.

Nick shifted uncomfortably. "What do you want me to say? Yes, it's bad out there—companies, governments, churches, people—all corrupt, all operating from a place of…" He wrestled with the word. "Evil."

Nick leaned in. "But you only told half the story. What about the helpers, the guardians, the martyrs, the saints—the people who, every day, resist the darkness and shine a light? They're still out there, toiling in the shadows, and you're going to wipe them out."

Monroe nodded a bittersweet smile. "It's true, some good people will be lost. But, in our grand story, it's just another chapter of evolution. War, famine, pestilence—they've all offered great resets throughout history. Ninety-nine percent of all species that ever lived are now gone. Extinction is the rule. Survival is the exception."

"In fact…" He picked up the bible and opened to the bookmark ribbon. "'God saw that the earth was corrupt and filled with violence, the wickedness of man was great, and that every imagination of the thoughts of his heart was only evil continually. And he spoke—Behold, I will bring a great flood upon the earth, to destroy all flesh, and every thing that is in the earth shall die.'"

He gently placed the bible down and straightened. "I am Noah, bringing the rains to cleanse the earth and begin mankind anew."

The office door burst open.

They both startled and stood.

Brian stumbled in, hands zip-tied behind his back, face cut and bruised, his posture hunched and defeated. Hunziker strutted in behind, shirt stained with blood, his face dark and battle-worn. Zoe followed, Blitzkrieg's hand on her lower back. Wiretap entered last.

"Compound's secure," Hunziker said with a tired rasp.

Shit—I thought they'd be gone by now.

"The girls, are they alright?" Monroe asked, his face concerned.

"They're good. All accounted for. Your docs are checking them out now, but…" Hunziker nodded at Brian. "Don't worry, he ain't the type. He cut a hole in the fence by the back corner of the compound, near the girl's dorm. They had a truck stashed in the woods, on the old gravel road—we brought it in. He put up a good fight, but not good enough." He slugged Brian in the stomach, doubling him over.

Monroe raised his hands with disgust. "General, please, not in my office. Take him outside."

"You can keep the girl," Hunziker said, "but these two…they're mine."

Monroe considered a moment, then nodded. "Drop her at the clinic for another exam. The others, do what you will."

Zoe clasped Brian's arm. "Dr. Teddy, please!"

"Let's go, sweetheart." Hunziker pulled her off Brian. "You too." He beckoned to Nick.

"I'm sorry, Nick." Monroe sighed. "But you shouldn't have come back."

"Dr. Monroe, wait," Nick pleaded as Hunziker pulled him toward the door. "We need to talk…give me five minutes…just hear me out."

Monroe sat and dismissed Nick with a backhanded wave. Hunziker gave a firm tug.

Blitzkrieg dragged a crying Zoe toward the door. The radio on his belt crackled, and he picked it up and spoke. "Come again?" He held it to his ear and strained to listen over the commotion. "Uhh, boss, we've got a vehicle at the gate."

Hunziker turned, concerned.

Monroe looked up, curious.

Blitzkrieg listened to the radio and repeated. "Two men, armed."

The room went silent. Hunziker and Monroe looked at each other, then at Nick.

"Is it a government vehicle?" Monroe rose from the desk and pointed at the radio. "Ask him."

Blitzkrieg turned up the radio. "Ronnie, does it look like Feds?"

The radio hissed. "Nah, it's a shitty pickup."

Hunziker looked at Blitzkrieg. "Go check it out. Don't engage unless—"

The radio crackled. "We got two more vehicles approaching. Three men in each, all armed. What's the order here?"

Monroe looked at Hunziker with panic in his eyes.

Hunziker drew his sidearm and leveled it at Nick's head. "What the *fuck* is this?"

Nick slowly turned to Monroe, a vengeful grin on his face. "You were right, it *was* a bluff. I've been trying to reach my brother for three days, but I can't get through. So I called someone else, someone much more powerful...more powerful than a senator...more powerful than congress...more powerful than the president." He cocked his head, as if sharing an interesting fact. "Did you know that T.J. Chandra has one hundred and twenty-five *million* followers on Zencryptic? That's a third of the U.S. population. That kind of reach...wow."

"Wiretap!" Hunziker lowered his pistol.

Wiretap tapped and scrolled. "Oh shit." He froze and his eyes went wide. He began to read. "'Penicillin is a hoax. I just found out that Dr. Teddy Monroe has a vaccine that is one hundred percent effective against Scratch 'n Sniff. It's held at the Monroe Sciences campus in Wolfeboro, New Hampshire. I'm on my way right now, meet me there. There will be a mad rush for limited supplies, so hurry and come prepared—hint hint. P.S. One-million-dollar reward to the first person who takes a selfie with the vaccine.'" Wiretap scrolled. "And then a bunch of hashtags—#Virus #Penicillin #ScratchnSniff #Monroe-Sciences #DrTeddy #SelfiePrize. It's already trending—thirty thousand likes, fifteen thousand reposts, and—"

"Four more cars!" Big Ron crackled. "What do we do here, General? We need backup."

Monroe stared into space, stunned. "They can't get the vaccine. It'll all be for nothing."

Hunziker holstered his gun and grabbed the radio. "Reinforce the front gate. Assume defensive positioning and do *not* fire unless fired upon."

Nick leaned toward Monroe and spoke calmly. "You might want to relocate the girls to a secure location. And if you call now, you still have a chance of putting the local police on crowd control before they decide to try for the selfie prize."

Monroe pointed at Hunziker. "Move the girls to your bunkers. Call Sheriff Thompkins. Tell him it's a hoax and we need crowd control *now*." He turned to Nick with rage in his eyes. "What have you done?"

"Let us go now, and T.J. will delete the post. It's only been out for…" Nick glanced at his watch. "…twenty-three minutes, so those guys are local. But by this time tomorrow, you'll have a thousand cars at your gate. It's not too late."

Monroe fumed. "How do I know—"

"You don't…it's unenforceable," Nick said. "But you've got no other choice." He stared at Monroe. "Tick-tock, Doctor. Every minute, ten savages set sail for paradise."

"Doc, you can't—"

Monroe raised a hand and cut off Hunziker. "If I let you go, you'll delete it?" he asked Nick.

Nick looked him in the eye. "As soon as we get back to T.J., he'll delete it. You have my word. He'll even post a retraction, say his account was hacked by Russian spies or something."

Monroe looked at Wiretap.

Wiretap shrugged and nodded. "We can promote it…it'll work."

Monroe turned to Hunziker. "Send a man with them. Make sure it gets done."

"Doc…" Hunziker wound up to object. "I'm not—"

"No," Nick said firmly. "We go alone. We walk out, right now, unbothered, and when we get home, we delete the post. Then we disappear. That's the deal. Take it or leave it."

Monroe stared at Nick for a long moment, then softly addressed Hunziker. "Let them go."

Hunziker stormed forward. "What? He shot sixteen of my guys! There's no way in hell—"

"Fifteen," Brian said, staring at the ground.

"The fuck you just say?" Hunziker stepped into his face.

Brian looked up and met his eyes. "I shot fifteen of your guys. The kid shot himself."

Hunziker put a hand on his sidearm—snarling, eyes wide.

Monroe touched his shoulder and spoke in a soothing tone. "Kurt, we *need* your leadership at the front gate. Sheriff Thompkins listens to you. Your men follow you. If we don't control this crowd, if they don't delete that post, everything will be lost."

Hunziker glared at Brian for a long moment, then whispered, "Get out."

Monroe gestured to Blitzkrieg. "Private Ratliff, remove their zip-ties."

Blitzkrieg cut them loose.

Hunziker raised the radio, fuming. "Three combatants are coming out of the medical staff building and heading to their vehicle at the back gate. They are cleared to leave the compound. Do not engage. I repeat, do *not* engage. All available units to the front gate, now."

Hunziker glared at Brian and Nick as they brushed past.

Monroe slumped behind his desk and buried his face in his hands.

When Nick reached the doorway he paused, then turned to face Monroe. "You got it backwards…"

Monroe looked up.

"God brought the rain. Noah built the Ark."

FORTY-EIGHT

THEY RUSHED DOWN the central road toward the back gate—Brian in front, scanning their surroundings, Nick in back, pinching a map on his phone, and Zoe in the middle.

"Zoe," Nick whispered as he pulled up alongside her. "Where's Abby?"

"They took her away when we arrived. Dr. Teddy said…" She winced.

"What?"

"He's doing a C-section."

Nick stopped short, gazing off into the horizon as he analyzed Monroe's motivation. He pulled up a satellite map of the complex and started frantically zooming around.

Zoe jogged back to him.

He alternated between inspecting the map and scanning the complex, looking for a clue as to where Abby might be. "Whatever they're using as a hospital, it's probably one of the newer buildings, maybe even—"

"It's that one." Zoe pointed to a large white building on the other side of the street. Nick looked up, surprised, then looked at Zoe. She shrugged. "They brought me in for an exam."

Brian rushed up to them. "Guys, what's wrong? We gotta go."

"Abby's in there." Nick pointed. "Let's grab her."

"What? Are you crazy? I'm getting Zoe out of here before Monroe changes his mind."

"The building is right here, and everyone's at the front gate." Nick gestured around the silent complex. "We can do it—in and out. If we don't get her now, we'll just have to come back later with something bigger and riskier. We've got a tiny window of opportunity here, let's take it."

"Dad, we can't just leave her here."

Brian's tired gaze jumped between their faces, and he sighed. "You're killing me, Nick." He grabbed Zoe's hand and started toward the hospital building, grumbling, "At least the Navy gave us time off between missions."

"You get time off," Nick called after him, then muttered with a shrug, "as soon as we reach New Zealand."

* * *

THEY CREPT down the fourth floor hallway of the hospital building.

"This is where they brought me," Zoe whispered. "Right into this—"

"Get off me!" Abby's voice echoed from down the hall, followed by shattering glass.

They rushed to an operating room door and pressed against the wall outside.

"Stop moving," a stern man said. "If we miss you could be paralyzed." Metal instruments clattered across the tile floor. "Fine! You don't want the epidural? We'll do it the hard way. Nurse Vargas, hold her hips. Nurse Jacobs, hand me that scalpel."

"Nooo!" Abby roared.

Brian burst through the door.

Abby was flat on the operating table, two nurses and two doctors holding her down. Her sweatshirt and leggings were pulled back to expose a beach-ball belly marked with a dotted black line. Another pair of doctors and nurses stood over her, poised to operate.

They looked up in shock at Brian menacing in the doorway—sweaty, blood-stained, bruised—his wide eyes jumping from face to face, scanning for combatants.

Nick stepped in from behind Brian and smirked at Abby. "Final boarding call, unless you'd rather stay here?"

Her eyes widened and she started to squirm out.

"You can't be in here, sir," the head doctor said, scowling at Brian through thick glasses. "We're in the middle of a medical procedure."

"Is that what you call this?" Nick said. "Let's go, Abby."

The doctor pointed his scalpel at Brian. "You need to leave, now."

Brian's eyes flashed wide and he advanced, tossing aside a surgical tray and closing on the doctor like an attack dog given a command.

The doctor threw the scalpel on the floor—his arms went vertical.

Brian stopped in his face and snarled.

Nick nodded to Abby. "Let's go."

She jumped off the table and fixed her clothes. As she rushed toward the door, she flipped off the head doctor with her gauze-wrapped hand. "First do no harm, asshole."

They moved into the hallway, Brian backing out last. "Everyone stays in here," he said to the frozen surgical team. "Come out, and I'll be standing there. I promise."

They raced down the hall and tapped the elevator button. "You OK?" Nick said to Abby.

She nodded and looked back. "Just get me out of here before—"

A shrill alarm startled them and emergency lights began to flash. A stern voice came over a loudspeaker. "Code Pink. We have a Code Pink."

The elevator dinged and opened.

Brian extended an arm, blocking Nick. "They called it in—look." He pointed out the window at a pickup barreling down the road toward their building.

"Come on." Abby beckoned. "I know another way."

She led them back down the hall. As they passed the operating room, Brian thumped the window with a hammer fist, flashed a wild glare, and pointed at the head doctor. Everyone's hands shot up.

They raced to a back stairwell, panting down four flights of cold concrete until they reached the basement level. They turned down a long hallway and sprinted to the steel door at the end.

"Through here." Abby pushed it open. "There's a way out on the other side."

They streamed into the room and automatic lights flickered over a large chemistry lab. Abby strode to a back door on the opposite side. She turned the handle and pulled. It didn't budge. She turned again and tugged. Nothing. Her eyes fell to a security pad with a red light.

"I had a badge." Brian patted his pockets. "I think they took it."

Nick looked back. "Break through now, or let's go back up—we don't want to get trapped down here."

Brian scanned the room, then looked down at the lab counter next to him. He scooped up a giant glass chemical bottle sitting beside a microscope. "What's this? Can it melt through the lock?"

Abby squinted at the label. "No, that's just—"

The front door burst open and Blitzkrieg rushed in, gun drawn. Behind him followed a hulking soldier with a name tag that read, "Big Dave" Dunnigan and a stumpy soldier named "Little Dave" Demarzo. Old Glory wobbled in last.

"Hands hands hands!" Blitzkrieg closed in, pinning the group against the back door with their hands up.

Monroe and Nurse Vargas scrambled in, red-faced and huffing. Old Glory mumbled into his radio and the Code Pink alarm went silent.

For a long moment, Monroe just stood and glared—blinking, face twitching—his usual air of academic prestige replaced by raw unfiltered rage.

"Dr. Monroe, the deal still stands." Nick stepped forward, hands up. "If you let us go now, with Abby, we'll delete the post in ten minutes. Better to lose one Mother than risk all thirty-three, right? And—"

"We are *done* negotiating." Monroe's voice trembled. "You've burned me twice. There will *not* be a third time." He turned to Old

Glory. "Lieutenant Dobbins, activate our backup location and ready the buses for departure."

Old Glory scurried out the door.

"Nurse Vargas, prepare the OR for an emergency C-section."

She rushed out.

Monroe closed the door and locked it. He slowly turned back to Nick, his face sinister. "Blitzkrieg…"

"Sir!" Blitzkrieg licked his lips, gun locked on Brian.

"Shoot them all. Not Abby."

Nick stepped forward. "Wait—"

Blitzkrieg turned his gun on Nick.

"Do it," Monroe said.

Blitzkrieg grinned, closed one eye, and aimed dead center on Nick's forehead. He squeezed the trigger.

Brian flashed, blasting Blitzkrieg's arm up as the gun cracked, shattering a glass case above Nick's head. The gun clattered away, and Brian drilled a stunned Blitzkrieg in the throat, sending him stumbling backward—eyes bulging, sputtering, clutching his neck.

Nick, Zoe, and Abby scrambled away as Big Dave and Little Dave raised their guns on Brian.

Brian launched the giant chemical bottle off the counter into a steel pipe above their heads, raining down glass shards and blue liquid. The soldiers frantically spat and swiped their eyes. With a single long step, Brian was on them, bludgeoning Big Dave with the base of a microscope and driving Little Dave through a glass cabinet.

Brian picked up the microscope and turned to Monroe, pulsing with bloodlust.

A shot rang out and everyone ducked. All eyes turned to the front of the lab, where a snarling Blitzkrieg held Zoe in a rear headlock, gun pressed to her temple.

Brian dropped the microscope and slowly raised his hands.

"Dad, I'm sorry." Zoe fought back tears.

He gazed at her with deep affection. "No, Zo, I'm sorry."

Big Dave rose and raised a pistol to Brian's head. "Good to go?"

Monroe nodded.

"Close your eyes, Z-Bird," Brian said sweetly. "I love you."

Zoe squeezed her eyes shut and winced.

Big Dave cocked back the hammer.

Brian gently closed his eyes.

"Stop," Abby commanded. "Let them go."

Everyone looked to the corner. She was standing with her back against an open supply cabinet, one hand on her belly, the other holding a small glass chemical bottle by her mouth.

"What are you doing?" Monroe asked, his voice a mix of confusion and concern. He eased closer, squinting at the label on the bottle. His eyes went wide with horror. "Abigail, are you out of your mind? Put that down right now."

Little Dave started toward her, and Abby tilted the bottle against her bottom lip, liquid dancing at the rim.

Monroe blocked his path. "Wait wait…stand down, Private," he said calmly, and began to drift toward Abby. "She won't do it. She won't hurt her babies." He closed in, palm extended. "She's going hand me that—"

Abby tipped the bottle—liquid splashed across her lips.

"Nooo!" Monroe recoiled.

Abby spit on the floor and roared, "Get *back*!"

Monroe reeled backward. "Everyone back! Give her room. Now!"

The soldiers backed up, startled by the doctor's panic.

Abby glared at Monroe, eyes vengeful and wild. "Badges."

Nick stepped forward, hand extended. "Badges here. Everyone."

Nick collected the badges, swiped the back door and opened it wide. Zoe and Brian rushed out into a concrete stairwell. He held the door and nodded to Abby. "Let's go."

"No no no." Monroe stomped forward, hands waving. "Blitzkrieg, if she sets one foot out that door, shoot them all…starting with Abby."

Nick glared at him.

"She stays." Monroe glared back. "That's the deal. Take it or leave it."

Abby death-stared at Monroe, her gauze-wrapped hand trembling the bottle, its little waves reaching for her lips. "Go," she said softly.

"No." Nick shook his head, racing through the options. "I just need—"

"Go!" she yelled, a lifetime of pain and frustration and sadness washing through her eyes like a dark, crushing wave.

"Come on, Nick." Brian pulled him out the door into the stairwell.

The lab door swung shut and locked with a sharp echo. Nick backed toward the stairs, his gaze locked on Abby shrinking in the little window frame, her eyes shimmering and darting between the soldiers and Monroe, like a fawn cornered by hungry wolves.

Brian dragged him to the stairs and shoved him forward. "Nick, let's go!"

Nick stumbled up the stairs, pausing halfway for one last look.

"I'm so sorry," he whispered.

FORTY-NINE

THEY RUSHED toward the back gate, Nick slowing to look back at the hospital building.

"Keep going." Brian pushed him forward. "It's like you said, we'll resupply in New Zealand and come back for her, and we'll keep coming back until she's free." He pointed ahead to the Ark glistening in the small parking lot, facing the open gate. "But right now, we need to go."

They reached the parking lot and Brian strode toward the driver's seat. Nick pointed Zoe toward the passenger seat. "You take front."

Nick opened the rear passenger door and stopped for one last look back—he gripped the door's edge, his mind racing.

There's no way to get her, we have to come back. By then Monroe will have moved to a backup location. If we could somehow track her—

A memory flashed in his mind, a brief moment stretched long across a wave of heartache: Abby staring into the falling snow with glassy eyes, tugging at the straps on her knapsack, kicking streaks into the fresh powder, her jaw chattering as she quietly argued with some invisible adversary.

Focus. How do you track her? Hide a phone on their bus? Give her a way to signal their location? Or check nearby—

Another memory flickered in his mind: Abby dunking a tube of cinnamon rolls, raising her arms… *"Touchdown!"*

Check nearby properties owned by Monroe Sciences and—

His focus cracked and the moments flooded in:

Abby spinning on the loading dock in the yellow apron… *"Ta-da!"*

Abby staring into the fireplace… *"If I'm a famous doctor, I'll always have a home."*

Frustration bubbled up inside.

Abby peeking over the comforter, giggling at his apron spin… *"You promise?" "I promise."*

Frustration swirled and thickened into rage.

Abby shrinking in the little window frame, her eyes shimmering and darting, a fawn cornered by hungry wolves… *"I'm so sorry."*

And then he smelled it…burning…everything burning, all at once…and strangely, he liked it, found comfort in it, savored it. He inhaled deeply.

Rage hardened into resolve.

A final image took hold: Dana gazing into his eyes, squeezing his shivering hand, whispering… *"Save the good ones."*

* * *

BRIAN STARTED THE ARK. "Alright, let's roll."

Nick's door slammed.

Brian revved the engine, the Ark roaring like a lion. He tapped their destination into the dash as he narrated the plan. "Ten minutes home, five minutes load up, ninety minutes to Moose River. We'll make it. Barely, but we'll make it."

Brian buckled his seatbelt. "Seatbelts on."

Zoe clicked her seatbelt. "On."

"Buckle up, Nick."

No response.

"Nick?" Brian looked in the rearview.

He spun and blinked at the empty back seat. "Nick?!"

"He's outside!" Zoe pointed out her window.

Nick was down on one knee, his back to the Ark, hunched over something on the ground they couldn't see.

"What the hell..." Brian lowered Zoe's window.

"What are you doing?" Brian shouted. "Let's go."

Nick dug through something in front of him.

"Nick! We need to move, now."

He kept digging.

Zoe looked nervously in her side-view mirror. "Dad?"

Brian checked his rearview. "In sixty seconds they're gonna be on us—get in!"

No response.

"Nick, I *will* leave you behind."

Nothing.

Brian threw the car in drive. "That's it. We're gone."

Nick stepped to Zoe's window with decisive speed, hand extended and dangling a jet-black pendant necklace. "Sixty-three fifty-three Wantabo Lake."

They looked down at the swinging necklace, then back up at Nick.

"Swipe this on the security pad at the front gate. The code is sixty-three fifty-three. Maia and Kora are expecting you."

Brian looked past Nick and saw the bug-out bag half unpacked on the ground behind him. "Nick..." he said with concern, "what are you doing?"

"I'm going back."

"Are you out of your mind? Get in, we'll game plan on the road."

Nick stared with iron resolve. "I'm not leaving without her."

Brian leaned in. "You go back, you're not leaving at all."

Nick didn't flinch. "I can live with that."

Brian squinted in his rearview—biting the inside of his lip, wincing, wrestling with a decision—then he looked down at Zoe. "Sorry, Nick, we'll see you at the ranch."

Nick nodded. "Go."

Zoe grabbed the necklace and Nick turned from the Ark.

"Hey Nick..." Brian called.

Nick turned back.

Brian extended a mighty hand to the window. “Give ‘em hell, brother.”

Nick clasped his hand with a solemn nod, a special nod reserved for soldiers charging into impossible odds. “Go time.”

* * *

Nick stepped back as the Ark peeled out in a cloud of burnt rubber and exhaust. He stood over the half-filled bug-out bag, surrounded by a spread of discarded prepper gear. He reached down into the bag, gripped a butane torch lighter, and slowly rose, squeezing the trigger, a blue flame hissing to life at his side.

Nick glared at the complex, a dark figure swirling in an iridescent mist of burnt rubber and gasoline…inhaling fumes, exhaling streams of smoke…his sinister face uplit by a steady blue glow.

FIFTY

Nick stuffed the torch in his pocket, threw the bag over his shoulder, and raced away from the back gate. He followed a footpath past the hospital building to a crossroads on the central lawn. A big informational placard declared he was on "Teddy's Campus Quad."

Nick did a slow spin, analyzing the perimeter: medical facilities, administrative buildings, pickup trucks, a groundskeeping shed, school buses, a small pond, a dining hall, patio seating, a long parking lot. All silent.

He completed the spin, set his watch timer for ten minutes, and took a deep breath.

"Go," he whispered, and started the timer.

Nick lowered the bag and pulled out an empty six-pack of soda. Shining a flashlight, he peeked inside the cans—Tracy's homemade smoke bombs had hardened beautifully, their wicks tucked discreetly inside.

"Perfect." He gave an impressed nod. "Boston's Queen of Comfort."

Nick grabbed his 15-in-1 multitool and used the pliers to fish inside each can and pluck out the wick. He tucked the six-pack under one arm and moved toward a brick building with big glass doors and shiny lettering: Central Administration.

He stepped inside, found the fire alarm, and pulled it, unleashing flashing lights and a deafening ring. He backed toward the entrance, pulled a can from the six-pack, kissed the fuse with his torch, and rolled it across the floor—a trail of inky black smoke filled the lobby.

Nick backed out of the building and watched the windows darken, lights flashing through the thick smoke like lightning in a thundercloud.

He glanced at his watch and repeated the attack on three more buildings: The Davis Research & Laboratory Center, Media & Public Relations, and The Gordon T. Chevalier Dining Hall.

Two cans left. Make 'em count.

He swung open the door on a beautiful old building and squinted at the lettering above the lobby desk: The Carol F. Emerson Library.

"Not the library," he muttered. "Everybody loves the library."

He gently closed the door and turned to the next building, a small modern structure with sparkling glass from top to bottom: Doctor Edward G. Monroe Biographical Museum and Archives.

Nick grinned and strutted over. He stepped inside and was welcomed by a life-size hologram of Monroe. "Hi there! I'm Dr. Edward G. Monroe, but you can call me Dr. Teddy. How did I get that nickname? Well, there was a young boy named Ben who was receiving my protocol at one of my clinics—"

Nick pulled the alarm, drowning out the speech. He sparked a can at Monroe's feet and backed out with a wave.

He trotted to the last building: IT & Communications.

Nick grabbed the fire alarm.

"Thompkins is here, sir. He's looking for you," a radio crackled across the lobby.

Nick turned to see a door ajar: Central Communications. He crept over and peeked inside the empty security room. The main wall was lined with two dozen camera monitors and surrounded by intercom controls, backup radios, telecom equipment, servers, computers, laptops, phones, and a big circuit-breaker box. The cameras covering the front gate showed six angles of chaos: twenty vehicles, plus police cruisers, and an uneasy standoff between armed locals, cops, and militiamen.

An idea struck.

Nick scrambled around the room opening cabinets, boxes, laptops, covers, server doors—anything with hinges. He swung back into the lobby, opened the emergency fire hose cabinet below the fire alarm, and walked the hose across the lobby into Central Communications. He secured the nozzle to a server rack in the far corner, opened the multi-tool's blade, and poked a hole through the hose every twelve inches from the nozzle to the door. He closed the door as much as the hose would allow, returned to the cabinet, and cranked the water to max flow. The hose inflated across the lobby floor. When it reached the room, there was a spurting sound followed by a loud hiss, then crashing and banging. Little streams of water trickled under the door. Nick grinned, pulled the fire alarm, and rolled the last smoke bomb.

He strode from the building, lights flickering behind him, and marched across a patch of grass to three school buses. He plunged the multitool's blade into the first tire and tugged it out with a loud hiss.

Say goodbye to your lifeboats.

He moved methodically from tire to tire—jab-pull-hiss.

He stopped at the last bus.

We'll leave one so the girls can get out safe. Not having enough seats will add to the panic, create conflict between Monroe and the militia.

Nick swung back to center, grabbed his bag, and headed for three pickups lined up by the groundskeeping shed. One by one, he soaked their front seats with lighter fluid and placed two camping-stove gas canisters on their dashboards.

He dug in his bag, then froze at a crackle behind the shed. "I want four more men on the wall, now!" Hunziker barked over a radio.

Nick crept behind the shed and found a long tarp pinned down with stones. One corner had blown loose, and a limp arm in a camo jacket hung out. Nick peeked under the tarp at the line of dead militiamen.

"Jesus, Brian."

He squatted and plucked a radio and a pistol off the first man's belt.

Nick thought a moment, pressed the talk button, then winced and released it.

He took a deep breath, nodded, and pressed the button again. "I need backup!" he yelled at a distance with a slight southern accent. "There's a pack of Black fellas storming the gun room. They cut the fence and snatched a Mother. Hurry!"

He scuffed the radio across his jacket, rose, and opened fire on the pickups, emptying the pistol across three hoods.

He released the talk button and waited.

Silence.

Was the accent that bad? Maybe there's no gun room? How could they not have a gun room? What if—

"This is General Hunziker—initiate Operation Alamo. I repeat, Operation Alamo. Anyone not at the front gate swarm the armory, now! Shoot to kill! Shoot to kill!"

A grin crept across Nick's face. He tossed the gun under the tarp and placed the radio back on the soldier's belt. He tore a strip of duct tape from his bag, carefully taped down the radio's talk button, and secured the tarp.

Enjoy the white noise.

Nick pulled a road flare from the bag and sparked it with the torch, the bursting flame casting a red glow across his smile. He tossed it on the truck's seat and flames roared through the cabin. Nick closed the door and moved to the next truck. As he slammed the third door, his watch went off. He stashed the bug-out bag behind the shed and strode back to center.

Nick slowly spun—torch in one hand, multitool in the other—and admired the scene: The entire complex was burning. Six buildings seeped thick smoke, their jet-black windows flashing an unsynchronized lightning storm. Water gurgled from IT & Communications. Two school buses slumped on empty tires. Three bullet-riddled trucks burned behind their windshields. It looked like an army had marched through and gone scorched earth.

Nick nodded and started toward the hospital building. Two pickups barreled down the path straight toward him. He pocketed the torch and multitool and took a hard left down another path. He was almost off the quad when another pickup skidded to a stop just ahead, and three soldiers leapt out, guns drawn.

Nick jogged to them, waving his arms and pointing back. "Help! They're back there. They just came through."

The soldiers stared past him—eyes wide, mouths open—scanning the quad with shock and awe.

"They had a girl with them…young, pregnant, white. She was crying."

They stared, dumbstruck.

Nick clapped. "Go! Before they get away."

The soldiers snapped from their daze and sprinted past, yelling into their radios, barking conflicting commands.

Nick left the quad and strode toward the hospital. As he reached the building, the front doors swung open—Big Dave and Little Dave burst out. They locked on Nick and stopped.

Little Dave smirked and reached for his sidearm. "Where do you think—"

A sharp explosion echoed from the quad.

They winced and ducked.

Two more explosions boomed, and their wide eyes followed three dark clouds rising behind Nick.

Nick pointed back. "Reynolds, Prewett, and Stine just spotted the Mother on the quad. The thugs must've set some kind of trap for them. You better go."

They brushed past Nick and sprinted toward the quad, Big Dave yelling into his radio. "We got booby traps on the quad, General. Do you copy? General?"

Nick stepped inside and marched through the building, past doctors and nurses huddled in dark rooms, down the rear stairwell. He reached the basement level, turned down the hallway, and froze.

Straight ahead, Blitzkrieg was gently closing the lab door as he backed into the hallway. He turned and stared at Nick for a long moment, then drew his gun and started stalking up the hall.

Nick stumbled backward out of the hallway and pressed against the wall.

He'll be here before you can make it up the stairs.

There are no other exits.

He's got a gun, you can't fight him.

You've got about seven seconds...

Nick spotted something on the opposite wall: a fire extinguisher.

He sprinted across the hallway opening, and a shot rang out. The light above him exploded, raining down sparks. The hallway dimmed.

Nick pulled the fire extinguisher from the wall, drew the safety pin, and squeezed the trigger handle, spraying a stream of white dust into the stairwell. He wedged the safety pin under the handle, locking the trigger in place, then squatted and rolled the fire extinguisher down the hall. A giant cloud of chemical dust filled the hallway and billowed into the stairwell.

Blitzkrieg screamed and coughed, then opened fire, five rounds flashing through the thick white haze, cement chips ricocheting around the stairwell.

Nick squatted by the hallway entrance like a sprinter on starting blocks. He drew the torch from his pocket and listened as the extinguisher hissed and clanged.

Come on, keep going...

It sputtered.

Wait for it...

Silence.

Go.

Nick held his breath and charged into the fog.

FIFTY-ONE

ABBY'S EYES jumped around the room as the bottle trembled at her lip:

Blitzkrieg's crazed smile.

Big Dave's stun gun.

Little Dave's zip-ties.

Dr. Teddy's concerned face.

"Abby, just stay calm," Dr. Teddy said. "Let's not do anything rash."

Rash? You've literally got me cornered. What do you expect me to do?

Dr. Teddy straightened and waved his hands. "Alright, everybody out."

The soldiers looked at him, confused. "Sir?" Blitzkrieg said.

"Out." Dr. Teddy ushered them out the front door. "I'll call you if I need you."

They shuffled into the hallway, disappointed.

Dr. Teddy placed a lab stool in front of Abby, sat down, and crossed his legs.

She glared at him.

He sighed. "You're smart, Abby—probably my smartest, most

promising Mother—so I'm going to be completely honest with you, because I respect you and because you'll know if I'm lying."

What is this bullshit?

"You and I, we're both scientists, and as I always say, good science is the pursuit of truth. So let's look at some hard truths." He started a count on his fingers. "Truth: You are all alone. Your friends are gone and they're not coming back. Even if they survive out there, even if they're crazy enough to come back, we'll be long gone."

It's true, they're on their way to the airport now.

He counted two. "Truth: You are not a killer." His face softened and he spoke with empathy. "You never wanted to be a Mother. You're a talented young woman just starting a long and successful career. Taking care of two babies?" He scoffed. "Good luck finding the time and energy for MCATs, med school, residency, boards, grants, research. I know you blame me, and that's OK, but you wouldn't harm the twins—after all, they're your babies too."

I don't want to harm them, I just...I never wanted this.

He counted three. "Truth: You belong here. You don't fit in out there, you never have. I bet you never had stable friends, or teachers, or coaches, or even family, right?"

She held her glare steady, but her vision started to blur.

"I know because I didn't fit in either. I've been there—you're too smart, too analytical...nobody understands your depth, your passion, your persistence...you're just the 'weird science kid.'" He paused and let the phrase sink in. "But you haven't fit in here either, and that's my fault—I paired you with Hunziker." He lowered his voice. "He's a brute, too thick for your talents and brain power. You belong among enlightened thinkers. The community we're building here will be filled with people just like you." He leaned in and whispered. "Two years from now, Hunziker and his apes will be long gone, trust me. Our community will ascend as the intellectual hub of humanity, and *you* will be one of our top leaders: a scientist, a researcher, a *doctor*." He sat up straight and returned to normal volume. "You're the future of this place, Abby. And the truth is, I need you."

Enlightened thinkers? Intellectual hub of humanity? Sounds like Harvard...

She lowered the bottle an inch and cleared her throat. "Where was all this a half hour ago, when they were about to cut me open?"

He nodded and raised his hands in submission. "I admit, I was upset. After the bleach incident...seeing you dragged back in here, half frozen...well, I was worried about your mental health and I wanted to protect our babies. But that was a mistake, I see that now, and I apologize."

Mm-hmm.

"I'd like to propose a compromise. Your babies are going to grow up in our community—that's non-negotiable—but your future is completely up to you. You can stay here with them or you can leave."

He held out his left hand, presenting the first of two options. "If you stay, I promise you'll have a safe home for as long as you like. You'll have unrestricted access to all my facilities. Whatever research you want—cancer, rare cancers, right?—I can get you everything you need: space, equipment, materials, funding, subjects, a complete blank check for rare-cancer research—every doctor's dream. I'll set up advisor relationships with the top doctors in my network, anyone you like. I'll pull you away from the Matchstick Militia and the juvenile Mothers and give you private accommodations among the medical staff. My nurses will take care of the babies, and as they grow you can spend as much or as little time with them as you want. If you'll give this place another chance, give *me* another chance, I'll give you complete control of your destiny."

I'd be a top cancer researcher by, like, tomorrow...

"And if I want to leave?"

He held out his right hand. "Then I will do everything I can to help you start a new life—money, transportation, supplies, housing, introductions, whatever you need. You can go anywhere in the world, you can even go join your new friends. And if you ever want to come back and visit the twins, you're always welcome."

He rested his hands on his lap. "Either way, I'll have Hunziker's adoption papers voided immediately. You can be my daughter until you're eighteen or get legally emancipated. Whatever you prefer, I'll have the lawyers draw it up. And you can deliver by C-section early or you can wait for natural birth. Your choice."

She squinted at him, weighing her options and his credibility as her hand trembled from fatigue.

"It's a win-win-win." He smiled and shrugged. "You get the freedom to pursue your life, your children get a safe home and a good future, and I get to see you all flourish, which is all I ever wanted." He leaned in. "But you need to choose, Abby, because they're not coming back, and you can't hold that bottle forever."

There was a hesitant knock at the door, and Blitzkrieg poked his head in. "Sir?"

"Not now." Dr. Teddy waved a hand without looking back.

"I'm sorry, sir, but it's urgent."

"What is it?"

The soldiers shuffled back in.

Blitzkrieg cleared his throat. "Some thugs broke into the compound and stormed the armory, sir. There's smoke and gunfire on the quad."

Dr. Teddy sighed and hung his head.

"Also, sir..." Blitzkrieg looked nervously at the other soldiers. "It sounds like they...they might have...grabbed one of the girls?"

Dr. Teddy's head shot up and he spun to face them. "What? Might have? What happened? Who is missing?"

"We don't know, sir."

"You two, go tell General Hunziker I want her back, whatever the cost. Blitzkrieg, you stay here and stand guard."

Big Dave and Little Dave rushed out. Blitzkrieg posted at the door.

Dr. Teddy turned back, teary-eyed, heartbroken. "This is what people are really like, Abby." He gave a weepy sigh. "Savages attacking science, destroying progress, kidnapping children." He gazed at her with haunted eyes. "The world is a nightmare, and we are the monsters. Sooner or later, evil comes for us all."

Woah, he's really upset...

He looked deep into her eyes. "I hope you'll stay here with us, I really do. I hate to think of you out there, all alone among the wolves.

But it's your choice, Abby. Either way, we need to get you to safety now, while we still can. Will you get on a bus? You can think about my offer. Whatever you decide, I'll honor it."

A distant explosion rumbled the lab—glassware rattled.

Dr. Teddy stood and looked at Abby with fear in his eyes.

Two more explosions followed.

He extended a hand. "Abby, *please*…"

He's right, they're all wolves.

At least with him I'll have a good home, smart peers, a path to becoming a doctor. It's better than being passed around out there again.

I mean, what choice do I really have?

Abby gave a defeated nod, placed the bottle on the table, and shook out her hand.

"Private Ratliff, scout ahead. Find us a safe path directly to the bus."

"Yes, sir." He backed into the hallway and gently closed the door.

Dr. Teddy put an arm around Abby and walked her toward the door. "Don't worry, an hour from now you'll be safe and warm in your new—"

A gunshot rang out in the hallway.

They froze.

Then a hissing and clanging…Blitzkrieg screamed and coughed… five wild shots.

They retreated to the back door, Dr. Teddy trying frantically to open it without a badge.

A series of thuds…silence.

They stared at the front door in terror.

The handle jiggled.

Dr. Teddy moved behind Abby and cowered. "Put your hands up. They won't shoot a pregnant girl."

The handle slowly turned, and the door swung open, spilling white fog into the room. A dark figure loomed in the hallway, an ominous silhouette in the swirling smoke.

Dr. Teddy gasped.

Nick stepped in—glistening with white dust and sweat, clothes ruffled and torn, a nasty bruise on his temple.

His eyes burned with savage intensity, and they grabbed her, and instantly she knew…felt it tingle down her arms…heard him whisper in her head, "Together, or not at all."

FIFTY-TWO

Nick watched the courage sweep across Abby's face. In an instant, she straightened and swung an elbow behind her, ramming Monroe in the stomach.

He grunted and doubled over.

She snatched the chemical bottle off the table and poured it over his head.

He howled and scrambled away, knocking over lab equipment as he groped toward the eyewash station.

Nick tossed Abby a badge and she opened the back door. They rushed into the stairwell and slammed the door. Nick started toward the stairs.

"No, this way." Abby pointed to a dim hallway underneath the stairs. They moved down a slim passage lined with craggy wet stone and dirty yellow lamps, a vestige of an earlier era. Abby stopped at a windowless steel door and looked back at Nick. "Hold your breath. Don't touch anything."

Two gunshots rang out behind them.

"He's shooting out the door." Nick nodded ahead. "Go." He sucked in a deep breath, and Abby burst through the door.

Automatic lights flickered on, illuminating four walls of floor-to-ceiling steel cages. Dozens of rhesus monkeys shrieked and banged as they watched Abby and Nick glide across the room toward the back door.

Nick's eyes jumped from side to side, and he instantly understood why he was holding his breath: The monkeys were infected with Scratch 'n Sniff. On the left, a large monkey was secured in the center of his cage with a tight rubber collar, his palms picked down to the whites of his bones, the newspaper under him crusted maroon. On the right, an emaciated monkey with his hands shackled to the top corners of the cage kicked frantically at the bars. By the back door, a dozen monkeys were split across two large cages, one filled with females and the other filled with babies staring blankly into space.

"Hurry!" Abby held the door and beckoned.

Nick rushed out.

She paused, stepped back inside, and opened the locks on the two large cages. She flipped off the automatic lights and closed the door tight.

They moved down the dank hallway to a single door at the end. As Nick touched the handle, screeching and clanging erupted from the monkey lab behind them. Monroe screamed and gunshots rang out. Nick pushed through the door, back into the main hospital.

"This way." Abby rushed down a long hallway, past several exam rooms, an operating room, a biosafety lab, and a long one-way mirror.

Nick slowed and squinted through the mirror. It overlooked a dark room that had recently hosted a party: there was a dining table lined with aromatherapy diffusers, a TV surrounded by empty beer bottles and cigar butts, a poker table with playing cards, a messy kitchenette, and two rows of cots.

"Come on!" Abby pulled him along. "We're almost there."

She swiped the badge and pushed through a set of large double doors. Nick followed inside, turning as he scanned the sprawling industrial warehouse. Enormous vents pumped cold dry air into the climate-controlled storeroom. Bright overhead lights hung above rows and rows of shipping pallets. Every pallet looked the same: cardboard boxes branded "Monroe Sciences" stacked eight feet high, plastic-wrapped, and ready to ship.

Nick leaned in and squinted, looking for labels. "What are these?"

She pulled him along. "I don't know."

They moved through the warehouse, passing row after row of pallets.

What is all this? There's no manufacturing here, this is corporate headquarters. Is it being stored here? Or shipped out?

They reached a heavy steel door next to the loading dock.

"This is it." Abby leaned into the door.

"Wait." Nick pulled the multitool from his pocket and drew the blade. "Just one second." He sliced down the side of a box, peeled back the cardboard, and squinted inside at stacked rows of vials. He pulled one out and read the label, "Monroe Science—Palmar Pruritus Virus (PPV) Vaccine." He slipped it in his jacket and nodded. "Let's go."

They stepped out onto the loading dock, ran down the cement steps, and turned onto the footpath. Abby slowed and looked back at the smoke rising from the quad. "Blitzkrieg said someone broke in…oh my god, how many were there?"

Nick smirked. "Eh, I'm thinking…one."

She spun. "*You* did this?"

"Well, yeah…" He shrugged. "I had to one-up your bleach panic."

She grinned, her eyes twinkling.

He pointed toward the back gate. "Come on."

"Wait." She grabbed his hand. "I know a better way."

* * *

NICK EXTENDED his hand across the shallow brook and Abby grabbed it, hopping effortlessly from one bank, to the flat stone, to the other bank. They climbed up the embankment and stepped onto the gravel road.

Nick started to run, then glanced back at Abby who was panting with her hands on her hips. He skidded to a stop. "Come on. We have to keep moving."

Abby coughed. "Hey, I'm nine months pregnant." She started into an exhausted gait. "And I've already done this run once today." She shot him a dirty look as she passed.

Six minutes later they spilled onto Cradle Cove and rested with their hands on their knees, puffing long clouds of mist.

"Now what?" Abby panted.

Nick shook his head. "I don't—" He wheezed. "I don't know."

"Well…" She straightened and gestured. "Talk it out."

He nodded. "OK…basically two options…run or hide."

"If we run, we need a car," she said. "No way we can outrun them on foot."

"Or a boat," he said. "I doubt they have boats, or the patience for a boat chase."

"And if we hide?"

"Well, we could go back to one of the original houses, or try a new house, or Herman found an old cabin in the woods. Basically just hole up somewhere and hope they don't find us. But we've got nothing. No supplies, no weapons, no—"

"Let's run," she said decisively.

"OK." He nodded. "Let's run. Which way do—"

"Shh! Do you hear that?"

He strained to listen, then he heard it, a low rumbling sound. They turned and stared back down the gravel road. The top of a yellow school bus bounced over the hazy horizon.

"He abandoned ship," Nick said.

A red pickup swerved wildly around the bus and soared past in a cloud of dust, barreling toward them with determined speed.

"Run!" Abby pulled him away from the gravel road.

They raced along the straightaway, then down a hill, toward a resort-style home.

"They'll have a boat." Nick pointed. "Come on!"

They swung into the driveway.

A vehicle roared behind them and screeched to a stop at the edge of the driveway.

They froze, raised their hands, and slowly turned.

The Ark glistened in a cloud of dust and exhaust, engine growling, driver's window down, Brian smirking in aviators and a leather flight jacket. "Need a ride?"

FIFTY-THREE

"You missed the flight?" Nick dropped his hands.

"Yeah, I tried to delay and they fired me." Brian shrugged. "Fuck 'em—I got a new job, T.J.'s personal assistant."

The rear door swung open—T.J. was sitting at the end of the row, his neck wrapped in a towel secured with duct tape. He turned his whole stiff body to look at Nick, his neck fat pressed up like a turtle. "Dammit, Brian, that's not what I was saying."

Nick grinned at T.J., then leaned inside to see Dana, Tracy, and Zoe smirking in the far back row.

Abby climbed in next to T.J.

Nick jumped in, slammed the door, and scooted forward. "They're coming. Get us out of here."

"What?" Brian looked back, alarmed. "How many?"

"All of them."

Brian threw the Ark in drive and slammed on the gas, the wheels screeching as they peeled out toward the entrance to Cradle Cove. As they hit the first curve, Hunziker's red pickup roared over the hill behind them.

They tore through the woods, riding the twisting road as it swerved around trees and boulders, rose over hills, swooped into ditches. Brian piloted like a stunt driver trying to break a record, accelerating into every straightaway, skidding around every corner.

A burst of automatic fire cracked behind them, chewing up nearby trees and sparking off rocks. Nick looked back to see a line of pickups snaking over the distant hill and he realized why Brian was going so fast.

He's trying to keep the woods between us and them. As long as they're not directly behind us, they can't get a clear shot.

Brian turned onto a short straightaway and slammed the gas, roaring ahead. As the Ark reached the next curve, Hunziker's truck skidded onto the straightaway behind them and opened fire. The Ark's back window exploded, spraying glass over the far back seats. The ladies screamed.

"Oh, come on!" Brian glanced in his rearview. "Not her window."

Tracy's head popped up. "Her?" She shook broken glass off her shirt. "I *know* you're not talking about the car right now."

The Ark screeched around a corner and bounced up a hill. The distant pickups fired wildly through the woods, several bullets making it through and thumping across the doors.

"Don't they know she's in here?" Dana leaned over Abby, shielding her body.

"They know." Nick turned to shield Abby's side. "They just don't care."

The Ark leaned hard around a curve and everyone slid sideways, bunching into each other.

"Ow!" T.J. yelled. "Goddammit, Brian! What happened to slow is smooth and smooth is fast?"

"It doesn't apply when you're getting shot at—hold on!" Brian stepped on the gas and veered off the road.

Everyone yelled.

They careened through a stretch of sparse woods, bumping and rocking as they shortcut a long curve in the road. When they reached the other side, the Ark tore out of the underbrush and skidded sideways onto the long straightaway that led to the little bridge. Brian peeled out, trying to gain distance from Hunziker before the general reached the straightaway behind them.

Nick watched the speedometer…50…60…70.

They tore past an old sign, "SPEED LIMIT 14."

"Slow down," Nick said.

"Brian! Slow down," Tracy yelled.

"Dad!" Zoe cried.

Brian accelerated, locked on the distant bridge, stone-faced behind his aviators.

Hunziker reached the straightaway behind them and opened fire.

Everyone ducked as bullets thumped and pinged.

"Brian, slow down!" Nick pointed ahead. "It's too tight."

The broken-down bridge raced toward them, barely wide enough to fit the Ark. The thick woods surrounding it funneled them toward the single narrow exit.

Brian accelerated.

Everyone screamed and closed their eyes.

With a whoosh they soared across, the Ark shuddering with inches to spare.

Nick looked back. "Jesus, Brian, that was close."

Brian slammed the brakes.

"What are you doing?" Nick said. "Go!"

The Ark fishtailed to a crooked stop in the middle of the road.

Brian threw the car in park, oblivious to Nick's protests. The Hell Frog was in command, executing with smooth, automatic precision. He stepped out and grabbed something off the floor. "Keep your heads down."

Brian slammed the door and stalked back toward the bridge, moving with deadly purpose, Herman's rusty shotgun held across his chest.

Hunziker barreled toward the bridge.

Brian aimed the shotgun high and off to the side. He fired and a furious boom echoed through the woods.

Hunziker accelerated, twenty seconds out.

Brian racked the shotgun, fired again.

Hunziker thundered ahead, fifteen seconds out.

Brian reached the center of the bridge and stopped. "Come on," he whispered. He racked and fired again.

Hunziker accelerated, ten seconds out.

"Dad, no!" Zoe screamed, and tried to scramble out the rear window. Tracy pulled her back.

Brian tossed the shotgun down. "Come on!" He beckoned at Hunziker.

Hunziker closed in on the bridge at unstoppable speed, five seconds out.

Brian stood his ground, unflinching.

A mighty roar thundered from the woods by the bridge's entrance, followed by a flash of black and red. A 1981 Chevy El Camino launched onto the road and slammed head-first into Hunziker's front wheel like a battering ram.

Glass, plastic, and metal sprayed across the bridge. A chunk of bumper tumbled to Brian's feet and rocked in place. Both vehicles hissed and smoked, a giant twisted heap of burning metal jamming the mouth of the bridge.

The El Camino's driver-side door creaked open and Herman stumbled out, a nasty gash below his eye. Mikey and Cadillac slipped out from the passenger side.

Hunziker's door swung open, and he fell out onto all fours. He spit blood and shook his head.

Herman started toward him.

Hunziker pulled himself up on the door and drew his sidearm, wincing.

Herman stalked straight ahead, fearless and committed.

Hunziker raised the gun and cocked it, his arm swaying.

With a final confident stride, Herman closed the gap and cracked Hunziker with a crushing boxer's hook. The general spun and slumped over his open door, his gun clattering across the ground.

Herman glared down at his KO'd opponent, then turned and started across the bridge.

Mikey shuffled up to Hunziker and jammed a finger in his unconscious face. "No!" he scolded, like he was disciplining a dog. He marched after Herman.

A line of pickups slowly approached.

Brian picked up the shotgun and racked it, staring them down with fire in his eyes.

The trucks eased to a stop a healthy distance away.

Herman clapped Brian on the shoulder as he strode past. Mikey did the same. They squeezed into the Ark and made a spot for Cadillac.

Brian backed away from the bridge and returned to the Ark. Without a word, he hopped into the driver's seat, closed the door, and buckled his seatbelt. He squinted at a tiny scratch on the dash and gave a disapproving grunt. He reached down and began to buff it out.

Everyone stared at him in silent awe.

The scratch disappeared.

Brian smiled into the rearview. "OK, where to?"

FIFTY-FOUR

THEY CRUISED north along a single-lane highway, through the mountain mist, past a blur of warm fall colors. Wind rippled the mylar blanket duct-taped over the Ark's shattered back window.

"So what are we going to do?" Abby asked Nick.

"I don't know." He sat back and sighed. "Start with shelter, then food and water—beyond that…I don't know."

Dana eyed the bruise on his temple. "Let me clean that up, Nick." She fished in Brian's bug-out bag and pulled out a first aid kit.

"Oh, that reminds me, I've got something for you." Nick drew the Monroe Sciences vial from his jacket and held it up to Dana.

She squinted, then her eyes went wide. "Is that…"

"I think so." Nick smiled.

Abby turned. "It looks exactly like the vaccine he gave me and the other girls. He passed it around during his big speech."

Dana fumbled through the first aid kit. "Well, then, let's take it."

"Now?" Nick said.

She pulled out a packaged syringe. "The sooner the better. Vaccines take time to work—if we want immunity in two weeks, we need to take it now." She grabbed the vial and drew the clear solution into the syringe. "I'll take it first. If I'm OK in forty-eight hours, we'll inject everyone else."

"You sure, D?" Tracy said. "Who knows what's in that thing."

"No, of course I'm not sure. But can we afford not to? How long until we need to go back out for food, water, medicine? What if we can't find a secluded place to stay? The virus is everywhere, it's coming for us—what choice do we have?"

Tracy nodded.

Dana rolled up her sleeve and aimed the needle at her shoulder. She held her breath and steadied her hand.

Nick grabbed her wrist and spoke softly, "It doesn't make sense."

She looked up, confused.

He shook his head. "Why unleash a deadly virus to destroy mankind and then stockpile enough vaccine to save everyone? It doesn't make sense."

"Money." T.J. turned like a stiff turtle. "It's the oldest game in the book—create the disease, sell the cure."

Nick released Dana's wrist. "That's not Monroe. He's got this grand vision—a fresh start for mankind, a great genetic reset, a peaceful paradise. Plus, he's already worth billions."

Abby nodded in agreement.

"Also," Nick said, "when I threatened to call my brother, he wasn't afraid of Washington finding his vaccine. He said he'd spin it as a miracle cure and enjoy the credit. Why would he do that?"

Nick and Abby stared at each other for a moment, both minds turning. Then it clicked, and their eyes went wide in unison.

"ACE," she whispered.

"ACE." He nodded. "Release a deadly virus worldwide, kill off the dumb and the desperate with a penicillin hoax, and then, when the moment's right, announce a miracle vaccine with ACE hidden inside."

"His sixth cure," Abby said.

"Fame, fortune, a return to the spotlight, but most importantly, anyone who's still alive rushes to take the vaccine."

"And gets ACE along with it," Abby finished.

Dana capped the needle.

"But wouldn't everybody figure it out?" T.J. asked. "I mean, as soon as people started getting vaccinated there'd be side effects. They'd stop the shots and bust Monroe within a week. Game over."

Nick furrowed his brow. "Hmm."

They considered in silence.

"Not if he used germline engineering." Abby turned to Nick, her eyes sparkling. "With a technology like CRISPR, it's easy to selectively alter germline DNA—sperm and egg cells—without impacting the recipient's somatic cell DNA. Basically, genetic changes only appear in future offspring, not in the person getting vaccinated."

"Right." Nick pointed and nodded. "So everyone gets the vaccine, they're protected from the virus, they seem fine, but their future offspring are all ACE-programmed—logical, reasonable, cured of irrational emotions."

Abby sat back. "And within one generation, the entire human genome is rewritten."

"By the time they figure it out, it's too late," Nick said. "Everyone's already vaccinated, mankind is forever changed, and the next generation is…"

He trailed off as he watched Abby stare down at her belly. She placed a hand on her bump and looked up at Nick, sadness in her eyes.

"When did he vaccinate you?" Dana leaned in.

They looked at her, confused.

"Before or after you were…" Dana looked down at Abby's belly. "Implanted."

Abby's face brightened. "After…he vaccinated us during the third trimester, a month before releasing Scratch 'n Sniff."

Dana and Abby smiled at each other.

"They're OK," Abby said.

"They were already formed." Dana nodded. "The last generation of humans with original code."

Abby turned toward the window, smiling and rubbing her belly as she watched the fall foliage stream past.

T.J. huffed. "So we have to avoid the virus long enough for the vaccine to arrive—a week, a month, a year, ten years, who knows—

and then we have to avoid that too? We're screwed either way." He looked at Nick. "What are we supposed to do?"

Nick shrugged. "We plan it out."

He patted his jacket pockets. "Focus on solving the first problem in front of us."

He patted his pants pockets. "And then the next, then the next."

He fished inside his jacket. "That's…uh…that's…"

Dana extended a red marker over the seats.

Nick smiled and took it. "That's all we can do."

FIFTY-FIVE

Nick, Abby, and Dana sat around the head picnic table, working by the light of the dining hall's grand fireplace. A faded wood-carved sign spanned the mighty stone chimney, "St. Gianna Girls Camp—est. 1935." Framed in the floor-to-ceiling windows, the setting sun cast a warm glow over the lake and glittered across overturned canoes on the beach.

"Whew, I think that does it." Nick tossed a sketchbook on the table and stretched.

The table was covered with crumpled paper, golf pencils, and eight sketchbooks, each labeled at the top with a symbol and survival category:

Airplane, "Transportation."

Fork, "Food & Water."

House, "Shelter."

Cross, "Health & Medical."

Shield, "Safety & Defense."

Dollar sign, "Currency & Assets."

Phone, "Communication & Continuity."

Book, "Leisure & Entertainment."

The top page of each was saturated with lists, circles, arrows, diagrams, and hub-and-spoke mind maps.

Dana skimmed down a ninth sketchbook titled, "Babies!" with a little drawing of a smiling swaddled baby. She looked up at Abby. "So, just to double check, you sure you're OK with a home birth?"

"Yeah, I mean, it's not like we can go to a hospital, right?" Abby shrugged. "As long as you're doing it, I'm good."

"I'll be there every step of the way." Dana placed a hand on Nick's shoulder. "And Nick will be my head nurse."

Nick made an eek face. "Uhh, I'll stick with diaper duty, thank you."

They laughed.

A side door to the dining hall swung open, and Zoe strode in, her arms filled with kindling. Brian stepped in behind her, his arms filled with chopped firewood. He closed the door with his heel and straightened. Zoe stared up at him, her eyes twinkling.

"Brian Donahue!" he said in a scratchy witchy old-lady voice. "Sit up and speak up, or kiss your recess goodbye!"

They burst out laughing.

"Oh my god," Zoe said, "so accurate it's scary."

They dropped the wood by the fireplace and plopped down at the table.

"Hey guys, what's up?" Brian eyed the spread of sketchbooks. "Got our future all figured out?"

Dana snatched the Safety & Defense sketchbook. "Well, actually—"

The front door swung open, and Herman and Mikey shuffled in and stomped off mud. Cadillac trotted between them and headed for the fireplace. "We'll take a look tomorrow," Herman said to Mikey, "see if we can't get her up and running."

They approached the table.

"We got twenty-two cabins, each with twelve beds," Herman said.

"Two hundred and sixty-four beds." Nick nodded. "Not bad."

Mikey gave an enthusiastic thumbs up. "Me and Cadillac are in cabin eight, next to the rope swing. Zoe, you're in cabin nine." He beamed at her.

"I love a good rope swing!" She gave him a high five.

"Now, hold on." Herman put his fists on his hips. "What makes you think this young lady wants to sleep right next to us? Let's give her some space."

"Next to *me*, Herman." Mikey put one hand on his hip and pointed toward the woods. "*You're* in cabin twenty-two, so we can't hear you snore."

Everyone laughed, and Mikey grinned as he looked from face to face, proud of his joke.

Herman crossed his arms. "Boy…what the…are you outta your mind? If you—"

"Herman, please, I'm joking." Mikey made a calm-down gesture and rolled his eyes. "Don't get bent outta shape."

"Bent outta…where…how in the—"

The kitchen double doors swung open, and Tracy and T.J. strode out, each carrying a steaming tray.

"Dinner's up!" Tracy said. "Hot dog mac and cheese with a side of curry rice."

"Oooh, brings me back to summer camp." Dana rubbed her hands together.

"Just wait for dessert," T.J. said, "we've got enough marshmallows to feed a small army."

"Mmm, sounds delicious." Dana stood to help them serve, giving Nick a little pinch on her way past.

Nick cleared the sketchbooks and pencils.

Two minutes later, everyone was seated, staring down at the steaming spread.

"Zo, you want to say grace?" Brian asked.

"Yes, please," Tracy said.

Mikey stood and sauntered around to Zoe, inserted himself between her and Brian, and clasped their hands.

Herman put a palm to his face and shook his head.

Nick took hands with Dana and Abby. He closed his eyes.

"Thank you, Lord, for watching over us and keeping us safe. Thank you for blessing us with this food and shelter. And thank you for the new lives you're about to bring into our world." Zoe took a deep breath. "Our hearts are with all the good people who are suffering, alone, afraid. Please watch over them and protect them in this time of darkness. Whatever tomorrow may bring, tonight we're grateful to have each other. Tonight we're a family. Amen."

Nick squeezed both their hands.

Everyone opened their eyes.

Brian grinned and rubbed his hands. "Let's eat."

* * *

"UGH, I'M STUFFED." Brian rubbed his belly.

"Delicious." Zoe blew a chef's kiss.

"Who knew mac and cheese paired so well with curry rice?" Dana said.

"T.J. knew." Tracy sent him a sly wink.

T.J. returned a humble little bow. "All credit goes to the Queen of Comfort."

Tracy gave a grateful nod.

They rested for a long moment, gazing into the crackling fire, basking in the soul-deep warmth that comes from feeling full, safe, and loved.

"Well…" Nick scanned the group. "Do you guys still want to…"

"Yeah, let's do it," Abby said.

Everyone murmured in support.

"OK." Nick stood and nodded. "Let's do it."

He pulled out his red marker, uncapped it, and moved toward the big window overlooking the lake.

"OK, so—"

"Wait, son!" Herman scrambled off the bench. "Wait just one second." He hustled around a corner, down a dark hallway. There was a squeaky rolling noise, and he emerged pushing a big whiteboard on wheels.

Everyone laughed.

Herman positioned it at the head of the table and gestured for Nick to proceed. Nick gave him a warm smile, put down the red permanent marker, and uncapped a green dry-erase marker.

Nick stepped to the board, took a deep breath, and turned to the group.

Everyone gazed up at him.

"OK, so, *if* we built a survival community here…how would we begin?"

AUTHOR'S NOTE

Dear Reader -

Thank you for taking this journey with me. There are a million ways you could've spent your time, and I'm truly grateful you chose to meet Nick and his family.

Writing *The Posh Prepper* was a labor of love. It started in September 2019, not so much as an idea, but as a feeling: What would you do with a twenty-four-hour head start on the end of the world? Where would you go? Who would you bring? How would you survive?

For six months, I sketched concepts and characters. Then the COVID-19 pandemic hit, and those questions suddenly felt real. Over the next three years, the rolling crisis provided a steady stream of inspiration for characters, settings, and themes. More than that, *The Posh Prepper* became my way of processing all thc pain I was seeing in the world.

During that time, my life changed a lot. I moved jobs, bought a house, got married, had a son, and I'm expecting another son any day now. Life was very, very busy, and there wasn't much time to write.

But Nick and Abby and their friends (and enemies) kept whispering in my ear, demanding to be brought to life.

It was not a smooth delivery—this story had to fight its way out. Inspiration struck while waiting at stoplights, emptying the dishwasher, shoveling snow, changing diapers. It was researched, written, and edited in a thousand drips and spurts. I thought about shelving it, more than once, but our friends kept calling. So my wife helped me carve out little pockets of time, and I powered through.

This is the first book I've ever written. It was hard. Very hard. Honestly, I don't know yet if it was worth it. I'm afraid the story won't move others the way it moved me. **So I have a small ask: Will you let me know what you thought?**

There are two ways:

1) If you would leave a review on Amazon or Goodreads, it would mean the world to me. I read every single one.

2) If you would send me a note and say hello, I'd love to hear from you. What was your favorite and least-favorite part of the story? What would you like to see in future books?

I really want to hear from you:

- Leave an Amazon review here or a Goodreads review here
- Send me a note at Todd@ToddKnightBooks.com
- Join my email list (deleted scenes, early access, free stuff) at ToddKnightBooks.com

A closing thought: This story was dark, because the world felt dark. But I hope our friends were able to shine a light for you, the way they did for me. Follow that light, you'll find the good ones.

- Todd
Boston, Massachusetts
February 15, 2023

ACKNOWLEDGMENTS

First, I want to thank my wife and family for their support. I spent many hours holed up in my office researching, writing, reading, acting, editing, and cursing at *The Posh Prepper*. Even outside my cave, I was often daydreaming, tapping notes on my phone, or itching to get back to my desk. Thank you for your love and patience.

Thanks to Amanda Ripley for her wonderful book, *The Unthinkable: Who Survives When Disaster Strikes - and Why*. And to Cade Courtley for *SEAL Survival Guide: A Navy SEAL's Secrets to Surviving Any Disaster*.

Many thanks to my beta readers and copy editors, your suggestions were a big help.

Finally, thank you, dear reader, for taking this journey with me. Sharing this story with you was one of the great joys of my life.

ABOUT THE AUTHOR

Todd Knight spent years working at tech companies before starting to pursue his true passion on the side: storytelling. *The Posh Prepper* is his debut novel, the first of many stories built around powerful themes and unforgettable characters.

Todd loves dark, gritty, character-driven, dramatic thrillers. Favorite books include *The Silence of the Lambs, Red Dragon, Let the Right One In,* and many works by Michael Connelly and Stephen King. Favorite shows include *Breaking Bad, True Detective, Deadwood, The Leftovers,* and *The X-Files.* Favorite movies include *The Dark Knight, Arrival, Mad Max: Fury Road, Contact, Children of Men,* and *Interstellar.*

Todd loves hearing from readers. Please say hello at:
Todd@ToddKnightBooks.com

You can follow Todd's writing, read deleted scenes, and get early updates on his next book at:
ToddKnightBooks.com

Printed in Great Britain
by Amazon

25680614R00243